WRITERS AT WORK

Eighth series

Previously Published

WRITERS AT WORK
The *Paris Review* Interviews

FIRST SERIES

Edited and introduced by MALCOLM COWLEY

E. M. Forster	Frank O'Connor
François Mauriac	Robert Penn Warren
Joyce Cary	Alberto Moravia
Dorothy Parker	Nelson Algren
James Thurber	Angus Wilson
Thornton Wilder	William Styron
William Faulkner	Truman Capote
Georges Simenon	Françoise Sagan

SECOND SERIES

Edited by GEORGE PLIMPTON and introduced by
VAN WYCK BROOKS

Robert Frost	Aldous Huxley
Ezra Pound	Ernest Hemingway
Marianne Moore	S. J. Perelman
T. S. Eliot	Lawrence Durrell
Boris Pasternak	Mary McCarthy
Katherine Anne Porter	Ralph Ellison
Henry Miller	Robert Lowell

SIXTH SERIES

Edited by GEORGE PLIMPTON and introduced by
FRANK KERMODE

Rebecca West	Kurt Vonnegut, Jr.
Stephen Spender	Nadine Gordimer
Tennessee Williams	James Merrill
Elizabeth Bishop	Gabriel García Márquez
Bernard Malamud	Carlos Fuentes
William Goyen	John Gardner

SEVENTH SERIES

Edited by GEORGE PLIMPTON and introduced by
JOHN UPDIKE

Malcolm Cowley	Arthur Koestler
William Maxwell	May Sarton
Philip Larkin	Eugene Ionesco
Elizabeth Hardwick	John Ashbery
Milan Kundera	John Barth
Edna O'Brien	Philip Roth
Raymond Carver	

Writers at Work

The *Paris Review* Interviews

EIGHTH SERIES

Edited by George Plimpton
Introduction by Joyce Carol Oates

VIKING

VIKING
Published by the Penguin Group
Viking Penguin Inc., 40 West 23rd Street,
New York, New York 10010, U.S.A.
Penguin Books Ltd, 27 Wrights Lane,
London W8 5TZ, England
Penguin Books Australia Ltd, Ringwood,
Victoria, Australia
Penguin Books Canada Ltd, 2801 John Street,
Markham, Ontario, Canada L3R 1B4
Penguin Books (N.Z.) Ltd, 182–190 Wairau Road,
Auckland 10, New Zealand

Penguin Books Ltd, Registered Offices:
Harmondsworth, Middlesex, England

First published in 1988
in simultaneous hardcover and paperback editions
by Viking Penguin Inc.
Published simultaneously in Canada

1 3 5 7 9 10 8 6 4 2

LIBRARY OF CONGRESS CATALOGING IN PUBLICATION DATA
Writers at work.
1. Authors—20th century—Interviews.   I. Plimpton,
George.   II. Paris review.
PN453.W739   1988   809'.04   87-31736
ISBN 0-670-82101-2

Printed in the United States of America by
R. R. Donnelley & Sons Company, Harrisonburg, Virginia
Set in Avanta

Contents

Introduction

The distinguished *Paris Review Writers at Work* series, of which this is the eighth volume, began auspiciously with an interview with E. M. Forster in the premier issue of *Paris Review* in the spring of 1953; the premier volume, published in 1958, though overseen by young novice editors, contained interviews with writers of the stature of Mauriac, Wilder, Moravia, and Faulkner. From the start the *Writers at Work* interviews have concentrated upon the art and craft of fiction—hence the "work" of the title; they have been characterized by the high quality of the interviewers (who are frequently writers) and of the conversations themselves—though the term "conversations" in this context is slightly inaccurate, suggesting as it does an oral exchange, in which deliberation, let alone artifice, is not the point. In the *Paris Review* volumes you will find no verbatim transcripts, no fumbling, groping, "spontaneous" utterances; no trailings off into baffled silence; no sense that the interviewer is the "active" component, and the interviewed the "passive"; no misstatements the subject dearly wished afterward to delete, but was prevented from doing so by journalistic exigency or malice. (Cynthia Ozick, for instance, for whom conversation is mere "air," insisted upon typing out answers to her interviewer's questions in his presence, and afterward amended the manuscript with oral comments that doubled its length; at a later date, she reviewed and revised her oral comments.) The book you hold in your hand is a book in the fullest and most deliberate sense of the word: the interviews are texts, intelligently, one might say lovingly prepared, edited, emended, expanded, revised. If the *PR* interviews are uniformly successful it is because they are highly stylized and collaborative. "No one really talks like that," someone once said of the characters of Henry James; and the apt reply was, "So much the worse for reality."

Yet the artifice of the form in no way interferes with the authenticity and consistently high worth of its contents. On the contrary, we are likely to be most faithful to our convictions when we have had time to contemplate them. "How do I know what I think until I say it?" is the classic question, to which the writer instinctively adds, "How do I know what I said until I have revised it?" The distractions of the moment, or of a vagrant, passing mood, even, in urban instances, the intrusions of the outside world, may yield a simulation of the revelatory, of the "real" self, but are more likely to be misleading. If I were pressed to say what the essential issue has been in the *PR* interviews over all, up to and including the present volume, I would say that it is a concern with recording the truth; and recording it in the best possible way. (As Robert Stone says, "If it works, you say that's real, that's truth, that's life, that's the way things are. 'There it is.' ") Thus the *PR* interview is known in the trade as the interview of record, and a number of the interviews have acquired reputations, with the passage of time, as masterpieces of their genre.

The present volume does, however, signal a departure in the series in that it includes, for the first time, not only "creative" writers—that inadequate, rather embarrassing term—but the essayist E. B. White, the biographer Leon Edel, the editor (and poet) James Laughlin, and the translator Robert Fitzgerald. It should not surprise us that these men bring to

their vocations the passionate, almost mystical intensity usually associated with the "creative" artist, nor that their insights into the processes of creation are as helpful, as
valuable, and occasionally as startling as those of Elie Wiesel,
Derek Walcott, E. L. Doctorow, Cynthia Ozick, Robert
Stone, *et al.* Leon Edel's remarks on the art of biography and
on his personal engagement in it constitute a sort of memoi-
rist monograph, brilliant in its personal no less than in its
theoretical revelations: "Everything seemed filled with mystery and promise," he recalls, when, as a young man, he discovered a treasure trove of hitherto uninvestigated materials
in the James family archive at Harvard, setting in motion the
course of his life's work. He tells us that choosing a subject
for biography is "a little like falling in love," and that he
invented as he went along the form of his magisterial five-
volume biography of Henry James: "The moment you start
shaping a biography, it becomes more than a mere assemblage of facts . . . you are creating a work of art." And: "All
this required what I like to call the biographical imagination,
the imagination of form." The late Robert Fitzgerald, one of
America's preeminent translators of the Greek classics, speaks
of the "music" of great poetry, which the translator must
create anew in his own language, and acknowledges that such
experiences approximate religious revelation. E. B. White
sounds like the most driven of Romantic poets in describing
the initial vertiginous stage of composition: "When I start to
write, my mind is apt to race, like a clock from which the
pendulum has been removed. I simply can't keep up . . . and
this causes me to break apart. I think there are writers whose
thoughts flow in a smooth and orderly fashion, and they can
transcribe them on paper without undue emotion or without
getting too far behind. I envy them." James Laughlin provides a brief history of American Modernism in his personal
recollections of Ezra Pound, William Carlos Williams, Gertrude Stein, Delmore Schwartz, Tennessee Williams, Denise

Levertov, and others whom New Directions published in its unparalleled shaping and re-shaping of American literature.

There is a camaraderie in diversity here, a common ground of profound seriousness about the writerly predicament. ("Putting black on white," as John Irving quotes Maupassant.) What is more natural than the writer's voice, yet more difficult to describe? What is more fundamental than motive, yet more enigmatic in the analysis? Elie Wiesel speaks of art as a vehicle for the cleansing and redemptive madness one might call mystical, in contrast to the merely clinical and destructive; in his practice as a writer it is this madness he must seek in determining the soul, or "melody," of a book: "Literature is a tone. It is a melody. If I find the melody of the book, the book is written. . . . Every book has its own. It's more than simple rhythm. It's like a musical key, major or minor. If you have that key, you know you can go on—the book is there. It's a matter of time." For E. L. Doctorow as well each book has its own identity, as distinct from that of the author: "It speaks from itself rather than you. Each book is unlike the others because you are not bringing the same voice to every book. I think that keeps you alive as a writer." And: "It's not calculated at all. It never has been. One of the things I had to learn as a writer was to trust the act of writing. To put myself in the position of writing to find out what I was writing. . . . The inventions of the book come as discoveries."

Similarly, John Hersey says: "When the writing is really working, I think there is something like dreaming going on. I don't know how to draw the line between the conscious management of what you're doing and this state. It usually takes place in the earlier stages, in the drafting process. . . . When I feel really engaged with a passage, I become so lost in it that I'm unaware of my real surroundings, totally involved in the pictures and sounds that that passage evokes." And: "The voice is the element over which you have no control; it's the sound of the person behind the work."

Cynthia Ozick, who acknowledges the compulsive nature of her writing, speaks even of reading as a part of her obsession with writing; finding herself a writer, and unable *not* to be a writer, she speculates on the genesis of a curious fate: "I think it's a condition, a given; content comes later. You're born into the condition of being an amphora; whether it's wine or water that fills it afterward belongs to afterward. Lately I think of this given condition as a kind of curse, because there is no way out of it. What a relief it would be to have the freedom of other people! Any inborn condition of this sort is, after all, a kind of slavery. . . . The beginning was almost physiological in its ecstatic pursuits . . . the *waiting-to-be-born* excitement of longing to write. I suppose it is a kind of parallel Eros." Derek Walcott speaks of the ritualistic nature of writing in religious terms: "If you think a poem is coming on . . . you do make a retreat, a withdrawal into some kind of silence that cuts out everything around you. What you're taking on is not really a renewal of your identity but actually a renewal of your anonymity so that what's in front of you becomes more important than what you are. Equally—and it may be a little pretentious-sounding to say it—sometimes if I feel that I have done good work I do pray, I do say thanks."

For Robert Stone and John Irving writing is primarily story-telling, but with a private, cathartic significance. "I would call it a coming to terms," Stone says, "a way of dealing with the violence in myself." Irving, who describes himself as a conventionally religious Christian, feels more of a kinship with nineteenth-century novelists than with the post-Modernist theoreticians who are his coevals: "Writing, in my opinion, is the opposite of having ego. . . . A writer is a vehicle. I feel the story I am writing existed before I existed; I'm just the slob who finds it, and rather clumsily tries to do it, and the characters, justice. I think of writing fiction as doing justice to the people in the story, and doing justice to *their* story—it's not *my* story. It's entirely ghostly work; I'm just the medium."

Joseph Brodsky, who sees the fundamental theme of his poetry as the nature of time—"what time can do to a man"—speaks too of an obsession with voice: "If there is any deity to me, it's language." And: "In the works of the better poets you get the sensation that they're not talking to people any more, or to some seraphical creature. What they're doing is simply talking back to the language itself—as beauty, sensuality, wisdom, irony—those aspects of language of which the poet is a clear mirror. Poetry is not an art or a branch of art, it's something more. If what distinguishes us from other species is speech, then poetry, which is the supreme linguistic operation, is our anthropological, indeed genetic, goal." As his own translator Brodsky finds himself in a unique and often frustrating position, as if he were required to look upon his own work "as the soul looks from its abode upon the abandoned body. The only thing the soul perceives is the slow smoking of decay."

The interview at its generic best is so intimate a literary form, so much in mimicry of a "real" meeting with a "real" person, we tend to come away from it slightly bedazzled, incapable of summarizing its significance as a whole. We are most likely to remember fragments, moments of unexpected revelation; amusing asides; self-contained anecdotes; stray remarks we would never have predicted, given their source. Who would have guessed that the British novelist Anita Brookner, for instance, would tell an interviewer that she does not consider herself an imaginative writer; that, were she happy, and married, with children, she would not be writing—"And I doubt if I should want to." What an admission, in an age of feminist orthodoxy! Where the art and craft of writing is for her fellow interviewees (including the only other woman artist in the series, Cynthia Ozick) a sacred task, undertaken with religious solemnity, if not dread, it has been for Brookner, at least by her account, hardly more than a means of escape from "the despair of living." Accordingly, she does not trouble to revise her work—"It is always the first draft."

Doctorow acknowledges the writing of prose fiction as a form of socially acceptable schizophrenia, in an aside that suggests a somewhat romantic notion of this mental disorder: "You can get away with an awful lot. One of my children once said—it was a terrible truth, too, and, of course, it had to be a young child who said this: 'Daddy is always hiding in his book.'" Robert Stone reminisces with nostalgia of a fatherless childhood spent with a schizophrenic mother, and sums up the Sixties glamour of Kerouac and Neal Cassady *et al.* as "just goofiness." Ozick imagines herself without readers—"I have been writing for years and years, without ever being read"— and suggests that revenge can be a seminal motive for writing: "Life hurts; certain ideas and experiences hurt; one wants to clarify, to set out illuminations, to replay the old bad scenes and get the *Treppenworte* said—the words one didn't have the strength or the ripeness to say when those words were necessary for one's dignity or survival."

John Irving tells a marvelous anecdote about an encounter in Iowa City he had many years ago with the Irish writer J. P. Donleavy—"this large, silly man with his walking stick"—who dared to snub John Cheever; Leon Edel speaks of James Joyce as a pathetic and pathological man who could not break the repetitious pattern of his self-myth as a victim of persecution, "even after the world honored and worshipped him." E. B. White confesses to have done startlingly little reading in his life: "I have never read Joyce and a dozen other writers who have changed the face of literature. . . . I have no special interest in any of the other arts. I know nothing of music or of painting or of sculpture or of the dance." James Laughlin says bluntly that American reviewing is "hopeless." Joseph Brodsky, pressed by his interviewer to say that he suffered "extreme duress" while serving his sentence of internal exile in

Russia, insists that, on the contrary, he did not greatly mind: "Because of some turn in my character, I decided to get the most out of it. I kind of liked it. I associated it with Robert Frost.... You get up in the morning in the village, or wherever, and you go to get your daily load, you walk through the field· and you know that at the same time most of the nation is doing the same. It gives you some exhilarating sense of being with the rest.... It gives you a certain insight into the basics of life." Derek Walcott, who has never felt that he belongs anywhere else but in St. Lucia, his birthplace in the Windward Islands, speaks critically of the West Indian temperament which simply wants "to have a damn good time, and that's it, basically." Elie Wiesel recalls his anger as a younger man, directed at "history, at the world, at God, at myself, at whatever surrounded me.... All my writing was born out of anger. In order to contain it, I had to write. If I had not written, I would have exploded." Such moments of candor, such turns of phrase, give these interviews their special tone. We hear, through the paraphernalia of tape cassettes, copyedited manuscripts, galleys, and Time, the cadences of voices hardly less resonant in our ears than our own.

Flannery O'Connor, attacked by critics for her "dark" and "pessimistic" vision of life, observed that no writer is a pessimist; the very act of writing is an act of hope. And so it is. And so do most writers perceive it, as a vocation, a privilege, a curse that nonetheless contains a blessing. John Hersey puts it most simply, and most honorably: "Writing is the only real reward." Writing, and such talk of it as conversations like these provide.

—JOYCE CAROL OATES

1. E. B. White

Elwyn Brooks White was born in Mount Vernon, New York, on July 11, 1899. As an undergraduate at Cornell University, he studied under William Strunk, whose *The Elements of Style* he would revise almost forty years later. After graduation, White headed to the West Coast in a Model T Ford he called Hotspur, but soon returned to New York, where he worked sporadically, and unhappily, as a reporter. In 1926 his essays caught the eye of *The New Yorker* editorial assistant Katharine Angell, who passed them along to Harold Ross, the editor of the magazine. Ross hired White, who within months became an integral part of *The New Yorker*'s staff. In 1929, the publication of *The Lady Is Cold* earned him notice for his poetry; *Is Sex Necessary?*, with James Thurber, sealed his reputation as a humorist. That same year also saw his marriage to Katharine Angell, a move he described as "the most beautiful decision of my life."

In 1938 White and his wife were offered the joint editorship of *The New Yorker*. The couple turned down the offer, instead to move permanently to the Maine seacoast of White's childhood vacations. There, White published books including *The Fox of Peapack*, a collection of his verse, and *One Man's Meat*, a collection of his monthly pieces for *Harper's* Magazine. Later work included *The Wild Flag* (1946), a volume of his editorials on world government; *Charlotte's Web* (1952), one of the most acclaimed children's books ever; *The Second Tree from the Corner* (1954), a collection of twenty years of his work; and several other volumes of essays, poetry, and children's fiction. White also edited *Onward and Upward in the Garden* (1979), a collection of essays on gardening by his wife, who died in 1977. E. B. White died on October 1, 1985, at the age of eighty-six.

topics
white

The question has been raised: is Russell Wiggins the man for the job? He has been named [as] our Ambassador to the United Nations. .The *Times*, as soon as it learned of this, jumped on it with both feet. "He is not the man for this job," said the Times.

This pronouncement struck me as a snap judgment. ~~It was easy to be sure whether Wiggins is the man~~ Who knows who is the man for a job? ~~for the job?~~ The Times complained that Wiggins had had no training in diploacy, and this is true. Wiggins is not a diplomat, he is the editor of a good newspaper. I looked up "diplomacy" in Webster's, and found a definition that said: "Artful management in securing advantages without arousing hostility." A newspaper editor, if he's any good, never gives a thought to arousing hostility, he goes ahead and prints the facts as he sees them. Maybe the time has come for our Ambassador to the United Nations to act with the same kind of ~~desire~~ abandon.

Wiggins has some very unusual qualifications for his new post. ~~He is unquestionably the only man to represent us in the United Nations who owns a Friendship sloop.~~ I think he bought the sloop ~~because the name~~ because he fell in love with the name Friendship. ~~Friendship sloops are not a dime a dozen——they~~ are a rare thing these days. They were built in Friendship, Maine, and were originally a work boat, mostly for hauling traps. They are very close-winded, have a deep forefoot, and a powerful ~~luxury~~ hull. Off the wind they are ~~[...]~~. On the wind, they ~~can eat up the sea~~

E. B. White manuscript page: New York Times *article.*

E. B. White

In the issue of The New Yorker *dated two weeks after E. B. White died, his stepson, Roger Angell, wrote the following in the magazine's "Talk of the Town" section:*

Last August, a couple of sailors paid an unexpected visit to my summer house in Maine: young sailors—a twelve-year-old-girl and an eleven-year-old boy. They were a crew taking part in a statewide small-boat-racing competition at a local yacht club, and because my wife and I had some vacant beds just then we

were willingly dragooned as hosts. They were fine company—
tanned and shy and burning with tactics but amenable to blue-
berry muffins and our exuberant fox terrier. They were also
readers, it turned out. On their second night, it came out at the
dinner table that E. B. White was a near neighbor of ours, and
our visitors reacted to the news with incredulity. *"No!"* the boy
said softly, his eyes travelling back and forth over the older faces
at the table. *"No-o-o-o!"* The girl, being older, tried to keep
things in place. *"He's my favorite author,"* she said. *"Or at least
he was when I was younger."* They were both a bit old for Stuart
Little, Charlotte's Web, and The Trumpet of the Swan, *in
fact, but because they knew the books so well, and because they
needed cheering up (they had done badly in the racing), arrangements were made for a visit to E. B. White's farm the next
morning.*

White, who had been ill, was not able to greet our small party
that day, but there were other sights and creatures there to make
us welcome: two scattered families of bantam hens and chicks
on the lawn; the plump, waggly incumbent dog, name of Red;
and the geese who came scuttling and hissing up the pasture
lane, their wings outspread in wild alarm. It was a glazy, wind-
less morning, with some thin scraps of fog still clinging to the
water in Allen Cove, beyond the pasture; later on, I knew, the
summer southwest breeze would stir, and then Harriman Point
and Blue Hill Bay and the islands would come clear again.
What wasn't there this time was Andy White himself: emerging
from the woodshed, say, with an egg basket or a length of line
in his hand; or walking away (at a mid-slow pace, not a stroll—
never a stroll—with the dog just astern) down the grassy lane
that turns and then dips to the woods and shore; or perhaps
getting into his car for a trip to town, getting aboard, as he got
aboard any car, with an air of mild wariness, the way most of
us start up on a bicycle. We made do without him, as we had
to. We went into the barn and examined the vacant pens and
partitions and the old cattle tieups; we visited the vegetable

garden and the neat stacks of freshly cut stovewood; we saw the cutting beds, and the blackberry patch behind the garage, and the place where the pigpen used to be—the place where Wilbur was born, surely. The children took turns on the old single-rope swing that hung in the barn doorway, hoisting themselves up onto the smoothed seat, made out of a single chunk of birch firewood, and then sailing out into the sunshine and back into barn-shadow again and again, as the crossbeam creaked above them and swallows dipped in and out of an open barn window far overhead. It wasn't much entertainment for them, but perhaps it was all right, because of where they were. The girl asked which doorway might have been the one where Charlotte had spun her web, and she mentioned Templeton, the rat, and Fern, the little girl who befriends Wilbur. She was visiting a museum, I sensed, and she would remember things here to tell her friends about later. The boy, though, was quieter, and for a while I thought that our visit was a disappointment to him. Then I stole another look at him, and I understood. I think I understood. He was taking note of the place, almost checking off corners and shadows and smells to himself as we walked about the old farm, but he wasn't trying to remember them. He looked like someone who had been there before, and indeed he had, for he was a reader. Andy White had given him the place long before he ever set foot on it—not this farm, exactly, but the one in the book, the one now in the boy's mind. Only true writers—the rare few of them—can do this, but their deed to us is in perpetuity. The boy didn't get to meet E. B. White that day, but he already had him by heart. He had him for good.

—ROGER ANGELL

INTERVIEWER: So many critics equate the success of a writer with an unhappy childhood. Can you say something of your own childhood in Mount Vernon?

WHITE: As a child, I was frightened but not unhappy. My

parents were loving and kind. We were a large family (six children) and were a small kingdom unto ourselves. Nobody ever came to dinner. My father was formal, conservative, successful, hardworking, and worried. My mother was loving, hardworking, and retiring. We lived in a large house in a leafy suburb, where there were backyards and stables and grape arbors. I lacked for nothing except confidence. I suffered nothing except the routine terrors of childhood: fear of the dark, fear of the future, fear of the return to school after a summer on a lake in Maine, fear of making an appearance on a platform, fear of the lavatory in the school basement where the slate urinals cascaded, fear that I was unknowing about things I should know about. I was, as a child, allergic to pollens and dusts, and still am. I was allergic to platforms, and still am. It may be, as some critics suggest, that it helps to have an unhappy childhood. If so, I have no knowledge of it. Perhaps it helps to have been scared or allergic to pollens—I don't know.

INTERVIEWER: At what age did you know you were going to follow a literary profession? Was there a particular incident, or moment?

WHITE: I never knew for sure that I would follow a literary profession. I was twenty-seven or twenty-eight before anything happened that gave me any assurance that I could make a go of writing. I had *done* a great deal of writing, but I lacked confidence in my ability to put it to good use. I went abroad one summer and on my return to New York found an accumulation of mail at my apartment. I took the letters, unopened, and went to a Child's restaurant on Fourteenth Street, where I ordered dinner and began opening my mail. From one envelope, two or three checks dropped out, from *The New Yorker.* I suppose they totaled a little under a hundred dollars, but it looked like a fortune to me. I can still remember the feeling that "this was it"—I was a pro at last. It was a good feeling and I enjoyed the meal.

INTERVIEWER: What were those first pieces accepted by *The*

New Yorker? Did you send them in with a covering letter, or through an agent?

WHITE: They were short sketches—what Ross called "casuals." One, I think, was a piece called "Swell Steerage," about the then new college cabin class on transatlantic ships. I never submitted a manuscript with a covering letter or through an agent. I used to put my manuscript in the mail, along with a stamped envelope for the rejection. This was a matter of high principle with me: I believed in the doctrine of immaculate rejection. I never used an agent and did not like the looks of a manuscript after an agent got through prettying it up and putting it between covers with brass clips. (I now have an agent for such mysteries as movie rights and foreign translations.)

A large part of all early contributions to *The New Yorker* arrived uninvited and unexpected. They arrived in the mail or under the arm of people who walked in with them. O'Hara's "Afternoon Delphians" is one example out of hundreds. For a number of years, *The New Yorker* published an average of fifty new writers a year. Magazines that refuse unsolicited manuscripts strike me as lazy, incurious, self-assured, and self-important. I'm speaking of magazines of general circulation. There may be some justification for a technical journal to limit its list of contributors to persons who are known to be qualified. But if I were a publisher, I wouldn't want to put out a magazine that failed to examine everything that turned up.

INTERVIEWER: But did *The New Yorker* ever try to publish the emerging writers of the time: Hemingway, Faulkner, Dos Passos, Fitzgerald, Miller, Lawrence, Joyce, Wolfe, *et al?*

WHITE: *The New Yorker* had an interest in publishing any writer that could turn in a good piece. It read everything submitted. Hemingway, Faulkner, and the others were well-established and well-paid when *The New Yorker* came on the scene. The magazine would have been glad to publish them, but it didn't have the money to pay them off, and for the most part they didn't submit. They were selling to the *Saturday*

Evening Post and other well-heeled publications, and in general were not inclined to contribute to the small, new, impecunious weekly. Also, some of them, I would guess, did not feel sympathetic to *The New Yorker*'s frivolity. Ross had no great urge to publish the big names; he was far more interested in turning up new and yet undiscovered talent, the Helen Hokinsons and the James Thurbers. We did publish some things by Wolfe—"Only the Dead Know Brooklyn" was one. I believe we published something by Fitzgerald. But Ross didn't waste much time trying to corral "emerged" writers. He was looking for the ones that were found by turning over a stone.

INTERVIEWER: What were the procedures in turning down a manuscript by a *New Yorker* regular? Was this done by Ross?

WHITE: The manuscript of a *New Yorker* regular was turned down in the same manner as was the manuscript of a *New Yorker* irregular. It was simply rejected, usually by the subeditor who was handling the author in question. Ross did not deal directly with writers and artists, except in the case of a few old friends from an earlier day. He wouldn't even take on Woollcott—regarded him as too difficult and fussy. Ross disliked rejecting pieces, and he disliked firing people—he ducked both tasks whenever he could.

INTERVIEWER: Did feuds threaten the magazine?

WHITE: Feuds did not threaten *The New Yorker*. The only feud I recall was the running battle between the editorial department and the advertising department. This was largely a one-sided affair, with the editorial department lobbing an occasional grenade into the enemy's lines just on general principles, to help them remember to stay out of sight. Ross was determined not to allow his magazine to be swayed, in the slightest degree, by the boys in advertising. As far as I know, he succeeded.

INTERVIEWER: When did you first move to New York, and

what were some of the things you did before joining *The New Yorker*? Were you ever a part of the Algonquin group?

WHITE: After I got out of college, in 1921, I went to work in New York but did not live in New York. I lived at home, with my father and mother in Mount Vernon, and commuted to work. I held three jobs in about seven months—first with the United Press, then with a public relations man named Wheat, then with the American Legion News Service. I disliked them all, and in the spring of 1922 I headed west in a Model T Ford with a college mate, Howard Cushman, to seek my fortune and as a way of getting away from what I disliked. I landed in Seattle six months later, worked there as a reporter on the *Times* for a year, was fired, shipped to Alaska aboard a freighter, and then returned to New York. It was on my return that I became an advertising man—Frank Seaman & Co, J. H. Newmark. In the mid-twenties, I moved into a two-room apartment at 112 West Thirteenth Street with three other fellows, college mates of mine at Cornell: Burke Dowling Adams, Gustave Stubbs Lobrano, and Mitchell T. Galbreath. The rent was $110 a month. Split four ways it came to $27.50, which I could afford. My friends in those days were the fellows already mentioned. Also, Peter Vischer, Russell Lord, Joel Sayre, Frank Sullivan (he was older and more advanced but I met him and liked him), James Thurber, and others. I was never a part of the Algonquin group. After becoming connected with *The New Yorker*, I lunched once at the Round Table but didn't care for it and was embarrassed in the presence of the great. I never was well acquainted with Benchley or Broun or Dorothy Parker or Woollcott. I did not know Don Marquis or Ring Lardner, both of whom I greatly admired. I was a younger man.

INTERVIEWER: Were you a voracious reader during your youth?

WHITE: I was never a voracious reader and, in fact, have done little reading in my life. There are too many other things I would rather do than read. In my youth I read animal stories— William J. Long and Ernest Seton Thompson. I have read a great many books about small boat voyages—they fascinate me even though they usually have no merit. In the twenties, I read the newspaper columns: F.P.A., Christopher Morley, Don Marquis. I tried contributing and had a few things published. (As a child, I was a member of the St. Nicholas League and from that eminence was hurled into the literary life, wearing my silver badge and my gold badge.) My reading habits have not changed over the years, only my eyesight has changed. I don't like being indoors and get out every chance I get. In order to read, one must sit down, usually indoors. I am restless and would rather sail a boat than crack a book. I've never had a very lively literary curiosity, and it has sometimes seemed to me that I am not really a literary fellow at all. Except that I write for a living.

INTERVIEWER: The affinity with nature has been very important to you. This seems a contradiction considering the urbanity of *The New Yorker* and its early contributions.

WHITE: There is no contradiction. New York is part of the natural world. I love the city, I love the country, and for the same reasons. The city is part of the country. When I had an apartment on East Forty-eighth Street, my backyard during the migratory season yielded more birds than I ever saw in Maine. I could step out on my porch, spring or fall, and there was the hermit thrush, picking around in McEvoy's yard. Or the white-throated sparrow, the brown thrasher, the jay, the kinglet. John Kieran has recorded the immense variety of flora and fauna within the limits of Greater New York.

But it is not just a question of birds and animals. The urban scene is a spectacle that fascinates me. People are animals, and the city is full of people in strange plumage, defending their territorial rights, digging for their supper.

INTERVIEWER: Although you say you are "not really a literary fellow at all," have you read any books, say in the past ten years, that deeply impressed you?

WHITE: I admire anybody who has the guts to write anything at all. As for what comes out on paper, I'm not well equipped to speak about it. When I should be reading, I am almost always doing something else. It is a matter of some embarrassment to me that I have never read Joyce and a dozen other writers who have changed the face of literature. But there you are. I picked up *Ulysses* the other evening, when my eye lit on it, and gave it a go. I stayed with it only for about twenty minutes, then was off and away. It takes more than a genius to keep me reading a book. But when I latch onto a book like *They Live by the Wind,* by Wendell P. Bradley, I am glued tight to the chair. It is because Bradley wrote about something that has always fascinated (and uplifted) me—sailing. He wrote about it very well, too.

I was deeply impressed by Rachel Carson's *Silent Spring.* It may well be the book by which the human race will stand or fall. I enjoyed *Speak, Memory* by Nabokov when I read it—a fine example of remembering.

INTERVIEWER: Do you have a special interest in the other arts?

WHITE: I have no special interest in any of the other arts. I know nothing of music or of painting or of sculpture or of the dance. I would rather watch the circus or a ball game than ballet.

INTERVIEWER: Can you listen to music, or be otherwise half-distracted when you're working on something?

WHITE: I never listen to music when I'm working. I haven't that kind of attentiveness, and I wouldn't like it at all. On the other hand, I'm able to work fairly well among ordinary distractions. My house has a living room that is at the core of everything that goes on: it is a passageway to the cellar, to the kitchen, to the closet where the phone lives. There's a lot of traffic. But it's a bright, cheerful room, and I often use it as a room to write in, despite the carnival that is going on all around me. A girl pushing a carpet sweeper under my typewriter table has never annoyed me particularly, nor has it taken my mind off my work, unless the girl was unusually pretty or unusually clumsy. My wife, thank God, has never been protective of me, as, I am told, the wives of some writers are. In consequence, the members of my household never pay the slightest attention to my being a writing man—they make all the noise and fuss they want to. If I get sick of it, I have places I can go. A writer who waits for ideal conditions under which to work will die without putting a word on paper.

INTERVIEWER: Do you have any warm-up exercises to get going?

WHITE: Delay is natural to a writer. He is like a surfer—he bides his time, waits for the perfect wave on which to ride in. Delay is instinctive with him. He waits for the surge (of emotion? of strength? of courage?) that will carry him along. I have no warm-up exercises, other than to take an occasional drink. I am apt to let something simmer for a while in my mind before trying to put it into words. I walk around, straightening pictures on the wall, rugs on the floor—as though not until everything in the world was lined up and perfectly true could anybody reasonably expect me to set a word down on paper.

INTERVIEWER: You have wondered at Kenneth Roberts's working methods—his stamina and discipline. You said you often went to zoos rather than write. Can you say something of discipline and the writer?

WHITE: Kenneth Roberts wrote historical novels. He knew just what he wanted to do and where he was going. He rose in the morning and went to work, methodically and industriously. This has not been true of me. The things I have managed to write have been varied and spotty—a mishmash. Except for certain routine chores, I never knew in the morning how the day was going to develop. I was like a hunter, hoping to catch sight of a rabbit. There are two faces to discipline. If a man (who writes) feels like going to a zoo, he should by all means go to a zoo. He might even be lucky, as I once was when I paid a call at the Bronx Zoo and found myself attending the birth of twin fawns. It was a fine sight, and I lost no time writing a piece about it. The other face of discipline is that, zoo or no zoo, diversion or no diversion, in the end a man must sit down and get the words on paper, and against great odds. This takes stamina and resolution. Having got them on paper, he must still have the discipline to discard them if they fail to measure up; he must view them with a jaundiced eye and do the whole thing over as many times as is necessary to achieve excellence, or as close to excellence as he can get. This varies from one time to maybe twenty.

INTERVIEWER: Does the finished product need a gestation period—that is, do you put a finished work away and look at it a month hence?

WHITE: It depends on what kind of product it is. Many a poem could well use more than nine months. On the other hand, a newspaper report of a fire in a warehouse can't be expected to enjoy a gestation period. When I finished *Charlotte's Web*, I put it away, feeling that something was wrong. The story had taken me two years to write, working on and off, but I was in no particular hurry. I took another year to rewrite it, and it was a year well spent. If I write something and feel doubtful about it, I soak it away. The passage of time can be a help in evaluating it. But in general, I tend to rush into print, riding a wave of emotion.

INTERVIEWER: Do you revise endlessly? How do you know when something is right? Is perhaps this critical ability the necessary equipment for the writer?

WHITE: I revise a great deal. I know when something is right because bells begin ringing and lights flash. I'm not at all sure what the "necessary equipment" is for a writer—it seems to vary greatly with the individual. Some writers are equipped with extrasensory perception. Some have a good ear, like O'Hara. Some are equipped with humor—although not nearly as many as think they are. Some are equipped with a massive intellect, like Wilson. Some are prodigious. I do think the ability to evaluate one's own stuff with reasonable accuracy is a helpful piece of equipment. I've known good writers who've had it, and I've known good writers who've not. I've known writers who were utterly convinced that anything at all, if it came from their pen, was the work of genius and as close to being right as anything can be.

INTERVIEWER: In your essay, *An Approach to Style,* your first rule for the writer is to place himself in the background. But recently you are quoted as saying: "I am an egoist, inclined to inject myself into almost everything I write." Is this not contradictory?

WHITE: There is no contradiction. The precept "place yourself in the background" is a useful one. It's true that I paid little attention to it. Neither have a lot of other writers. It all depends on what's going on, and it depends on the nature of the beast. An accomplished reporter usually places himself in the background. An experienced novelist usually does. But certainly nobody would want B. Cory Kilvert to place himself in the background—there would be nothing left. As for me, I'm no Kilvert, neither am I a reporter or a novelist. I live by my wits and started at an early age to inject myself into the act, as a clown does in the ring. This is all very well if you can get away with it, but a young writer will find that it is better discipline to stay in the background than to lunge forward on the assumption that his presence is necessary for the success of the occasion.

INTERVIEWER: Since your interest with Strunk on style, have there been any other such books you would recommend?

WHITE: I'm not familiar with books on style. My role in the revival of Strunk's book was a fluke—just something I took on because I was not doing anything else at the time. It cost me a year out of my life, so little did I know about grammar.

INTERVIEWER: Is style something that can be taught?

WHITE: I don't think it can be taught. Style results more from what a person is than from what he knows. But there are a few hints that can be thrown out to advantage.

INTERVIEWER: What would these few hints be?

WHITE: They would be the twenty-one hints I threw out in Chapter V of *The Elements of Style*. There was nothing new or original about them, but there they are, for all to read.

INTERVIEWER: Thurber said that if there was such a thing as a *New Yorker* style, possibly it was "playing it down." Would you agree?

WHITE: I don't agree that there is such a thing as *New Yorker* style. The magazine has published an enormous volume of stuff, written by a very long and varied roster of contributors. I see not the slightest resemblance between, say, Cheever's style and the style of the late Alva Johnston. I see no resemblance between, say, Thurber's style and the style of Muriel Spark. If sometimes there seems to be a sort of sameness of sound in *The New Yorker*, it probably can be traced to the magazine's copy desk, which is a marvelous fortress of grammatical exactitude and stylish convention. Commas in *The New Yorker* fall with the precision of knives in a circus act, outlining the victim. This may sometimes have a slight tendency to make one writer sound a bit like another. But on the whole, *New Yorker* writers are jealous of their own way of doing things and they are never chivvied against their will into doing it some other way.

INTERVIEWER: Do you think media such as television and motion pictures have had any effect on contemporary literary styles?

WHITE: Television affects the style of children—that I know. I receive letters from children, and many of them begin: "Dear Mr. White, My name is Donna Reynolds." This is the Walter

Cronkite gambit, straight out of TV. When I was a child I never started a letter, "My name is Elwyn White." I simply signed my name at the end.

INTERVIEWER: You once wrote that English usage is often "sheer luck, like getting across a street." Could one deduce from this that great writers are also lucky?

WHITE: No, I don't think so. My remark about the ingredient of luck in English usage merely referred to the boghole that every writer occasionally steps into. He begins a sentence, gets into the middle of it, and finds there is no way out short of retracing his steps and starting again. That's all I meant about luck in usage.

INTERVIEWER: Could we ask some questions about humor? Is one of the problems that humor is so perishable?

WHITE: I find difficulty with the word "humor" and with the word "humorist" to peg a writer. I was taken aback, the other day, when I looked in *Who's Who* to discover Frank Sullivan's birthday and found him described as "humorist." It seemed a wholly inadequate summary of the man. Writing funny pieces is a legitimate form of activity, but the durable humor in literature, I suspect, is not the contrived humor of a funnyman commenting on the news but the sly and almost imperceptible ingredient that sometimes gets into writing. I think of Jane Austen, a deeply humorous woman. I think of Thoreau, a man of some humor along with his bile.

INTERVIEWER: Dorothy Parker said that S. J. Perelman was the only "humorist" around and that he must be pretty lonely.

WHITE: Perelman is our dean of humor, because he has set such a high standard of writing and has been at it so long. His virtuosity is unchallenged. But he's not the only humorist around. I can't stand the word "humorist" anyway. It does not seem to cover the situation. Perelman is a satirist who writes in a funny way. If you part the bushes, I'm sure you will find somebody skulking there—probably a younger, if not a better, man. I don't know what his name is.

INTERVIEWER: She makes a great distinction between "wit" and "wisecracking." She said that the satirists were the "big boys—those boys from the other centuries."

WHITE: I agree that satire is the thing but not that it is the property of "other centuries." We have had Wolcott Gibbs, Russell Maloney, Clarence Day, Ring Lardner, Frank Sullivan, Sid Perelman, and Don Marquis, to mention a few. Satire is a most difficult and subtle form of writing, requiring a kind of natural genius. Any reasonably well-educated person can write in a satirical vein, but try and find one that comes off.

INTERVIEWER: You were also an artist. What did Thurber and the other *New Yorker* artists think of your drawings and *New Yorker* covers?

WHITE: I'm not an artist and never did any drawings for *The New Yorker*. I did turn in a cover and it was published. I can't draw or paint, but I was sick in bed with tonsillitis or something, and I had nothing to occupy me, but I had a cover idea—of a sea horse wearing a nose bag. I borrowed my son's watercolor set, copied a sea horse from a picture in Webster's dictionary, and managed to produce a cover that was bought. It wasn't much of a thing. I even loused up the whole business finally by printing the word OATS on the nose bag, lest somebody fail to get the point. I suppose the original of that cover would be a collector's item of a minor sort, since it is my only excursion into the world of art. But I don't know where it is. I gave it to Jed Harris. What he did with it, knows God.

INTERVIEWER: You did write the famous caption for the Carl Rose drawing of a mother saying to her youngster: "It's broccoli dear"—with his reply: "I say it's spinach, and I say the hell with it." Why do you think it caused so much reaction as to become, as Thurber said, "part of the American language"?

WHITE: It's hard to say why a certain thing takes hold, as that caption did. The Carl Rose drawing turned up in the office with an entirely different caption—I can't recall what it was, but it had nothing to do with broccoli or spinach. The drawing landed on my desk for recaptioning, and I abandoned the theme of the Rose caption and went off on my own. I can't say why it got into the language. Perhaps it struck a responsive chord with parents who found it true of children, or, more likely, true of what they liked to *think* a child might say under such circumstances.

INTERVIEWER: Many people have said that your wife, Katharine S. White, was the "intellectual soul" of *The New Yorker* in the early days, and her enormous influence and contributions have never been recorded adequately.

WHITE: I have never seen an adequate account of Katharine's role with *The New Yorker.* Then Mrs. Ernest Angell, she was one of the first editors to be hired, and I can't imagine what would have happened to the magazine if she hadn't turned up. Ross, though something of a genius, had serious gaps. In Katharine, he found someone who filled them in. No two people were ever more different than Mr. Ross and Mrs. Angell; what he lacked, she had; what she lacked, he had. She complemented him in a way that, in retrospect, seems to me to have been indispensable to the survival of the magazine. She was a product of Miss Winsor's and Bryn Mawr. Ross was a high school dropout. She had a natural refinement of manner and speech; Ross mumbled and bellowed and swore. She quickly discovered, in this fumbling and impoverished new weekly, something that fascinated her: its quest for humor, its search for excellence, its involvement with young writers and artists. She enjoyed contact with people; Ross, with certain exceptions, despised it—especially during hours. She was patient and quiet; he was impatient and noisy. Katharine was soon sitting in on art sessions and planning sessions, editing fiction and poetry, cheering and steering authors and artists along the paths they were eager to follow, learning makeup, learning pencil editing, heading the Fiction Department, sharing the personal woes and dilemmas of innumerable contributors and staff people who were in trouble or despair, and, in short, accepting the whole unruly business of a tottering magazine with the warmth and dedication of a broody hen.

I had a bird's-eye view of all this because, in the midst of it, I became her husband. During the day, I saw her in operation at the office. At the end of the day, I watched her bring the whole mess home with her in a cheap and bulging portfolio. The light burned late, our bed was lumpy with page proofs, and our home was alive with laughter and the pervasive spirit of her dedication and her industry. In forty-five years, this dedication has not cooled. It is strong today, although she is out of the running, from age and ill health. Perhaps the nearest thing to an adequate glimpse of her role with the magazine is a collection of books in our upstairs sitting room. They are the published works of the dozens of fiction writers and poets she edited over the years, and their flyleaves are full of words of love and admiration and gratitude. Everyone has a few lucky days in his life. I suspect one of Ross's luckiest was the day a young woman named Mrs. Angell stepped off the elevator, all ready to go to work.

INTERVIEWER: Is there any shifting of gears in writing such children's books as *Charlotte's Web* and *Stuart Little*? Do you write to a particular age group?

WHITE: Anybody who shifts gears when he writes for children is likely to wind up stripping his gears. But I don't want to evade your question. There *is* a difference between writing for children and for adults. I am lucky, though, as I seldom seem to have my audience in mind when I am at work. It is as though they didn't exist.

Anyone who writes *down* to children is simply wasting his time. You have to write up, not down. Children are demanding. They are the most attentive, curious, eager, observant, sensitive, quick, and generally congenial readers on earth. They accept, almost without question, anything you present them with, as long as it is presented honestly, fearlessly, and clearly. I handed them, against the advice of experts, a mouse-boy, and they accepted it without a quiver. In *Charlotte's Web*, I gave them a literate spider, and they took that.

Some writers for children deliberately avoid using words they think a child doesn't know. This emasculates the prose and, I suspect, bores the reader. Children are game for anything. I throw them hard words, and they backhand them over the net. They love words that give them a hard time, provided they are in a context that absorbs their attention. I'm lucky again: my own vocabulary is small, compared to most writers, and I tend to use the short words. So it's no problem for me to write for children. We have a lot in common.

INTERVIEWER: What are your views about the writer's commitment to politics, international affairs? You have written so much (*The Wild Flag*, etc.) about federal and international issues.

WHITE: A writer should concern himself with whatever absorbs his fancy, stirs his heart, and unlimbers his typewriter. I feel no obligation to deal with politics. I do feel a responsibility to society because of going into print: a writer has the duty to be good, not lousy; true, not false; lively, not dull; accurate, not full of error. He should tend to lift people up, not lower them down. Writers do not merely reflect and interpret life, they inform and shape life.

For a number of years, I was thinking almost continuously about the needless chaos and cruelty of a world that is essentially parochial, composed of more than a hundred parishes, or nations, each spying on the others, each plotting against the others, each concerned almost solely with its own bailiwick and its own stunt. I wrote some pieces about world government, or "supranational" government. I didn't do it from any sense of commitment, I did it because it was what I felt like writing. Today, although I seldom discuss the theme, I am as convinced as I ever was that our only chance of achieving an orderly world is by constructing a governed world. I regard disarmament as a myth, diplomacy as a necessary evil under present conditions, and absolute sovereignty as something to outgrow.

INTERVIEWER: Can you suggest something about the present state of letters, and, perhaps, the future of letters?

WHITE: I don't suppose a man who hasn't read *Portnoy's Complaint* should comment on the present state of letters. In general, I have no objection to permissiveness in writing. Permissiveness, however, lets down the bars for a whole army of non-writers who rush in to say the words, take the profits, and foul up the room. Shocking writing is like murder: the questions the jury must decide are the questions of motive and intent.

INTERVIEWER: In a country such as ours, which has become increasingly enamored of and dependent upon science and technology, what role do you see for the writer?

WHITE: The writer's role is what it has always been: he is a custodian, a secretary. Science and technology have perhaps deepened his responsibility but not changed it. In "The Ring of Time," I wrote: "As a writing man, or secretary, I have always felt charged with the safekeeping of all unexpected items of worldly or unworldly enchantment, as though I might be held personally responsible if even a small one were to be lost. But it is not easy to communicate anything of this nature."

A writer must reflect and interpret his society, his world; he must also provide inspiration and guidance and challenge. Much writing today strikes me as deprecating, destructive, and angry. There are good reasons for anger, and I have nothing against anger. But I think some writers have lost their sense of proportion, their sense of humor, and their sense of appreciation. I am often mad, but I would hate to be nothing but mad: and I think I would lose what little value I may have as a writer if I were to refuse, as a matter of principle, to accept the warming rays of the sun, and to report them, whenever, and if ever, they happen to strike me. One role of the writer today is to sound the alarm. The environment is disintegrating, the hour is late, and not much is being done. Instead of carting rocks from the moon, we should be carting the feces out of Lake Erie.

INTERVIEWER: How extensive are the journals you have kept and do you hope to publish them? Could you tell us something of their subject matter?

WHITE: The journals date from about 1917 to about 1930, with a few entries of more recent date. They occupy two-thirds of a whiskey carton. How many words that would be I have no idea, but it would be an awful lot.

The journals are callow, sententious, moralistic, and full of rubbish. They are also hard to ignore. They were written sometimes in longhand, sometimes typed (single spaced). They contain many clippings. Extensive is the word for them. I do not hope to publish them, but I would like to get a little mileage out of them. After so many years, they tend to hold my attention even though they do not excite my admiration. I have already dipped into them on a couple of occasions, to help out on a couple of pieces.

In most respects they are disappointing. Where I would like to discover facts, I find fancy. Where I would like to learn what I did, I learn only what I was thinking. They are loaded with opinion, moral thoughts, quick evaluations, youthful hopes and cares and sorrows. Occasionally, they manage to report something in exquisite honesty and accuracy. This is why I have refrained from burning them. But usually, after reading a couple of pages, I put them aside in disgust and pick up Kilvert, to see what a *good* diarist can do.

INTERVIEWER: Faulkner has written of writers, "All of us failed to match our dreams of perfection." Would you put yourself in this category?

WHITE: Yes. My friend, John McNulty, had a title for a popular song he always intended to write and never did: "Keep your dreams within reason." We both thought this was a very funny idea for a song. I still think it is funny. My dreams have never been kept within reason. I'm glad they've not been. And Faulkner was right—all of us failed.

INTERVIEWER: Could you say what those dreams were?

WHITE: No. Here I think you are asking me to be specific, or explicit, about something that is essentially vague and inexpressible. Don Marquis said it perfectly:

> My heart hath followed all my days
> Something I cannot name.

INTERVIEWER: What is it, do you think, when you try to write an English sentence at this date, that causes you to "fly into a thousand pieces"? Are you still encouraged (as Ross once wrote you after reading a piece of yours) "to go on"?

WHITE: It isn't just "at this date"—I've always been unstable under pressure. When I start to write, my mind is apt to race, like a clock from which the pendulum has been removed. I simply can't keep up, with pen or typewriter, and this causes me to break apart. I think there are writers whose thoughts flow in a smooth and orderly fashion, and they can transcribe them on paper without undue emotion or without getting too far behind. I envy them. When you consider that there are a thousand ways to express even the simplest idea, it is no wonder writers are under a great strain. Writers care greatly how a thing is said—it makes all the difference. So they are constantly faced with too many choices and must make too many decisions.

I am still encouraged to go on. I wouldn't know where else to go.

—GEORGE A. PLIMPTON
—FRANK H. CROWTHER

2. Leon Edel

Leon Edel is best known for his five-volume *Life of Henry James,* a project that took over twenty years to research and write and for which he won both the Pulitzer Prize and the National Book Award in 1963. In 1976, Edel received the Gold Medal in Biography from the American Academy and Institute of Arts and Letters. Edel also completed E. K. Brown's biography of Willa Cather in 1953 (Brown died while at work on it), and in more recent years has written a group biography, *Bloomsbury: A House of Lions* (1979), a volume of essays on literary psychology, *Stuff of Sleep and Dreams* (1982), a widely disseminated pamphlet-life of Henry David Thoreau (1970), a great deal of material about James Joyce, and also about the psychological novel. He has recently completed a four-volume edition of Henry James's *Selected Letters,* and has edited four volumes of Edmund Wilson's journals, the most recent of which, *The Fifties,* was published in 1985. In addition, Edel has spoken and written extensively on the art of biography. *Literary Biography,* taken from his series of Alexander Lectures, was published in 1957, and *Writing Lives,* an updated compendium of his work on the subject, was published in 1984. A one-volume edition of the *Life of Henry James* was published in November, 1985.

Leon Edel was born on September 9, 1907, in Pittsburgh, Pennsylvania, and spent most of his childhood in Canada. After the war, in 1949, Edel published his first work on Henry James: edited versions of James's *Complete Plays* and *The Ghostly Tales of Henry James.* He later held the Henry James Chair in English and American Letters at New York University from 1966–1973. Edel lives with his wife, the writer Marjorie Sinclair, in Honolulu, where from 1972–1979 he occupied a post-retirement chair at the University of Hawaii called the Citizens Chair.

A first draft of Leon Edel's review of Robert Holmes's Footsteps, *written for* The Washington Post.

Leon Edel inspecting the garden at Monk's House, home of Virginia and Leonard Woolf.

Leon Edel

About biography, Lytton Strachey once wrote, "We do not reflect that it is perhaps as difficult to write a good life as it is to live one." In our own time, Leon Edel—a literary biographer for over fifty years—is the most notable practitioner of his craft.

When the prospect of an interview on the art of biography first came up, so did the issue of geography. Quite simply, Edel was in Honolulu, the interviewer, New York. With characteristic generosity, Edel offered a solution. "Will you come to Honolulu?" he wrote, "an ocean and a continent away? You are welcome to conduct the sessions here in my study on a hilltop overlooking the city, a fine green place with an intrusive sleek cat, plumeria trees, cooing doves and general quiet." Tempting as it was, the meeting in Hawaii was preempted by the Edels'

*visit to New York in the spring of 1985. This interview was
conducted in their room at the Westbury Hotel during two
consecutive mornings in mid-May. Now in his seventies, Leon
Edel is a small man with a soft voice and a ready smile. We
sat in armchairs by the window of his hotel room, with a tape
recorder on a glass tabletop between us. Often, to stress a point,
Edel would lean in toward the machine and raise his voice
slightly to be sure he was heard over the rumblings of traffic on
Madison Avenue. At other times, Edel would quote long passages by memory, then double-check the quotation in one of the
many books or notepads piled neatly beside him. A seasoned
biographer, Edel is well aware of the importance of accuracy—
yet his assiduous checking proved to be mere formality. He
invariably got each quotation right, word for word, a feat he
noted with a broad smile and a slight twinkle in his eyes. After
our last session together, the Edels took me to a celebratory
lunch, where we discussed everything from Marjorie's work—
she has recently written the biography of a Hawaiian princess—
to Edmund Wilson's sex life, and shared the first wild
strawberries of the season.*

INTERVIEWER: What moves one to write a biography, to
spend that much time in somebody else's life?

EDEL: It's a little like falling in love; at any rate that's the
way it usually begins. You never know how long the affair or
the infatuation will last. Of course, it's a one-sided love affair
since the love object is dead or, if alive, relatively unwooable.
Most biographies are begun out of enchantment or affection;
you read a poem and want to find the poet, you hear a states-
man and are filled with admiration, or you are stirred by the
triumphs of a general or an admiral. In the writing of the life
changes occur, discoveries are made. Realities emerge. The
love affair, however exhilarating, has to be terminated if a
useful biography is to emerge. Sometimes there is disenchant-
ment and even hate; the biographer feels deceived. Isn't that

the way all love affairs run—from dream and cloud-journey to earth-firmness?

INTERVIEWER: Of course, we're talking about one kind of biography here; there are other kinds.

EDEL: Yes, the kind written by journalists and hacks to cash in on a new reputation or a horrendous crime; the quest for the Boston stranglers and the off-beat kinkiness that leads to murder; the material of *In Cold Blood* and *The Executioner's Song* . . . though the latter are not the works of hack writers, but novelists trying to put reality into fiction. The great and important biographies, however, derive from feelings akin to love and are written because the biographer feels a need to explore the given life regardless of publisher interest and possible success. Since we are focusing on biography as an art, let me put it this way: biography for better or worse is an involvement with another person; if the biographer forms an attachment or is "hooked," the affair can last for years. It acquires, at any rate, a history of its own, a very complex history.

INTERVIEWER: How did you originally become interested in Henry James?

EDEL: That's indeed a complex history. It began when I was a student of eighteen. And it started with James Joyce, not Henry James. In 1926, I heard stories about Joyce's banned book *Ulysses* and what an oppressed author he was; nobody wanted to publish him. I sympathized; I explored. I finally got a smuggled copy. For a youth of eighteen the prose was dazzling. I thought of Joyce as a kind of Paganini of prose: a trickster who carried all English literature in his head. I was fascinated by the way Joyce tried to put the reader into the minds of his characters—that long soliloquy of Molly Bloom's, the way Joyce flitted from Bloom's thoughts into street smells and street incidents and then back into the stream of consciousness. Great stuff! Did I fall in love with Joyce? No, he wasn't lovable. But he was a great performer and youth likes performance. So I went to my favorite professor and announced I would write a dissertation on the "stream of consciousness" in Joyce. "Impossible," said the professor. Joyce was forty. His book wasn't available. There were only some poems, *Dubliners,* and *Portrait of the Artist as a Young Man.* And anyhow, he was alive; at that time you wrote dissertations only on the dead, whose work was complete and who could be fully appraised.

INTERVIEWER: How did Joyce lead you to Henry James?

EDEL: My professor said to me during our conversation that James seemed to him really the man who had anticipated all the new writers. "Henry James? Who's he?" I asked. My professor told me he was an American writer, just ten years dead, and I would find all his works in the library. Off I went, and there he was: thirty-five volumes of novels and tales in the old Macmillan edition, blue and gold, very crisp and new. His titles were beautiful—*The Wings of the Dove, The Portrait of a Lady, The Golden Bowl.* I carried home the two-volume *Wings* and started reading. Often I only half understood. It moved slowly and with difficulty, but it was startling and strange to someone like myself who had read Charles Dickens and Mark Twain and James Fenimore Cooper. I began to dip into the two volumes of his letters. They were grandiose. And then I read that he had tried to write plays for five years and been booed off the stage. Somehow that episode fascinated me; it shocked me that a man so delicate and refined could receive this kind of treatment. I went back to my professor and we ended up with a compromise: I could write on James as a psychological novelist and smuggle in a chapter on Joyce, and Virginia Woolf, whom I also was reading. That was how I came to the moderns, at that early time.

INTERVIEWER: Where did you go from there?

EDEL: I had put myself through college working on a local paper in Montreal. After graduation and a year's work I found myself dissatisfied—the life of a reporter somehow wasn't what I wanted. So I applied for a fellowship to go abroad. I thought only of Paris and the Joycean world. In Quebec at the time the government had sold a great deal of liquor in their liquor-control stores to thirsty prohibition-starved Americans who crossed the border weekends, creating a great tourist industry. The provincial government decided to make a gesture out of its opulence to humanism and the arts; the result, a dozen fellowships a year for European study. I was carried across the Atlantic on the alcoholic profits, ostensibly to study French journalism. In Paris, I hung around the writing crowd, admired Hemingway from a distance, watched Joyce at the opera applauding an Irish singer, frequented Sylvia Beach's bookshop where I met the young Cyril Connolly; I went to Brittany for a holiday, to Concarneau, a port filled then with red and blue sails of the tuna fleet, ran into Allen Tate and Caroline Gordon, and Léonie Adams, who were there, and they took me in Paris to meet Ford Madox Ford so he could talk to me about Henry James, which he did, leaning on a grand piano and wheezing like a walrus. I was a junior hanger-on of the expatriates in Montparnasse, hearing the far-off rumbles of panic and the Wall Street crash. Then I pulled myself together. It dawned on me that I would go back to a changed world and I had better find something to show for my stay abroad. Also, I had to have progress reports to get my fellowship renewed—it was good for three years if I showed myself serious and industrious. I made friends with a gifted young Canadian from Toronto named E. K. Brown, whose life of Willa Cather I would later complete when he died prematurely. It was he who took me to see the French professor of American Literature and Civilization, and this professor, Charles Cestre, urged me to go on with my Jamesian studies. I offered to do a dissertation on James's five years of failed playwriting.

INTERVIEWER: So your study of James's plays anticipated the biography?

EDEL: The idea of a biography never occurred to me at that time. I had to investigate those mysterious five years of drama-writing, which I began to call James's "dramatic years."

INTERVIEWER: How did you launch your investigation?

EDEL: First, I read all of James's published novels: all thirty-five volumes, and magazine stuff still uncollected. Then I made inquiries and learned that James's produced plays were in London, but I'd have to get permission from the James executor to get at them. The plays were in the Lord Chamberlain's Office where copies had been placed at the time of production to fulfill British censorship requirements. Would you believe that this old custom was still observed until late in this century? James had four plays produced; and after getting permission from the family, I sat in a little office in St. James's Palace—very appropriate!—where I was allowed to bring my typewriter. Of course, this was long before the age of Xerox. One thing led to another. I met James's last secretary, Theodora Bosanquet, a remarkable woman, and she looked up her old diaries and told me James had corresponded with Bernard Shaw. So I wrote to Shaw who immediately received me and gave me a discourse on how good James's plays would have been if he had written them like Shaw plays. He was marvelously articulate; he marched up and down his long study talking *at* me, but actually losing himself in his spoken prose. He talked in completely punctuated sentences. Anyway, the end result of my researches in London and Paris, during which I met various persons who had known James—including Edith Wharton—was that I wrote two dissertations for a Sorbonne *doctorat-d'état*, appeared before a board of examiners, five solemn French professors who gave me a hard time—it's a public event—and finally grudgingly declared me a doctor of letters. Then I went back to Canada, and to the Depression.

INTERVIEWER: With the thought of doing a biography of James?

EDEL: No, I felt I'd done with James. And I needed a job. So I drifted back into journalism—where I remained, locked in that dead end for the next seventeen years. I did think I might turn my French thesis into a book, and having established relations with James's executor I received his permission to edit the complete plays of the novelist. There were twelve in all. But the drudgeries of journalism, the Depression of the thirties, flattened me out. Finally, however, I got a Guggenheim Fellowship to edit the plays. I returned to Europe and found new material, and then went to Harvard to continue my researches. The Jameses had deposited the family archive in the basement of the Widener Library and were expected to give it to Harvard, but for the present they still controlled access to it. I was supposed to deal exclusively with James's plays—but in an archive one has to look at everything in order to find the particular things one wants. That was how I found myself one day in a long underground room with very long tables and boxes and trunks and papers and letters everywhere: William James to Henry, Henry to William, Alice to her brothers, all neatly lined up, also letters of mama and papa James, piles of manuscripts, assorted books, and a large wooden box like an army footlocker labeled "Henry James." The secretary in charge said as far as she knew it had never been opened. I opened it. Neatly labeled items in the handwriting of Theodora Bosanquet, James's last secretary, were typescripts of the very plays I was looking for; also a few sheets labeled "Last Dictation." I read these and decided I would copy them—they were all about Napoleon and I wanted to study them. The dictation was like "stream of consciousness." A note from Bosanquet said that James during his last illness called for her and dictated these fragments, signing them "Napoleon"! Some time later I learned that the executor ordered the dictation destroyed because it showed the "disintegration" of Uncle Henry's mind. But I had put *my* copy in a safe-deposit box and published it years later, after the executor was dead. I also found a number of scribbles in James's handwriting with all kinds of notes, some about the plays. I decided I'd copy these too. I think it was in that room, with all those treasures around me opening the doors of the past, that I discovered my vocation as a biographer.

Everything seemed filled with mystery and promise; there were all kinds of answers in those papers to the puzzles and secrets the novelist had left behind, residues of his complex being. But a number of years would elapse before I would really face this truth—the truth that I wanted to write a life of this man.

INTERVIEWER: What held you back?

EDEL: For one thing, I hadn't delivered on my project, the editing of the plays. I was sure of myself in that work, but otherwise I felt unsure and overwhelmed by what was involved. Years of journalism lead to a kind of sloth—unless you are in one of its special branches and have made it your career. I hadn't. I felt like someone who had access to a kind of fortune, but didn't know where to turn. Didn't know how to use it. So I decided I'd begin by copying a few pages of the hurried scribbles in James's notebooks, and spend the rest of the time reading the plays and examining their successive revisions, so as to establish publishable texts. Then one day I had an extraordinary experience. I came on a passage in the notes which confirmed my long-ago hypothesis—that James's play-period had profoundly influenced the creation of his later novels. In that passage, James wrote, "Has a *part* of all this wasted passion and squandered time (of the last five years) been simply the precious lesson, taught me in that roundabout and devious, that cruelly expensive way, *of the singular value for a narrative plan too* of this (I don't know *what* adequately to call it, the) divine principle of the Scenario . . . a key, that, working in the same *general* way fits the complicated chambers of *both* the dramatic and narrative lock?" My old hunch, that had grown into my Paris thesis, found itself validated in the Master's own words. I suppose this discovery gave me a measure of confidence. But by the time I'd finished my Guggenheim year, the Hitler war was upon us. I ended up taking three years out for soldiering under Patton in Europe, and a year in Germany, in the military government.

INTERVIEWER: And through all this, did you still think of James and Joyce?

EDEL: As you may imagine, my mind was on other things. I dreamed of trying to write a novel like *War and Peace,* now that I had been a soldier and moved in a great swirl of history; but that was just a passing fancy, a Mitty-dream, and I told myself that my real skills lay in biography—that this was the way I best could express myself. Yet, even so, James followed me. During the war itself, I dug up some of his letters.

INTERVIEWER: How was that?

EDEL: It's a funny story. I was at the liberation of Paris. I was in a special group of French linguists who went into Paris with De Gaulle—he was at the head of our procession. I met a publisher one day who had heard that I was interested in James. He asked me if James had been translated into French; he was interested in publishing him (and he did, he published quite a bit of James after the war). I said to the publisher, what I really want to know is if James's letters to Alphonse Daudet are still around, and the publisher said, "His son Lucien is in the phone book. Why don't you call him up?" So I called, and there was this tired voice at the other end. I said I was an American soldier who was interested in Henry James, and I had some spare hours at the end of the day, could I come and see him? He had a very courteous and gentle voice. He said, come along. I didn't ask him on the phone if he had any letters, but I asked if he remembered James. And he said, yes, he remembered James's visits to his family. I trotted over to his place; he was still in the old family apartment on the Left Bank, near the Invalides. It was a very elegant apartment. When I arrived, he was bundled up in bed—there was no heat then, and he was a very old man. And when I walked in, there were the James letters laid out. He said, "I found James's letters to my father, here they are. Take them!" I said, "You're *giving* them to me?" He said, "Yes, I'm an old man, I'm going to die. They'll end up in the garbage if you don't take them." So I said, "I'll take them, but I'll see they get into a permanent collection. I'll donate them in your name." I read them, they were very good. I copied them, and mailed them to Harvard.

INTERVIEWER: When did the biography project actually come into being?

EDEL: Three years after I got out of the army, and had finally brought out my long-delayed *Complete Plays of Henry James*, an eight-hundred-page book, I signed a contract with Lippincott, the old Philadelphia firm which had published the James plays, to write a life of Henry James.

INTERVIEWER: And did you originally plan that this would be a five-volume work?

EDEL: Oh no. I planned a single volume, in three parts: the fledgling years, the middle years, and the age of mastery. I wrote the young James in three years and called it *The Untried Years*. This was Part One. I asked Lippincott to put it in their safe. I now had very comprehensive research to do for the middle years. Very soon George Stevens, their trade books chief and a man of considerable literary distinction, took me to lunch and asked me whether I'd mind if they published Part One as an independent book. "If that's the young Henry James, it can stand by itself." I became panicky. "What if I want to insert some further chapters? What if I find new letters?" He wasn't troubled by that. "This book stands by itself. If you want to insert some chapters do it now." I took it home and reread it. It was tempting to get the book out. But I warned him that he was committing me to serialization. He and my English publisher agreed that *The Untried Years* could stand even if I didn't write any sequels. I did insert some chapters. And I knew then, thinking of all the letters still unread—and that vast archive now presented to Harvard by the Jameses—that I'd have to face some knotty problems later on.

INTERVIEWER: What knotty problems?

EDEL: Well, I knew James's dramatic years [1890–95] in great detail but I still had a tremendous amount of research to do. There were thousands of letters to read, the greater part of all the material I had seen at Harvard. I was in New York and had just started teaching at New York University. My first volume had attracted attention and I was no longer a young man beginning a career. I was, to be exact, forty-six when *The Untried Years* came out.

INTERVIEWER: What sort of reception did the first volume get?

EDEL: In England, the book received considerable praise, from those who had known James—Max Beerbohm and Harold Nicolson among others, and a newer generation like Graham Greene, Joyce Cary, and Herbert Read. In the States, I got cautious reviews from the academics, but very little general notice—still, a good climate was created. Suddenly, I was recognized as the ranking Jamesian expert. Even though others had been breaking ground, I had a longer backward reach. After all, I had had a quarter of a century novitiate.

INTERVIEWER: So here you were, starting a new teaching job at NYU, and buried in research.

EDEL: Yes, and pretty soon I was floundering. The residual Jamesians abroad went to their attics and, with their sublime confidence in the British Post Office, kept mailing me big bundles of his letters—without even registering the packages! My desk was piled. I knew the grand lines of James's career, but I had by no means sorted out the details. And I had very little time to go to Cambridge to read steadily in the James archive. It took me ten years to get my bearings and master my materials, including an entire year at Harvard dictating data from James letters and other documents into a tape recorder. It was clear to me that my subject was large enough to require some hard thought about how it might be treated. The unexpected letters that belonged in the first volume did turn up, and then I began to realize I was free to devise my own form. I could use flashbacks for new materials that, chronologically, belonged earlier. And as I kept finding surprises of one sort and another, I created a kind of fluid nonchronological episodic story. I'd startled too many hares in the published volume to be able to turn back to conventional chronological biography. I was creating a serial and it could be a cliffhanger if my material allowed for this.

INTERVIEWER: If you didn't really have anything more than a general plan, then you had no idea where you would end up, what shape the biography would take?

EDEL: No. I invented my form as I went along. At one point, for example, it became clear that I had to deal with the strange friendship between James and Constance Fenimore Woolson—she an old maid who loved him, he a fastidious bachelor who was being kind to her but keeping himself distinctly at a distance. I decided to drop one part of my story to tell this phase. In effect I was doing what all the old novelists did: tell one part of the story, then turn to another part; then turn back—the narrative mode of suspense, as old as Homer. In the first volume I'd intuitively planted all my themes in the first four chapters; like Ibsen, I placed my pistols in the first act, knowing the audience would expect me to produce them in the third. Having James's last dictation about Napoleon, I planted the Napoleonic theme; then the "museum world" theme; the relationship with his brother, and so on, and my structure took its form from my themes. Expediency, you see, made me artful. My total work was built on a series of continual discoveries and adjustments. Then my volumes grew longer; the second volume became two volumes.

INTERVIEWER: For which you won both the Pulitzer Prize and the National Book Award.

EDEL: Yes, though why they gave me the Pulitzer before I'd finished my entire job I can't imagine. I suspect they thought I *had* finished it. Then, my final volume broke into two and there they were—five volumes. My morbid fear was that public interest would peter out, but it didn't. My last volume sold much more than the first. The movement was upward all along.

INTERVIEWER: I want to come back to something you said earlier. Is biography really an art or is it, in fact, a structural piecing together of fragments—a form of carpentry?

EDEL: There is carpentry involved, of course, but what I was doing was finding a form to suit my materials as I went along, having from the first given myself a large design. The moment you start shaping a biography, it becomes more than a mere assemblage of facts, mere use of lumber and nails—you are creating a work of art. I think I was performing like a dramatist when I planted my pistols ahead of time, and like a novelist when I did a flashback—incorporating retrospective chapters as I moved from theme to theme, character to character, showing the hero making mistakes and correcting them, facing adversity and learning from experience, growing older and having his particular kind of artistic and intellectual adventures, writing novels applauded in England and decried in America or being attacked in England amid the cheers of his countrymen back home. I had James's Europe as my scene, and his bold way of annexing foreign territory to his American subjects. Above all, I was working toward what would be the climax of my serialization—those five intense years of dramatic writing, when he failed miserably, and then pulled himself together to write his last novels. All this required what I like to call the biographical imagination, the imagination of form. As biographers, we are not allowed to imagine our facts.

INTERVIEWER: How would you describe the nature of the biographical art beyond the technique of narrative?

EDEL: I believe the secret of biography resides in finding the link between talent and achievement. A biography seems irrelevant if it doesn't discover the overlap between what the individual did and the life that made this possible. Without discovering that, you have shapeless happenings and gossip. The difference between one kind of biographer and another may be measured by the quantity of poetry infused into the narrative of life and *doing*—the poetry of existence, of trial and error, initiation and discovery, rites of passage and development, the inevitabilities of aging, or the truncated lives, Keats, Byron and others, who died young and yet somehow burned like bright flames. This kind of writing requires patience, assiduity, also enthusiasm, feeling, and certainly a sense of the biographer's participation. The biographer is a presence in life-writing, in charge of handling the material, establishing order, explaining and analyzing the ambiguities and anomalies. Biography is dull if it's just dates and facts: it has for too long ignored the entire province of psychology and the emotions. Ultimately, there must be a sense of the inwardness of human beings as well as outwardness: the ways in which we make dreams into realities, the way fantasies become plays and novels and poems—or the general who fights a great battle, Nelson and Trafalgar, Wellington and Waterloo, Washington and Valley Forge, the defeated Napoleon and *his* Waterloo—the strivings and the failings. It involves finding the links between the body and the spirit or soul in which human beings seem to rise above weakness and struggle.

INTERVIEWER: The links between poet and poem, politician and politics, generals and battles are one distinct part. Isn't there a lot more?

EDEL: Oh yes! To continue our building metaphor, the reader must get a sense of the girders, the structural steel, the consistencies and ambiguities of existence, the ways in which individuals grow and shrink and shrivel, or suddenly burst into flame and burn up. The world is full of snapshots; but these are single moments of existence, brief flashes of public or private history and often arranged beforehand by the photographer or TV camera. The biographer must be inside the narrative as well as outside—a quest for an active imagination at its work: James writing *The Wings of the Dove,* or Churchill at the helm of a world war. There is the teller and the tale, and the teller must be capable of handling the poetry and the humor, the richness and poverty of existence. And there's more: the use of words, the question of style, the way the materials are melted down, the supreme art of summary, the delicate use of other persons' mail, the modes of saying and doing, and now with the sexual revolution the capability to be frank about physical matters, which Victorian biography always kept hidden. There is all this. Each subject establishes its area of relevance. Hemingway offers us the *macho* relevance. Thoreau's self-contemplation is at the center of his using Walden as a huge mirror for himself. And then the complex ones—Napoleon who seemed to possess the art of facing the impossible, the art of contingency, and so on.

INTERVIEWER: So then, what is the essential difference between a biographer and a novelist?

EDEL: The difference between a novelist and a biographer resides in the biographer's having to master a narrative of inquiry. Biography has to explain and examine the evidence. The story is told brushstroke by brushstroke like a painter, and the biographer often has to say he simply doesn't know—he cannot fill in the gaps. There's so much that can never be known, whereas the omniscient novelist can be—well, omniscient, something impossible in biography.

INTERVIEWER: Can you talk a bit about a biographer's relation to the subject?

EDEL: You'll remember I began by saying most biographies start with a love affair, a very peculiar one. There are endless mementos, a kind of created relationship, because biographer and subject move on the same level of history. You read your subject's letters, you make friends and enemies with the subject's friends and enemies, you are often as identified with the image as a novelist is identified, while writing a novel, with the hero or the heroine. Sometimes the love collapses during the research; at other times it is reinforced. There is always an air of mystery—every box of letters you open, every attic in which you rummage, becomes filled with the emotions of the biographer's involvement. Freud long ago described this as a latching-on to some aspect of the subject that has belonged to one's earlier years; the subject may have a familiar smile, or a facial resemblance, or offer some hint of some likable person in the past, a parent, a favorite uncle, a nanny, some figure of our schooldays. It's a little like America's love affair with Ronald Reagan. He could recite nursery rhymes on TV and his admirers would say, "Isn't he great? Doesn't he communicate!" But what does he communicate? Something upbeat, a grin, a wisecrack; he tells us that this is a glorious world and he will take care of everything. That's the early phase of biography in which a subject can do no wrong, an infatuation stage. In psychology, this is called a "transference."

INTERVIEWER: In what ways does biographical transference manifest itself over time?

EDEL: If the biographer remains infatuated we get a hero-worshipping biography. Many such are written. But a biographer in touch with realities sooner or later comes out of the involvement. Biographical transference takes many forms. It can be so powerful that the biographer after spending a lifetime gathering materials isn't able to get the life down on paper. Some strong inhibition occurs. I've known such would-be biographers—one young biographer who followed a living novelist all over Europe, drank with him, developed a friendship, they corresponded, the subject was helpful and willing to be questioned . . . and then the friendship stood in the way. Nothing the young man could put down seemed good enough; or, in the fantasy, there remained a fear that perhaps the subject wouldn't like it. The history of Boswell's dilemma after Johnson died fits what I'm saying. He'd had a long friendship with Johnson and it was one of continual admiration; Johnson had also liked Boswell's own genial candor. Boswell struggled to get the book written, but he finally had to get the help of a great scholar, Edmond Malone, who, being an outsider, could help give the narrative an objectivity Boswell didn't always have.

INTERVIEWER. [...] in the past who act[...] with his subject.

EDEL: Well, with him i[...] [...] [...]e Queen *Victoria*, he wrote *Elizabet*[...] [...] take it any way you want. He was a homo[...] [...]as a queen, too. He identified with them. He wanted to [...] [...] queen. Ruling, presiding over the destiny of other people.

INTERVIEWER: I wanted to get back to James and ask how you get started tracking your subject, especially one no longer living.

EDEL: You start almost anywhere. I've already described how I began by tracking James's plays. I wrote to the eldest son of William James, who was his father's and uncle's executor, and it was he who gave me permission to read the plays at the Lord Chamberlain's. Then there were the actors who had been in the plays. One was still acting in London. He didn't tell me much, but he brought some letters he got from the wife of the actor-manager who'd staged the play. He mentioned another individual who had known James; I wrote to him. I've described how from James's secretary I learned there'd been correspondence with Shaw. Shaw in turn told me that Granville-Barker read some of James's plays. A former actor, Allan Wade, working in the British Museum (now the British Library) heard I was reading up on James as a playwright and came to my desk, and he was full of valuable information; we became very good friends.

INTERVIEWER: James was one of those people who feared his biographer and who sought to foil him, right?

EDEL: Well, James was a secretive person; he tried to frustrate future biographers by burning all the letters he received, but he couldn't burn those he had sent to others. I soon discovered everybody saved them because they were so warm and written in such an inimitable style. James invited his future biographers to seek him out in what he called the "invulnerable granite" of his art. That's so Jamesian—the "invulnerable granite." Well, I sought him there; it wasn't invulnerable at all. He talked in his travel writings about himself. He wrote two remarkable volumes of autobiography and left a fragment of a third. Even before I entered that room in the Widener which first housed his papers and the family's, I knew that I was going to be overwhelmed by material and that I'd have to find some way of dealing with it.

INTERVIEWER: It sounds like a potentially endless undertaking. You mention that James wrote thousands of letters. Did you ever become so overwhelmed with material that you gave up?

EDEL: I gave up a number of times. In a letter in the two volumes of James correspondence Percy Lubbock edited in 1920, I found James mentioning to his brother William that he had spent a weekend with Manton Marble. That was an odd name, but I found him in the *Dictionary of American Biography.* He had been one of Pulitzer's editors on the *World,* and a world authority on bimetallism. A biographer develops a curious graveyard memory. I pigeonholed the name. Once at the Library of Congress, looking over a list of the library's accessions, my eye caught the fact that it had just acquired the papers of Manton Marble. I went promptly to the manuscript division. Great libraries can't card index every item when they have a massive archive, they can only deliver boxes of stuff, and let you rummage. I was told the Marble papers were in huge scrapbooks; he had pasted in all his correspondence and masses of clippings. They wheeled in a cartload covering certain years and told me there were other cartloads I could have. Library carts are of varying sizes, and these were big, like luggage carts at a railway station. I spent three days turning pages. There was vast correspondence in the likely years—but it yielded me only three thank-you notes from James. I would have to spend months turning the pages of bimetallic letters to and from very famous people, and I then and there decided that I would skip Mr. Marble and take the chance of being called negligent.

INTERVIEWER: And were there any repercussions?

EDEL: No, but there was an interesting sequel. About eight or ten years later I received a letter from the librarian of the London Library, then Mr. Simon Nowell-Smith, a dear friend. "I suppose this is the cross you have to bear," he wrote. Apparently, a lady had just called on him with more than a hundred letters from Henry James to Manton Marble, and asked whether she could present them to the library. Luckily, there were also typescripts of the letters and these Nowell-Smith sent to me. It was just as well I hadn't wasted several weeks in Washington turning pages of those folio scrapbooks. It also proved that a library may have an individual's papers and still not have everything. James's letters had been held out from the Marble archive.

INTERVIEWER: Were any interesting?

EDEL: Just two, as far as I was concerned. A good letter about Shakespeare, in which James asserts Bacon didn't have enough poetry in him to have written the plays and sonnets; and another letter admitting he had written a review of *Drum Taps*, attacking Whitman when the volume came out, but adding that nothing would induce him to reveal "the whereabouts of my disgrace." The whereabouts were given in the bibliography I compiled with my collaborator, Dan H. Laurence.

INTERVIEWER: You mentioned the social notes to Marble. Don't social notes reveal little things too?

EDEL: Sometimes—dates, names, occasions. It's always difficult to recover details of social events and by and large they remain unrecorded. The great hostesses often don't write their memoirs. Also, social notes often are deceptive. One never knows, when James declines an invitation, whether or not he's indulging in the white lies of social duplicity.

INTERVIEWER: You also cite the importance of laundry lists,

unpaid bills, and check stubs—things that might reveal clues to the personality of the subject.

EDEL: One never knows what these things may reveal. Eliot said, if we found Shakespeare's laundry lists, we might very well know something more about Shakespeare. We *might* know whether he was a man who was scrupulously clean, or whether he was a slob. We might. All these things tell us something. With James, for instance, it's the handwriting. He used to sign himself, Henry James, Jr. And after a while, the "Junior" got to be less and less. He hated being a junior, he hated number two. Papa was number one. There are a lot of juniors like that, who try to get around it some way, with numbers for instance: Vanderbilt I, Vanderbilt II, Vanderbilt III, etc. What's interesting is the way that the "Junior" in James's signature becomes, finally, just a little curve, a tiny curve with a dot over it. And in a matter of days after his father dies, he writes a letter to his publisher and draws a hand pointing to his signature—it's "Henry James," without the junior—saying, "this is the way I sign my name now." That's graphics. He didn't like being number two, he didn't like being number two to William either. I always look at things like that. There was one old notebook where James scrawled his expense accounts . . . that told me something. I haven't found any of James's checks, though I found checks written to him, which told me how much he was getting paid for his stories. Of course, I was very interested in that. An earlier biographer suddenly had the idea to look up the account books of magazines and sure enough, he found payments made to James for work he had done which, when it came out originally in the magazine, was unsigned. There are something like three hundred items of James's writing that were identified merely through the bookkeeping of some of these magazines. His early review of Whitman was found that way. Those fugitive writings can tell us so much.

INTERVIEWER: Fugitive writings?

EDEL: The odd little things that writers toss off spontaneously, which sometimes don't even get recorded in their bibliographies. Biographers search for them, if you can get any clues to them. There's another case of discovering one of James's great letters, of which I found a mention in a literary journal. Sometimes, you just look through the journals of the time that you knew the writer was involved with in some way. In one journal I found a little item that said, "Mr. James had advice for would-be novelists at the Deerfield Summer School." It quoted one sentence from the letter. So I thought, perhaps a fuller version of the letter is quoted somewhere else. Following that kind of reasoning—and this is the sort of "sleuthing" part of it—I did some straight thinking. I said, "Well, the first place to look is *The New York Tribune.*" That was the most influential newspaper of the time. And I decided to look at the Sunday issues of that year starting in January through June. I went and looked, and sure enough, somewhere along the line there was James's letter to the Deerfield Summer School. The Summer School had written and asked him for the letter, and he had sent them back four paragraphs. That's a good example of the plain, hard digging you do in biography—I came upon one fact, and just sat down and reasoned the rest out.

INTERVIEWER: So there's a great deal of speculation in biography.

EDEL: Inevitably. We can never know everything. We can't even be sure of the dates on letters, unless we have some verification. Letters often are misdated. What we hope for from most biographers is informed speculation. I usually set the facts in front of a reader and if necessary say "we may speculate" or "we may conjecture," if I think the facts add up to this or that conclusion. There are gratifying moments when you speculate and then find proof of accuracy; there are less gratifying moments when you find your conclusion was far-fetched.

INTERVIEWER: You play a hunch?

EDEL: It isn't quite a hunch. It's often a subliminal bit of computer-work in your mind. I once asked myself why James had called his collected novels and tales "The New York Edition." This struck me as curious. The edition was being published in New York and in London. But he didn't call the one in London "The London Edition." He called it "New York" there as well. The logical answer seemed that he was somehow relating his collected works to the city of his birth. When I was given access to the Scribner archive—they published the edition—I found a very Jamesian memorandum which confirmed my hypothesis. "If a name be wanted for the edition, for convenience and distinction, I should particularly like to call it the 'New York Edition.' My feeling about the matter is that it refers the whole enterprise explicitly to my native city—to which I have had no great opportunity of rendering that sort of homage." And I have already described how my original thesis, that James's play-writing years consciously made him reconsider his novelistic techniques, was validated in James's notebooks.

INTERVIEWER: To get to the point where you can use supposition effectively, you must have to know your subject very well.

EDEL: A biographer gets to know a subject better than the subject ever knew himself or herself, because the biographer has read everything. Can you furnish a list of all your correspondents? All the writings you did long ago? And yet a lot probably are lurking in some trunk or attic. A couple of years ago a high school friend of mine died and his widow sent me all the letters I had written him when I was fourteen and fifteen, he having been then in England. It was astonishing how much of my lost young life I recovered in these letters, how much I saw of my young and rather priggish self! All I remembered was that we had exchanged a few letters when he was staying in Birmingham and I was on the prairie. I had written more than a hundred letters. T. S. Eliot once asked me about all the letters James had written, and I remember he made a gesture to his wife that *his* letters would fill a book—and he held up two fingers to show a very thin book. Now the widow is going to publish his letters; she has found trunksful. There will be, I am sure, several very fat volumes. After a while I got to be pretty expert in appraising James's correspondence. I once called on a woman in England who had an important batch, and told her I figured there might be eighty or ninety. She counted them out to me as if she were shuffling a pack of cards. There were eighty-nine. The length and nature of the friendship, the general size of such batches, enabled me to hazard a guess. I remember once urging Harvard to get Morton Fullerton's letters because I thought them important. When they got them, I read them with a sense of disappointment. There were eighty or so and they told me very little. This was like the Manton Marble story. I was sure there must be others. And in due course I found the really important batch at Princeton. Fullerton had given his best letters to his sister or cousin, and she passed them on to Princeton. And then later, one or two other good ones turned up in auctions. You see, biographers have to be like dogs, always following a scent.

INTERVIEWER: Were there other kinds of material besides correspondence?

EDEL: James discovered the telegram at the turn of the century. That got to be a sport. I've seen long Proust telegrams, as long as letters. But James's are brief and he's having fun. "Deprecate attendance at station. Opulent choice of cabs."

INTERVIEWER: You are currently editing Edmund Wilson's papers. A major difference between your work on James and your work on Wilson is that you knew Wilson, knew him well. Are you running into the same problems of accuracy and discretion that you did with James?

EDEL: I am not writing Wilson's life; the problems are different. I am editing Wilson's journals, diaries, and notes. With Wilson's papers, even so, I have to verify as much as I can, because people forget, they make mistakes . . . I've come now to the part where he and I know each other, and he often misquotes me. Or, I'll tell him some little biographical fact that I've learned, I'll mention a name, and he gets the name wrong. So that makes me very careful about what he said to other people. And then, where the people are still alive, I write to them and try to check and make sure—I don't want to get involved in any libel suits!

INTERVIEWER: In addition to the nature of the work being different, there is also the difference between the two men.

EDEL: Fundamentally, Wilson and James belonged to different eras and had distinctly different minds and temperaments. They can't really be compared, except that both had fine minds, and both tended to be aloof in spite of their gregariousness. James had a transfiguring imagination; Wilson was concerned with concretions. A daffodil was, to Wilson, a daffodil, and he could describe it charmingly. To James it was a yellow essence, a distinct form and shape, an embodiment of shade and color, texture and sunlight. James abstracted reality into new realities and generalities. Wilson interrogated, assembled, dissected. James was the novelist par excellence; Wilson struggled to write the two or three novels he produced, and they are by no means his best writing. So with sex—allowing for the difference between the Victorian-Edwardian James, and the modern Wilson. Wilson dealt with sex in all its physicality. He was direct, confronting, copulative. James translated sex into spirituality, into varied forms of reticence and avoidance. It assumed highly nuanced forms; it was all indirect. James would have called Wilson a literalist. Wilson could not quite get into Jamesian depths—the novelist was too subjective for him and Wilson had the same difficulties with him that he had with Kafka.

INTERVIEWER: Wilson had, well, quite a busy sex life, as you've just alluded to. Is that presenting a problem for you?

EDEL: There are whole sections in Wilson's journals in which he is very candid about his sex life. You couldn't have published that in the twenties. Now I've been doing it, though there are parts I've had to omit because the people don't want to appear, and I have to respect their wishes.

INTERVIEWER: Even if it's at the expense of telling the whole story?

EDEL: That's right. I can't. When the people are still alive, they're entitled to their privacy. Fortunately, by the time he was old, a great many of his sexual partners were old ladies and I don't think that I've been indiscreet . . . but in one or two cases, I did get indignant letters, where the ladies suddenly recognized themselves in an early volume, even though their names were disguised. They were very unhappy about it, but at least they weren't litigious. One has to take the attitude that later biographers, of later generations, will rectify and deal with that. It's up to them. I can only do what I can do now. I have to go by the present situation.

INTERVIEWER: That must be frustrating.

EDEL: Sometimes it can be. What was frustrating was to find Mary McCarthy giving her papers to Vassar recently, and some of her quarrels with Wilson appearing in the press, whereas I had avoided using such details in the last volume. I can understand her reason for withholding the papers until now. She could feel that her privacy was being invaded. And I think that's quite right, quite fair. Biographers and editors have to practice a certain ethic in this kind of work. They're dealing with human situations and human lives, and if the people are still living one cannot ride roughshod over them. That's why I was very careful not to offend the Jameses, although they gave me complete freedom. And as I say, I tell the story, but I always try to tell it very cautiously and not give them too much mental anguish. Sometimes, you can cause a lot of mental anguish. Anyway, I suppose *now* I could restore some of the McCarthy material. Do a retrospective or a flashback or something—if I were writing Wilson's life.

INTERVIEWER: You've said many biographies need to be re-written. Why?

EDEL: Like humans, biographies grow old. New generations need new versions of past history in the generation's new language. In the past thirty years our attitudes toward sex—toward the physical being of men and women—have changed drastically, and most biographies were written before these changes occurred. We have had the new feminism. And we have also the "new biography."

INTERVIEWER: By which you mean—

EDEL: New ways of writing lives, new approaches. During the past fifty years there has been a remarkable revolution in psychology and our understanding of human behavior. That doesn't mean that every biography needs to be rewritten. There are memoirs, and brief lives of many persons, which serve the general need. But every now and again a new generation will want to take a new look at FDR, or Napoleon, or Churchill. Also new material keeps turning up. Look at the Mary McCarthy example. An older generation often sits on a good many secrets which come to light as the generation dies off. The rewriting of biographies is a natural process and follows the curve of a new generation's curiosity and the continuing work of historians. What I did to Thoreau is a good example.

INTERVIEWER: What did you do?

EDEL: I was asked to write a fifty-page pamphlet on Thoreau. I did a lot of reading, and rereading. I came to him quite freshly. The biographers had been using their received image of him for a long time. He had become very popular in the 1960s. He was at the center of two myths: one was that he had built his hut in the wilderness and escaped from the tyrannies of civilization. The other was that he went to jail to defy a form of taxation and so stood up for civil disobedience. Both myths had in them not the truths of what Thoreau did, but the wishes of most Americans at the time. When I had looked afresh at all the data, it was clear Thoreau had not moved into the wilderness. He moved one mile from his home into the woods at Walden Pond, within walking distance of the life he had always led. So it was a gesture. And his civil disobedience had been considerably rewritten, as it were, by Gandhi, and it had worked for Gandhi. I wasn't trying to debunk the magic of Thoreau's myths, but I saw that Thoreau himself wasn't at all the Thoreau of legend which biographers and folklore had built up. The biographers had all told the story of how Thoreau, in a dry season, fried some fish in a tree trunk and set fire to the Concord woods. What I saw was that he had come to be hated by the townspeople, that he was a meditative narcissist with more feeling for trees and plants than for humans. I had asked myself the question: Why did he *really* at that moment of his life move a mile down the way to the edge of the pond? The answer was because he had become very unpopular in the town.

INTERVIEWER: How did you arrive at your conclusions?

EDEL: I arrived at my conclusions—they have been picked up since by others—by reading the psychological signs and signals of Thoreau's personality and his actions.

INTERVIEWER: How can you be sure you read the signs correctly? What is the psychological evidence?

EDEL: The ways in which we act; the things we say whose meanings we can read today, though earlier generations did not have the perception of them. The Freudian slip which tells what people really are thinking. The aggressive practical joker, the funny man who is really depressed, the suicide who jumps rather than swallows pills—these are all, as we now know, signatures of the self. All these details need to be observed and pondered. That's what I mean by reexamining our materials and our conceptions. Of course you can't prove all your inductions, but in lives we have repetitious patterns. Joyce repeated his myths about himself again and again—and everyone thought what he did brilliant and funny; but a new and careful look shows them to have been pathetic and pathological. He constantly proclaimed himself a victim of persecution, even after the world honored him and worshipped him. T. S. Eliot's stance, his structured prose, the very subjects he chose for his essays, tell us much about him. His essay on "Tradition and the Individual Talent," behind its great show of impersonality, is a most personal essay about his stuffy family and his impatience with his own stuffiness, his striving to break away into "the new," as Ezra Pound had urged him. He's very much involved with being a sort of "Prince Hamlet."

INTERVIEWER: You've been known to use the term "literary psychology."

EDEL: A doctor defines a patient's illness in part by looking at symptoms. A biographer (who is by no means a doctor and certainly not a therapist) defines the subject's nature by looking at what the mind brings to the surface and transforms into language. What I like to call "literary psychology" is the only kind of psychology a biographer can practice, for there's no question of putting his subject on the couch—as critics of biography and the psychological approach claim. A biographer is merely someone looking at evidence—circumstantial, psychological, documentary. We must remember that human beings are psychological entities as well as physical; and that above all, in biography, we are watching their imagination of themselves.

INTERVIEWER: You've been both admired and criticized for your use of psychology in biography.

EDEL: Well, there are the convinced and the unconvinced. Biographers who have felt shortcomings in their own works, when they saw what I had done and what I demonstrated, faulted me. But most of my readers reacted quite differently. You must remember there's still a great resistance to certain simple truths about the human animal. Everything points to our being creatures of habit and "conditioning"—but there are still some who give us absolute free will and laugh at this kind of determinism. Academe hates what it calls "psychologizing," because they fear it. And then there's been a great deal of half-baked psychologizing.

INTERVIEWER: Let's talk about determinism.

EDEL: Shakespeare's great line about determinism is in Hamlet—the special providence that exists in the fall of a sparrow. Our lives are determined, if you want to take the religious view, by God—but God gave us parents, or surrogate parents, and their behavior forms us in childhood; a loved baby behaves differently from a neglected baby. Our entire sensory apparatus goes into play the moment light and air and sound—the entire world—assail us as we emerge from the womb. All this is in the textbooks, and yet most people dismiss it. Our bodies and our psyche take their shape from the way in which all of us have been fashioned. There are phases and stages of our bodily as well as our mental education. The habits we form, the clothes we wear, the furniture we put into rooms all are in one way or another signatures of ourselves. A great part of biography is the study of these signatures. Biography has for too long studied the artificial trappings, the clichés of lives. Everything has in reality been determined, including the ways in which we cope with the determinings, and the ways in which we defend ourselves. A biographer tries to figure out, if he follows this path, how the subject feels—or fails to observe, or shuts out feeling—the fundamental things of humanity and human behavior. The inhibited person will act predictably different from the unbuttoned person.

INTERVIEWER: Isn't there a danger of overpsychologizing in biography?

EDEL: A biographer mustn't overdo anything. Readers need evidence in reading a biography and the biographer needn't underline to excess. Let me give an example. In James's early stories, I found a few which deal with the ways in which marriage proves fatal to one or the other party. In "Longstaff's Marriage," for example, a man is ill and wants to marry a young woman on his deathbed. She refuses. He recovers. Then later she is dying, and he marries her, and *she* dies. Isn't that a strange fantasy? There are other stories like this one, and there is James's favorite story by Mérimée, about the young man who puts his engagement ring on the finger of a statue of Venus. She comes to his bed to claim him in marriage—and crushes him to death. You will recognize that when I found in James's notebooks his playing with names, as he often did, the rhymes Ledward, then Bedward, then Dedward—and then as if for emphasis Deadward—I saw his association of these names as defining the stories he had been writing. My conclusion was "To be led to the marriage bed was to be dead. James accordingly chose the path of safety. He remained celibate." All this did embody his genuine fear of women—and he wrote a number of vampire stories. The stories, the rhymes, James's attitude toward marriage, his entire psychosexual makeup, about which I offered a long chain of evidence, warranted my reaching this conclusion and making this remark. But you should have heard the howl biographers and critics let out when I first launched my hypothesis. A short story written by an author is fabricated in every detail in the mind of that author. It is fiction, but all the fictional elements have been thought, conceived, worked and reworked in the fancy of the writer. They are daydream stuff—and they tell us a great deal. What we need is validating evidence. I don't think I was overpsychologizing.

INTERVIEWER: What was your own background in psychology?

EDEL: My wanting to write about the "stream of consciousness" when I was eighteen will suggest to you that I was interested in the inner workings of the mind, in free association. I was indeed at that time excited by Joyce's attempting to set down not only the intellectual thoughts but the perceptual world, and I found Faulkner's *The Sound and the Fury*, his giving us the mentally retarded Benjy's sensory perceptions, a veritable revelation. I have told in *Stuff of Sleep and Dreams* of my meeting with Alfred Adler in Vienna. I also read a great

deal in William James and I first read Freud in French translation in the late 1920s. But reading is not always feeling; we get
only an intellectual conception of psychology. It wasn't until
I came out of the army in 1946, at forty, that I found myself
in such a state of confusion and despair that I went to an
analyst. During the three years of this analysis I underwent an
entirely new education—insight into the nature of my dreams
and fantasies. I was mentally attracted to the entire process—
the analysis wasn't just therapy, it became for me an entire
schooling—and as I began to read more widely and talk with
therapists, I was struck by the misapplication of therapeutic
concepts to literature. Van Wyck Brooks and Edmund Wilson
had both undergone therapy and used it—Wilson more successfully than Van Wyck Brooks. I went on to ask myself what
in Freud, Jung, Erik Erikson, and the others *belonged* to literary study and what belonged to the realm of helping people in
their problems. When I started using what I had learned—and
I kept up my discussions and readings—I recognized that the
only part of psychoanalytic psychology that belonged to literature was what Freud had discovered about the human capacity
for imagining, dreaming, experiencing, observing, our tendency to delude ourselves, our rationalizations, our need for
pleasure, our defense against pain—these human things belong
to literature. Talking about "oral" and "anal," using the adjec-
tive Oedipal, and all the other lingo of the analysts, has nothing
to do with us—these are theoretical constructs. The first paper
I wrote after my exposure to analysis was an appeal to fellow
biographers to translate the technical language into human
language. Do you know that in all my five volumes of the Henry
James I do not once speak of "sibling rivalry," though I describe the rivalries between the brothers? What people have
called my "Freudianism" isn't that at all. I do not apply "constructs" to my material. I look at my material and deal with
what it contains from the psychological orientation I have
described. But this can't be explained to one who hasn't been

through the excitement or anguish of seeing dream symbols as part of one's experience of feeling and life; intellectual discussion of emotion doesn't convey the actual *lived* feeling of emotion. An individual who hasn't been in the depths of depression has no conception of what being depressed means.

INTERVIEWER: You've frequently talked about the biographer discovering the "life myth" of the subject. What do you mean by that?

EDEL: The inner, unconscious and invisible drive in an individual, what we popularly call the "life-style," is in reality a coalition of fancies springing from what the individual would like to be. Hemingway is an easy illustration because his myth is so obvious. Every minute of the day, in all that he did, he was trying to prove himself—how he was a fighter, a slayer of animals, a "slayer" of women sexually. He had to fight battles, to get into wars. Something drove him: big animals, the biggest fish, and he had to be "the greatest," the supreme writer. And he himself didn't understand this; he merely asserted himself in this way. Something teased his mind and created his directed physical energy. The self-myth is a covert myth, and Hemingway had to go on living it even after he had succeeded far beyond the expectations of most writers. The myth of "achievers" offers one key to unlock the inner individual. Thoreau revealed his life myth in what he must have thought a pretty little fable—but what a sad fable it is! He talked about having lost a hound, a bay horse and a turtle dove and sometimes he heard them in the distance, but he could never find them. Thus his fancy told a truth he himself didn't begin to understand. He was describing longing and need. He named the three elements missing in his life: the faithfulness of the dog, that is affection; the strength and virility of the horse, in other words his sexuality; and the dove, the symbol of peace and the Holy Ghost that is love. Without guides (aptly selected from the animal kingdom) Thoreau kept looking in nature for the things absent in his psyche, and with an aggressivity that undermined the sweetness of his life. A man who decides to be, or finds himself to be, a loner must accept the consequences of that decision. Thoreau's life is a tragic life, that of a man of enormous feelings that have shriveled up within him.

INTERVIEWER: What about Henry James's personal myth?

EDEL: James wore an extraordinary mask. He presented himself and thought himself the quietest of men, all meekness and acceptance and resignation. He wrote and read and talked for fifty years; it was a sedentary writer's life with some social life on the side, during which he displayed much wit and charm. From the beginning, he announced he would not marry. He lived by himself, but in one respect he met the world grandly— he gave of his work in abundance; that abundance in itself was a part of his hidden drive to power. His novels are about power, not love. He gives an impression of involvement in personal relations, but he is distant and cool, and seems to possess the kind of wisdom in which an individual never flounders; he knows where he is going. He needed money and success. He earned enough to live decently and stylishly. Society accepted him. He tried for years—he was tenacious—to earn theatrical success, and failed. This was a man who wanted and achieved greatness. His planning of *The Portrait of a Lady* as a literary coup is very much like Flaubert's planning of *Madame Bovary* (who wasn't a lady). By his tenacity, James brought it off—and made himself a literary power even when he had a limited audience. He became an oracle, a "Master" as the young called him. The myth of his drive to power was revealed in his death-bed dictation when in his delirium he dictated letters signed "Napoleon." The military Napoleon would not accept the word "impossible." James wouldn't either. Nothing was impossible to a man of imagination, he maintained. He believed in *gloire* in the exalted French sense of the word. As Napoleon annexed territories by waging wars, James annexed, in his imagination, the whole of Europe to the American novel. He created the "international" novel—he foresaw the drama of

America's encounter with Europe which today we watch in every foreign policy debate, and he saw too the dangers of America's ignorance of the rest of the world. What he could not have dreamed is the way in which we have been great colonizers of the American dream and Coca-Cola. James became a theorist of fiction, a lawgiver. Thus some individuals act out their covert dreams and the world accepts these as it accepted Hemingway and James; Hemingway the writer for the masses, James the artist for a distinct and profound civilized minority—Matthew Arnold's "saving remnant," which cannot, I'm afraid, stay the rising tide of barbarism.

INTERVIEWER: You've just talked about James's deathbed dictation. Is it true that he said something like "Ah, here it is, that distinguished thing!" when he was dying?

EDEL: I'm not sure he said it, but it's a beautiful bit of apocrypha. It sounds like something Max Beerbohm might have put into James's mouth. But what you're thinking of originated in Edith Wharton's memoirs. She says that when James had his first stroke, at the beginning of the last illness, he heard a voice—distinctly not his own—saying, "So here it is at last, the distinguished thing!" Mrs. Wharton got it from James's old friend Lady Prothero. But the flat-footed facts of biography tell us James woke up and felt ill. He got out of bed to call his valet, Burgess; in reaching for the bell-button he grabbed the cord to his bed-lamp. He shouted as he crashed to the floor and help came. That doesn't preclude his hearing the voice; and he may have later polished the story a bit if he was able to tell it; subsequent strokes quickly clouded his mind. We do know he asked for a thesaurus to find a better word for "paralytic."

INTERVIEWER: In what way will biography be changed in the future?

EDEL: We can foresee great changes as a result of the sexual revolution. The biographer now can write with greater openness. Homosexuality was totally underground; today we at least face it. The Victorians so often suppressed the idea that men and women were physical—that is, sexual—entities. The problem will be how and where the lines will be drawn between privacy and the unbuttoned self. The exhibitionists will be out in force, and the voyeurs. New codes will be advanced—but the cry will be to "tell it all," and biography will probably move closer to pornography. But freer discussion and consideration of humans as psychosexual beings is a great gain for the biographical art and for truth.

INTERVIEWER: Do you yourself think James was homosexual?

EDEL: Somehow, homosexuality in James's mode of life seems out of character. He was too fastidious, too afraid of sex altogether—and contented himself by being publicly affectionate, giving his friends great hugs and pats on the back. That was why I use the term homoerotic. He had more erotic feelings towards men than women; we have a great deal of evidence in his work and in his late letters to younger men. But there was something avuncular about this. Somerset Maugham's story that Hugh Walpole once offered himself to James and James said, "I can't, I can't, I can't," rings true, and I was told by Stephen Spender once that Walpole himself confirmed this. What I did find was that James, who in seventeen out of his twenty novels couldn't write about love (he always turned it into power), in his last three finest and most powerful novels wrote believably about love, especially in *The Golden Bowl*. This suggests that once he had reached old age, and the time of diminished passions, he could open himself to feel love in ways that he had not been able to feel when he was channeling all his emotions into his inexorable power-drive. Some such hypothesis seems to me valid.

INTERVIEWER: James had a lot of female friends.

EDEL: As homoerotic men do. But they were elderly ladies, mostly mother figures. They were his best friends, when London society opened its arms to him: one was eighty, one was eighty-five. They were a marvelous mine of information about the society of the past. The actress Fanny Kemble—he'd visit her once a week, he was loyal to her. She was in her late seventies, early eighties. And the young girls . . . he loved young women, after all. And he wrote *Portrait of a Lady*. He understood them, but then, he was totally identifying with them. He was a young lady in so many ways. A Victorian lady. Somewhere inside him, there was an adolescent girl. And he understood adolescents very well.

INTERVIEWER: I'd like to ask you about the recent tendency to equate biography with fiction.

EDEL: Biography cannot be fiction. I have said a novelist is free to do anything—the novel is as much a work of the imagination as the writer wants to make it. The novelist creates the characters, supplies their background. Turgenev used to give each character a lengthy dossier as if the person had a police record. The biographer doesn't have that freedom. The characters are real. The dossiers have to be real. Lytton Strachey once gave Queen Elizabeth a jewel to wear at a great occasion, but when asked, he admitted he put the jewel there to add a touch to his picture. That was a piece of fictional "property" imported into the story. George Kennan once admitted that in one of his histories he put a goat into the landscape between Russia and Finland when he was describing the departure of some important diplomat or personage from Russia to Finland. This was historic license. But he did add that he had usually seen goats in that landscape even though he didn't know whether there was one there on that particular day. These of course are small details but they define the difference between fiction and history. Truman Capote, to get around this, wrote an account of real criminals and real murders but called it "a non-fiction fiction." That was his way of explaining he had done some fictionalizing. Norman Mailer calls his *Executioner's Song* a novel, not a biography. There are biographies that have imitated fiction, and there are fictions that have imitated biography—Woolf's *Orlando* for example, which contains real-life materials about Vita Sackville-West.

David Copperfield and *Tristram Shandy* also pretend to be biographies.

INTERVIEWER: Did you ever imitate the techniques of fiction?

EDEL: Yes, I did it twice in the James life. I created a small scene for which I found all the data, or a lot of it, in his autobiography, where he describes his call on his ailing cousin Minny Temple, in New Rochelle, before leaving on his tour of Europe—his first independent tour. There are two or three vivid sentences and I used them as if the scene were taking place; I dramatized the material. But every item came from the novelist—how Minny looked, what she said, what he replied. The other details were in the letters they wrote subsequently to one another. It was the last time he saw her; she died before he returned. My second imitation was when I found a sentence from James to a friend saying he had that morning visited Millbank prison to get material for a scene in a novel he was about to write. The visit to the prison is quite minutely described in the novel. I made a pastiche and had James actively mounting steps (as he described) and going through clanging doors, and seeing the prisoners. James reported the sounds, the smells, all that his senses had absorbed. His travel writings had demonstrated to me how accurate his descriptions could be. I could have quoted this stuff, but it was more dramatic to have James actively gathering his material. This is part of the shaping and telling in biography. Not a single fact has been imagined. Only my narrative form.

INTERVIEWER: So the moment comes when you must start writing. You've gathered all your material. Where do you begin?

EDEL: You begin, I suppose, the way all storytellers begin. Remember, a biography is a narrative, and the biographer has a story to tell. Inside the mind there is the classical beginning: "Once upon a time . . ." In my Thoreau I found my first sentence an expression of my thematic sense of Thoreau's narcissism. I began something like this: "Of the creative spirits that flourished in Concord, Massachusetts, it might be said that Hawthorne loved men but felt estranged from them, Emerson loved ideas even more than men, and Thoreau loved himself." A cruel beginning, but I think the reader wants to go right on. In the James, I began, well, *at* the beginning, with the coming of the first Jameses to America. I had made two decisions before I started writing: one was to enunciate all my themes in a kind of prologue called "Interrogation of the Past," the second was that I had so much material I'd bog down if I didn't find a selective principle. I determined to find a series of characteristic episodes in the lives of the Jameses, almost as if I were doing a scenario, and the biography would consist of the ways in which I strung the episodes together. As I wrote one episode, the next took its shape. Usually when I found a title, I had the essence of my given episode. I moved chronologically but also I had to juggle events in sequence, and events which occurred simultaneously and needed arranging in some sort of cogent order. The questions in writing I paid most attention to were those of narrative interest, drama where possible, and *pacing.* No one knows how to write biography if they can't pace the story. Too many biographies are jerky bundles of indigestible fact.

INTERVIEWER: As you went on with your twenty-year project, surely your relationship to James must have changed?

EDEL: My relationship with James became increasingly businesslike. I sometimes wished I could ask him questions, but in his absence I played the biographer's game of putting the question to myself and then writing down all the possible answers. Sometimes you succeed; sometimes you overlook the most obvious possibilities. My psychological studies helped me out of the "transference," I think, when I found myself saying, "Here is that strange queer talkative man, a wanderer in London . . ." and when I recognized what an *ego* he had! Most biographers blindly overlook their involvement and simply report facts and believe themselves to know the answers to all unanswered questions.

INTERVIEWER: Did you ever feel like arguing with James?

EDEL: Not often. I did like his balanced view of life, his calm, his general "cool" compared to my own impulsive way of approaching life. But I think I can best answer your question by telling you the one dream I had about him. I never dreamed about him when I was working on the biography. But when I had finished, I one day dreamed I was a journalist again and with a group of journalists at Lamb House, his country house in Sussex. I remember that in the dream I was worried what he might think about all I had written about him. I hung back, and when the rest of the press went away I walked into his study. He was sitting behind his desk. I sat down and said, "Mr. James, I must tell you, I've had great difficulties establishing the hierarchies of your friendships." He looked sadly at me and replied, "You know, I never got them sorted out myself." I think what I did in that dream was to give myself James's blessing. The dream also enunciated a biographical truth. The subject of a biography has never had a chance to bring order to a life so constantly lived and involved in action. It is the biographer who finds the frame, sorts things out, and for better or worse tries to bring order into a life story—create a sense of sequence and coherence.

INTERVIEWER: Do you ever feel "possessive" of James now, as though he is your subject?

EDEL: Certainly not. I never did. But I was criticized and often bitterly attacked for defending my priorities. Academics are great raiders; they love to pounce on other people's work and grab a letter and rush off and publish it. The point which they always overlooked was that I was committed to a long-range project, I had devoted years to it and it had cost me a great deal. In simple business terms, I wasn't going to tolerate trespassers. There were plenty of other subjects in the world open to them; the old frontier spirit of my childhood asserted itself. I had established my territory. I didn't see why I shouldn't exercise my rights. There were times when the academics were like a bunch of little nibbling mice and if one allows them to nibble away, your work is endangered, the best gets eaten up. I wanted my books to take the public by surprise, to have novelty and freshness. There were, along the way, certain professional invaders as well and I had to use whatever resources, not least the law, to protect myself. There were also plagiarists who borrowed my structure and order and development of the story, and often my quotes, arguing that they had seen the same material—but you see, what they didn't know was that for every letter I used there were perhaps a hundred others of the same sort I could have used. It was too much of a coincidence that they should choose the selfsame letters and the exact quotes, and the order I imposed on this vast material. There have been famous lawsuits about this kind of thing, and the courts have upheld the originality of the created work, the originality of a design.

INTERVIEWER: Let's talk about the gender of a biographer and that of the subject. Does it have an effect on the work?

EDEL: If you mean women can only write about women and men about men, that's nonsense. Henry James wrote *Portrait of a Lady* and I believe portrayed his lady better than most women writers would have done. You might get a biography written by a woman-hater, and I have seen some biographies by feminists which were a bit biased in dealing with men. The male biographers of famous women have usually had their love affair with these women in their "transference," and what you get then might be the usual intersexual bluntings, obfuscations, fantasies. We all have male and female components, and I am inclined to believe that the problems I have discussed exist on either side of the sexual line. You can have homoerotic loves in biography and also lesbian loves. And the results have to be judged by the completed book.

INTERVIEWER: You spoke of using the tape recorder. How

did biographers obtain lengthy, accurate interviews before the invention of the tape recorder? How did Boswell interview Johnson?

EDEL: We know that Boswell kept regular minutes, written retrospectively, of his talks with Johnson. In my time, I did the same; sometimes just brief jottings. A biographer, like a reporter, has to judge whether pulling out a notebook will frighten the interviewed person, or inhibit, or render the subject expansive. My own theory was that a notebook interfered; I suspect tape recorders today interfere. I simply engaged in conversation and wrote notes afterwards. I'm sure that in my talks with Edith Wharton, we would have had a much more formal relation if I had ever pulled out my pencil, let alone a notebook. Ask me today what Edith Wharton was wearing the first time I met her in 1930, and I think I could tell you.

INTERVIEWER: Say, what was Edith Wharton wearing when you first met her?

EDEL: The image I got, as she stood on the walk where the car drew up, was of a short dumpy woman, very expensively dressed. She wore an off-the-face hat, of the kind that was stylish in the twenties. I was too young to observe detail, but I seem to recall a mauve suit of very fine weave and a mauve or lavender blouse. What stayed with me above all was that I was looking (after I had met her eyes and her welcoming smile) at the Legion of Honor *bouton* carefully pinned to the blouse, resting below a fine piece of jewelry. (I was dressed in an ill-fitting suit, had a wisp of a mustache, and wore a beret.) On a later occasion I remember her wearing the same sort of outfit for a walk in the garden and then saying she would use up one of the two times she was allowed, by her doctors, to climb the stairs daily, to put on a fresh "frock" for lunch. It was a lovely frock, as I remember, gold and black I think—but I don't trust my memory on colors. The *merlan frite* and the Montrachet, however, were delicious.

INTERVIEWER: What do you think about the biographical

value of "oral" biographies, like Jean Stein and George Plimpton's *Edie* about Edie Sedgwick, or Peter Manso's *Mailer,* in which snippets of numerous people's accounts are woven together, like an oral mosaic?

EDEL: I haven't read these, but I've seen others, like Michael Ondaatje's book about New Orleans jazz. They are like film documentaries or collages. They are distinctly cinematic and vivid, but the evaluating eye of the biographer, screening the testimony, is absent. You take the story for granted, as you do a film. They are built on the theory that pictures don't lie, which isn't always true, and that a visual is worth a thousand words, which I deny—words can do many things pictures can't. A picture hits an emotion; words explain and offer nuances and delicate overtones in addition.

INTERVIEWER: You've just cut your James down from five volumes into one.

EDEL: Yes, I'm happy to have done that. It gives me, at my age, a sense of completion. The cutting was done by my editor, Catharine Carver, and it was splendid. Then I sewed up some of the truncations, and grafted in new material, and wrote some new chapters, and I think it is now a fresh and independent work, a reworked biography, for our new time. All biographies *can* be put into a single volume, but the many-volumed serialization exists because of the richness and abundance of material; it provides more backgrounds, and then there is a different kind of pacing. But sometimes the big fat ones exist only because the biographer didn't bother to summarize, didn't know what to put in and what to throw out. I used to say that if I had done that, I would have ended up with twenty-five volumes. And then there is the question of exploring our greatest literary genius.

INTERVIEWER: Do you think that of James?

EDEL: I'm not the one who first made that claim. R. P. Blackmur called him the Shakespeare of the American novel. And I noticed that recently Joseph Epstein ranked him with the great names of British literary history—with Milton and Dryden, and the great line of prose writers. Certainly he was our greatest literary imagination; and the way in which he is constantly quoted and referred to suggests that his dream of *gloire* has been confirmed by time. But many Americans are put off by him.

INTERVIEWER: Why?

EDEL: Because he had so many phases—because his style grew intricate. Because he was often critical of America. Because he was wholly committed to art. Because, they say, "why can't he say it out plain"—as his brother William always demanded. I think his late style has floored many.

INTERVIEWER: What was the reason for his late style, how did it evolve?

EDEL: He began dictating directly to the typewriter. It's a case of the medium being the message and with dictation he ran into longer sentences, and parenthetical remarks, and when he revised what he had dictated he tended to add further flourishes. In the old days when he wrote in longhand he was much briefer and crisper, but now he luxuriated in fine phrases and he was exquisitely baroque. It's a grand style but not to everyone's taste.

INTERVIEWER: And no one noticed a change in the style at the time?

EDEL: His friends did, and some of the reviewers. And then people began to parody him. James Thurber, in our time, wrote wonderful parodies of his late manner; earlier, Beerbohm; and there were others. Parody demonstrates, I believe, the high individuality of a style. And one must distinguish between true style and a series of tics, like Hemingway's. I think you'll find James's late books can be read aloud, because they are written in a dictated style.

INTERVIEWER: What about you? Do you write in longhand or directly on the typewriter?

EDEL: I used to write always in longhand and then type. But

now I write best on the typewriter, it gets my thoughts down faster. But I really mess around and can go from one to the other. My way of writing is hard to describe because I don't completely think through what I am going to put down—I just start and a lot of nonsense and bad writing comes out on the page. I keep on rewriting, in longhand or on the typewriter, until somehow out of my subliminal self there emerge all kinds of thoughts and ideas I hadn't known to be tucked away inside me. Then I edit myself drastically. At some point a final version appears. It's largely an unconscious process. My Bloomsbury book, which was an experiment in group biography that almost immediately (as a method) had an influence on other writers, came very quickly and easily, because I loved my subject, and the whole idea of the book. I have just rewritten the introduction to Wilson's *The Fifties* twenty times—and finally it has jelled.

INTERVIEWER: Is it true you type with only two fingers?

EDEL: Yes. That's why I couldn't make my peace with a word processor. My wife gave me a lovely one for my seventy-fifth birthday, but I didn't like the machine's insolence. It tried to make me its slave. If I were seventeen or so, I would have had to master it, but I was too old. Yet my friend John Hersey swears by it, he thinks it's done wonders for him. But then, John's a little younger than I am. . . . I went back to cutting and pasting, sorting and retyping. I wear myself out typing too much: slumped shoulders, aching back, cramped fingers. Too many years of sloppy and untrained working of machinery; but longhand now makes me impatient.

INTERVIEWER: What about the end of twenty years' work? When you finished the last of the James biography, did any sort of postpartum depression set in?

EDEL: I suppose a vague sort of separation anxiety, but also a sense of triumph. And then I had so many other projects—I was committed to the Bloomsbury book, four volumes of James's letters, the five volumes of the Wilson journals. I couldn't tell you how many books I've seen through the press in the last ten years—but about one or two a year. Last year I had the final volume of James's letters, and my book *Writing Lives*. This year I have the one-volume James and the fourth Wilson. For next year, I am to revise my volume of the James plays, and am editing in collaboration James's complete notebooks, as well as doing the last of the Wilson volumes, and also a one-volume edition of selected James letters. And I like to keep up book reviewing, a few reviews a year.

INTERVIEWER: You've been doing a lot of work on writers in old age.

EDEL: I have watched myself aging, and in line with my theory that the greatest enemy of writers is depression, which they can't avoid, I have studied in detail the old age of writers to see how they handled themselves. My essay "Portrait of the Artist as an Old Man" is widely known, and this year I published "The Artist in Old Age." The first dealt with Yeats, James, and Tolstoy; the second with Willa Cather, Edmund Wilson, and William Carlos Williams.

INTERVIEWER: What, if I may ask, is the answer to old age?

EDEL: The answer to old age is to keep one's mind busy and to go on with one's life as if it were interminable. I always admired Chekhov for building a new house when he was dying of tuberculosis.

INTERVIEWER: Aren't you currently working on your memoirs?

EDEL: Yes, but I have not yet found a form for these. I don't want to do a formal autobiography, or a confessional book. I am going to select certain specific areas of memory. All my writings have been a search for form, really experiments in form. Critics will someday see this in the James—it's the last thing they look for nowadays. I gave a form to the life of Willa Cather, which I finished after my friend E. K. Brown died in the fifties and left three or four chapters unwritten. My Thoreau was an experiment in condensation and reinterpretation.

Bloomsbury was a stringing of different lives together as one strings beads. My memoirs will deal with my prairie years, but I don't intend to dwell on seventeen years of journalism. The war will be the center. And then the James project. With, of course, all the personalities I met in my various lives. One learns always from the past. I studied Boswell to understand modern biography; now I am studying Gibbon's memoirs— which though fragmentary have some important lessons. I'd be happy if I could write a single sentence like Gibbon. Like James, he had a grand style—it can't even be parodied.

INTERVIEWER: So your memoirs are your next project?

EDEL: Yes, I'm very much absorbed in the problem of how to handle the story of my own life.

—JEANNE MCCULLOCH
May 1985

3. Robert Fitzgerald

Robert Fitzgerald was born in 1910 and grew up in Springfield, Illinois. He attended the Choate School and then Harvard College, from which he graduated in 1933. Fitzgerald is best known for his translations of Homer's *Iliad* (1974) and *Odyssey* (1961), and more recently Virgil's *Aeneid* (1983). His early translations, carried out in collaboration with Dudley Fitts, include Euripides' *Alcestis* (1936) and Sophocles' *Antigone* (1939) and *Oedipus Rex* (1949). In addition, he translated works by Valery, St.-John Perse, and Borges. Fitzgerald was also the author of three books of poems, collected in *Spring Shade: Poems, 1931–1970* (1971).

While an undergraduate at Harvard, Fitzgerald made the acquaintance of James Agee, and the two worked together at *Time* magazine in the forties. After Agee's death in 1955, Fitzgerald edited his collected poems and short prose. Fitzgerald was also the literary executor of Flannery O'Connor's estate and the co-editor of her posthumously published occasional prose, *Mystery and Manners* (1969).

In the late forties, Fitzgerald was an instructor in literature at Sarah Lawrence College and poetry reviewer for *The New Republic.* Later, he held visiting professorships at Notre Dame (1957), the University of Washington in Seattle (1961), and Mount Holyoke College (1964). From 1965 to 1981, he was Boylston Professor of Rhetoric and Oratory at Harvard. Fitzgerald died at his home in Hamden, Connecticut, in January of 1985.

ὅρκοι. Τειχοσκοπία. Ἀλεξάνδρου καὶ Μενελάου μονομαχία.

ΙΛΙΑΔΟΣ Γ

αὐτὰρ ἐπεὶ κόσμηθεν ἅμ' ἡγεμόνεσσιν ἕκαστοι,

Τρῶες μὲν κλαγγῇ τ' ἐνοπῇ τ' ἴσαν ὄρνιθες ὥς,   1) ὄψ voice shout

ἠΰτε περ κλαγγὴ γεράνων πέλει οὐρανόθι πρό,

αἵ τ' ἐπεὶ οὖν χειμῶνα φύγον καὶ ἀθέσφατον ὄμβρον,   winter's gloomy storm;

κλαγγῇ ταί γε πέτονται ἐπ' ὠκεανοῖο ῥοάων   3)

ἀνδράσι Πυγμαίοισι φόνον καὶ κῆρα φέρουσαι·   Pygmies "Thumblings"

ἠέριαι δ' ἄρα ταί γε κακὴν ἔριδα προφέρονται.

οἱ δ' ἄρ' ἴσαν σιγῇ μένεα πνείοντες Ἀχαιοὶ

ἐν θυμῷ μεμαῶτες ἀλεξέμεν ἀλλήλοισιν.

Robert Fitzgerald's worksheet for his translation of the opening of the Third Book of the Iliad.

Robert Fitzgerald

Robert Fitzgerald met us in his office in Harvard's Pusey Library one morning in August 1983. The day was muggy; Fitzgerald was wearing a blue seersucker suit and a sport shirt. He carried a worn bookbag over his shoulder, announcing, "I've brought some exhibits!"

Pusey Library is a new building and Fitzgerald's office is a small, durably carpeted room, somewhat longer than it is wide. A bookshelf hangs over a desk. In the room there's just enough space for an easy chair and a straight chair. Standing at the door, we could see out a narrow window at the opposite end of the room onto a courtyard, where grass and a few thin trees were trying to grow. Fitzgerald shook an old, pocket-sized copy of Virgil out of his bag onto his desk. We sat down, and the interview began.

Fitzgerald speaks slowly and very deliberately. When he finds a quotation or phrase or word that seems particularly telling, he marks the occasion with a small click of the tongue. We talked for about an hour and a half, and then went to lunch.

INTERVIEWER: First, we thought we'd ask you what made you want to be a writer?

FITZGERALD: I don't think it comes on that way . . . wanting to be a writer. You find yourself at a certain point making something in writing, and this seems to be great fun. I guess in high school—this was in Springfield, Illinois—I discovered that I could put words together and the results were pleasing to me. After I had discovered the charms of verse, I wrote verse all the time. Then when I was a senior, a great, kinetic teacher named Elizabeth Graham conducted something called the Scribbler's Club for a few seniors. It was a class, but it called itself a club, and was engaged in writing throughout the year. They put out a little magazine. I guess that was when the whole thing came to a head. I wrote a lot of verse and prose. So it wasn't so much wanting to be a writer as having a knack or fondness for putting things into verse.

INTERVIEWER: Were there any writers whose work you particularly admired at that time?

FITZGERALD: Well, I was greatly taken by a story called "Fifty Grand" in *Scribner's Magazine,* which came into the Scribbler's Club. I thought it was really wonderful. That was Ernest Hemingway's story about the boxer who's offered $50,000 to throw a fight and, though double-crossed and fouled, still goes on to throw it. It's a faultless story. I was also greatly taken at that time by Willa Cather's *Death Comes for the Archbishop.* And in verse, well, you know, you come across the work of William Butler Yeats at a certain point and your head endures fraction.

INTERVIEWER: Where did you go when you left Springfield?

FITZGERALD: I went to the Choate School in Wallingford, Connecticut. When I got out of high school in Springfield, Illinois, in 1928, I had applied for and had been admitted to Yale. My family felt that since I was only seventeen, it would be a little premature to put me in college. So, I went to Choate for a year. While at Choate, I met Dudley Fitts, who was one of the masters there. He had been at Harvard, and I got the idea that where Fitts had gone to college was the place for me to go.

INTERVIEWER: What sort of influence did Fitts have on you?

FITZGERALD: He encouraged me to learn Greek. I would never have gone in for it unless he had dropped the word that it was nice to know a little Greek. So when I got to Harvard, I enrolled in a beginning course. And Fitts was up on Pound and Eliot and Joyce. He read me *The Waste Land*, which changed my life.

INTERVIEWER: Your early poems are full of dislocated, unidentified speakers, images of night and darkness, glinting lights. What drew you to such imagery?

FITZGERALD: I think that the life of the undergraduate, now and certainly in those days, was nocturnal, quite a lot of it.

INTERVIEWER: Do you still feel close to those poems?

FITZGERALD: I recognize them as my own and I don't disown them or feel silly about them. I think some of them are still pretty good, for what they are. I wouldn't have put them in my collection unless I thought they were worth including.

INTERVIEWER: One of your poems, "Portraits," is a portrait of John Wheelwright. How did you get to know him?

FITZGERALD: It must have been Fitts who introduced me to Wheelwright, and also to Sherry Mangan, a very spectacular literary figure. Both of these gents were socialists and political thinkers. Eventually, Sherry Mangan, whose early poetry was highly stylized and affected, settled into a life of dedication to the Trotskyite cause: socialism without the horrors of Stalinism. Wheelwright, too, was of this persuasion. Well, you probably know something of Wheelwright's place among the eccentrics of Boston of his time. He was always in his great big raccoon-skin coat and he belonged to the best Boston society of the time. Yet after an evening with friends, wherever the Brahmins of the time congregated, he would go out and do a soapbox turn on the Common, lecturing the cause of socialism in his tux and so on. He was also a devout Anglo-Catholic. These figures, along with B. F. Skinner, who was the white-haired boy of psychology around here at that time, and a physicist named Cuthbert Daniel, were all intellectuals of considerable—what?—presence and audacity and interest. None of them had any money and at that time— this was '32, '33—this country had already felt the very cold grip of the Depression. The mystery of what in the world was going on to deprive people of jobs and prospects, and of what was the matter with American society, occupied these guys constantly. I remember that my senior year I went in to see my tutor and I found this man, a tutor in English, reading *Das Kapital.* When I noticed it, he said, "Yes. I don't intend to spend my life taking care of a sick cat"—by which he meant capitalist society.

INTERVIEWER: Were you sympathetic to revolutionary causes too?

FITZGERALD: Not very, although I had to realize that something was going on. It had been taken for granted in my family that I would go to law school after college. It turned out that the wherewithal to go to law school had vanished, so I had to go to work. I went to work on a New York newspaper, the *Herald Tribune.* But I could never get passionate about revolution, at that time or later—it was a passion that was denied me.

INTERVIEWER: So that when, in the poem about Wheelwright, you speak of "the class machine" . . .

FITZGERALD: I've forgotten.

INTERVIEWER: It goes:

> But [he] saw the heads of death that rode
> Within each scoundrel's limousine,
> Grinning at hunger on the road
> To incorporate the class machine;

FITZGERALD: Those were images drawn from Wheelwright's own work and his way of looking at things.

INTERVIEWER: Do you admire his work?

FITZGERALD: Well, up to a point. I think it extremely peculiar and difficult and always did. The fantasy can be wonderful, figuring "some unworldly sense." Lately, there's been a little fashion of taking it up. John Ashbery, for example, thinks highly of it. A lot of it simply baffles me and I'd rather not get into it.

INTERVIEWER: Another early poem of yours, "Counselors," is about someone who considers resorting to various professionals for advice, experts in this and that, but decides that on the whole it wouldn't be worth his while. Did you think of Vachel Lindsay, or T. S. Eliot, or Yvor Winters, perhaps, as true counselors?

FITZGERALD: I thought that Vachel was a really great fellow, *molto simpatico,* and very good to me. I wrote about him, by the way, in a recent issue of *Poetry.* And later, Winters always seemed to me, crotchety as he was, to have applied himself with great independence and great purity to the literary business. When I was working at *Time,* in New York, I suppose I held him as an exemplar of serious application to the problems of poetry and literature. I remember in June 1940 I was sitting in my office when the office boy came in with the afternoon paper, which was the old *World-Telegram,* and threw it down on the desk. The front page consisted of nothing but one large photograph of the Arc de Triomphe, with German troops marching through it down the Champs Elysées. The headline was: *Ici Repose un Soldat Français Mort pour la Patrie.* That was all. Think of a New York newspaper doing that! That's when I knew that in a year or so we'd be in that affair. There was no question. So, I walked into the managing editor's office and said, "I resign." I'd saved up enough money to live on for a year and I thought I'd do what I could with my own writing until I got swept up in what I knew was coming. They very kindly turned my resignation into a year's leave of absence. I thought, "Now's the time to see Winters." I went to Palo Alto, got a room in a hotel, and called on him. Winters was very kind. He suggested I go to Santa Fe if I were going to make my effort. So, eventually, I'd say in September or October, I found myself, and my then-wife, in Santa Fe, working at poetry, working at Greek—I translated *Oedipus at Colonus*—and spending the year as best I could.

INTERVIEWER: What was your experience of the war?

FITZGERALD: It was very mild. I was in the Navy, and I worked at a shore station in New York. Late in '44, I was assigned to CINCPAC—the Commander-in-Chief Pacific Ocean—at Pearl Harbor, and when that command moved to the Marianas, to Guam, I went along on staff, to do various menial jobs. From, say, February to October of that year, I had nothing to do when I was off-duty but to read. I took three books in my footlocker. One was the Oxford text of the works of Virgil, one was the *Vulgate New Testament,* and the other was a Latin dictionary. I went through Virgil from stem to stern. That's when I first really read the *Aeneid.* I never took a course on Virgil in college or anything like that. I think that's of some interest . . . that with reference to my eventually doing the translation, my first real exposure to the *Aeneid* was hand to hand, with nothing but a dictionary—no instructor, no scholarship, nothing but the text itself, and the choice, evening after evening, of doing that or going to the Officers' Club and getting smashed.

INTERVIEWER: In your memoir of James Agee, which appears as the introduction to Agee's collected short prose, you speak of how difficult it was to write during the thirties and forties; you seem to mean that it was not only financially difficult to get by as a writer, but also that it was hard to know what to write. Was that so?

FITZGERALD: Well, let's take my first job on the *Herald Tribune*. There was no newspaper guild, no union. It was a six-day work week. For a good part of that year and a half I was coming in, as everybody did, at one-thirty, two o'clock in the afternoon, to pick up assignments—you'd get two or three. Then off you'd go on the subway, up and down the town. From two to six you'd gather the dope. You'd come in around six and knock off, if you could, two or three of these stories. These would be small stories and the result would be a couple of paragraphs each, if anything. Then you'd go to the automat, let's say, and eat something, and then you'd come back and get more assignments. You'd be through, with luck, around midnight. It would be a ten-hour day, and you'd have six of these in a row. I can promise you that on your seventh day, what you did, if you could manage it, was to stay in bed. I can remember literally not being able to move with sheer fatigue. How then were you going to arrange to turn out three hundred Spenserian stanzas per year? What added to the difficulty, for me, was that I do not and never could write fast. God knows how I got through it. I really don't. There was the same problem at *Time*, with the additional element that you had to be pretty clever. A *Time* story had to have a good deal of finish, in its way.

INTERVIEWER: Agee and you once planned a magazine. What was it to be like?

FITZGERALD: I have his letters but I didn't keep copies of mine, so I don't know what I was proposing. Anyway, it was to be the perfect magazine.

INTERVIEWER: How did you meet T. S. Eliot?

FITZGERALD: I got to know him earlier, when I was in England in '31–'32. Vachel had written to him, and he wrote me at Cambridge to invite me, saying, "Do drop in." You know, at Faber and Faber. I did. I went to see him and we talked about Cambridge, where I was working in philosophy. He was familiar with the people at Cambridge who were then my teachers or lecturers, C. D. Broad and G. E. Moore. This, of course, was a continuing interest in his life. He had, after all, done his dissertation on Bradley. Had he gone on in that direction, he was going to be a philosopher in the philosophy department here at Harvard. I think on the second or third of my visits I had the courage to hand him a poem. He looked at the poem for a long time. Great silence. He studied it, then he looked up and said, "Is this the best you can do?" *Whoo!* Quite a thing to say! I didn't realize then what I realized later—that it was an editor's question: "Shall I publish this or shall I wait until he does something that shows more confidence?" What I thought at the time, and there was also this about it, was that it was fraternal. Just talking to me as one craftsman to another. A compliment, really.

INTERVIEWER: You've said that *The Waste Land* shook your foundations, and that *Ash Wednesday* always seemed to you something that was beyond literature. How so? Particularly *Ash Wednesday*.

FITZGERALD: Well, the music is unearthly—some of it. It seemed that way to me then, and it still does. And the audacity! "Lady, three white leopards sat under a juniper-tree." *Whoo!* Who is the lady? Whose is the juniper tree? What are the leopards doing there? All these questions were completely subordinate to the audacity of the image—and in what would be called a very religious poem. It needs to be said of Eliot that although in the end the whole corpus has settled in people's minds as a work that comes to its climax with the *Four Quartets,* and is definitely religious (Pound in his kidding way referred to him as the "Reverend" Eliot), that the genius was *a fury, a real fury!* Only a fury could have broken the molds of

English poetry in those ways at that time. That's what excited us all. *The Waste Land* was a dramatic experience too. It's very hard, in a few words, to get across the particular kind of excitement, but people ought to realize that at its height this gift was the gift of a Fury—capital *F*.

INTERVIEWER: What led you to translate Homer?

FITZGERALD: Now we come to, say, 1950, '51, '52. We were living in Connecticut and having a baby every year, and I was frantically teaching wherever I could, whatever I could, in order to keep everything going. It occurred to me one day—I was teaching at Sarah Lawrence at the time—driving from Ridgefield, Connecticut, to Bronxville, that the best place to get help with the household and the children was overseas. And how could I manage to get abroad? Well, at this time, in the colleges and universities, humanities courses were being developed, and everyone agreed that a good verse translation of the *Odyssey* was something they would love to have. There weren't any. Lattimore had done the *Iliad*, published, I think, in '51. I had reviewed it, admiring it very much. I wrote to Lattimore and I said, "Do you plan to do an *Odyssey* or not?" And he wrote back and said he did not. He had other things he wanted to do. So I thought, "Why don't I try for a Guggenheim with the project of translating this poem?" I felt quite confident I could do something with Homer. Then I went to a publisher, to see if I couldn't set up a contract to do this, maybe entailing advance of a royalty. There was a very bright young man named Jason Epstein, just out of Columbia, who had invented the quality paperback (Anchor Books) at Doubleday, and had made a great killing with these things. So I ended up in the Doubleday office talking to him and, by God, he gave me a contract for an *Odyssey*. This was extraordinary at the time, gambling on me with this contract which assured me of three thousand dollars a year for five years while I was doing the translation. *And* I got the Guggenheim. So, Guggenheim, advance—off we went, to a part of the world where domestic help could be obtained. That's how that worked out. Just a number of favoring circumstances, a concatenation of things, combining to assure me of support, or enough support. We lived very frugally in Italy for several years—no car, no refrigerator, no radio, no telephone—everything was very simple. And so the work began and got done. It was the hand of Providence, something like that, working through these circumstances.

INTERVIEWER: You've said in the past that you came to translate Homer as a kind of amateur or free-lancer, without a full-blown academic background in classics. How did that affect your work?

FITZGERALD: It may have had some ill effects; it wouldn't have done me any harm to have been a better scholar. It wouldn't have done me any harm to have known German. During the whole nineteenth century, you know, German scholars were *it* in Homeric studies. That was a disadvantage.

INTERVIEWER: But don't you think that laboring under that disadvantage perhaps contributed to the immediacy and continuity of your contact with the text?

FITZGERALD: Right. Weighing one thing against the other, I'd rather have had that immediacy than the scholarship. A direct and constant relationship between me and the Greek— that was indispensable. Having the Greek before me and the job of matching the Greek, if I could, from day to day, hour to hour—that was what kept it alive.

INTERVIEWER: Did you set to work with any inviolable principles of translation?

FITZGERALD: Yes, one or two. One was that it didn't matter how long it took. I'd stay with it until I got it right. The other was, roughly, that whoever had composed this poem had imagined people in action and people feeling and saying things out of what they felt; that work of imagining had to be redone. I had to reimagine it, so that it would be alive from start to finish. What had kept it fresh for so many centuries was the sensation you had, when reading it, that *this* was alive.

INTERVIEWER: What considerations went into finding an English equivalent for Homeric Greek?

FITZGERALD: Diction. One wanted the English to be, as I've already said, fully alive. That this should be so, the colloquial register of the language had to enter into it. How far should you go with colloquialism? Would slang be useful? Answer: practically never. One would avoid what was transient in speech. The test of a given phrase would be: Is it worthy to be immortal? To "make a beeline" for something. That's worthy of being immortal and is immortal in English idiom. "I guess I'll split" is not going to be immortal and is excludable, therefore excluded.

INTERVIEWER: Were there any modern English poets who gave you some insight into what kind of line to take in doing the translation?

FITZGERALD: There was, of course, Ezra Pound and his fondness for the *Odyssey*. He had helped W. H. D. Rouse. Rouse was trying to do a prose version and there was a correspondence between them. I always felt that Pound was really dissatisfied and disappointed in the end with what Rouse did. Before I went to Europe, I went to see Pound at St. Elizabeth's. I wanted to tell him what I was going to try to do. I told him what I felt at the time—which was that there was no point in trying to do every line. I would do what I could. I'd hit the high spots. He said, "Oh no, don't do that. Let him say everything he wanted to say." So I had to rethink it and eventually I did let Homer say everything he wanted to say. I sent Pound the first draft of the first book when I got that done in Italy that fall. I got a postcard back, a wonderful postcard, saying, "Too much iambic will kill any subject matter." After that, I was very careful about getting singsong again. Keep the verse alive, that was the main thing. That's what he meant. And then, at a certain point I came across the *Anathemata*, by David Jones, which I thought was beautiful, like a silvery piece of driftwood that you could carry around with you. I carried it around just because of the texture of parts of it, a wonderful texture. I really couldn't pinpoint or put my finger on anything in my work that was directly attributable to David Jones. It was a kind of talisman that I kept with me.

INTERVIEWER: Did you find your trip to Greece and Ithaca to be useful?

FITZGERALD: That was wonderful. It corroborated my sense of the place. There, for example, was the wine-dark sea.

INTERVIEWER: How did you work on the translations?

FITZGERALD: I had this whole routine worked out while doing the Homer. I wrote out every line of Greek in my own hand, book by book, a big notebook for each book. One line to two blank lines. As I went through the Greek and copied it out in my own hand, I would face the difficulties—any crux that turned up, questions of interpretation—and try to work them out. I accumulated editions with notes and so on as I went along. So before I was through, I had acquired some of the scholarship that was relevant to my problems. But always, in the end, it was simply the Greek facing me, in my own hand, in my own notebook.

INTERVIEWER: How different is it when you compose your own verse?

FITZGERALD: You don't have any lines of Greek. And you're not riding the ground swell of another imagination as you are in translating. You have your own imagination.

INTERVIEWER: Would you revise as you went along, book by book, or did you wait until it was over with?

FITZGERALD: Both. It was heavily revised before I got the typescript more or less as I wanted it. Then the routine was for me to send in to the publisher what I had done during that year and at the same time send revisions for what had been submitted the year before. Then at the end, I spent a summer going through the whole damn thing from start to finish. Revising was interminable.

INTERVIEWER: How long did it take altogether?

FITZGERALD: Seven years of elapsed time. I'd say six full *working* years went into this poem.

INTERVIEWER: What were the peculiar satisfactions of translation?

FITZGERALD: Well, this is exaggerating a little bit, but one could say that I eventually felt that I had him, the composer, looking over my shoulder, and that I could refer everything to him. After all, it was being done for his sake, and one could raise the question with him, "Will this do or won't it?" Often the answer would be no. But, when the answer was yes, when you *felt* that it was yes—that is the great satisfaction in writing. It's very precious. Writing is very difficult. It's pure hell, in fact, quite often. But when it does really click, then your little boon is at hand. So that happened sometimes.

INTERVIEWER: Your own poems seem to have fallen off since you began translating Homer.

FITZGERALD: I wonder if they did. I don't know. I think that what roughly happened with my own poems was that, indeed, I had taken on a very large job. The magnitude of that job did rather put in the shade the adventure of making a wonderful page, which is, as I would put it, the pleasure and satisfaction of making a poem: to make which really has about it something wonderful, as a good lyric poem has. On the scale of what I was trying to do, that rather faded away, and I guess I would no longer feel the complete satisfaction that in the old days had come of making a poem. I must have begun to feel that there was a slightness in comparison with the big thing. That's one way of looking at it. And then I think that when I got to Harvard and began teaching, and putting a lot into the teaching, that also took care of a certain amount of what had been taken care of in the old days by making a poem. Instead of making a poem, I was helping other people make poems, and on quite a steady basis too. I was handing it out to other people instead of keeping it. Maybe, anyway. That's possible.

INTERVIEWER: After you finished the *Iliad*, you said that you weren't going to do any more translations. What led you to take up Virgil?

FITZGERALD: Well, the circumstances are really very clear. My first teaching job after the war, at Sarah Lawrence, was to give a course in poetry. I could do anything I liked, so I devised a little course called "Virgil and Dante." Each year I would take a small group of students through the *Aeneid* and through *The Divine Comedy,* using the original languages. When I moved to Harvard after the long interval with Homer, I devised a little course called "Studies in Homer, Virgil and Dante." That kept the Virgil, so to speak, abreast of the Homer. Kept it alive in my mind. So, in 1978, four years after the completion of the *Iliad,* I was sitting in Boston's South Station waiting to get a train, and going over in my mind the Latin of certain lines at the beginning of Book Two of the *Aeneid.* I found these Latin lines taking English shape in my mind. Aeneas is beginning his remarks to Dido, the queen: a little story of the fall of Troy. So, he says:

Infandum, regina, iubes renovare dolorem,
Troianas ut opes et lamentabile regnum
Eruerint Danai . . .

And he goes on:

Et iam nox humida caelo
Praecipitat suadentque cadentia sidera somnos.

"The humid night is going down the sky . . . and the sloping stars are persuading slumber"—a literal translation, the sort of translation that a kid would make in class. So, I found myself uttering *this* sort of thing:

Now, too, the night is well along, with dewfall
Out of heaven, and setting stars weigh down
Our heads toward sleep.

Well, I said to myself, "My God, I've got that!" *Now, too: dewfall*—the end of the line is symmetrical with the beginning of the line. *Out of heaven, and setting stars weigh down: Out* at the beginning of the line; *down* at the end. The secrets of music in this business are very subtle and strange; I did not see these sound patterns at the time, but eventually I realized that what I had had that kind of quality to it. Having done that, I said to myself, "Hmm, if I can do a few lines with this pleasure, why don't I do the whole thing?" And so I did.

INTERVIEWER: Translating Homer, you avoided Latinisms as much as possible and made words of Anglo-Saxon origin the backbone of your language. But in the Virgil you seem to have employed a more Latinate vocabulary. Is the effect of Latin words in Latin really akin to that of Latin-derived words in English, where they've developed new connotations?

FITZGERALD: It's absolutely true that I avoided Latinisms in doing Homer; the Latin forms of the names of people and places were avoided in favor of the Greek. I wanted the *Greekness* of the thing to come across, and a lot of Latinate phrases would irresistibly have taken you back to the neoclassical, which I wanted utterly to skip . . . I wanted to skip Pope and Chapman because they all came to Greek so much through Latin. Their trots were in Latin, and kids in school, of course, learned Latin so thoroughly. Greek was always second for educated people in the seventeenth and eighteenth centuries. I wanted to skip all that and, if possible, to make it a transaction between Homer, 700 B.C., and Fitzgerald, 19-whatever. Between that language at that time and our language at this time. I don't think that these criteria were very much altered in doing the Virgil. A living English in our time had better be careful about Latinisms. Latinisms are so associated with mandarin English, with the English of Englishmen, not of Americans.

INTERVIEWER: In your introduction to Dryden's translation of the *Aeneid,* you speak of Dryden's clear perception of the difficulties any translator of Virgil faces. In Latin words there are, on the whole, as many vowels as consonants, whereas English words are cluttered with the latter. Latin is inflected, English is not, so that Virgil could rearrange word order at will for musical effect. Virgil exploits a nearly endless stock of figurative terms. How did you grapple with these problems?

FITZGERALD: Well, Dryden's despair, you know. I wouldn't say that I was overthrown very often by it, though it is true, toward the end of the poem, that more and more of what Dryden calls "figurative, elegant, and sounding words" keep coming in. The vocabulary is freshened. One copes with that. One keeps on doing the best one can with the problem of the moment, whether it be in speeches or in narrative, always, first of all, making sure that it's idiomatic English . . . that it's not muscle-bound or stiff.

INTERVIEWER: Arnold said that the distinguishing feature of Homer's verse is its rapidity. What quality of the *Aeneid* did you consistently try to bring over into English?

FITZGERALD: Well, I ventured to put as an epigraph to the book the line *"Aeternum dictis da diva leporem,"* from *De Rerum Natura* of Lucretius. This is a plea that the goddess (whom we may understand as Venus in Lucretius' case, or indeed as the Muse) should give eternal charm. Charm to the work. That the product should have an incantatory quality, as a charm, pronounced in the enchanter's way. Insofar as one can make a conscious effort to achieve this kind of thing, I suppose that here and there I've made it. "And setting stars weigh down/ Our heads toward sleep" is an example.

INTERVIEWER: When you speak of the music of poetry, what exactly do you mean?

FITZGERALD: Well, take from *Ash Wednesday:*

A pasture scene
And the broadbacked figure drest in blue and green
Enchanted the Maytime with an antique flute . . .

That's music. And one notices in the sounds. "Enchanted the Maytime with an antique flute"—*ant, ant, flute.* What comes into the Maytime thing, the colors blue and green, what the air is like on a day in mid-May, under the magnolias, the lilacs. The little echoing in the line—that's a kind of music, it seems to me. *"Formosam resonare doces Amaryllida silvas."* This is from the First Eclogue. *Ryllida, silvas*—again an echoing, like a note in the bass on the piano, although in fact the right hand is carrying another melody, so you have this repetition in the left hand which insists on doing a second melody there. What the line is saying is one melody. What in counterpoint these little repetitions of sound are doing is another. The music is enriched as the music in a fugue is enriched by two things going on at once.

INTERVIEWER: In translating, do you try to mimic the music of the original?

FITZGERALD: That, or make an equivalent. It's what I meant when I said in the afterword to the *Odyssey* that translating the Greek of Homer into English is no more possible than translating rhododendron into dogwood. On the other hand, suppose you make dogwood?

INTERVIEWER: But wouldn't you want some relation?

FITZGERALD: You would like to convey as exactly as possible what is being conveyed in the Latin narrative. You want what is happening to be exactly what's happening in Homer's imagination, if you can, and then you want an English equivalent of the Latin music. The Latin music is very elaborate. Listen to this:

Vertitur interea coelum, et ruit oceano nox,
Involvens umbra magna terramque polumque
Myrmidonumque dolos.

That's the full orchestra, really, the full orchestra. Let's see what the Latin turns out to be in English:

As heaven turned, Night from the Ocean stream
Came on, profound in gloom on earth and sky
And Myrmidons in hiding.

There is at least the matching of the series of long vowels—
night, ocean, stream, came, profound, gloom, sky, hiding—long
open vowels that by their succession and echoing give something like the effect of the Latin. But it's English, it's carrying
the story on. You don't have to listen to this music. If what you
want to hear is the story, read the story.

INTERVIEWER: Robert Lowell wrote a little piece on epics in
which he said, "Homer is blinding Greek sunlight. Virgil is
dark, narrow, morbid, mysterious, and artistic. He fades in
translation." What do you think of those adjectives Lowell
racks up?

FITZGERALD: Well, too much has been made of texture.
One of the things that I tried to bring out more fully, as I
went along, was the pure narrative interest of this thing as a
story. It's Aeneas's story, some of which he tells himself, and
most of which he doesn't. The narrative, if it's properly rend-
ered, is extremely interesting and exciting. What happened
to Virgil (partly because of the curse of his being a text in the
fourth year of secondary school, and also because of his having supplied so many tags for speakers in the House of Lords)
is that the poem has been fragmented. The arc, the really
quite magnificent arc of the original narrative, has been
rather lost to view. Nobody ever reads the entire *Aeneid*.
They read in school, if they read anything, Books Two, Four,
Six, *maybe*, if they're lucky. That's it. Nobody ever reads the
last six books. Yet in the last six books the whole thing happens, really. That's the man at war. That's the *arma* and the
virum. I would love to think that the whole story will be
restored to view. People can read it, and will read it, because
it turns out to be readable.

INTERVIEWER: It certainly seems that in the first half, Aeneas is an oddly stunned sort of hero, while in the second half he is commanding, even horrifyingly so.

FITZGERALD: Exactly. The tragic import of all this is what happens to a man wielding power, especially in hostilities of that kind. He goes as berserk as anybody. The point is very abundantly made that the Roman state was founded on war, on their being very good at war. I happened to reread Caesar, *The Battle for Gaul*, during the composition of the last six books, to see what, in fact, war was like in the generation preceding Virgil. Virgil certainly knew, as every Roman did, what it cost, and the exertion that was made to defeat these hordes of extremely hard-fighting Germans and Gauls. No doubt about the carnage, the incredible carnage: field after field left absolutely soaked in blood, with dismembered individuals for miles. The scene was one of great terror and desolation, all of this in order that Julius should become first consul and have his career. One does sense throughout the *Aeneid* the tragic import of Roman power, of what they were proudest of: their ability to defeat the tribes that came against them and then to create some kind of civil order in the provinces they conquered. But the cost of that, and the dreadful effects of these encounters of armed men, is very vividly brought out, and is one of the things that Virgil meant to bring out, along with the *pro forma* praises of the Roman heroes. A Roman *gladius*, or short sword, honed on both edges, was like a cleaver! A two-edged cleaver! Just imagine turning twenty thousand men with two-edged cleavers loose on the opposition!

INTERVIEWER: You once said that English poetry "hungers for a sound metaphysic," but that its history is largely a record of a failure of supply. What did you mean?

FITZGERALD: English poetry "hungers for a sound metaphysic"? I was, I think, at the time, interested in the superior precision of Aristotle's *De Anima* as contrasted with Coleridge. I was thinking in particular of the difference between the Aristotelian and the Coleridgean views of what happens in creative work of the mind. I made my remarks, that's it. I never went out to argue.

INTERVIEWER: In the Agee memoir you speak of your brotherhood in the arts with him. Did you have a similar relationship with Lowell or Berryman or Auden? Did you consult them when you were working on your translations?

FITZGERALD: I certainly did. Not W. H. Auden, though, because we met so rarely. John Berryman saw what I was working on at the time and made a suggestion or two on word order which I adopted. Randall Jarrell also saw what I was working on one summer. He had an excellent notion. His notion, to put it briefly, was that if you're going to be colloquial, you can achieve the colloquial thing by gradation. You depart from the formality a little bit and then a little bit more, and then you're colloquial, and then you modulate away from it— modulate toward and modulate away from it. Such a beautiful idea! I don't know whether I really obeyed this or not. And Cal Lowell just said, "You've got it! This is a bullseye!" There is, after all, a brotherhood among people who are working at the same craft, who show each other what they're doing from time to time. The result's likely to be more helpful if your pal simply runs his hand down the page, stops, and does not say a word. Just stops. You see something's wrong where the finger's pointing, and that's enough.

INTERVIEWER: How did you get to know Lowell?

FITZGERALD: I met him through Randall Jarrell. Jarrell was teaching at Sarah Lawrence the first year I taught there, and we therefore saw one another every week and got to be friends. He brought Lowell along some evening or other and we had the evening together.

INTERVIEWER: Nowadays people tend to praise Jarrell's criticism and downplay his poetry. Do you think that's fair to his work?

FITZGERALD: No, I don't. I think quite a few of his poems are very good indeed. No one ever did anything remotely like

what he did for the Air Force, for the ca~
rest of that.

INTERVIEWER: You've often s~
should be "chiefly hair-raising." ~wever,
you've spoken of the desirabili~ ~etween the
poet and the community he ~ that you seem to
believe has been broken in ~ ~s. Do you see any
contradiction or tension betwee~ ~cial concern and the
requirement that poetry be, above ~ hair-raising?

FITZGERALD: Well, don't we have Emily Dickinson, the won-
drous lady of Amherst, as an authority for that: 'It's a poem if
it makes you feel as though your head were taken off'? And A.
E. Houseman: 'If while I am shaving a line of poetry strays into
my mind, my beard bristles so that I can't cut it'? This is an
extreme, and this kind of poetry is part of the extreme literary
experience—extreme both for the maker and for the reader.
That's at one end of the spectrum. At the other end there is
Dryden, sitting in his coffeehouse, turning out couplets to
insult someone whom he feels like insulting. So, one has the
gamut between what is essentially a private, we might say a
metaphysical experience, and the other which is simply a refinement of prose—verse devoted to wit, or to the quotidian
purpose of making something clear or making somebody
ashamed, of exposing somebody, of putting into a witty form
someone's foibles . . . which can be read with amusement and
without a touch of the other extreme, which is private and rare
and precious. I don't see why we can't live with a decent
consciousness of these two poles of poetic experience. I once
said, too, that poetry is at least an elegance and at most a
revelation. That says it pretty well—"is at least an elegance"—
something that is well-formed, readable, and then again something that takes you *up*.

INTERVIEWER: How close is the revelation of poetry to the
religious experience of revelation?

FITZGERALD: Very close, I think. Very close indeed.

INTERVIEWER: You've spoken of a "third kind of knowledge" that came out of moments of vision you had as a young man. How important were they?

FITZGERALD: Terribly important. I don't think that anything could be more important than to be reminded that, as Flannery O'Connor used to say, "The church is custodian of the sense of life as a mystery." We get so used to it that we lose the sense. To have the sense restored to us—which the religious experience does and which the poetic experience at its extreme does as well—is a great boon.

INTERVIEWER: You say that you came back to the Church with a "terrific bump." What brought you back?

FITZGERALD: Well, a number of things that I really don't think I can satisfactorily speak of in this context.

INTERVIEWER: Do you think that the integration of poetry and the university since World War II has been harmful?

FITZGERALD: Maybe. At Harvard in my time there was Robert Hillyer's course in versification, and beyond that, very little indeed in the way of writing courses. An exceptional teacher at that time would be *au courant* with what was living and exciting about writing. Hillyer was exceptionally the other way. He was deliberately blind, deaf and dumb to what was going on in the avant-garde. I think one felt, in general, one wasn't going to get much attention from the faculty. If you wanted to put things in the undergraduate literary magazine, *The Advocate*, okay. *The Advocate* was . . . *The Advocate*. I don't think that people on the faculty paid much attention to these half-baked manifestations of literary ambition on the part of the undergraduates.

INTERVIEWER: Can we ask you about Flannery O'Connor and how you came to know her?

FITZGERALD: Flannery O'Connor came with Cal Lowell. Lowell and she and Elizabeth Hardwick turned up in New York together. They'd been at Yaddo and there was a dustup at Yaddo in which I'm afraid Lowell had begun to go off his trolley. At that point nobody really understood that this was the case, but we all understood it before it was over, very thoroughly. It was one of Lowell's very early, maybe his earliest breakdown. We met Flannery in the course of that, really, and then, of course, we went on independently of Lowell.

INTERVIEWER: You seem to have been something of a counselor to her. She would send her work to you, seeking your comments.

FITZGERALD: I wouldn't want to build myself up. No, no, she knew what she was about. Owed nothing, I don't think, to me so far as the essence of these things was concerned. I supplied her with one title, "The Life You Save May Be Your Own." I'd been driving through the South, and it just happened this was something one saw on the road signs. And I supplied her with some reasons for undertaking a revision of her novel, *The Violent Bear it Away*, which she did. I think she was better pleased with it after she'd done the revision. Those would be practically the only instances in which I had any effect on what she did. She was a good friend. One liked to see what she was working on. That was always great fun to see.

INTERVIEWER: Are there any younger poets whose work strikes you as outstanding?

FITZGERALD: I think that Robert Shaw has done quite beautiful work. He's a good critic and a good poet. He was here ten years ago; he was in my classes and performed very well in them. He went on to teach here and at Yale. Now he's at Mount Holyoke. He's very good. Who else? Brad Leithauser. He was in my writing class and turned out some amazingly good poems. His wife, Mary Jo Salter—she's also very good. And Katha Pollitt. James Atlas went on to do that good biography of Delmore Schwartz. I risk forgetting others who are just as interesting.

INTERVIEWER: So you think the world of poetry prospers apace?

FITZGERALD: That reminds me of Eugenio Montale's great

piece on the encouragement of poetry, particularly by the state—National Endowments and things like that. He was very skeptical about the utility of encouraging poetry on a grand scale. Is encouragement what the poet needs? Open question. Maybe he needs discouragement. In fact, quite a few of them need more discouragement, the most discouragement possible.

INTERVIEWER: Has your career so far differed from your early expectations of it? Or didn't you have any expectations?

FITZGERALD: I don't know that I had any. I just hoped to keep on. I suppose I'd have been amazed when I was twenty to hear that before I was through, I would have translated Homer and the *Aeneid.* The notion that I should go in for these gigantic labors would have been completely out of this world. As I remember, when I was signing Elizabeth Bishop's *Iliad* for her, her only remark was, *"My,* all that *work!"*

—EDWIN FRANK
—ANDREW MCCORD
August 1983

4. John Hersey

John Hersey was born in 1914 in Tientsin, China, the son of a Protestant missionary. He attended Hotchkiss and Yale, and studied for a year at Clare College, Cambridge, on a Mellon Fellowship; after returning from England, he worked for a summer as private secretary to Sinclair Lewis. He then spent several years at *Time* magazine, first as a staff writer and later as a war correspondent in the South Pacific, China, Japan, North Africa, and elsewhere. His first novel, *A Bell for Adano*, won the Pulitzer Prize in 1945; but he is perhaps best known for the book that followed—*Hiroshima*, a nonfiction account of the first use of the atomic bomb. It first appeared as an entire issue of *The New Yorker* in 1946. Reproduced in newspapers and read over radio stations throughout the world, it was a social and a literary sensation; in its paperback edition, it remains one of the best-selling books of all time. Since then, Hersey has written twelve novels—among them *The Wall* (1950), *A Single Pebble* (1956), *The War Lover* (1959), *The Child Buyer* (1960), *Too Far to Walk* (1966), *My Petition for More Space* (1974), and *The Call* (1985)—and six works of nonfiction, including *The Algiers Motel Incident* (1968), *Letter to the Alumni* (1970), and *The Writer's Craft* (1974). His most recent work is *Blues* (1987), a meditation on the subject of fishing, in the form of a dialogue between two fictional characters, a Fisherman and a Stranger.

CHAPTER FORTY-TWO

The Election to Stay

1

"Prayer is not helping me, ~~enough," he wrote in his diary.~~

He was finding the return to "normalcy"--his rounds of the
villages on the saddle of his Indian--hard to ~~adjust to.~~ make. "It's as
if I had ~~different colored glasses on from before;"~~ new eye-lenses." It was hard now
to ~~feel~~ think sustain a passionate belief that the most ~~important~~ urgent issue in ~~life~~ his time-span was which handful of
country words would make their way into basic literacy texts. David
had ~~seen a man killed in cold blood five feet away from him.~~ heard a click at the temple gate of his skull. He had ~~been~~ a pure man
shot in the face. ~~He twice affadavit~~ ~~~~ before the blood dried, ~~Then~~ had to try to make ~~that death~~ murder seem an aspect of God's wisdom to the
~~man's~~ widow. ~~At an~~ Even more disturbing, ~~level,~~ he had felt, as he
noted in his diary, "my will crouching in ~~the~~ a back room of my brain" as
he tried to come to terms not just with the ~~gore and~~ rage in China's
~~too painful~~ ordeal of renovation, but with "something dark in the
human mind I have not been ~~sufficiently~~ aware ~~aware~~ enough of all these years."

~~Friends in Sha~~ (they had not actually seen) He ~~had felt~~ the dying afflatus leak. ~~Eaten out~~ of the body before the blood dried. ~~from where the mouth had been~~

John Hersey

Early in his career—"before," he says, "I was really even a writer"—John Hersey decided to restrict his public expression to the medium in which he was most comfortable; that is, to the written rather than the spoken word. He has kept to his decision. This is only the second interview he has ever granted; the first was with Publishers Weekly *in 1984.*

Since retiring from his professorship at Yale three years ago, Hersey and his wife Barbara have divided their time between homes in Martha's Vineyard, Massachusetts, and Key West, Florida. I visited them shortly before their annual move south, in typical autumn weather on the island—clear, bright, and unexpectedly cold. He and I talked on a glassed-in porch, carpeted and comfortably furnished, which afforded a spectacular view across Vineyard Haven Harbor; his study, directly upstairs from where we sat, offers the same lovely distraction. The ferry

*which runs to and from the mainland passes in front of those
windows, its horn blasting, every half hour or so. Also visible,
moored just offshore, is the small gray boat aboard which Hersey
frequently goes fishing and does what he calls his "back-of-the-
head work."*

*The Herseys were extremely hospitable during my three-day
stay; but in the four-odd hours when the tape recorder was
running, there was no small talk and no break. Unused to, and
a little distrustful of, the process, he clearly felt it demanded his
full concentration. He spoke very slowly, and paused frequently,
looking out across the water as if trying to envision his words
upon a page before releasing them. The house was absolutely
silent; we were never interrupted, most likely by design.*

INTERVIEWER: How long did you live in China?

HERSEY: I was eleven when we left China. My father contracted encephalitis on a trip into the back country on famine
relief work; that turned out to have a sequel of Parkinson's
disease, and he had to retire. So we came home in 1925.

INTERVIEWER: Was that the first time you had ever been to
America?

HERSEY: No, most missionaries got furloughs every seven
years, and an earlier furlough of my father's coincided with the
First World War. When I was three, my father was assigned
by the YMCA to go to France to help with the Chinese Labor
Corps. There were nearly two hundred thousand Chinese coo-
lies who were taken to France to dig trenches and unload ships
and relieve troops from the front. While he was there, my
mother and my two brothers and I came to this country. We
lived in Montclair, New Jersey, for a little more than a year.
It was a segment of my life so different from the childhood I
had known, and subsequently knew, that I do have some odd
visual memories of Montclair—for instance, of finding some
old newspapers in the attic of the house we were renting and
taking them out to sell to various neighbors. A few sharp

pictures stay in my mind. And then in 1919 we joined my
father and went back to China, around the world the rest of
the way.

INTERVIEWER: What sort of schooling did an American child
in China receive?

HERSEY: I went first to a British grammar school which was
right next door to us. It was run on old-fashioned English lines.
The headmaster was a strict character who had a whip in his
office, used on bad boys, which we were all quite aware of. On
the other hand, there was a motive to learn and to do well
there; my oldest brother went right through that school, and
his name was carved in wood up on the wall, in the inscriptions
of honors winners there, for me to look at and think about. I
was only in that school for a couple of grades. After that I went
to a new American school, which had only about thirty students. That school got me started on languages—we studied
French in the early grades—and on an early interest in music;
I remember we had opera records played to us. I played the
violin then. My father, when he was with the coolie corps in
France, had bought a three-quarter-size violin. He found a
White Russian refugee in the city who was a violinist, and Paul
Federovsky gave me lessons. He later came to this country and
played with the Boston Symphony for the rest of his life. In
later years I used to go and see him frequently, after his concerts. And he never forgave me for giving up the violin in favor
of writing, which he said anybody could do. He was a very
gifted man, and in those China years he excited me enough to
make me think I wanted to be a concert violinist. There was
a period before I went to college when I practiced four to six
hours a day; I was serious about it. I gave it up in college,
making a choice between that and writing, and I haven't dared
to touch the violin since then. My son Baird gave me one for
Christmas about eight or ten years ago, and I never opened the
case.

INTERVIEWER: Do you think the kind of formative reading

you did, both in and out of school, was any different than it might have been had you grown up in America?

HERSEY: It may have been, I suppose. There was a certain amount of reading that many American boys would have done: Ernest Thompson Seton, the Terhune books. Animal stories of one kind or another, I remember I loved. There were also some semi-inspirational things—Lamb's essays, books about mythological heroes—the common currency of that sort of world; I guess those things pushed me eventually toward other kinds of reading, about heroes or their equivalents, in works by writers I came to admire later on, Malraux and Silone. Much of my early reading was commonplace. My father was a shy, studious, contemplative man, and I spent a lot of time in his study in our house in China. I was into *The Book of Knowledge* all the time, and later the *Encyclopedia Britannica.* I was allowed to play, I guess you would say, on his typewriter at a very early age. My mother kept scrapbooks of everything any of her children did all their lives, and among my scrapbooks are newspapers that I wrote on the typewriter at the age of six, The Hersey Family News, with ads offering my older brothers for various kinds of hard labor at very low wages.

INTERVIEWER: You mention in *The Algiers Motel Incident* that there was a class system in China of which you were always aware . . .

HERSEY: It was my natural world, and I can't say I consciously questioned that world, though I did have feelings of dislocation and discomfort every once in a while. It was a world in which I was a foreigner, a member of a minority, but the dominant minority. We lived in the British Concession, where the Chinese were not supposed to live, though some wealthy Chinese rented houses from foreigners there—some who had been thrown out of the government, perhaps some who were afraid of being beheaded if they were at large, and some who just liked the idea of luxuries, living like foreigners. I rode to school in a rickshaw, paid a human being very few coppers for pulling me there, and sometimes when I was feeling lazy I would ride home from school, too, and get the coppers from the cook's bag in the kitchen. We had three servants—cook, number one boy, and coolie, in that order—though my father was paid very little, something like $200 a month. Even considering how much more valuable dollars were then, by American standards we were poor. Yet there we lived in a rather fine two-story house, with servants' quarters. As I say, that was my natural habitat, so I didn't really question much of it at the time. Though beggars in the streets, and some of the coolies who were beasts of burden in the British concession, did trouble me. I remember once going home from school, I came on a water cart—water was brought from the river to sprinkle on the dusty streets to keep dust down so the foreigners wouldn't be troubled by it. It was a terrifically heavy burden when a two-wheeled wooden cart, with a rectangular cask of probably ten cubic feet, was filled with water. A coolie had stopped his cart, that day, propped the shafts up with a stick. I had never seen the inside of one of these things, and was barely tall enough to look over the edge; I reached up and grabbed one side to take a look, and upset the cart. The water spilled, and the coolie's labor of hauling it all the way there from the river was lost. He was not supposed to shout at a white child, but I understood why he did. His rage at me was something I have never forgotten.

INTERVIEWER: Did that system change the way you looked at American society?

HERSEY: I've considered myself a foreigner all my life, in ways. I was born a foreigner. I grew up bilingual; no matter that my spoken Chinese was that of an eleven-year-old—it was native to the ear. When we came back to this country, the ambiance here was so different from the one I had grown up in that from late boyhood until, say, college, I felt I was a little different. Those early years got me somewhat in the habit of thinking of myself not exactly as an outsider but as someone who came from another culture. I think that's affected my adult years, though I feel very much an American now. Still, my prevailing interest has been in the world as a whole, and in the place of a person in a larger setting than one defined by national boundaries.

INTERVIEWER: It must really have seemed another world to go from China to Hotchkiss and Yale.

HERSEY: I went first to a local high school in Briarcliff Manor, New York, for two years. Hotchkiss had taken in a number of missionaries' sons; I was admitted there on a scholarship. The scholarship boys cleaned classrooms, waited on tables, and were in one sense in a separate social class. But that seemed to me to be perfectly normal; in fact, in ways I saw it as an advantage. Waiting on tables, you were at the nerve center of gossip and understanding—you knew everybody, what they were like, what they were about. I didn't feel that the work was demeaning in the least. A great teacher in my life was the headmaster of the school, George van Santvoord, a man of enormous erudition. Van Santvoord was an eccentric, and a model of great value in a school that might have seemed to build pressure for conformity. Quite the contrary, he encouraged dissent and independence. He had a crude Socratic method of his own; he used to sneak up on you in the school corridor when you were talking freely and foolishly with other boys, and you'd feel his hand come into the crook of your elbow, and then he would ask you an odd question. The first question he asked me, when I was a homesick child at the very beginning of my stay there, was, "What was Stradivarius's first name?" I didn't know. The second question, some days later, was, "Is it true that eeny, meeny, miney, moe is counting in Chinese?" I knew that it wasn't, and I counted to him correctly in Chinese, and that gave me a great boost. What I didn't realize at the time, though I do now, was that he had known both that I played the violin and that I had been born in China.

He had given me an identity by asking me these questions, something I very badly needed at that point.

INTERVIEWER: Were the violin and writing already competing when you were there?

HERSEY: Yes, to some degree. There were teachers there who started me thinking about writing. One was Gordon Haight, who would later become the world's leading authority on George Eliot. Another, a teacher named John McChesney, an eccentric like the headmaster, got me at a period when I was wasting my eyes on Galsworthy and put *The Sound and the Fury* in my hands—this was in 1930, when Faulkner was so far relatively unknown. I did play the violin; I played in a string quartet with, among others, John Hammond, who was later a catalyst in introducing black jazz musicians to the recording world—the patron saint of recorded jazz of the thirties and forties.

INTERVIEWER: How did you wind up working for Sinclair Lewis? It seems an unusual first job.

HERSEY: I had applied for a job at *Time* magazine; my brother roomed with Henry Luce's brother Sheldon at Hotchkiss, and that gave me an opening. Luce promised me a job after graduation, but then I was offered a Mellon Fellowship to Clare College, Cambridge, and I decided to take it; I asked Luce if I could still have the job when I got back. He said I could. When I did get back, though, he seemed to have forgotten his promise. So I applied for a job in the regular way; I was given something called a *Time* Test, which consisted of their handing you all the research a writer would have writing a *Time* story, and asking you to write what you thought would be the appropriate story based on the material. I took the test, and after that could never get past a certain Miss Schultz, secretary to a man named C. D. Jackson, who was an assistant to Luce. So I began looking elsewhere. I heard about the job for Sinclair Lewis through a friend who worked at the *Herald Tribune*, and applied for it, and worked for him for several months, beginning in the late summer of 1937.

INTERVIEWER: What did the job entail?

HERSEY: He had just finished a novel called *The Prodigal Parents*, and my first job was to read the manuscript and tell him what I thought of it. The novel was about the relationship between some parents and their college kids. It wasn't very good, but I didn't have the courage to do anything but correct him on some lapses in student slang. Mainly, though, I took dictation and retyped his work. It was a wonderful summer for me. I didn't know at the time that he had been a heavy drinker. The reason I got the job at all was because he had gone off on a tear with a man named Florey, then his factotum, and the pair had disappeared; Lewis's wife, Dorothy Thompson, who wrote for the *Herald Tribune*, began calling inns all along the coast, thinking he would have wandered off that way somewhere. She finally called one in Old Lyme, I believe, where he was in the throes of delirium tremens. She went and got him, and, finding that Florey had been drinking with him, she fired Florey. So Lewis needed someone. I called him, and he invited me to come up to the Essex House on Central Park South, where he was staying. We talked for a while about Yale, and about the American Legion, which was having a convention in New York at the time, one thing and another, and then he suddenly said, "Excuse me, I have something else I have to do." And I thought oh, that went badly, and went back to reading *Gone With the Wind*, which I was in at the moment. But he called me the next morning and asked me to come up. This time he talked about being married to a columnist, about women in general, again one thing and another, and again dismissed me. He called me the *next* morning. As we were talking, the phone kept ringing; it was clear he didn't like the phone. He came back from one call, and said, "John"—by this time he was calling me by my first name—"there's a young man downstairs in the lobby who's applying for a job as my secretary. I have to shave and change, do you mind interviewing him for me?" That was the signal that I had been hired—being asked to interview someone applying for the job I thought I was applying for. I was able to tell Lewis that the young man was a good stenographer but I didn't think he'd really work for him. Lewis gave me a month to learn Gregg shorthand, and to convert from hunt-and-peck to the touch system in typing. And then I took my first dictation from him.

INTERVIEWER: Was he a model for you in any way?

HERSEY: He was past his important work—this was a couple of years after *It Can't Happen Here.* But he was wonderfully important to me; I was able to see the life of a man totally given over to writing. Even though he was not producing important novels anymore, he was so gripped by what he was doing that it was very impressive to me. He would get up in the middle of the night, cook up some coffee, and work for two or three hours and then go back to bed. He led an irregular life, but a life that was passionately devoted to his work. I was exposed to someone who lived for writing, lived *in* his writing, in a way. That summer he became interested in theater, and was writing what turned out to be a very bad play about a mythical Balkan kingdom. He wanted to learn everything about the theater. There was a summer-stock company in Stockbridge, Massachusetts, where we were, and every night he would have the casts over to his house. He was like a student trying to learn fundamentals; he would ask them how you get people on stage and off stage. His utter wholeheartedness was an important example for me.

INTERVIEWER: He must also have been an example of the darker side of the writer's life.

HERSEY: Yes, he was a very troubled man. He was on the wagon then, and wanted to be in Stockbridge in order to be near the Riggs sanitarium. He wasn't under treatment, but he felt safe being near the psychiatrists, in case he tumbled. He was haunted in ways, it was clear; at the same time, he wanted

to please, he was very entertaining and outgoing, and he com-
pensated for some of his dread and pain, I think, by being
charming. I have gathered that it was another story when he
was drinking; I understand—though I never saw him that
way—that he could be nasty when he was tight. But he was
wonderful the summer I was working for him. When he moved
back to New York, after several months up there, he didn't
need me as much as he had in the country, and he encouraged
me to leave him and make a million dollars, so as to be free to
write whatever I wanted. With a war brewing, he thought
making toy soldiers would be profitable, and he sent me to
F. A. O. Schwarz and other stores to study their lead-soldier
lines. But I decided I had no gift for money-making—an insight the years have confirmed—and I chose to try *Time* again.
I took the *Time* Test again, and this time, having been nettled
by what had happened before, I wrote a piece that was as far
from *Time*'s style as I could make it be. I wrote a twenty-four-
page essay on how rotten *Time* was.

INTERVIEWER: That one got past Miss Schultz?

HERSEY: I was hired the next day. My first job was as writer
for Milestones, Miscellany, People, and Animals, four different
columns, each of which now, I assume, would be the work of
at least three people. Thirty-five dollars a week, and hard work.
Time was in an interesting phase; an editor named Tom Mat-
thews had gathered a brilliant group of writers, including James
Agee, Robert Fitzgerald, Whittaker Chambers, Robert Cant-
well, Louis Kronenberger, and Calvin Fixx—the father of the
avatar of jogging who died jogging. They were dazzling. *Time*'s
style was still very hokey—"backward ran sentences till reeled
the mind"—but I could tell, even as a neophyte, who had
written each of the pieces in the magazine, because each of
these writers had such a distinctive voice. Working for the
magazine was, I think, a valuable training because it taught me
the importance of what's left out. There were absurd tasks
sometimes—very complex and important issues having to be

dealt with in two hundred words, so that often you were forced in a way to cheat and lie in order to compress as much as you had to. In the end I differed with Luce on a number of things, in particular his China policy. But on the whole, the training in tightness and concision was something I've come, in retrospect, to value. I also made some friendships that have been important to me over the years. Robert Fitzgerald was a close friend up until his death last year.

INTERVIEWER: But you stayed at *Time* long enough to be a correspondent for much of World War II.

HERSEY: I went first to China in 1939 and then to the South Pacific after the war began, as a war correspondent with the Navy on the aircraft carrier *Hornet.* Then on Guadalcanal. And later in North Africa and Sicily, and Russia. I did some writing for *Life* then as well.

INTERVIEWER: Somewhere in the midst of all that traveling, you managed to find time to write a first novel.

HERSEY: My first book was about MacArthur; I came to dislike it a lot, and asked Knopf, my publisher, to take it out of print in the early years. Then I wrote a book called *Into the Valley* about the Guadalcanal campaign, and it was after that, when I went to North Africa and Sicily, that I got the material for *A Bell for Adano.* I outlined the book and drafted a few possible pages of it in Sicily and North Africa. Then I came home and had a vacation from *Time* for a month, and I wrote the novel on that vacation.

INTERVIEWER: In a month?

HERSEY: Yeah. It was written in a sort of white heat.

INTERVIEWER: Was it that natural a move, to go from writing nonfiction to writing fiction?

HERSEY: I guess I'd been thinking from the very beginning, and had been experimenting a little bit in the pieces I did for *Life,* with the notion that journalism could be enlivened by using the devices of fiction. My principal reading all along had been in fiction, even though I was working for *Time* on fact pieces. As I said, Malraux, Silone, John Dos Passos of those years, Hemingway, Faulkner, were all writers who had excited me; the kind of skepticism and challenging of the norms that Van Santvoord had put to me had attracted me to writers who were trying to break the molds in various ways. In Sicily I wrote some *Life* pieces about people there who interested me very much. I couldn't take their stories in nonfiction beyond the articles I had written; but implicit in what they were like was the possibility of a novel. So I just plunged in. The book almost wrote itself. I was working under pressure of time—I had a month in which to work. I now look back on it as a naïve book, and an imperfect one. But the example of Silone, who spent his last years rewriting his novels, has cautioned me against trying to repair *A Bell for Adano,* to make it better. Silone went around a long curve from left to right, and I think he wanted to take the political errors of his youth out of his early books. But instead he took his youthfulness out of them, and I think damaged them badly. As did Fitzgerald when he tried to straighten out *Tender Is the Night. A Bell for Adano,* as I see it now, had a value when it came out, flawed as it is, because it presented to the American public, at a time when the war was far from won, the spectacle of an American general who seemed to represent the very things we were fighting against— General Marvin, loosely based on Patton, who was I think rather seriously deranged during the Sicilian campaign.

INTERVIEWER: Didn't you lose the manuscript to the novel at one point?

HERSEY: I had flown back from Europe with a colonel—I've forgotten his name, but let's say it was Wilcox—and I rode in a taxi with him from the airport. I had been in two airplane accidents my last few days in Sicily; one plane crashed when it landed in a bomb crater in the Licata airport, and shortly after takeoff the other ran into the anchoring cable of a barrage balloon, which had inadvertently been put up by the Navy in the takeoff path of the Army field the night before. I had a little

Olivetti typewriter which had been badly bent up, and I was
bringing it home as a souvenir of the accidents. I was fortunately not very badly bent up myself. I had tucked my draft
chapters, and the outline I wanted to follow, in the case of the
typewriter. When we got into New York I was so excited about
getting home that I left the typewriter in the taxi with Colonel
Wilcox. He went on, and I realized of course right after I'd
gotten out of the taxi that my work was lost. I called the
Pentagon and got a very friendly lady who said she would be
willing to look up the Wilcoxes; she found there was one who
came from New London and was indeed on leave, and she gave
me his address. I called the telephone company and asked for
the phone at that address. I rang the number. There was no
answer. The telephone information operator, who had stayed
on the line, was a wonder. She said, well, I'll get the number
of the people across the street. I called *them* and they said yes,
they'd heard that Colonel Wilcox was coming on leave but he
wasn't home yet, they thought he was going to be there in a
few days. So I waited a few days. I called him, and he said yeah,
he'd taken that thing in with him, he was supposed to meet
his wife in the Commodore Hotel, and she was an hour late.
He was so mad that when she came, he got up and walked out
and left the typewriter there. I called the Commodore Hotel and they said yeah, it's here in Lost and Found, come and
get it.

INTERVIEWER: How did you hear that the book had won the
Pulitzer Prize?

HERSEY: On the tennis court. I was playing tennis with a
friend of mine named Richard Lauterbach, who later died of
polio; he was then working for *Life.* We were at Rip's Tennis
Courts on 54th Street and Sutton Place. And Rip or his assistant came out of his shed onto the court and said, "I just heard
on the radio that you won the Pulitzer Prize." And I said,
"Lauterbach, you bastard, you're trying to pull a fast one on
me. I know it!" We went on and played the rest of the set, then

I went home and found out that it was true. That also happened to be V-E Day, as it turned out.

INTERVIEWER: Were you still at *Time* when all this was going on?

HERSEY: No, I had left *Time* by then and had gone up to work for *Life*. I went to China and Japan a few months after that on an odd assignment for *Life* and *The New Yorker*—two magazines that hated each other. But I made separate arrangements with them to do a given number of articles for each one.

INTERVIEWER: Was that the trip on which you interviewed the subjects for *Hiroshima?*

HERSEY: Yes. I went to China first and did several pieces there, and then went from there to Japan, did the research for that piece, came home and wrote it. It was published in *The New Yorker* in August of 1946.

INTERVIEWER: Was that why you went to Japan—with the intention of doing that particular story?

HERSEY: Yes. Before I went on the trip I had lunch with William Shawn, who was then the number two to Harold Ross on *The New Yorker,* and we talked about various possible stories. One that we thought about was a piece on Hiroshima. At that point, what seemed impressive was the power of the bomb, and almost all the reporting had had to do with the devastation it had caused, the physical devastation; it was really in terms of the destructive power of the bomb that Shawn and I envisioned the story. But as I thought about it in advance, while I was working in China, I thought more and more that I wanted to try to do something about the impact on people rather than on buildings, on the physical city. One of the assignments I worked on for *The New Yorker* involved a trip on the LST—a Landing Ship for Tanks—which was transporting Chinese troops from Shanghai to the north to fight against the Communists. I was horrified on that trip by the way the American naval officers treated the Chinese. This reaction may have been some kind of reverberation from the sense of dislocation I'd had as a child in China, I suppose. Anyhow, I was very upset and feverish by the end of the voyage, I thought from anger, but it turned out I had a mild case of the flu. I was taken on a destroyer from there back down to Shanghai. Some crew members brought me books from their library, one of which was *The Bridge of San Luis Rey* by Thornton Wilder. Reading that, I sensed the possibility of a form for the Hiroshima piece. The book is about five people who were killed when a rope suspension bridge over a canyon in Peru gave way, and how they had happened to find their way to that moment of fate together. That seemed to me to be a possible way of dealing with this very complex story of Hiroshima; to take a number of people—half a dozen, as it turned out in the end—whose paths crossed each other and came to this moment of shared disaster. So I went to Hiroshima and began right away looking for the kinds of people who would fit into that pattern. I went first to some German priests, because I'd read a report to the Holy See on the bombing by a German Jesuit who had been there. One of the priests—Father Kleinsorge, about whom I wrote in the Hiroshima piece in the end—spoke some English, and he began to introduce me to others. Through him I met the Protestant minister, Tanimoto, who spoke very good English, having studied at Emory University before the war. And both of them then introduced me to still others. I must have talked to forty or fifty people, trying to find the ones that would work for what I wanted to do. I narrowed it down to the six I finally wrote about, and got their stories. I spent about three weeks doing that, and came home and wrote it, in about a month, I guess.

INTERVIEWER: Was this designed from the beginning to be a piece which would take up a whole issue of *The New Yorker*?

HERSEY: It was originally intended as four separate pieces to be run in four successive weeks. One of the problems in handling it serially was that of giving enough clues in the second installment about what had happened in the first so that the reader who hadn't read the first would be able to pick up on it. But not so much as to stop someone who *had* read the first from wanting to read the second. That difficulty led Shawn finally one day to say, "Look, we just can't, we'll have to do this all in one week." He took the idea to Ross, who a few days later called me and said that he wanted to give an entire issue to the account. So we then went back and untangled it all—made it consecutive, for one issue.

INTERVIEWER: Was the Wilder book a model in terms of style as well? That flat style that characterizes *Hiroshima*?

HERSEY: Not really. Wilder's was a much more ornate and meandering style than mine would be. My choice was to be deliberately quiet in the piece, because I thought that if the horror could be presented as directly as possible, it would allow the reader to identify with the characters in a direct way. I've thought quite a lot about the issue of fiction and journalism as two possible ways of presenting realities of life, particularly such harsh ones as we've encountered in my lifetime. Fiction is the more attractive to me, because if a novelist succeeds, he can enable the reader to identify with the characters of the story, to *become* the characters of the story, almost, in reading. Whereas in journalism, the writer is always mediating between the material and the reader; the reader is conscious of the journalist presenting material to him. This was one of the reasons why I had experimented with the devices of fiction in doing journalism, in the hopes that my mediation would, ideally, disappear. I believe that the reader is not conscious of the writer of fiction, except through the author's voice—that is, you are conscious of the person *behind* the work. But in journalism you are conscious of the person *in* the work, the person who's writing it and explaining to you what's taken place. So my hope was, by using the tricks and the ways of fiction, to be able to eliminate that mediation and have the reader directly confronted by the characters. In this case, my hope was that the reader would be able to become the characters enough to suffer some of the pain, some of the disaster, and therefore realize it.

INTERVIEWER: What were some of the tricks of fiction that you tried to employ?

HERSEY: Well, there's the whole issue of point of view, presenting each of the characters from his viewpoint. There are six points of view in the book, and each section devoted to Tanimoto, Miss Sasaki, Dr. Fujii, and so on, enters into each survivor's state of mind without representing his thoughts—it's all done in terms of action, of what happened to them, what they saw, heard, and did. The reader looks at what is happening through the eyes of each of these characters, as he would in reading through a point of view in fiction. Then there is the means of building suspense in fiction: the writer takes a given episode up to the verge of some kind of crisis, and then cuts away from it to another scene, making the reader want to get back to the first to learn the outcome. One of the other fictional elements in *Hiroshima,* I feel, is the way in which time is opened up. The first passages are very tight in time, and then time gradually pulls out as you go through the story, to a more—not to a casual pace, but to a pace which one hoped would open out into a sense of a long and terrible future— which has since indeed come to pass.

INTERVIEWER: What was the initial reaction to the piece at *The New Yorker?*

HERSEY: It was a very big step for them to devote the entire space to a single piece. This meant that they gave it wonderful editing. It was the first experience I had had with editing as careful as that. At *Life,* they had a lot of confidence in their writers, sometimes to the extent that—well, I know of articles I wrote for *Life* which no single editor read from beginning to end. On the Hiroshima piece, I must have spent ten hours a day for twenty days with Ross and Shawn on it. Ross's kind of editing was to put hundreds of questions in the margins of the proofs—*The New Yorker* puts things in galleys the minute they arrive, so the editors can see them as *New Yorker* pieces, I guess. Ross wrote many, many queries. A typical query of his was this: I had written of ruined bicycles near the epicenter of the bomb as "lopsided bicycles." Ross's query was "Can something which is two-dimensional be lopsided?" As Shawn and I came to this, we realized that Ross was right, it couldn't. That happened late one evening after we'd been working for hours, and so we both said, let's deal with that tomorrow morning. So I went home, thought about it, and decided that the only word I could use in place of "lopsided" would be "crumpled." Got in the next morning before Shawn; the galleys were on his desk and he'd written "crumpled" in the margin already. That was an example to me of the way he becomes the writer he's dealing with. I see Shawn as a kind of editorial Zelig; it's a wonderful gift he has, to be able to think in the vocabulary of the writer he's editing and to find a way of dealing with the text that's exactly appropriate to that person.

INTERVIEWER: Were you prepared for the reaction to the piece when it finally appeared?

HERSEY: The reaction was explosive, simply because this was such an unprecedented thing for the magazine to do; to have this heavy thing take up a whole issue of a magazine which normally carried lots of humor, cartoons, light pieces, and so on. It caused a sensation. That's all been paraded in one way or another. It was broadcast over networks, and reproduced in a lot of newspapers, so it did get a lot of readers right on the spot. And has had a lot, over the years; I get letters all the time now from kids at school who are reading it, being exposed now. Now it has a different significance, because these are young people who are vaguely fearful of "the bomb" but have never had any way of imagining what that fear stood for.

INTERVIEWER: Was it something like that feeling, that a new generation has never known the bomb's effects, that led you to go back to Hiroshima recently, to write the book's new concluding chapter?

HERSEY: I had corresponded with Tanimoto over the years, and he had told me a little about what had happened to each of the other five people. It was quite clear that the shadow was longer than the one year about which I had written in the original piece. The shadow was much, much longer. So I thought there might be some value in going back to find out what had happened to the six over the time since 1946. Though these six people were by no means representative of a cross section of Hiroshima's population, the kinds of consequences of the bombing that they suffered were probably fairly true of the way the shadow fell on everyone.

INTERVIEWER: What evidence did you have that, as you say in the postscript's last sentence, "the world's memory . . . had grown spotty"?

HERSEY: Well, let me put it another way around to begin with. I think that what has kept the world safe from the bomb since 1945 has not been deterrence, in the sense of fear of specific weapons, so much as it's been memory. The memory of what happened at Hiroshima. I think that an argument can still be made that it would have been better to demonstrate the bomb somewhere else, rather than dropping it on a city. That might have brought an end to the war. Yet I wonder whether we might not have experienced another use of the bomb, since then, if there had been only a demonstration on a desert island. The demonstrations at Hiroshima and Nagasaki were so powerful that we have been able, so far, to extrapolate from them what it would be like to have a much bigger bomb dropped on a center of population. But if memory had been fully active, fully functional, we would long since have had some agreement on the use—or rather the nonuse—of these weapons, some curbs on their manufacture and deployment. For some, the memory is certainly still there; but it seems to me very spotty in the centers of power. A Caspar Weinberger or a Richard Perle, it seems to me, must never have grasped the meaning of the Hiroshima bomb, the way they go on about a future with bigger and better nuclear weapons. In the Soviet Union, there's probably very little memory of it. The control of information there is such that I wonder how many really know what happened in Hiroshima. Then, you have to remember that two generations have come along since the bombs were dropped. A very large number of citizens of this country, of every country, have no memory at all of what happened. The memory isn't even there.

INTERVIEWER: What do you think is memory's role in the creation, rather than the effect, of literature? I guess this is a question that has more to do with fiction . . .

HERSEY: A writer is bound to have varying degrees of success, and I think that that is partly an issue of how central the burden of the story is to the author's psyche. The things that have worked best for me have been the things that really mattered in some deep way to me. Another way of saying this is that a measure of whether a book works or not is the degree to which the author's memory is fully drawn into the undertaking. I don't mean by that that the substance of the book has to come from what the author remembers; but it seems to me important that the fiction should have the kind of relationship to the writer's memory that dreams may have. The dream material doesn't often seem to have any direct source in the person's life, but it must have been constructed from what the writer remembers. So I think a measure of the power of a work lies in the depth of the memory that is drawn on to fabricate the surface of the work.

INTERVIEWER: We've talked about the use of fictional techniques in nonfiction; but you are known as well for your use of nonfictional devices in your novels. The first manifestation of that was *The Wall*, the novel which followed *Hiroshima*.

HERSEY: I wrote most of a first draft of *The Wall* from the universal point of view, that of an all-knowing author—1085 longhand pages—and then realized that since I hadn't experienced any of the life in the Warsaw ghetto, the novel needed an authority I couldn't bring to it. And so I gave the book then to Noach Levinson, and rewrote it, or *he* did, in diary form. I had heard about a mass of documents called the Ringelblum Archive—they later were translated and published here, but long after *The Wall*—which suggested the archival device I used. But I wasn't breaking any ground; the epistolary form has been used for a long time.

INTERVIEWER: I read one criticism of *The Wall* which maintained that the book suffered mainly from its author not being a Jew. Whether or not that's valid, it must have crossed your mind during the writing.

HERSEY: Oh yes. I had had, as a child, quite a lot of Old Testament tossed my way, and I spent the better part of a year and a half reading not only about Judaism, but as well writings by people like Sholom Aleichem and Peretz and Buber. All that I could get my hands on, to try to identify as much as I could with what it meant to be a Jew. I think that, to the extent I was able to overcome being a non-Jew, the sources must have been in the childhood I was talking about, in having been a foreigner in the culture in which I lived. And so, I was able to try, at any rate, to identify with what it meant to be a Jew in the circumstances of Warsaw in those years.

INTERVIEWER: It must not have been an easy decision, to rewrite something as long and ambitious as *The Wall* almost from scratch. Did you have any colleagues, any writer friends whose opinions you could solicit in these matters?

HERSEY: I didn't have much experience of that kind of friendship and help, and I'm not sure how widespread that is in American life—or was; it may be more common now than it was then. My readers were family and friends rather than writers. I don't think I had as much editing as I would have liked to have on my books. My experience working with Shawn and others on magazine pieces suggested ways in which I might have had a more searching editing of the books. On my last book, *The Call*, I did get wonderful editing from Judith Jones at Knopf. I've had a wonderful relationship with her; she is, I would say, one of the few remaining editors who fulfill the whole range of the editor's function. But for many years, I was overtrusted by Knopf.

INTERVIEWER: What is that "editor's function"?

HERSEY: One of the things that has been bad for American publishing was the invention of the person called a copy editor, an expert who knows grammar and can spot inconsistencies: a technician of text. Many copy editors are very good at what they do, but the creation of that function has taken away from the principal editor a basic interest in the text. Most editors, with some notable exceptions, have become packagers now, rather than close editors. And I think that publishers are more interested in acquisitions from their editors than they are in developing to the fullest extent the craft of each writer they deal with. Publishing has changed in my years. I've worked since the era of Alfred Knopf Sr., who had as contemporaries people like Alfred Harcourt, Horace Liveright, Charles Scribner Sr., all essentially book men. In the case of Knopf, he was dazzled by authorhood; he cared more about his relationship with authors than he did about his relationship with books. His concern was the full career of the writer. He lost many authors, he was crusty, many writers moved on to other firms. But Knopf's concern was always for the growth of the person as a craftsman. Now—again with some worthy exceptions—the heads of firms are more apt to be businessmen. That's been a loss, I think.

INTERVIEWER: It is notable that you've been with Knopf through forty-odd years and twenty-one books.

HERSEY: All my life. I've had a very happy relationship with them.

INTERVIEWER: If we can talk a little bit about how you write: I understand you are a great fan of the word processor. Does it change the way you write in any way?

HERSEY: I was introduced to the idea very early. Alvin Eisenman, the head of the design department of the Yale School of Art, came to me in 1972 and said that a young electrical engineer, Peter Weiner, was developing a program called the Yale Editor on the big university computer, with the hope that there would be terminals in every Yale office. They were curious to see whether it would work for somebody who was doing more or less imaginative work, and they asked me if I'd be interested in trying it. My habit up to that point had been to write first drafts in longhand and then do a great deal of revision on the typewriter. I had just finished the longhand draft of a novel that was eventually called *My Petition for More Space,* so I thought, well, I'll try the revision on this machine. And I found it just wonderfully convenient; a huge and very versatile typewriter was what it amounted to. It could remember what I'd done, and help me find mistakes, and so on. If I used an out-of-the-way word and had a dim memory of having used it a hundred pages earlier, I could simply type the word and ask the machine to find it, and there it would be, in its context, right away, instead of my having to riffle through a hundred pages and spend two or three hours looking for it. It was simply a time-saver. It took about a month to get used to looking at words on a screen, almost as if in a new language; but once that was past, it seemed just like using a typewriter. So when these badly named machines—processor! God!— came on the market some years later, I was really eager to find one. I think there's a great deal of nonsense about computers and writers; the machine corrupts the writer, unless you write with a pencil you haven't chosen the words, and so on. But it has made revision much more inviting to me, because when I revised before on the typewriter, there was a commitment of labor in typing a page; though I might have an urge to change the page, I was reluctant to retype it. But with this machine, there's no cost of labor in revision at all, so I've found that I've spent much more time, much more care, in revision since I started using it.

INTERVIEWER: Some writers think that what one starts out to write will come out differently if one uses a word processor. Not "corrupt," necessarily, but different . . .

HERSEY: I don't think so. You know, the classic question that the ladies in the audiences of writers' lectures ask—or used to ask, in old days—was, "Do you write with a pencil or a typewriter?" I think every writer becomes habituated to a way of working that may matter to him a great deal. Disturbing the rituals surrounding writing may be very confusing, very difficult. I think there are a lot of things that are annoying about modern computers, particularly the ones that are interactive and keep giving you cute questions to answer as you work. That kind of thing would madden me. But I have a very simple, old-fashioned, "dedicated" word processor that doesn't inflict any of that on me. I think of it as a useful tool.

INTERVIEWER: You mentioned Silone and Dos Passos and Faulkner as some of the writers who excited you when you were starting out. Are there any contemporaries that you especially admire?

HERSEY: I think I'll duck that one. I wrote book reviews in the very early days, before I had become a writer, in a sense; but when I felt that I had become one, I drew back from judging my contemporaries. I think I'd rather not do that. I'll talk with you about that some other time.

INTERVIEWER: When you set out to write a novel, where does it begin for you? What comes first?

HERSEY: I think the first impulse comes from some deep emotion. It may be anger, it may be some sort of excitement. I recognize in the real world around me something that triggers such an emotion, and then the emotion seems to cast up pictures in my mind that lead me towards a story. To give you an example, the impulse to write *The Wall* came from seeing some camps in Eastern Europe when I was working as a correspondent in Moscow for *Time*. We were taken first to Estonia, and there we saw a camp where the Germans had had orders to kill everybody before they left; they had done it in a crude and awful way, making the prisoners build their own pyres before shooting them. We went later to Poland, and though the Warsaw ghetto itself was completely razed, we saw a couple of camps where the same thing had happened, the Germans had been ordered to kill everybody. In each case, there had been a few survivors to talk to. This came at a time when the West had not yet known very much about the Holocaust; there had been some vague rumors of the camps, but we had no real pictures of them. To see these bodies, to hear from the people who survived, created a sense of horror and anger in me that made me want to write. I thought at first to write about one of the camps like Auschwitz, and I did a lot of research on that; then it appeared to me, later on, that the life in the ghettos was at least something like real life for a long time, and so would, I thought, lend itself better to a novel. But it was the sense of distress, fear, anger that I felt seeing those camps that got me launched on that work.

INTERVIEWER: Do you always know where you're headed once you begin?

HERSEY: No, I don't. I work by all sorts of methods. In some cases I've wanted to have the whole book outlined before I started. In others I have simply begun writing and let the story take me where it would. *A Single Pebble* was an example of the latter. I had thought through *The Wall* pretty thoroughly before I started writing. But it's almost invariably been the case, when I've tried to plan through to the end, that I've had to modify the plan very sharply as the characters became—*if* they became—real to me, and began behaving in ways I couldn't control quite so easily.

INTERVIEWER: In the introduction to *The Writer's Craft*,

you say that the writing of imaginative literature seems to require "an altered state of consciousness." How would you characterize it in your case?

HERSEY: When the writing is really working, I think there is something like dreaming going on. I don't know how to draw the line between the conscious management of what you're doing and this state. It usually takes place in the earlier stages, in the drafting process. I would say that it's related to day-dreaming. When I feel really engaged with a passage, I become so lost in it that I'm unaware of my real surroundings, totally involved in the pictures and sounds that that passage evokes. So I think it's a kind of dream state of some sort, though it has baffled most people who've tried to analyze just what takes place in the creative process. Even Freud, who gave up on almost nothing, seemed to have given up on that. It remains mysterious; and it's probably a good thing that it does. It may be that the mystery is among the things that attract those of us who write.

INTERVIEWER: Your novels vary greatly in style and subject matter, sometimes taking on various nonfictional disguises—the unearthed diary in *The Wall*, or the transcript of legislative hearings in *The Child Buyer*. What is the relationship between that kind of variance and the consistency of the fictional "voice" you speak of?

HERSEY: The voice is the element over which you have no control; it's the sound of the person behind the work. I suppose there are some more or less conscious elements in voice; that is to say, a self-conscious manipulation of rhythm that may become habitual. But even the rhythms, it seems to me, stem from personality rather than from something acquired or mechanical. They're the tremblings of individuality. A person whose mind blurts will blurt in prose, and a person whose mind flows will flow in prose. Even writers who have experimented can't avoid this—a model would be Faulkner, who tried so many different ways of solving fictional problems, yet the voice was always clearly Faulkner's. He was helpless in that respect; his voice was his voice.

INTERVIEWER: At the risk of asking another back-of-the-lecture-hall question: do you keep to a regular schedule, and has it changed since you stopped teaching?

HERSEY: As I said, I think there's a great deal of habit in writing, and I have worked to the same schedule ever since I cut away from *Time* and *Life*. During the years when I was teaching, I didn't try to do any new work in term time. On *The Call*, for example, which took me six years to write, I would spend the time when I was teaching doing the research for the next chunk of the novel, and the rest of the year doing the writing work. It was one of the reasons why I taught just one term of the year, to be free the rest of the year to do my own work.

INTERVIEWER: Some writers say they find the teacher's life constricting. That didn't seem to be the case with you.

HERSEY: I backed into teaching. I had thought that it would be constricting, most of my working life. In the early sixties we'd been living in the suburbs of New York, in Southport and Weston, and were thinking about trying city life. We looked at New Haven, and heard about a house on the market there, that belonged to Yale. I asked Kingman Brewster, whom I had known, if we could look at it. He said yes, and we did and found it too big for us. A week or so later, at a social gathering of some kind, Brewster took my wife and me aside and said, "I think I can solve your real-estate problem. There's a house on Park Street," which happened to be the Master's House of Pierson College, "and you're welcome to take that if you take on the job of being Master." I had no idea what that meant; but within a couple of hours, my wife and I said, let's shake our lives up and try it. So we lived in Pierson for the last five years of the sixties, a wild time. And I was truly shaken up by it. I found being around the young rejuvenating, and often trying: very difficult times, the sixties. But I enjoyed it a great deal. And then after I left I found that I'd become addicted to the company of the young. So I began, first very tentatively and then with growing pleasure and enthusiasm, teaching a couple of seminars every year.

INTERVIEWER: Was that as rewarding, or as trying, as your role as Master?

HERSEY: I found the struggles of students who were trying to find themselves as writers fascinating and very moving. I think that their struggles somehow had echoes in my own continuing struggles. A writer never really finds his voice, but is always striving, I think, to find it. This is one of the reasons I've had a horror of repeating myself. I believed that if I ever concluded that I knew exactly what my voice was, I would stagnate. The writer grows, has experiences, feels joys and pains that somehow accrete and change him, so that the voice that was appropriate when I wrote *A Bell for Adano* was not appropriate when I wrote *The Call.* What I'm saying is that I think I learned from students that the struggle that was so intense in their case was still appropriate for me.

INTERVIEWER: What aspects of writing did you try to teach, or feel could be taught?

HERSEY: It's simply a matter of helping the student to set gifts free. That's about all you can hope for.

INTERVIEWER: A hot topic now among writers and academics is the value of graduate writing programs—some say they not only don't help, but actually hurt the young writer.

HERSEY: There's long been argument among writers about whether they should let themselves be captured by the academic world, whether they don't stultify there, and so on. I have always had the view that it really doesn't matter what a writer does; the argument that you should go out and meet raw life, work on the crew of a freighter, take part in revolutions and whatnot, doesn't seem to me valid. What matters is how a writer responds to the life around him. When I arrived in Pierson that first term, I had thought of the university as an ivory tower, and had been afraid that if I was incarcerated there I would stagnate. But in the very first term we had every human manifestation that I could think of except for murder. And we almost had that, from time to time. We did have violent death, and suicide, and rape, and everything in degrees up to those traumas. So the life is around you wherever you are, whatever you do, and it's a matter of how keenly and sensitively you respond to what's happening.

INTERVIEWER: You said in several places, most notably in *Letter to the Alumni*, what great hope and expectation you placed in the energy and generosity of the students of that time. Were you disappointed by what you saw in the years following?

HERSEY: There certainly has been a deep shift in the center of gravity of motive among students since the sixties—and not only among students, but in the culture as a whole. The deep impulse that I wanted to try to write about in *The Call* was, I think, a very American one, of wanting to be useful and helpful in the world. It's not by any means simply a Christian or missionary impulse; it's manifested in the Peace Corps, and in the kind of response the starvation in Africa has brought. But it seems to me that in the last twenty-five years the impulse of greed has grown in this country, the self-centered drive that makes people primarily fight for their own. The whole swing of the dominant political force toward the right has been, I think, a reflection of and stimulus to this move toward self-centeredness or greed. I find it very distressing.

INTERVIEWER: You taught fiction writing for fifteen years. Did you ever have any sense of seeing trends in the classroom emerge a few years later as trends in contemporary fiction?

HERSEY: Much more the other way around. In the effort to find a voice, young writers will try on various models to see whether they fit. But the gifted students never let themselves be beguiled by fashion. They write out of what they have. One of the things that has been happening in recent years is that the new forms of communication, particularly radio and television, have tended to make people's attention spans shorter. There's a much greater tendency to write in telegrams than there used to be. The pressure is for a kind of tightness, that must be influenced somehow by the 45-second commercial and the evening news. We're bombarded by these swift images—by "we" I mean even writers who don't watch television very much, yet who must be responsive to a readership that largely does. So there's been a great pressure for speed, concision, tightness, that has changed the nature of short stories particularly. But still, writers who have vigor and power form their own way and pay no attention to that sort of thing.

INTERVIEWER: You mentioned mediation in nonfiction, and how, in *Hiroshima,* you tried to eliminate it. Yet in *The Algiers Motel Incident,* your account of one event during the Detroit race riots of 1968, you made a very conspicuous entry into the narrative. What was different about that circumstance?

HERSEY: That was the first time I had done that. I tried to face it that the situation of the black in America had a kind of urgency, and put demands on me as a white of a kind that made it impossible for me to withdraw, for me not to be there as a mediator. The whole burden of Ellison's *Invisible Man* is that whites refuse to look at blacks; and I didn't want to be, couldn't afford to be blind in that respect, and so had to, I thought, come out in the open. Much as one may try to disappear from the work, there is a kind of mediation that takes place in journalism, no matter what. By selecting 999 out of 1,000 so-called facts, you are bringing your own bias to bear. In that case, I thought that the biases which I recognized—to my distress, having thought myself fairly clean in that respect—had to be stated; I had to get them out.

INTERVIEWER: Do you think that that "situation" has been, or is being, resolved?

HERSEY: I think it's been pushed to one side, in a way that is bound to haunt us in the long run. The situation has improved in some ways. I went down, for instance, to Mississippi in 1964, the summer when all the students went down there. I lived with a black farmer who was in great danger on account of my living with him. It was scary to me, but to him it was mortally dangerous. There was that summer the beginning of an effort to register people to vote, and he had the courage to register, and to take other blacks to do so. Everywhere we went, when he drove me around, there was a pickup behind us with a shotgun showing. So it was a very scary thing. We were in Holmes County, the center of which was a town called Tchula. Tchula recently elected a black mayor. So there have been changes, probably more profound in the South than in the North. But the fundamental problems of race and class have not been faced by our society. And I think that we are bound to have to face them sooner or later. The paradox is that trouble will probably come when we have a freer, more liberal administration; the opening up of possibilities will probably create a more dangerous situation. It is a paradox, and an unhappy one, that a repressive administration like this one seems to make the problem go away. But it doesn't. It stores up the powder.

INTERVIEWER: Are we in, do you think, anything like the "age of American repression" you warned of in *Letter to the Alumni*?

HERSEY: No, but there are signs that it might be in the making. We have a wonderfully healthy Constitution, and the one hope is that things may correct themselves every four years, or every eight years. Or every twelve years. The issue would be whether there would be time enough.

INTERVIEWER: You have been cited, to your chagrin, as an "ancestor" of the New Journalism. Yet there seems to be much in it that you disapprove of; as you wrote in your essay "The Legend on the License" in *The Yale Review* a few years ago, "I am one worried grandpa. The time has come to redraw the line between journalism and fiction."

HERSEY: I think it is true that I was one of many who began to experiment, early on, with ways of using the devices of fiction in journalism. I was certainly not alone in that. It was a valid movement, and one that has opened up journalism a lot. The important thing that was taking place was that journalists were making it more possible for readers to identify with the figures and the events about which they were writing. The fictional mode made it easier for the reader to imagine that these events were happening to him. But eventually two things polluted the so-called New Journalism. The fictional methods tempted some writers to cross the line, touch up their nonfiction—to invent. And then the fictional voice that transferred to journalism became more and more audible; the element of the subjective that appears under the surface of fiction came to the surface in the journalism, so that in the end, the figure of the journalist became more important than the events being written about.

INTERVIEWER: You mentioned doing the "research" for *The Call*. What do you think is the role of factual, historical research in the writing of fiction?

HERSEY: It's a substitute for memory, I suppose; though I also suppose that Tolstoy in writing *War and Peace* must have done a lot of reading about a period fifty and sixty years earlier, which he hadn't lived through. Not that I mean to compare *The Call* with *War and Peace*. But Flannery O'Connor said in one of her essays that fiction is an incarnational act; you're trying to make flesh and blood of things that are remembered. And in order to do that it's absolutely essential to make the past concrete. There have to be real, palpable objects, things seen, things heard. So either memory or a substitute for memory has to operate to bring those things into the fields of vision and hearing. Research in this case was partly a substitute, partly a supplement, to memory. I had at least a child's memory of the world of China, and I went back four years ago and refreshed my memory. I had gone a couple of times as a journalist in the meantime. But I also needed the memory of others to make the world I was writing about as real as possible. The need for concreteness was put wonderfully by García Márquez, in an interview in your magazine, when he said, "If I say I saw elephants flying, nobody would believe me; but if I say I saw twenty-four elephants flying, they might." There is something about exactness of detail that makes imagined things seem to come true.

INTERVIEWER: One of the notable things about *The Call* is that your father, Roscoe Hersey, appears as a minor character in it. Was that to discourage people from thinking that the main character, David Treadup, was modeled after your father?

HERSEY: Partly, I suppose; but really to reinforce the verisimilitude. Again, I think of a line of García Márquez's about that: "One word of falsity in journalism destroys the whole, but one actual fact in a fiction may make it seem believable." I think that's what I was after in using my father's name.

INTERVIEWER: Was this a book you had been meaning to write for a while? Had you been saving it in any way?

HERSEY: I suppose in ways it should have been my first novel; usually, a first novel is a trip back into childhood. I'm glad that it came as I am practicing to enter second childhood, rather than when I was coming out of my first one, because I think I could bring more of the experience of my life to that scene of memory than I could have when I was very young. I had never made earlier stabs at the book. Probably it was only with the deaths of my mother and father that I began to think more about them and about the past. I'm trying to think where it welled up from; I can't remember any moment at which I decided that it was time to write that book.

INTERVIEWER: But in *A Single Pebble,* for instance, you went back to China in a sense.

HERSEY: Yes, and there the missionary figure is displaced by the figure of the engineer. I suppose, in a way—though I've tried to avoid repetition—that there are repetitions of the same figure throughout my books. Major Joppolo in *A Bell for Adano,* I suppose, displaced the same character. Or perhaps Noach Levinson or Berson in *The Wall.* But I don't think that any of this is conscious—I've not thought of this sort of connection until now. I tend, when I finish a work, to put it out of mind completely, and go on to something else.

INTERVIEWER: It's fair to say that your nonfiction has had a considerable social impact. What kind of impact do you think your fiction, or fiction in general, has? Does fiction teach?

HERSEY: I believe that writers of fiction have somewhere always a motive of first trying to figure out for themselves how life can be less difficult than it seems to be. Indirectly, they may have a motive of trying to share whatever's learned with a reader. I think that *The Wall,* being very early in opening up to the American consciousness what had happened during the Holocaust, had a value of revelation, and may have helped people to understand things they hadn't understood before. Since then, many much more authentic works have come from people who lived through the Holocaust, and so the experience has gone deeper, and the understanding has gone deeper for people who've read those works. I don't think I have an impulse to teach in my writing. I do have a deep need to try to understand. In my effort to understand, I may hope that I can help readers to understand more about life, more about the stressful events I'm writing about. But I found the experience of teaching, when I actually did it, very different from the experience of writing. Mainly because in teaching, I'm trying to explore the student I'm dealing with, and in the writing, I'm trying to explore myself.

INTERVIEWER: You are on record in several places as dismissing the idea that the novel is dead. What do you think is its current state of health?

HERSEY: I think it's more alive than ever. Fiction has no

boundaries. Just as we're getting farther and farther out into space, I think we're opening up the boundaries of fiction more and more. The fact that we don't recognize three or four giants in the world of fiction now, as we tended to when, say, Faulkner and Hemingway and Fitzgerald and Dos Passos were operating, doesn't mean that there aren't remarkable pieces of writing being done. It's just that there are so many vivid writers going now that it's very hard to say that we have just this handful that matter. The range from the somewhat traditional Bellow to Pynchon and Barth and Barthelme, and to people even farther out on the edges of consciousness than those three, is very great these days. There is a violent competition from other forms of entertainment now; and yet the world of readers doesn't seem to be diminishing proportionately. There are too many books published, and consequently publishing has become a lottery. Many good books disappear, never to be seen again, or possibly not until they're rediscovered many years later, as some novels have had the good fortune to be—as Henry Roth's *Call It Sleep* was some years ago, for instance.

INTERVIEWER: After the success of *Hiroshima,* you concentrated almost exclusively on fiction. Was that a conscious decision?

HERSEY: I can't say that it was anything I thought through very deliberately. I was attracted to fiction for the reasons I gave before; I thought that there was a better chance, if what I did worked, to get the reader to experience the material than there would be in journalism. Sometimes, the stuff is too raw and immediate to be dealt with in fiction. There's a need for distance from the material that only time can give; so when something like the Detroit riots came along, I still resorted to nonfiction as a way of dealing with it. Then I wanted to try to experiment some; I've had a horror of repeating myself and running down on that account. So I began to try a number of things, some of which worked and some of which didn't. But they were always challenging and fun to try. I think in ways I was lucky to be hit by an early success—if the Pulitzer Prize and two or three books that did well represented success—because it left me free to do what I wanted to do. You know, I kept talking to my classes about the fact that the writing itself is the only real reward. I think I was able to learn that very early, and so have been able to take pleasure from some kinds of writing that I knew were not going to be accepted in the way that some of the early work had been. I still got pleasure from the doing.

—JONATHAN DEE
October 1985

5. James Laughlin

James Laughlin IV was born on October 30, 1914, in Pittsburgh, Pennsylvania, heir to the Jones-Laughlin steel fortune. His early schooling—at Le Rosey, in Geneva, the Eaglebrook School, and Choate—sparked his interest in literature, but when he went to Harvard, he found it "stultifying" and decided to take a leave of absence after only a year. He headed for Europe, traveling first to Gertrude Stein's home in France, where he lived with her and Alice B. Toklas for a month. Laughlin then went on to stay in Italy with Ezra Pound. Pound advised Laughlin not to write but to publish.

When Laughlin returned to Harvard in 1935, he followed Pound's advice, editing a supplement to *New Democracy* titled "New Directions in Literature." These pages soon evolved into New Directions, a publishing house and literary magazine whose initial contributors included Pound, William Carlos Williams, e. e. cummings, T. S. Eliot, and Marianne Moore. In the years since its inception, New Directions has continued to publish outstanding writers and has become especially known for its attention to foreign literature.

Laughlin himself continues to write poetry, much of which is gathered in *James Laughlin: Selected Poems 1935–1985.* Previous volumes of what Laughlin calls sentimental but other poets have termed "exquisite and distinctive" verse include *Some Natural Things* (1945), *Report On A Visit to Germany* (1948), *A Small Book of Poems* (1948), *The Wild Anemone & Other Poems* (1957), *The Pig* (1970), *The Woodpecker* (1971), and *In Another Country: Poems 1935–1975* (1978, ed. Robert Fitzgerald).

Laughlin lives with his second wife, Ann Resor, in Connecticut.

~~LINES FOR EZRA POUND~~

A COLLAGE FOR E.P.

At the Ezuversity

(Lead off with a tag from somebody like Socrates (Plato) or Cicero
   on the aims of education??) *Epictetus, II, xiv is The best*
                           "And so now I am your teacher—

So I came to Rapallo, I was ~~18~~ eighteen then,

And y̶o̶u̶ accepted me into your "Ezuversity,"

Where there was no tuition, the best beanery since S̶a̶l̶a̶m̶a̶n̶c̶a̶ Bologna,

And the classes were held at meals in the din̶ing room of what you
      called the Albuggero Rapallo,

Where Gaudier's b̶i̶g̶ head of you sat in the corner, an a̶s̶t̶o̶s̶h̶m̶t̶ aston-
      ishment to the tourists,

Because it was too heavy to tote up to the fifth floor of Via Marsala
      12/V

And might have c̶o̶l̶l̶a̶p̶s̶e̶d̶ bust through the floor.

And y̶o̶u̶ showed me with some relish that if o̶n̶e̶ looked at the back of
      the cranium it was quite clearly a scrotum.

Literature (pronounced literchoor), you said, is news that stays news, (checkO

Abd, quoting Harry Stottle (was he a buddy of Harry-Stop-Her-Knees?)**:**
      ut p̶o̶t̶e̶s̶t̶ doceat ut moveat ut delectet.   (check it
                                          Was Harry)

Yes, you taught me and you moved me and you gave me great delight!

Your conversation was the wittiest show in town,

What"ver you'd ever heard or read was in your head as fresh as when
       it came there first.

The books you loaned me were filled with caustic marginalia,

And I found where you'd gotten your City of Dioce in Herodotus,   (why does

And the world's greatest liar (better than Fordie) said that the   EP drop
      towers of Ectaban were plated with silver & gold,   the Gk s?)

But

A̶n̶d̶ you wrote:

     "To build the city of Dioce whose terraces are the colour
         of stars."

(which is a far more elegant image)

And in de Maille's <u>Histoire de la Chine</u> (Paris, 1777) you'd put a
      big star

Beside the part where he tells how Emperor   had MAKE IT NEW   (get his
      painted on his bathtub.   name)

A James Laughlin manuscript page.

James Laughlin in the old office in the stable at Norfolk, 1941.

James Laughlin

A frequent traveler since the thirties, James Laughlin has always returned to the family home in rural Connecticut where he runs New Directions' affairs from Meadow House, a simple frame structure beside a pasture, where often a small flock of sheep graze. Just inside the door of the house, in the front hall, is a long table used to accumulate mail. Precariously balanced stacks are everywhere, with piles divided into manuscripts, letters, newspapers, and journals. There are six to eight stacks, each at least twelve inches high. Straight ahead is a large, signed photograph of Ezra Pound; the mammoth, fan-shaped wicker chair in which he is seated seems to dwarf him.

Beyond the hall is the living room/study. The room is open and spacious, with three separate sitting areas, one of which functions as Laughlin's workplace. The high ceiling, the wide picture window overlooking the meadow, and the French doors contribute to the sense of openness. The built-in bookcases are stuffed with books and records. There are Oriental rugs, but the furniture is modest, selected primarily for comfort and durability. His desk is covered with books, file folders, manuscripts, office supplies, memos, letters, an old typewriter, tobacco, and numerous pipes.

Laughlin is tall—over 6' 5"—and his size could easily intimidate others. It does not, though, because he is a soft-spoken, unassuming man who seems intent on avoiding the spotlight as much as possible. He takes pleasure in acknowledging that readers appreciate New Directions books, and his poetry. At the same time, he is clearly uncomfortable with the celebrity status that has been thrust upon him by well-intentioned colleagues, grateful writers, and respectful academics.

The interview took place July 19–20, 1982, during a record-breaking heat wave. On the ground floor, the Laughlin home is air-conditioned only in the kitchen, so the discussions were intermittently placed in abeyance to permit Laughlin and the interviewer to drink iced tea, drive over to Tobey Pond for a swim, or escape to the comfort of the air-conditioned kitchen.

INTERVIEWER: You've mentioned numerous times that your family was not especially literary. What was life like at home that made you so passionately concerned with literature?

LAUGHLIN: I don't think there was really anything in the life at home in Pittsburgh which started me on a literary course. My family didn't read a great deal, except the Bible. Occasionally my mother did read very bad novels by Lloyd Douglas, but that was about the extent of her literary aspiration. She did paint—very pretty watercolors, mostly landscapes. Most of the pictures we had in the house were framed watercolors that she had done in various parts of the country or down in Mexico, where she went sometimes in the winter for vacation. I painted a little bit myself along with her. We'd go out together in the country and I'd dabble away, not very successfully. So there was a concept of painting as something which people did. And, of course, we traveled almost every summer in Europe, where we dutifully went to the museums to look at great paintings. But there was no compulsion toward art that I remember.

INTERVIEWER: In Europe did you ever encounter writers or literary people?

LAUGHLIN: The family knew no writers at all. I did pick up, when I was quite young, an interest in writing plays. I wrote a play every Christmas. I had seven first cousins living next door. Every Christmas I wrote a little blank verse melodrama which we would perform on the night before Christmas. These were very romantic, highly dramatic plays with a great deal of sword-fighting in them and fair ladies locked in towers and stuff of that kind. The problem was to get the cousins to learn their parts. They weren't very keen.

INTERVIEWER: Did your interest in writing poetry develop integrally from writing plays?

LAUGHLIN: I don't think I began writing poetry until I was exposed to poetry in boarding school at Le Rosey in Switzerland. All of the classes were in French, of course, but one of the masters loved poetry. He would have us learn fairly long passages of classical French poetry, things like Lamartine and Du Bellay and Sully Prudhomme and Victor Hugo. We had to learn the poems by heart and then recite them. When I got back from Switzerland and went for a year to Eaglebrook School in Deerfield, Massachusetts, there was a remarkable old English teacher, a Mr. Gammons, who was steeped in English poetry of the past. He started me reading Wordsworth, Keats, and others. So that brought it along. We were very attached to one another.

Then, of course, at Choate, where they had a marvelous English faculty, I was thoroughly exposed to poetry, especially through Dudley Fitts and Carey Briggs. Briggs held all his classes in the library. His theory was to expose boys to books and let them dig out what interested them. He said on the first day of his class, "Gentlemen, here are the books. It's up to you what you get out of them." Each boy had to choose a project for the term. My project was poetic prose. I dug out everything on it in the library, beginning with writers such as John Lyly and Sir Thomas Browne, and going up through Rimbaud. Fitts was a very inspiring composition teacher; he got me writing prose. It was largely through him that I became editor of the Choate literary magazine. He was my introduction to modern poetry. He gave me Pound and Eliot to read.

INTERVIEWER: You have noted that even though you spent a good deal of time in the offices of the *Advocate,* you were something of a loner at Harvard. Yet you seem a very personable individual.

LAUGHLIN: I was socially retarded and not good at getting on with people. Harvard was very cliquish and socially conscious. Coming from Pittsburgh, I didn't rate with the boys who had been to Groton or Milton. Harvard was an aloof place then. In the dormitory where I lived (and I roomed with a very nice boy from Choate), we shared a shower with two boys from aristocratic families, Anthony Bliss and Peter Jay. But throughout the entire year we never exchanged a word with them, or they with us. It was the way things were at Harvard in those days. You sat in lecture halls always in the same seat next to the boy whose name was alphabetically next to yours. I remember that in History 1, I sat next to a boy from Boston. We never spoke. I'm sure it's not that way anymore.

INTERVIEWER: You have also indicated your debt to Harvard.

LAUGHLIN: You could get to the professors. I was close friends with Ted Spencer. I played tennis with him. I was friends with F. O. Matthiessen. And earlier on, I'd received much hospitality from E. K. Rand, the Latin scholar. He liked his students. He'd invite them out to his house on a Sunday; there might be four or five people sitting around and sipping tea and having a good time with the old boy. I think I was more aggressive than many students about making contacts. I wanted contact with my professors; I wanted to be close to them.

Of course, one of the greatest influences on my publishing work (after Ezra Pound and Kenneth Rexroth) has been Harry Levin—a man of enormous learning and taste, and in many literatures. You could always go around to Harry's and he'd give you a drink and you could talk to him and learn so much. Such wit. He's wonderful. He very kindly came to the poetry reading I gave up at Harvard in 1982 and we got to the little poem about the former director of the Metropolitan Museum, Mr. Rorimer. It's called *"Ars Gratia Artis."* After I read the poem I called over to Harry: "Harry, is that a tag from Horace?" He said, "No. It's from MGM." He told me afterwards how MGM had gotten their motto from some bird in France. I'd always thought it was Horace, and it isn't Horace. Harry knows everything.

One astonishing thing about Harry was that when, at New Directions, we were reissuing W. C. Williams's novel, *A Voyage to Pagany* (that's the one about Williams's trip abroad), we wanted an introduction. I thought it was a very long shot, but I asked Harry if he would be interested in writing it. To my happy surprise—he writes so gracefully—he said he would.

The first thing New Directions did with Harry was his *James Joyce,* which to my mind is still the best book about Joyce. Recently we did his beautiful book, *Memories of the Moderns,* which is one fine essay after another. But I had never seen anything he had written on Williams. Yet very quickly he turned out one of the best, most comprehensive, most perceptive essays that has ever been written on Williams. Harry had the scholarly capacity to "get up" Williams in a couple of months—although I was only going to pay him maybe $200 for the piece. But he cared enough and he wanted to know about Williams, so he found out.

INTERVIEWER: You have also reported Harvard as rather dull.

LAUGHLIN: Well, that was just after I got there, which was in 1933. I took a leave of absence and went to Europe halfway through my sophomore year. It happened to be a period of transition just then. The great men, the old fellows like Kittredge, Lowes, and the rest of them had retired, and the new young lions, F. O. Matthiessen and Ted Spencer, hadn't come on yet. The resident poet was Robert Hillyer, who'd send you out of the classroom if you mentioned Pound or Eliot. So it *was* dull, and it seemed a good time to get away. I went to Europe to try to write, both stories and poems, and to travel.

INTERVIEWER: That was the summer you met Gertrude Stein.

LAUGHLIN: I met her through a distinguished French professor with a limp, Bernard Faÿ, whom I met that summer at the Salzburg music festival. I used to go swimming every day in the public swimming pool and that's where I met him. It turned out that one of his best friends was Gertrude Stein. I told him that I had been reading Stein back in the U.S. and that she sounded fascinating. He wrote her that he'd met this young American in Salzburg who might be useful to her. He asked if he could bring me to Bilignin, in Savoie, which was her country place. I went and stayed about a month. It was a lovely place, what they call a *château ferme*—not quite a chateau but more impressive than a farm—with a view down over the rolling hills. She put me to work. She was quite a utilitarian!

INTERVIEWER: What did she have you do?

LAUGHLIN: Well, the next year she was going on her famous lecture tour through America, and somebody had suggested that in each city where she was scheduled she should hand out a press release explaining what she was going to be talking about. That was my job—to take these lectures and produce a one-page presentation for each. It was not easy at all. The *Lectures in America* are philosophical and dense. To try to identify their central themes and translate them from Steinese into American newspaperese was quite a task. I would try, carrying my attempts to her, and she would say, "No, no, you've missed the entire point. Go back and try again." That's why I stayed there a month. It took me that long to get these releases done to her satisfaction. The two of us sat out on the terrace in the mornings, working. Then in the afternoon we'd tour the countryside in her little Ford with Gertrude, who drove, sitting in the front seat with Alice B. Toklas, while I sat in the back with those two awful dogs—Basket, who was a white poodle, and Pepe, who was a nasty little black Mexican nipper. Trying to control the pair of them back there, I saw very little of the Savoie countryside. That part of the Savoie is a favorite place for hikers. They'd lose nails out of their hiking boots, and almost invariably the little Ford's tires would get a puncture. Gertrude would pull off to the side of the road and she and Alice B. Toklas would take out their picnic things from the car and find a nice cozy spot to overlook it all. They'd sit and chat and eat while I would change the tire, harassed, as you can imagine, by Basket and Pepe.

INTERVIEWER: What were your impressions of Stein?

LAUGHLIN: She had great natural charm, tremendous charisma. Marvelous head. Those wonderful flashing eyes. A deep, firm voice. So I couldn't help but be very much impressed by her at times, except that often she'd erupt with crazy ideas. She thought Hitler was a great man . . . this *before* the war, of course, but how a Jewess could be attracted to such a notion at any time is difficult to understand. She was certainly a woman of strong opinions—indeed to the point of megalomania. She felt she had influenced everyone. We had a big fight one day when I mentioned I was reading Proust. She said, "How can you read junk like that? Don't you know, J., that Proust and Joyce both copied their work from *The Making of Americans*?" She finally cooled on me. I simply didn't accept everything she said. That was disrespectful.

INTERVIEWER: And then you met Pound that same year?

LAUGHLIN: Dudley Fitts, my old teacher at Choate, who had been corresponding with Pound for a number of years, gave me a letter of introduction to him. Fitts was a great linguist; he'd read everyone. He was a wonderful letter writer—his letters entranced Pound because here was someone who'd read in all the languages. Pound must have remembered. Because that fall, after my experience with Gertrude Stein, I went up to Paris, lived in a tiny room in an insurance office which I rented for seven dollars a month, and after a while, I wrote to Ezra, not expecting a reply, really, just asking if I could come down to Rapallo to see him . . . and to my astonishment he sent me a telegram: "Visibility high." So I went down then to Rapallo. Ezra and I hit it off immediately. He found me an eager student, and certainly he was the thwarted professor. He found a room for me in the flat of an old German lady and I was enrolled in what he called the "Ezuversity." No tuition.

INTERVIEWER: How did the courses go?

LAUGHLIN: The Ezuversity instruction was mostly a monologue about the mail he'd received that morning. His mornings were devoted to his correspondence. He used to say that postage was his highest living expense. Then we'd have lunch in the dining room of the Albergo Rapallo, and then after the snooze he'd take, we would go swimming or play tennis. One of the wonderful things about those monologues was his mimetic ability. He could imitate Joyce, how he talked, or how Yeats talked. His stories were endless, and very funny, and what I remember about them—over all those years—was that I never heard him tell an off-color story.

INTERVIEWER: But he could be prickly.

LAUGHLIN: Oh, you could never predict what he was going to do—even from the very first. I remember that one summer we drove up to Salzburg—Ezra, Olga Rudge, and my Harvard classmate John Slocum—to the *Festspielhaus,* where Toscanini was conducting Beethoven's *Fidelio.* Ezra didn't think much of Beethoven. After about twenty minutes into the opera, Ezra rose up and said in a very clear voice, "No wonder! The man had syphilis!" He started out, and all of us, of course, felt we had to file out with him. Toscanini was absolutely unfazed. He continued to conduct.

INTERVIEWER: How did Pound help you get started with New Directions when you got back to Harvard?

LAUGHLIN: He wrote letters to all his writer friends—to William Carlos Williams, to Kay Boyle, Cocteau, dozens of them, saying, "If you have a manuscript send it to this worthy young man." I started all this with complete innocence. The first book we published was a very funny one called *Pianos of Sympathy* by Wayne Andrews, who in those days called himself, for some reason, Montague O'Reilly. It was printed by the people in Vermont who printed the *Harvard Advocate*—delicious stories about old gentlemen with long hair and a fetish about piano strings—two hundred copies in blue covers, and then two hundred more in red covers. That was the start.

INTERVIEWER: What was the reception when you started publishing books while still at Harvard? Were other students aware that you were doing it?

LAUGHLIN: The people around the *Advocate* were aware; and they were interested. They thought it was different and enterprising. But the general student body took no interest whatever.

INTERVIEWER: Was there any sense among the folks over at the *Advocate* that this was a precocious, ambitious project?

LAUGHLIN: I think the *Advocate* crowd were, by the time I started doing books, rather used to me because the first step in my publishing was when I began, with a couple of friends, such as John Slocum, to infiltrate texts by non-Harvard people into the magazine. These were writers whom I had met through Pound and others. I remember we printed a Pound *Canto* and a Henry Miller story which was banned by the police. It was a piece called "Glittering Pie," which by present standards would be considered very innocuous, but it was Miller enough for the young lawyer who was running for district attorney in Cambridge to have the issue seized and get himself a lot of publicity in the newspapers about decadence at Harvard. It was such a harmless piece. In it was a joke about leis, you know Hawaiian leis, as a double entendre. It was charming and very funny. Henry could be extremely funny. The way we got out of that scrape was this: through some friends in the athletic department, we got the district attorney candidate two seats on the 50-yard line for the Harvard-Yale game. So he forgot about it.

INTERVIEWER: The name that has probably come up more than any other in interviews about your life has been your Aunt Leila. What made her so special for you?

LAUGHLIN: She was a very loving, and at the same time, powerful-minded woman. I came to live with her here in Connecticut, shortly after I started going to boarding school, because I didn't care for Pittsburgh at all. She more or less adopted me and spoiled me. At the same time she was constantly telling me what I should do and what I shouldn't do. Although our personalities and interests were greatly different, we became very attached to one another. She was a symbol of the family tradition. She had all the old virtues.

INTERVIEWER: So, in a sense, she became your family.

LAUGHLIN: Yes. I adored my father, who was a marvelous man, very unlike a businessman. In fact, he wasn't a businessman. He stopped working in the steel mills when he was forty, the day that his father died, and devoted the rest of his life to gentlemanly pursuits, such as fly-fishing and duck shooting. We were very close. If I asked him for money, he'd say, "Are you going to publish some more of those books that I can't understand?" And I'd say, "Yes." And he'd give it to me. I was fond of my mother, too. But I simply could not get on in Pittsburgh.

INTERVIEWER: What was it about Pittsburgh that made things difficult?

LAUGHLIN: There was no one for me to talk to. I didn't have any friends interested in literature, and most of the kids were tearing around raising hell. It was a country-club existence, which didn't appeal to me at all. It was a stifling town. So I moved here to Connecticut.

INTERVIEWER: Was your Aunt Leila modern in her attitude about literature?

LAUGHLIN: She was very down on certain books I published; she couldn't stand Henry Miller. I was very careful not to undertake the *Tropics,* because I knew it would set the whole family on its ear. She thought he was obscene and an anarchist.

INTERVIEWER: There are obvious disadvantages to being this far away from New York City; what are the advantages that made you decide to stay in the country all through the years?

LAUGHLIN: I liked the country. My aunt converted a stable into an office for me. She was very good about being nice to the various writers who came to work for me here—the Patchens, Jimmy Higgins, Hubert Creekmore, and others. It was a pleasant place to function. New Directions didn't move away from here until the business became so big I could no longer run it from the country; it was hard to keep help and there was no close access to printers and binders. At a certain point it became obvious that I couldn't handle the work from here with floating literary helper staffs.

INTERVIEWER: Were you deliberately using writers as floating helpers?

LAUGHLIN: It was a definite part of the program to try to provide employment for writers I knew who didn't have a job. Of course, it wasn't much of a job for them, because in those days we were selling very few books and the wages that I was able to pay were at subsistence level. It did give them some writing time.

INTERVIEWER: How much?

LAUGHLIN: It was up to them. I was usually somewhere else.

In those days I was often out on the road trying to sell books, or I was out at the ski resort in Alta, Utah, where I had business interests. Most winters I was in Utah for months. So I corresponded with the office by daily letters and they would send letters out to me. As long as they got the books and the bills out and kept things rolling, they were pretty much on their own.

INTERVIEWER: How did you manage to get Ezra Pound to come to New Directions?

LAUGHLIN: At the time we started he was being published by Farrar and Rinehart, a distinguished old firm, but they made the odd mistake—though how could they have known?—of sending him at Christmastime a copy of his latest book, bound in leather. His judgment of this, quite unjustified, was, "They must be crooks." I have no idea what his rationalization was. So he took his work away from them and gave it to me. I doubt if it bothered Farrar and Rinehart very much, because in those early days his work wasn't selling. We published *Polite Essays*, which weren't at all, and *ABC of Economics*—a text I'd still recommend to anyone who's puzzled about inflation. We've done, I'd think, a total of twenty books of Ezra's, and I am proud to say that, with one or two exceptions, all of them are in print.

INTERVIEWER: Do they continue to sell?

LAUGHLIN: The *Selected Poems, ABC of Reading.* And the *Cantos,* of course. As for the rest of them: three or four hundred copies a year.

INTERVIEWER: How much of an influence did Pound have on you—that is to say in those first days with him in Rapallo when you were nineteen years old?

LAUGHLIN: I think that perhaps in earlier interviews or talks I may not have sufficiently stressed the way that Ezra completely changed, to use one of his phrases, my *forma mentis,* my way of looking at the world. I went to him with fairly conventional views about almost everything, and I left him

with either very eccentric or radical views about everything—
views which have persisted with me to the present day.

INTERVIEWER: Social Credit?

LAUGHLIN: Social Credit, political things, literary concepts.
Poets whom I still like to read for my own pleasure are the ones
he told me I should, the Pound canon as you find it in the *ABC
of Reading.* Pound pushed me away from the kind of literature
which was embalmed in the "beaneries" to a much more
interlingual, international literature. That has persisted to this
day. A great deal of what we do now at New Directions is still
translations of foreign books. Last winter we did a Swedish
novel, a Hungarian novel, and a Brazilian novel. And if you
look at our annual anthology you'll find that often a third of
it is made up of translations of foreign poets from all over the
world. That concept came largely from Ezra, who in his critical
writings was always saying that you could not understand poetry if you only worked with one language. He was a compara-
tist in the good sense of actually looking at texts in different
languages and seeing what the writers were doing with them
and comparing them one with another. He loved to compare
Flaubert with Henry James, for example. He made judgments
of that kind. To him it was all one world literature, even
including the Chinese.

INTERVIEWER: Did he get you learning foreign languages—
Italian, for example?

LAUGHLIN: I learned a certain amount of Italian from going
with him to the Italian cinema in Rapallo. The movies were
simply awful, but Ezra loved them. He'd sit up in the first
gallery with a cowboy hat on and his feet up on the rail, eating
peanuts, roaring with laughter. I only went because through
the roar of his laughing I was able to add . . . well, a little to
my understanding of the language. Pound also arranged for me
to have Italian lessons with an aged spinster named Signorina
Canessa, who hated Mussolini because he had put a tax on
canaries. She must have been at least ninety years old. We'd

converse and I read the Italian newspapers and talked to people around town. I was gradually building up my Italian, but it was still strange to me, and it still is strange to me now. In the filming job last summer when we were working on the Pound documentary, I had to interview a lot of people in Italian who had known Pound. I could do it, but it was still a foreign language to me; whereas French, which I got earlier in my Swiss school, is still a foreign language, but much less so.

INTERVIEWER: Have we gotten to most of the things you wanted to add about the Rapallo experience?

LAUGHLIN: There was the wonderful friendship with Dorothy Pound, who was such a lovely lady, so kind to me. She used to read Henry James to me after tea—short stories. She meant a great deal to me. She was at meals, the lecture meals, when Ezra would hold forth, and she'd chime in. And she'd make tea for us after we'd finished playing tennis or swimming. Then Ezra would take a little snooze, and she'd take me into her studio—she was a very good painter in the Vorticist tradition—to read to me.

INTERVIEWER: Did you have any other interests outside your life at New Directions?

LAUGHLIN: I think you have to bear in mind the skiing mania. It's been a big part of my life. I was crazy about skiing and did a lot of it. I got involved in a ski resort out in Utah. I spent a lot of time out there in the early days. I married a Salt Lake girl, who liked skiing. I lived there in a suburb of Salt Lake and went up to the ski place every day to work. It was a very strong drive.

INTERVIEWER: Was there any relation at all to the literary?

LAUGHLIN: It was pretty much apart. It was a much more physical activity than writing. Some of my poems come out of that period. "The Mountain Afterglow" was written at Alta. There are often references in the poems to snow or to tracks in the snow. And I wrote magazine articles about skiing.

INTERVIEWER: What was it about skiing that was so attractive?

LAUGHLIN: The incessant movement, the rhythm, and the beauty of the mountains. Skiing is a very good sport because you never get to the end of it. There's always more you can do to ski better, more you can perfect in your technique. This is a challenge, especially when you're ungainly like me.

INTERVIEWER: What kind of skiing did you do when you were skiing competitively?

LAUGHLIN: I did them all. I did downhill and slalom, I jumped a little, and I did cross-country.

INTERVIEWER: That must have been interesting when you jumped, given your height.

LAUGHLIN: I never got anywhere; I flapped around in the air. Jumpers are compact, like good golfers.

INTERVIEWER: You suggested that you didn't see too much connection between the publishing or the writing on the one hand and the skiing on the other. Did they conflict with one another?

LAUGHLIN: No, because the mail would come out to me from the office every day. I'd ski for a few hours, then I'd go in to the typewriter and answer the mail. It worked very nicely. I wasn't in an office all day; I was in a pleasant place.

INTERVIEWER: When W. C. Williams got upset with you in the 1940s and the early 1950s, he implied several times that your passion for skiing was interfering with your work at New Directions. Do you think there was anything to his reaction?

LAUGHLIN: I could have been more attentive had I been East, so I think his criticism was justified. But skiing meant a lot to me and I wasn't going to give it up. In that connection, there's a nice postcard that Ezra sent me about my skiing mania. He wrote, "ARE YOU DOING ANYTHING? Of course, if you spend 3/4s of your time sliding down ice cream cones on a tin tea-tray. If you can't be bothered with detail, why t'hell don't you get Stan Nott[1] who could run it. Then you could scratch yr arse on Pike's Peak to your 'eart's content." And then in another card he said:

Here lies our noble lord the Jas
Whose word no man relies on.
He never breathed an unkind word,
His promises are pizin.

And that of course comes from Rochester's epitaph on Charles II, which reads:

Here lies our sovereign lord the king
Whose promise none relies on.
He never said a foolish thing
Nor ever did a wise one.

INTERVIEWER: When it got to the point where skiing was such an important element of your life, were you losing interest in New Directions?

LAUGHLIN: Not at all. But I saw the ski resort, apart from the pleasure of skiing, as an opportunity to make a little money to support the publishing, so that I wouldn't have to keep going begging to my father and my aunt. It didn't make much money at first, but now it's in the black.

INTERVIEWER: You still have it?

LAUGHLIN: Yes, my family group is the majority stockholder, but I don't run it anymore. I have excellent managers: I go out occasionally. But now on a Sunday at Alta there are four thousand people skiing. They're like ants on the slopes. Whereas when I was out there, some days there would be only five or six people on the mountain. It was lonely and beautiful.

INTERVIEWER: Do you see finance and economic issues having a direct influence on art?

LAUGHLIN: Oh yes. That, of course, was what Ezra was

[1]Stanley Nott, the London publisher of Pound's "Money" pamphlets.

always talking about, that business and wealth did not support the artists and writers. That, in fact, was one reason Ezra became interested in Mussolini. He knew that Mussolini was an intelligent, rather cultivated man. He'd been a Socialist journalist. Ezra hoped that Mussolini would throttle the banks and could be converted into a patron of arts and letters. You remember the Renaissance princes, such as Sigismondo Malatesta. Ezra admired Sigismondo not because he went out and beat up other princes' hired armies, but because he brought the best Greek scholars, such as Gemistus Plethon, and Italian artists such as Alberti and Duccio di Buoninsegna and Piero della Francesca, to his court and he built the Tempio Malatestiano in Rimini for his girlfriend Isotta.

INTERVIEWER: Did Pound succeed in any measure in getting his views to Mussolini?

LAUGHLIN: As far as I know, he never succeeded at all with Mussolini. He had one audience in Rome with him, which he arranged through the secretary, who put out a copy of the *Cantos* on Mussolini's desk. Ezra marched in and Mussolini picked it up and said, *"Ma questo é divertente."* That pleased Ezra very much. Then they talked for ten minutes about economics. Ezra told Il Duce what he should do about the Italian banks, and that was the end of the audience and the end of a beautiful friendship. That was the only time he saw him.

INTERVIEWER: They didn't become disenchanted with one another?

LAUGHLIN: I think Mussolini's aides had told him that Ezra was a crackpot, but he felt he should see him because he was a famous poet.

INTERVIEWER: Where did you have your most serious difficulties in getting New Directions off the ground?

LAUGHLIN: The learning process was difficult. I had to learn so much so quickly, how to make a book, and how to market a book. That was the greatest difficulty. But there was never any shortage of manuscripts. First beginning with Ezra's

friends and then going to Williams's friends and then moving
through Yvor Winters's group, there were always plenty of
manuscripts to do. That was no problem. In those days—it was
fairly soon after the Depression—the big publishers just
weren't doing much literary publishing.

INTERVIEWER: What was it like to be developing the press
on your own?

LAUGHLIN: It was very exciting. It was something new and
different and gave me a sense of action or accomplishment even
though the books didn't sell. It kept me busy. I enjoyed it.

INTERVIEWER: Was the excitement in the variety?

LAUGHLIN: There were so many different things I had to do.
I had to keep in touch with the authors and read the manuscripts, and I had to copyedit manuscripts, and I had to find
printers and binders. Then I had to get up ads and do the
catalogs. I had to try to sell the books. Publishing, when it's a
one-man operation, is an extremely varied occupation. It isn't
like a big firm where each person does a different job. I don't
know that I looked at it very objectively; I just did it. It seemed
to come, although I knew nothing about it when I started—I
was a quick learner in some ways, though I never learned
promotion and never will. The printers and the binders taught
me a lot, what to do and how to do it. There were good printers
around Cambridge. The man from whom I learned the most
about the beauty of a book was Giovanni Mardersteig of the
Officina Bodoni in Verona. He was the greatest hand printer
in Europe until he died a few years ago. I would visit him when
I was in Italy. He did three or four superb books for me. Gide's
Theseus, two Pound texts, and a Dylan Thomas. They were
limited editions, very expensive. He showed me a little bit
about how he designed books, which was very valuable in
establishing a criterion. Peter Beilenson taught me an enormous amount. He was a printer in Mount Vernon, New York,
who died much too young. He printed many of my books in

the old days, including those early fat annuals. He was a fine craftsman and designer.

INTERVIEWER: Rexroth has talked about the fine, limited editions you did in the early days and was upset that you had worked into other formats. Does what he said make sense to you?

LAUGHLIN: His rendition wasn't exactly correct. The early books were done in Harvard Square and they were not limited editions. They were just, I think, quite nicely printed books. Rexroth always had this romantic concept that he was going to become editor of New Directions and we would only do beautiful limited editions. But it was more in *his* mind than in mine. I have always liked to do hand-printed editions; there have been ten or fifteen of them over the years.

INTERVIEWER: One of your objectives with New Directions has been to make quality literature available to people who might otherwise not be able to afford it. That philosophy conflicts with limited editions, doesn't it?

LAUGHLIN: It does, but the two can go together. In the early days we were able to do that. The Poets of the Year series sold for, I think, fifty cents each in pamphlet form and one dollar each in paper over boards. I could do that then because I could get those thirty-two-page pamphlets printed for $300. But we gave up that series—after we did forty-two numbers. We wanted it to be on a subscription basis, but we could never build up a subscription list. People preferred to pick and choose. I think the subscription list only got up to about six hundred copies. The early New Classics series sold for a dollar and a half. You could do that in those days before inflation. Then I started the paperbacks. Those we were selling, some of the thin ones, for a dollar and the thick ones for a dollar and a half. Now the same books are $5.95 because of the damn inflation. So the concept of trying to produce cheap classics has just gone out the window.

INTERVIEWER: Were you given much advice in the early days at New Directions . . . working with writers such as Pound and Williams?

LAUGHLIN: Both were such tremendous people, and their letters were so interesting. In the same letter Ezra could be both very sweet and very cranky. He'd want me to reissue the autobiography of Martin Van Buren and the collected works of Alexander Del Mar. Del Mar was a minor official in the U. S. Treasury in the reign of Grant. He was an early credit crank and monetary theorist who wrote about eight books, the most famous of which is called *A History of Monetary Crimes.* Ezra loved him. He was always after me to publish it.

INTERVIEWER: You never did, did you?

LAUGHLIN: No, but Ezra did finally get some Del Mar published. One of those disciples of his at St. Elizabeth's Hospital put it out in the Square Dollar Series.

INTERVIEWER: How did he react when you "declined" to publish people he was pushing?

LAUGHLIN: Among his postcards there are any number of funny comments. Do you want me to try to find a typical one? "Possibly a politic move on Jas's part. Great deal of sewage to float a few boats. Possibly useful. Nasty way to educate the public. Four percent food. Ninety-six percent poison."

INTERVIEWER: He called you "Jas"?

LAUGHLIN: Yes. E. P. called me "Jas," as his family and "Poundians" still do.

INTERVIEWER: Do you recall any moments when you wondered whether you really wanted to stay with New Directions?

LAUGHLIN: I've never had any doubts about that. New Directions is my life.

INTERVIEWER: Did any low moments arise because an author was threatening to leave New Directions?

LAUGHLIN: I was terribly upset when Paul Bowles's agent stole him away from us. Can't remember her name. Paul's first book, *The Sheltering Sky,* had been turned down by every

publisher in New York. Paul was a friend of Tennessee's.
Tennessee brought the manuscript around and asked, "Would
you like to publish this?" I read it and said, "You bet." We did
very well with it; it went through seven printings. Then this
agent got a big offer from Random House for Bowles's next
book. Random House was one of the ones that turned down
the first book. I couldn't meet the advance, and so they stole
him away. That really hurt me and made me mad.

INTERVIEWER: That doesn't fit with the basic publishing
ethic.

LAUGHLIN: There are no ethics in publishing. This goes on
every day. Of course, Tennessee Williams was wonderfully
loyal. We had an understanding that we would do the plays and
stories and poetry. If he wanted to write something special,
he'd go out and get some big money for it.

INTERVIEWER: Do you know why Tennessee Williams stayed
with you?

LAUGHLIN: Maybe it was because we were the first to publish
him. He knew that I liked his poetry and his stories very much,
which were important to him, as well as the plays. And it's just
the way he was. I think he trusted me. I'm a trustee for one
of his sister's trusts. She's not well, and I guess he knew that
I'd take care of things. I was really shook up when Tennessee
died. I wrote the following lines for him a few hours after I
heard about it. I know they are sentimental, but that's the way
I felt:

TENNESSEE

called death the sudden subway and now he has taken that train
but there are so many good things to remember
first the young man in sloppy pants and a torn grey sweater
whom I met at Lincoln Kirstein's cocktail party
he was very shy and had hidden himself in a side room
I too was shy but we got talking

he told me he wrote plays and that he loved Hart Crane
he carried the poems of Crane in his knapsack wherever he
   hitch-hiked
then his first night of glory in Chicago
when he and Laurette Taylor made a new American theater
I remember happy days with him in London and Italy and Key
   West
and how often friends and writers who were down on their luck
told me how generously he had helped them
(but you would never hear about that from him)
so many fine things to remember
that I can live again in my mind
until it is my turn to join him on the sudden subway.

INTERVIEWER: Back at the beginning, it must have been a satisfying feeling when Williams's career really took off.

LAUGHLIN: It was very exciting. Here was a man who had an almost impoverished youth, who was struggling to publish with great difficulty. He had tough times, only occasionally placing a story in some small magazine. Then he arrived at the pinnacle with his first play. Suddenly, with *The Glass Menagerie,* everything changed. I went out to Chicago for the opening there with Laurette Taylor. It was fun and wonderful. I was very happy for him. Then, of course, he had a personal problem in handling success. It frightened him a little because he wasn't used to it.

INTERVIEWER: What are some of the other landmark moments that made you say, "Well, that's really satisfying"?

LAUGHLIN: It was pleasing when Jack Hawkes first had a full-page review in the Sunday *Times'* book section. He should have gotten it for his first book, *Cannibal,* twenty years before. It was just as brilliant a book, but there is always the time lag with original work. It took Jack years to get proper attention. And some reviewers still say he's "too difficult." What do they think Joyce is?

INTERVIEWER: Do you think that response arises because he writes difficult material in the European tradition?

LAUGHLIN: That's only a part of it. There are some pretty difficult writers who get as much attention as Jack. Barth, Pynchon, Barthelme. Perhaps it's something about his special sensibility.

INTERVIEWER: Do you mean the macabre element?

LAUGHLIN: Yes. That's very hard for some readers. They say: "I can't swallow this."

INTERVIEWER: In your own poetry you've always striven for clarity, yet you've published so many writers in recent years who are relatively difficult and obscure.

LAUGHLIN: Ezra always used to say that some poetry had to be difficult because of its content. He cited Cavalcanti, who is difficult. And Dante, who is in parts not easy. I agree that with poetry some subject matter requires, I hope not obscurity, but complexity of approach and language. For example, a great poet, Robert Duncan, has created his own imaginative and spiritual world to the point where he has to use new language and new syntax and new form to express it.

INTERVIEWER: How does the work of Hawkes and Abish fit in with your own tastes?

LAUGHLIN: I like their work. I understand what they're doing. I don't insist that everyone write light verse the way I do.

INTERVIEWER: That doesn't seem like a fair description of your work.

LAUGHLIN: I like to be understood by ordinary people. But many poets aim higher, and they should. George Oppen wants to speak to philosophical poets. So does Gustaf Sobin. They need this kind of metaphysical complexity to express themselves.

INTERVIEWER: Do you publish people like that because you like what they're doing?

LAUGHLIN: Yes, if we publish someone, I feel there's something good there. Occasionally we do something I'm not mad about because one of the staff wants to do it very much. I accept their taste and their judgment. But with me a book has got, as Gertrude Stein said, "to ring the bell."

INTERVIEWER: Have there been writers you've really wanted and just didn't get?

LAUGHLIN: We were speaking of the fact that I don't "lift" authors. I had been a friend of "Cal" Lowell from college days at Harvard, and I would have loved to publish him, but he was published first by Ronald Lane Latimer. Since he was being published by a small press I made no move, and then the first thing I knew, Harcourt Brace had made a move, and there he went. But we remained good friends all our lives. I admired him very much. Then there is Guy Davenport, who I think is tremendous. I've known Guy for a long time. But he didn't publish much in magazines and I hadn't really followed his writing. I didn't write to him, and North Point Press took him on. Then there's this young lady I met out at Centrum in Port Townsend, Carolyn Forché, an absolutely beautiful poet. Rexroth had told me about her, oh, six or seven years ago. I wrote to her—no answer. When I met her at Centrum, the first thing she said was, "The reason I didn't answer your letter was that I didn't have any new poems then. But the next one I write I'm going to send to you." She's being published by Harper, so she's tied up. I think she's going to be the next Denise Levertov.

INTERVIEWER: What have been the most surprising publishing ventures—the ones that made you say: "I just didn't expect that to happen"?

LAUGHLIN: I think, on the positive side, it would be Hesse's *Siddhartha.* Henry Miller pushed me into doing that, and it became a great best-seller. Another book which became a great best-seller was Ferlinghetti's *Coney Island of the Mind.* It's a wonderful book, but I didn't expect it to sell over a million copies when I took it on. On the other side there have been cases where a very good book just did nothing. The stories of

Tommaso Landolfi, for example; his collection called *Gogol's Wife and Other Stories*. Also the English poet Edwin Brock's autobiography, *Here. Now. Always.* A strong book and beautifully written. Nothing happened. You're so much at the mercy of the reviewers. If you don't get reviews, if people don't hear about the books . . . Another disappointing case was the *Selected Writings* of Blaise Cendrars, who was another great enthusiasm of Henry Miller's.

INTERVIEWER: Is there any pattern to these particular disappointments, a similar feature in the work?

LAUGHLIN: It's harder to get a foreign writer known.

INTERVIEWER: Helen Wolff has said that the critical problems in this country are poor quality reviews, but even worse, prejudice among the reviewing community against foreign writers.

LAUGHLIN: I think that's true. We did four foreign novels in 1981 and 1982, by Johan Borgen, Lars Gustafsson, Istvan Orkeny, and Lêdo Ivo. Now we were lucky on the Gustafsson because John Updike liked it and reviewed it in *The New Yorker*. It's into a second paperback edition. The Ivo and the Orkeny haven't done as well. They're all very good.

INTERVIEWER: So in a sense, a lot of your disappointments have come out of lack of reaction—

LAUGHLIN: Neglect of books that I thought were important.

INTERVIEWER: W. C. Williams once took you to task for what he referred to as an "insufficiently refined palate" in choosing writers for the New Directions anthology.

LAUGHLIN: He was probably right.

INTERVIEWER: Do you believe that you've gotten some "breakthrough" people precisely because you didn't strive for the highly refined palate?

LAUGHLIN: The annuals varied in quality a great deal from year to year. Probably the best was the one in the blue cover that you can't find now, ND 1939. An extraordinary number. That had the Lorca play, *Blood Wedding*, probably the first

Lorca play translated here; it had my piece on the Samuel Greenberg manuscripts, which showed how Hart Crane stole from Greenberg; it had Harry Levin on Joyce; it had three chapters of Henry Miller's *Tropic of Capricorn.* It was a knock-out issue. But I couldn't do that every time. The material wasn't offered, and I didn't have the money to commission things.

INTERVIEWER: Williams went on to say you've got to decide not to publish people who aren't ready yet or people who've been ready but have slipped.

LAUGHLIN: I disagree with him. I have always wanted to encourage the young. That has been one of the primary purposes of the annual. So I have printed a lot who perhaps weren't yet ready but who became good later. As for the good writers who were slipping, they needed encouragement, too.

INTERVIEWER: Have your feelings over the years about New Directions changed at all?

LAUGHLIN: I don't think they've changed much, although in the early years I was much more belligerent. I felt that we were the only ones who were doing anything good in literature and all the other publishers were a bunch of bums. I remember writing a letter to Bennett Cerf: "Dear Bennett, You have just committed one of the great crimes against American culture of our day. You have let Stendhal's *Chartreuse de Parme* go out of print. Sincerely yours."

INTERVIEWER: Have you mellowed because things have changed?

LAUGHLIN: I've come to accept that we live in a very imperfect publishing world and that we cannot expect people who have to make a living out of it, as I don't, to do the impossible. I've just relaxed and said, "We'll hoe our little row and not fuss about the others." But in the early days I was spikey as hell.

INTERVIEWER: Is more being done by other publishers now?

LAUGHLIN: Yes. Take Gordon Lish at Knopf. He's now publishing Ray Carver, which is a pretty courageous thing to do.

There are people like Gordon in most of the big houses. Jonathan Galassi at Random House is another "discoverer" and great on foreign translations. Call them hidden spies of literature who are working under cover and slipping things through. The other thing that I think is very encouraging is the good stuff that is being done by the small presses. Ferlinghetti's books, Jonathan Williams's books, Capra Press, John Martin's Black Sparrow books, Scott Walker's Graywolf Press, and David Godine are all very good. And the North Point Press—obviously modeled on New Directions, as William Turnbull, who backs it, told me when he was here. And that's very flattering. He came here to receive the laying-on of hands, which I was delighted to give him. He has very good people working for him. He's using good paper, he's Smyth-sewing instead of gluing, he is using headbands, and he is doing books of high literary merit.

INTERVIEWER: So the libraries are not going to have the problems with North Point books falling apart the way so many other books are now.

LAUGHLIN: I can't touch my set of *The Little Review* now because the paper flakes. There is a related story about Djuna Barnes. We were planning a special hardbound edition of *Nightwood*. She insisted she had to have paper that would last a thousand years. We asked the paper dealers, and they said, "No, it's impossible. You can't unless you go to an Italian or French handmade paper, which would be exorbitant. We cannot *produce* a paper that we will guarantee for more than five hundred years." So we finally printed the book on Curtis Rag, which the manufacturer guaranteed for five hundred years, but Djuna was never happy about it.

INTERVIEWER: Did you ever ask her how she was going to check the guarantee?

LAUGHLIN: No.

INTERVIEWER: You've arranged for a New Directions trust. What does that involve?

LAUGHLIN: The way this trust is written it will provide money for New Directions to go on for many years. But it is up to the trustees to be certain that quality is being maintained. If it isn't, they can terminate it.

INTERVIEWER: You mentioned you don't go out after authors. Do you solicit manuscripts?

LAUGHLIN: Oh yes. If one of us, myself or someone on the staff, reads something in a magazine that seems promising, he or she will write: "Can we see a manuscript?" The annuals also feed into books.

INTERVIEWER: How tough has it been to keep things fresh at New Directions?

LAUGHLIN: Very difficult, because my taste, in poetry especially, goes back to the days of Pound and Williams. While I can recognize the genius of a Carolyn Forché or an Allen Grossman or a Gustaf Sobin, I don't have much flair for picking from the latest crop. New Directions is moving strongly into publishing the remaining works of the great moderns. We've got ten books of both-sided Pound correspondence under contract. We have books of W. C. Williams correspondence under contract. And we have a program for publishing the unpublished manuscripts of William Carlos Williams that are in the Yale and Buffalo libraries. Very interesting things. And the unpublished work of H. D. [Hilda Doolittle] that is at Yale.

INTERVIEWER: Could you describe the process by which you make a publication decision?

LAUGHLIN: First one of the editors reads a manuscript; then the others read it. If the first reader likes it and if they all like it, they send it up to me.

INTERVIEWER: Do you have the final say?

LAUGHLIN: It has to be a majority decision. A few times I have thrown my weight around when I cared passionately about a book.

INTERVIEWER: Let's move into some questions about your

relationships with New Directions writers. What features of Pound's art do you admire?

LAUGHLIN: The metrical innovations, the collage structure of the *Cantos,* the ideogrammic method. I think he was a tremendous technician. Perhaps the greatest of the century. He will endure. His criticism is remarkable and his translations are superb.

INTERVIEWER: Pound and Williams wrote poetry that was so different in many ways. Why do you think they were such good friends during the early years?

LAUGHLIN: They became friends in college at Penn in 1902. They were kindred souls who loved literature. Later Pound helped Williams to change the nature of his poetry from bad Keats to good modern. Ezra was a very loyal person who liked Bill and was supportive. Of course, they fought a lot, but it was a real friendship. Ezra was one of the first to appreciate *Kora in Hell* when few others but Marianne Moore and Kenneth Burke understood it. And that meant a lot to Bill. Ezra was a strong rooter for *Life Along the Passaic River* and for *White Mule.*

INTERVIEWER: This despite the fact that Pound was so very condescending toward him?

LAUGHLIN: Very condescending, but Bill took it. Bill was infuriated with Ezra for doing the Rome broadcasts. Bill had two boys in the service then, and Bill told him to go to hell, but when Ezra landed in St. Elizabeth's Hospital, Bill felt sorry for him and went down to see him and made peace.

INTERVIEWER: In a recent book—*The Roots of Treason: Ezra Pound and the Secret of St. Elizabeth's*—a psychiatrist named E. Fuller Torrey argued that Winfred Overholser, the Superintendent at St. Elizabeth's Hospital, had protected Pound from prosecution on treason charges. Was Pound really as sane as Torrey argues?

LAUGHLIN: Not at first. When Ezra was brought to Washington from Italy I asked my lawyer, Julien Cornell, to go talk to him. Cornell called me up and said, "Jas, I can't do much to

help this man. He's out of touch with reality. He has no
conception that he has done anything wrong. He can't keep his
mind on track. What will we do?" We corresponded with
Dorothy Pound's lawyer in England and he said, "Go for
insanity," and that's what we did. A few days after I'd heard
from Cornell I went down to see Pound when he was still in
Gallinger Hospital. He was hopelessly confused. But he was
given very good care in St. Elizabeth's, where he rapidly improved. He got over a lot of his paranoia and confabulation, but
elements of it remained. After a year or so he was able to work
and he seemed not unhappy. I'd go down to see him and he'd
be cheerful, telling stories, but he still had some strange ideas.
After three years Cornell wanted to try habeas corpus to get
him out on the grounds that there had never been a treason
case in law where a man had been held indefinitely for insanity.
But Ezra wouldn't let Dorothy, who was his guardian, sign the
habeas corpus papers. He said, "I will never leave here except
with flying colors and a personal apology from the President."
He was not realistic. He thought he'd been right all along, that
we should have been fighting the Russians, not the Germans
or the Italians.

INTERVIEWER: Was Pound aware of the heat that you were
taking for publishing him during those years?

LAUGHLIN: I don't think he paid any attention to it. There
were some Jewish booksellers who wouldn't order his books,
but, generally speaking, there wasn't too much stink about it.

INTERVIEWER: Did you ever feel that your differences with
Pound on his anti-Semitism affected your relationship with
him?

LAUGHLIN: When I was in Rapallo, in 1935, there were
not-quite-nice jokes about Sir Montagu Norman, the Governor
of the Bank of England, and other Jewish bankers. I was upset.
This despite the fact that I'd been raised in Pittsburgh in a very
anti-Semitic atmosphere. But by 1935 I'd gotten some sophistication. I went after him on it, but all he said was, "How do

you think a man whose name is Ezra could be anti-Semitic?" He wouldn't face up to it. Dr. Overholser later explained it to me. Anti-Semitism was a recognized symptom of paranoia. One should not, he said, judge Ezra on moral grounds but on medical grounds. Once Overholser, who was eminent in his field, had told me that, I accepted it. I have saved a characteristic postcard from Ezra. It was time to bring out another section of the *Cantos* and it had some rather unpleasant anti-Semitic lines in it. I wrote to Ezra to ask if I could take those out. He wrote back: "Again in *Cantos,* all institutions are judged on their merits. *Idem* religion. No one can be boosted or exempted on grounds of being a Lutheran or a Manichaean. Nor can all philosophy be degraded to a status of propaganda merely because the author has one philosophy and not another. Is the *Divina Commedia* propaganda or not? From '72 on we shall enter the realm of philosophy, George Santayana, etc. The publisher cannot expect to control the religion and philosophy of his authors. Certain evil habits of language, etc. must be weighed and probably will be found wanting. I shall not accept the specific word *anti-Semitic.* There will have to be a general formula covering Mennonites, Mohammedans, Lutherans, Calvinists. I wouldn't swear to not being anti-Calvinist but that don't mean I should weigh Protestants in one balance and Anglo-Cats in another. All ideas coming from the Near East are probably shit. If they turn out to be typhus in the laboratory, so is it. So is Taoism. So is probably all Chinese philosophy and religion except Confucius. I am not yet sure." I never could get anywhere with him on his anti-Semitism. At one point I censored him. In one of the *Cantos* he talks about the Rothschilds and calls them "Stinkshilds." At the time a Rothschild family member was living in New York. I thought it might be libelous to call her "Stinkshild," so I just put a black bar through the name and that survived for several printings.

INTERVIEWER: You've been working recently on a film about Pound in Italy. What can you tell me about that project?

LAUGHLIN: It's being produced by a very interesting group called the New York Center for Visual History, which hopes to get the financing for a series of ten documentary films about poets, beginning with Walt Whitman and Emily Dickinson and coming up through Hart Crane, Lowell and William Carlos Williams. They started with the Pound project because they wanted a contemporary figure who stood out as a key maker of modern poetry. We began in Venice, interviewing Olga Rudge, for so many years Pound's best friend, and then we shot scenes in Venice which Ezra had written about in the *Cantos* or elsewhere. Last summer we did Provence, or rather the Dordogne, up in the northern part of Provence, where Pound and T. S. Eliot and Dorothy Pound had made a walking tour in 1919 to find old troubadour castles. We were able to follow their route because every day Dorothy had written a postcard to her mother in London. These gave us the dates and where they'd been. The postcard would say, "We found Mareuil today and it was like this. . . . Today we walked to Hautefort." We had a great time shooting those old castles. We got Yves Roquette, considered the leading speaker of traditional Provençal poetry, to read Bertran de Born for us from the battlements of Hautefort. And we got another man who plays the *vielle à roux,* an ancient instrument, to sing *canzone* of Arnaud Daniel at Excideuil. It was a beautiful experience. Then we went to Italy, to Rapallo, where Pound had lived. We were lucky in being able to get permission from the present owners of his old apartment to shoot the Gulf of Tigullio from his terrace. We shot the little house in San Ambrogio where he lived during the war. Next we went up to Sirmione on Lake Garda, one of Pound's "sacred places," where the famous first meeting with Joyce took place. Then we shot the church of San Zeno in Verona, which Pound considered the finest piece of architecture of the Middle Ages. We also went up to his daughter Mary's castle at Tirolo di Merano. We got a wonderful interview with her. We went down to Siena, a place that he loved, and shot some good things there. Then down to Rome, where I was able to recite the *"Nox mihi candida"* from "Homage to Sextus Propertius" on the Palatine Hill, but the director wouldn't let me wear a toga.

INTERVIEWER: What came to be your role in this film?

LAUGHLIN: It was doing whatever they asked me to do. Literary advice. Interviews. Commentary. Voice-overs. The film's going to have a lot of poetry in it, using the latest electronic techniques. I had to interview some people in Italian, old people who had known him, which was quite a strain since I've forgotten most of my Italian.

INTERVIEWER: Is anybody playing parts?

LAUGHLIN: No. Just interviews with people who knew him. But no one will play Pound, which is good. It would be impossible to find an actor who could play Pound.

INTERVIEWER: With respect to Pound's aesthetic theory, did you agree with him for the most part?

LAUGHLIN: I agreed with him almost completely. I reread his literary essays for a course I gave last spring at Brown and it continually astonished me how smart he was about distinguishing between good and bad writing and what in various traditions should be preserved and followed and what shouldn't. I'm amazed at his flair for that kind of discrimination. He was perhaps the first to recognize that Yeats was a *great* poet. He spotted Joyce and he spotted Eliot.

INTERVIEWER: I want to move on to some questions about Rexroth. You said in an earlier interview that "the role of Ezra in my life was taken over by Rexroth in that he advised me what to do and put me onto things." Could you elaborate on what kinds of things he was doing?

LAUGHLIN: It's odd; Kenneth was very much like Pound temperamentally, though he detested him because he considered Pound fascist and Kenneth was an anarchist. But their wide-ranging interests in everything literary and philosophical were parallel in many ways, though certain things Rexroth emphasized more than Pound. Rexroth was a great teacher, as was Pound. Pound was one of the greatest talkers I ever knew, and Rexroth was right next to him. He'd ramble on about everything. He was very helpful to me, telling me what to read. He would lend me his books, just as Ezra had done. He took over as my teacher where Pound left off. Obviously their specialties were different, but they were both stimulating.

INTERVIEWER: Did the mentorship with Pound diminish at the beginning of World War II?

LAUGHLIN: Yes. He was in Italy and no mail got through.

INTERVIEWER: How early did Rexroth come into the picture as mentor?

LAUGHLIN: I became involved with the ski resort at Alta, Utah, about 1939, and I went down often to see Kenneth and stay with him on Potrero Hill in San Francisco during the war. We spent a lot of time together, camping and skiing in the mountains, in the Sierras. We went on trips in the early spring when there was still a lot of snow. We climbed into the mountains, and Kenneth would dig a little cave in the snow, lining it with fir branches, where we slept. This was very fine. When I was staying with him in San Francisco we often went rock climbing down the coast. Rexroth was a good rock climber, very much the outdoorsman. He loved nature and understood it in a philosophical way. That shows in his greatest poems, such as "The Signature of All Things." I miss him. He was a unique character. He was cantankerous; he loved nothing better than going to read at a college and being the "insulting author." He was a naughty fellow. I used to get angry with him about that. I said, "Kenneth, you know you're hurting the sale of your books by antagonizing professors." He just laughed.

INTERVIEWER: You mentioned earlier that one of your other special relationships was with Thomas Merton. What made you feel so close to him?

LAUGHLIN: He was so nice, so jolly. He wasn't a dour monk at all. He was a kind friend and interested in everything. I often went down to visit him at the monastery in Kentucky. The Abbot would give him a day off, and I'd rent a car. Tom would get an old bishop's suit out of the storeroom and start out in that. Then we would stop in the woods and he'd change into his farmworker's blue jeans and a beret to hide his tonsure. Then we'd hit the bars across Kentucky. He loved his beer, and he loved that smoked ham they have down there. He was a wonderful person. He wanted to read contemporary writers, but the books were often confiscated, so we had a secret system. I sent the books he wanted to the monastery psychiatrist in Louisville, who would get them to Merton. I sent him everyone he wanted to read: Sartre and Camus, Rexroth and Pound, Henry Miller and many more. We talked a great deal about the Oriental religions. He was very ecumenical. We talked about his situation and why he stuck it out in the monastery. Once I asked, "Tom, why do you stay here? You could get out and be a tremendous success in the world." He answered that the monastery was where God wanted him to be.

INTERVIEWER: Did you feel he was misplaced in a monastery?

LAUGHLIN: He would have been misplaced if he hadn't been so determined to get what he wanted in the monastery—his own hermitage among the hills. He couldn't stand the "social life" in the monastery with all the monks talking sign language, having to go to church six times a day, going to chapter, and making cheese. He finally did persuade the Abbot to build him a hermitage. Tom was a shrewd operator. He got out of sleeping in the communal dormitory by learning how to snore so loudly that the other monks got together at chapter and said, "Father Louis has got to leave the dormitory." So Tom was allowed to use one of the old bishop's rooms. He believed that the old monastic tradition was so strict that it could no longer foster true spirituality.

INTERVIEWER: Robert Lowell has complained that Merton's poetry is soft; yet you have made a case for Merton as one of the underrated poets, especially in terms of the personal epic. Could you elaborate?

LAUGHLIN: He wrote only one personal epic, *The Geography of Lograire*, which he started about four years before his death. What he wanted to do was obviously modeled on Williams's *Paterson*, but he executed it very much in his own way. This was going to be the geography of a man's mind and interests based on his reading. He read widely in many fields. Unfortunately, he completed only one volume of *Lograire*. I was disappointed because it only got two serious reviews. I think it will some day be recognized as one of the big modern poems. What is particularly strong in it, apart from his continually imaginative treatment of his material, is his use of parody and myth, with which he does fantastic things.

INTERVIEWER: What is he parodying?

LAUGHLIN: Anything that came into his head. There's one section called "The Ladies of Tlatilco," where he's writing about the beauty of the ancient Mexican Indian women; it is almost entirely cribbed from the ads in *The New Yorker*, for ladies' beauty products and clothes. It's exquisitely funny. He does that often. He will take a text of something he's been reading in anthropology and parody it. With myth he also does extraordinary things, as with the Cargo Cults literature and the stories of the Dakota Indians' ghost dances. He had a great gift for selective condensation from his reading. Pound had this, too. He was able to select the kernel, the core, the colorful detail that dramatizes history. Williams did this in *In the American Grain*.

INTERVIEWER: In an earlier interview you mentioned, with respect to Merton, that he was able to create an extremely vivid world; you went on to note that most of the great poets were also able to do that. What is the appeal in creating a "world"?

LAUGHLIN: Many people want to get out of the world they're in. They want to get into someone else's world that's more exciting and more interesting. The great poets create their personal worlds. Pound made his diachronic and intercultural world, Williams made *Paterson*, Robert Duncan is busy making his world, Merton made his in *The Geography of Lograire*, Hart Crane made his in *The Bridge*.

INTERVIEWER: Is there any shared element in these various poets' "worlds," or are they all in a sense idiosyncratic visions?

LAUGHLIN: I think the best poets since Pound have taken something from him. Williams did, even though *Paterson* is unlike the *Cantos*, except in elements of its structure. Both are collages, big mosaics, built by association out of memory and reading.

INTERVIEWER: What was it Williams borrowed?

LAUGHLIN: Certain attitudes about how you write poetry and what you think about. Duncan has drawn on Pound. Over the centuries poetry is a continuous process of reformulation and adaptation. At a certain point Eliot and Pound decided that free verse had become squashy. So they read the Bay State Hymnbook, the poems of Théophile Gautier and Tristan Corbière; they read the Greek poet Bion, and out of that mix came the strict forms of Eliot's hippopotamus poems and Pound's "Hugh Selwyn Mauberley." (By the way, Basil Bunting says that Pound once told him that "Mauberley" was a hoax, inspired by a hoax perpetrated by Samuel Butler. Well, for a hoax it's a great poem.) There is a continual plowing up of old poetic ground, from which elements are given new life. Poets have this instinct to seek forebears, to seek ancestors. Yet they want to be new, to do their new thing, to "make it new," as Ezra said. Pound was constantly drawn to the past, picking out from the past what he thought was "the live tradition."

INTERVIEWER: What was it like to have Delmore Schwartz working for you?

LAUGHLIN: Delmore, again, was one of the great talkers, particularly as a parodist. He was a marvelous mimic and fantasist and confabulator. He didn't do a great deal of work at New Directions. He put much of the work off onto his wife Gertrude, except the night the Charles River flooded in Cambridge. Then Delmore had to carry up the books from the basement. But he more than made up for it with his charm. Before he went off his head, he was utterly charming. He was very helpful in reading scripts. He had excellent taste.

INTERVIEWER: Did you realize right from the start when he began attacking you that there was something terribly wrong?

LAUGHLIN: I knew that he was ill and arranged to have him go to a psychiatrist. The psychiatrist didn't do him much good. It became clear that he had a problem, and all his friends knew that. There was increasingly difficult and quarrelsome and eccentric behavior. I guess he was paranoid.

INTERVIEWER: You've mentioned several times in the past that you think Henry Miller is underrated. By way of developing the case for Henry Miller, could you offer some detail on what you value so highly in his work?

LAUGHLIN: One problem with Miller is that he wrote so much you must pick and choose to get at the best. *Tropic of Cancer* is a marvelous book. Did I tell you how I got to know about Henry? One day I was having lunch with Ezra in 1935 in Rapallo, and he threw a paperback across the table. "Well, Jas, here's a dirty book that's pretty good." I wrote to Henry and we got into correspondence. I arranged to do a selection of his pieces called *The Cosmological Eye*. When Miller is good, he is very good. Probably his best book is *The Colossus of Maroussi,* the one about Greece. But he wrote many fine shorter pieces. You'd have to go through and sort them out.

INTERVIEWER: Isn't this the case with Gertrude Stein? You've described changing tires and rewriting copy to try to help her present her lectures in the States. But later things seemed to change quite a bit. You said in several interviews that you were afraid she wasn't moving on.

LAUGHLIN: I don't think that she did move on from her remarkable early work. She got deeper and deeper into automatic writing, which she was beginning at the time I worked for her. Automatic writing is a dead end. You go on writing "automatically" and what do you write? If you look at those later books that Yale published for her after she gave them her papers, they're pretty boring.

I used to watch Gertrude at it. That summer I spent in Savoie writing those press releases for *Lectures in America,* I'd watch her sitting in a bath chair on her terrace with a big notebook, writing just as fast as she could, the pen flying, no pauses whatsoever. No rewriting. And then Alice B. Toklas, sweet person—well, not all that sweet, *sort* of sweet—would be given these notebooks to type out. Her best work came early: *Three Lives, Blood on the Dining-Room Floor,* parts of *The Making of Americans, Portrait of Mabel Dodge at the Villa Curonia. Four Saints in Three Acts* was beautiful, and some of the other plays, the opera plays. She really needed someone like Virgil Thomson, whom she respected, to sit on her a bit and make her devise some plot. In the automatic writing pieces there's no plot movement; they just roll on and become tedious.

INTERVIEWER: What's your feeling now about her importance?

LAUGHLIN: What's interesting is that now so many of the younger writers are reading her seriously, people such as David Antin, Jerome Rothenberg, and Robert Duncan, among others. I think this indicates that something significant *is* there. Then, too, Williams was so much influenced by her. Those two essays he wrote about her. It's clear if you read Williams's "Imaginations" that he had been profoundly influenced by the work of hers which he saw in Alfred Stieglitz's magazine *Camera Work.* This doesn't come out in Williams's autobiography because Gertrude and Floss Williams had a fight. You know how Gertrude and Bill broke up? One evening at her place in Paris she took out a big stack of her manuscripts and asked Bill what to do with them. Bill replied in his "Billyums" way, "I'd pick out the best one and throw the rest away." This was an impossible thing to tell Gertrude, who believed her every word was Great Art. Alice B. Toklas showed the Williamses to the door.

INTERVIEWER: Many times you've talked about how you met Tennessee Williams, but could you comment on why you think so much of him as a poet?

LAUGHLIN: He's a wonderful romantic poet. He comes right out of Romanticism, and no one else has done that kind of thing so well recently. He has beautiful imagery. His line is perhaps a little loose, but he's a fine poet. I think that if he hadn't written his great plays, he'd be more recognized as a poet. Some of the poems have wonderful humor, such as "Life Story." The poem about his sister Rose (the Laura of *The Glass Menagerie*), "The Paper Lantern," is a little masterpiece.

INTERVIEWER: Do you think his poetry is good enough that readers will begin to recognize him as a poet?

LAUGHLIN: His poetry was swamped by his being such a famous playwright. Readers tend to pigeonhole writers. He was a magnificent story-writer. There are few storywriters today who touch him for pure narrative drive, psychological penetration, and that lovely fantastic, light, self-mocking style.

INTERVIEWER: Dylan Thomas. What was your relationship with him like?

LAUGHLIN: It was difficult, because he always wanted to drink. I went on one bender with him in London which lasted for two days and three nights. We ended up sleeping on the floor of some lady's apartment and neither of us knew who she was. He always wanted to drink, but I'm not such a great drinker.

INTERVIEWER: Did his drinking get in the way for you?

LAUGHLIN: Yes. When he came to New York he'd come in the office at ten o'clock in the morning and say, "Let's go to the White Horse Tavern." I'd say, "Dylan, I've got work to do." So he'd go off to the White Horse and meet various cronies and sycophants. Sometimes I'd join him late in the evening. He was a sad case, Dylan; he was basically a nice person, and when he started boozing he was very amusing, but he would never stop; he'd go on and on. It's very hard to get close to a drinker. There was always that thing between us, the boozing. He was a great talker, too; he was a wonderful talker, but I had work to do. When Dylan drank he wanted people to be with him, to listen to him. It was a method of attracting people. But he was very indiscriminate about whom he would attract. He had a bunch of hangers-on in New York, such as that jerk Oscar Williams, who were crumbs. That was a barrier, because he'd be with such crummy characters. You couldn't really have a conversation with Dylan when he was drinking. It wore me down. John Davenport had a good name for Dylan. He called him "Old Messy." He was. He was messy because of the drinking. You couldn't count on him. If you wanted to do something you couldn't count on his turning up sober or on time.

INTERVIEWER: How about your relationship with Kenneth Patchen?

LAUGHLIN: Kenneth I knew very well. He and Miriam worked here in the Norfolk office. I was deeply fond of them both. I was sorry for him; he seemed to have a chip on his shoulder about life. He had those big sad brown eyes. He had unendurable pain from his bad back. He was sometimes difficult to work with. He was a most conscientious employee, but as a writer he could be difficult to work with because he wanted to design his own books, and he wasn't that good a designer. His layouts were a bit heavy-handed.

INTERVIEWER: Did you get along pretty well with him?

LAUGHLIN: Except for a few arguments. When we did the *Collected Poems* there was a fuss because he'd written so many poems. If we'd included all of them it would have made a two-thousand-page volume. We argued over what length the book could be and what should go into it. He was mighty unhappy about that. But it just wasn't practical to do a two-thousand-page book. His public, mostly young people, couldn't have bought it. And he was uneven. Some poems were very good and some were not. I thought that I was doing him a favor by cutting out the repetitive poems.

INTERVIEWER: What attracts you to Denise Levertov's work?

LAUGHLIN: For me, she's the best of the organic form poets. She has that so important ability that Williams had: she knows where to end the line. Very few poets know where to end the line. This is terribly important in free verse. Pound had it. His finest free verse is in the "Homage to Sextus Propertius." He knew where to end or break the line. And so does Denise.

INTERVIEWER: Is that something she's had to work at?

LAUGHLIN: Yes. Her first book, *The Double Image,* was somewhat in the vein of the so-called New Romantic School in London—rather conventional, not very original in technique. Then she married Mitch Goodman, an American GI, came to this country, and began reading Williams. Almost immediately she figured out from Williams how to write good free verse. Her two early American books sounded much like Williams's voice. She was beginning to learn his technique, but the voice was what colored them. Then when she found her *own* voice, when she was completely herself, she became terribly good. One thing that I admire so much in Denise is her social commitment, the way she goes to jail for things that she believes in and climbs over fences to picket nuclear plants. This is admirable. Carolyn Forché has the same dedication.

INTERVIEWER: What do you think of her discipline as a poet?

LAUGHLIN: She constructs her poems with the greatest care. Listen to the sound patterns of her lines and look at the way the lines are placed on the page. She is a superb technician. She makes it sound free and easy. But you examine it and you'll see it isn't. It's very disciplined, very carefully done. I think a time comes when poets find that discipline becomes almost spontaneous. The line arrives in their heads in the shape and form they want.

INTERVIEWER: What is it that "rings the bell" for you with Gary Snyder's work?

LAUGHLIN: The limpidity of it; his sure, good technique; the mixture of thought content with human examples. Most of his poems are about a subject, but he will bring in persons to illustrate what he's talking about.

INTERVIEWER: Have you developed a fairly close personal relationship with Snyder?

LAUGHLIN: We write back and forth. We visited him once at his place in the Sierras and had a fine time. The little house that he built is a mixture of Japanese and Indian (American Indian) style. We met his nice Japanese wife and his two boys. He's a happy person to be with. Maybe it's his Zen training. He has a deep spiritual quality, but without any pretension. There's no pretension about Gary at all. He's one of the people I feel really has a soul. Gary is a charismatic figure. His ecological work is so important. I sometimes wish he would sacrifice his private life a bit to be more a public figure. He is such a good speaker and so charismatic that he could have wide popular influence if he would become, not a politician, but someone like a Ralph Nader, working to save the earth.

INTERVIEWER: Does this statement about Snyder fit in with your notions from way back about the poet as leader?

LAUGHLIN: He is a leader already. His books are widely read. But he could do more. He did make an attempt when Jerry Brown, the former Governor of California, put him on his Arts Council. I haven't seen Gary since then, and I don't know how much he was able to accomplish. But that is the sort of thing I'd like to see him do more of.

INTERVIEWER: There seems to be an unusual consistency in the quality of the personal relationships you've had with many of your writers. Do you have any sense of why you're able to maintain those relationships, even though you don't see these authors very often?

LAUGHLIN: I write to them occasionally and see them when

I can. I hope they feel I'm someone they can turn to if they need something—advice or attention or a loan.

INTERVIEWER: Sounds as though you're returning to Pound's dictum—do something useful. Is that something you do instinctively?

LAUGHLIN: It's instinctive. You like someone, and you do what you can to help him out. I don't make anything of it. I've just been lucky to pick authors who happen to be great people. I look back over the people I've published and I think there've only been two stinkers.

INTERVIEWER: Can you say who these two "stinkers" are?

LAUGHLIN: That would not be in good taste. *De mortuis nihil nisi bonum.*

INTERVIEWER: You spent five years working for the Ford Foundation on *Perspectives.* What effect did your years with *Perspectives* have on your acquisition of Oriental titles?

LAUGHLIN: I met Raja Rao in Trivandrum and was greatly impressed with him. He's a remarkable writer and a true Vedantist. He put me on to his book *Kanthapura,* which is perhaps the most authentic novel of South India. *Kanthapura* carries on the tradition of village oral literature in India, which goes back thousands of years. Most of the population there couldn't read Sanskrit, so they got their religion and history through the village speaker. Raja Rao has picked this up in the narrative voice of the old woman in a typical village. She tells the story of life in the village and how Gandhi affected it. It's a powerful and perfect little book. Then I met the Frenchman Alain Danielou, the brother of the Jesuit Cardinal Danielou. He had gone to India as a young man and had become a Hindu. He was living, when I first knew him, in a tiny palace on the banks of the Ganges in Benares. I liked him immediately and we've become great friends. He told me about a wonderful old-time Tamil classic, the *Shilappadikaram: The Ankle Bracelet,* a beautiful mythic novel of early Chola days. He had already translated it into French. He's perfect in English, so I persuaded him to retranslate it into English. It is certainly one of the most important Indian books that I have published.

INTERVIEWER: Had you intended to concentrate so heavily on Asia?

LAUGHLIN: No, that came along later. The original project was to do *Perspectives* in four languages: English, French, German, and Italian. There'd been a big gap during the war when nothing cultural from America came to Europe, and the magazine was planned to fill that gap. We had articles on architecture, art, philosophy, etc., and, of course, stories and poems. The idea was to give a catch-up course in recent American culture. Then later the Indian project got started. They sent me out there to work on the Indian Southern Languages Book Trust, which I set up and which was a glorious flop, because the Indians had trouble doing distribution in a businesslike way. At the outset, *Perspectives* was all "outflow" from the U.S.A. Then we decided that since cultural exchange should be a two-way street we must have some "inflow," presenting the culture of other countries. To do that, rather than try to set up our own magazine with all the expense of building a circulation, we rode piggyback on the *Atlantic,* courtesy of Ted Weeks. Ted gave us forty-eight pages at the back of the magazine. They paid for the printing and distribution, so all we had to do was get the material together. We did nine of these special supplements. I edited the *Perspectives* of Burma and Germany and had a wonderful time in those countries.

INTERVIEWER: Do you continue to be able to draw the Oriental titles?

LAUGHLIN: Bob MacGregor, my former managing director, was the one who thought of reprinting the Irving Babbitt translation of the *Dhammapada.* It's one of the basic scriptures of Buddhism. We've not done much Orientalia recently— though there is a collection, called *Rasa,* of the essays and translations of a curious and very interesting Frenchman, René Daumal. Ferlinghetti published his beautiful little symbolic novel, *Mount Analogue*. *Rasa* is a strictly scholarly book, but it appealed to me very much because of my interest in Oriental religion from the time I'd spent in India and also the two years I spent working on Merton's *Asian Journal*, when I had to read, in order to verify his texts and quotations, so many Buddhist and Hindu sacred books.

INTERVIEWER: Your eyes seem to light up when you start talking about some of the German literary figures. Is there something about German literature in general that attracts you?

LAUGHLIN: I should say first that I find German very difficult. It's a language that I've never been able to master; the abstract words all sound too much alike to me. But I read a lot of Goethe and Schiller when I was in Harvard. I was crazy about Hölderlin, Kafka, Rilke, Celan, and Kleist. Kleist is one of my favorites. I think *Prince Friedrich of Homburg* is one of the great plays of world literature.

INTERVIEWER: Have you had much personal contact with your foreign writers? Michaux, for example?

LAUGHLIN: Michaux I knew when I was living in Paris. I loved Michaux. I was brought to him by Richard Ellmann. Ellmann translated a selection of his poetry for New Directions. And we did Sylvia Beach's translation of his travel book, *A Barbarian in Asia*. But then I dropped away from Michaux. I didn't like his drug books. I couldn't understand them. First of all—what was he talking about? And I've never been very sympathetic to the whole idea of drugs. Michaux became annoyed with me when I didn't take on those books. However, he seems to have forgiven me and we'll be doing his little book on Chinese ideograms. This is the book Pound wanted to translate in his old age but hadn't the strength.

INTERVIEWER: Céline?

LAUGHLIN: Céline I met. I once went out to see him when he was living in Meudon, an industrial suburb of Paris near the Renault plant. He had a small house, and outside it there was a high barbed-wire fence. He had two very fierce dogs that barked at me when I rang the gate bell. He had to come out and tie up the dogs. This was because Robert Denoël, his publisher, had been murdered on a street in Paris. Denoël had been a collaborator, too. Céline was rather paranoid, but he was friendly to me. I had had contact with his wife, who was a ballet dancer. While they were in exile in Denmark during the war, she couldn't get ballet shoes for her practice. So she used to write to me and I'd go down to Capezio in New York to buy her ballet shoes and airmail them over to her.

INTERVIEWER: That's an interesting publisher service.

LAUGHLIN: She went through a lot of ballet shoes.

INTERVIEWER: Outside Europe, where are the strongest concentrations of writers?

LAUGHLIN: Latin America.

INTERVIEWER: Do you locate most of your foreign writers through contacts with individuals in the country?

LAUGHLIN: It varies. There's no general plan. Many manuscripts come to us from translators who are professors in American colleges who've gotten interested in a given writer. But others come on the recommendations of French or Italian or German publishers with whom we're in touch. Others come on the recommendation of writers we've published.

INTERVIEWER: Earlier we talked about some of the problems foreign writers have and Helen Wolff's comment that the foreign writers often do not get the reviews they need. Do you have any ideas about solutions or ways of going at the problem?

LAUGHLIN: No. American reviewing is hopeless. I think that Harvey Shapiro at *The New York Times* did his very best. He tried to be evenhanded and review all different kinds of books, but there are just too many. Generally speaking, there aren't enough places where reviews of serious writing appear. *The New York Review of Books* is good but can't cover much with such long reviews. There's also the space problem. The newspapers don't want to give space to an industry which doesn't advertise much. New York publishers usually confine their advertising to *The New York Times* and three or four other papers. So papers that don't get advertising won't give space for reviews. The good thing about the London *Times Literary Supplement* is that, except for the lead article, they keep their reviews short. Thus they can get in reviews of fifty or sixty books. That means exposure for many titles.

INTERVIEWER: You wrote admiringly in the thirties and forties in the New Directions anthology of the "pure" writers. Who are the pure writers today who are refusing to betray their genius?

LAUGHLIN: Jack Hawkes, Walter Abish, Raymond Carver, Jerry Rothenberg, Annie Dillard, Russell Haley, and a good number of others. They're doing their new things, paying little attention to whether the books sell or what the critics say about them. I think Abish's *How German Is It?* is a very "pure" book. I always tell the New Directions writers, "Don't read your reviews."

INTERVIEWER: Have you seen direct, negative examples where writers have started paying attention to reviews?

LAUGHLIN: Jack Hawkes reads his reviews. Sometimes he'll call me up, upset by a review. I tell him, "Jack, do your thing. Don't pay any attention to those bastards. How often does a good enough critic review your work so you're going to learn anything from him?" Many critics talk about themselves and then give very superficial opinions about the work. We don't have many Edmund Wilsons around these days. But a writer should pay attention to what John Updike writes. Or to what Hayden Carruth says in his poetry reviews.

INTERVIEWER: How did you happen to come across Kafka's *Amerika*?

LAUGHLIN: It came from England. Edwin Muir and his wife translated it in England and for some reason Schocken, who publish Kafka here, had not done it.

INTERVIEWER: It's clear that a large number of your acquisitions have come because you've listened to other writers and scholars. Do you think commercial publishers listen enough?

LAUGHLIN: I don't know. Fran McCullough listened, kept her ear to the ground, and then Harper and Row fired her after sixteen years. Said her books didn't make enough money. There are others who listen—Gordon Lish, for example. He reads the little magazines, and he gets around. Bob Giroux must listen because he is our greatest literary editor.

INTERVIEWER: You've said at one time or another that formal discipline is essential for good writing.

LAUGHLIN: There was a period when Delmore Schwartz wrote a sonnet every day. He didn't really like sonnets, but he wrote them for discipline. It certainly helped him. If you look at his best short poems, they're not sonnets, but they're very well structured. So too with Pound. There was a time early on when Ezra used to chant his lines to a metronome, though he gave it up after a while—another way to learn verbal discipline and control.

INTERVIEWER: What role has creative writing played in your own life?

LAUGHLIN: From boarding school on I wanted to be a writer. I didn't want to go into the family steel business. I was not *then* attracted to the academic world, though I am *now*. I wanted to be a writer. I wrote a story, which won the *Atlantic* Prize. I won the *Story* magazine prize twice. I was writing unplotted stories and enjoying it and writing little poems.

INTERVIEWER: When Pound advised you in 1935 not to pursue a career as a poet, what was your reaction?

LAUGHLIN: I guessed he was probably right.

INTERVIEWER: Had you had your own doubts before he said what he did?

LAUGHLIN: No. I was trying. But I knew I wasn't turning out much that was up to his standards. I showed him my things.

He'd mark them all up and tell me what was wrong with them. I wasn't much surprised that he told me to become a publisher, not a writer.

INTERVIEWER: Have you ever regretted allowing that exchange to lead you into publishing and in the process to minimize the amount of time for your own writing?

LAUGHLIN: No, because I don't think, to put it very simply, that I was ready in 1935 to do my later kind of poetry (which is quite different from what I was writing when I was with Pound). And when I *was* ready to do it, Bill Williams encouraged me. The new metric began to work for me, but it was entirely different from what Ezra had seen.

INTERVIEWER: Your self-imposed guidelines are visual, but the force of the American idiom comes through.

LAUGHLIN: That comes from Williams. The cadence in my poems is a natural-breath, American speech cadence. But to get tension I manipulate the line lengths.

INTERVIEWER: Have you ever wished that you had more time to write?

LAUGHLIN: I'd like to. I'd write more stories if I could think up plots. I've written a few lectures about the work of Pound and Williams which I "perform" at colleges. A friend has persuaded me to start on a book of literary recollections. In *New Directions 45* we included a story from my "Paris period" called "The River." Reprinting it was pure sentimentality and nostalgia.

INTERVIEWER: It's a nice story.

LAUGHLIN: It's a tribute to and an imitation of Gertrude Stein; it uses her repetition. No plot; nothing much happens. A mood piece. But in my poems I try to make things happen quickly. They all come to me from somewhere in space (or my subconscious?); they arrive whole. So I don't need much time to write them. They arrive in my head in the cadence of colloquial speech; the beginning and end are there. Then I need only type them out and tailor the lines to nearly equal lengths in each couplet. I'm a "typewriter versifier." We are typewriter, and now word-processer, people. Occasionally if a word won't fit the pattern, I'll have to find another one which sounds the same but is longer or shorter to replace it. I know this sounds crazy, but for my ear and eye it works. "Cal" Lowell once wrote in *The Hudson Review* that I learned this bizarre metric from Williams. In fairness to Williams this should be corrected. He was a master of visual patterns, but he never counted typewriter characters.

INTERVIEWER: You seem ambivalent about the publication of your poetry and writing, but you have continued to publish all through the years.

LAUGHLIN: I put out five tiny poetry books—all privately printed—and I've sent out poems to magazines. Then Lawrence Ferlinghetti and Robert Fitzgerald persuaded me to have a commercial book with City Lights. It is called *In Another Country*. I wouldn't have done it if Fitzgerald hadn't agreed to make the selection of poems for it. I didn't feel confident in my own critical ability to make the choice.

INTERVIEWER: In the *festschrift* that *Conjunctions* did for you, an impressive array of well-recognized poets said your poetry should get more attention.

LAUGHLIN: That was very kind of them.

INTERVIEWER: Denise Levertov said, "Laughlin hasn't given himself the pleasure that one should derive for poetry well-wrought, and his is well-wrought poetry."

LAUGHLIN: Denise, bless her, has been a great fan. Another friend who often urges me to write verse is Hayden Carruth. Marjorie Perloff has been encouraging me. She likes my love poems. And Aleksis Rannit and David Gordon help me. But poetry for me has always been just a hobby, for personal satisfaction, and I'm quite content to keep it that way.

INTERVIEWER: Does the prospect of attention beyond your circle of close friends bother you?

LAUGHLIN: I'm always nervous when I do poetry readings.

The verse is so eccentric and so personal. Brendan Gill once said to me (he had read something of mine): "You have a pretty hard time, don't you?" I said, "What do you mean, Brendan?" He said, "Sorting out your private and public personalities."

INTERVIEWER: Is that perhaps the reason you've been reluctant to have it go any further?

LAUGHLIN: I think so. Eliot told someone that when he gave a poetry reading he always felt it was a kind of indecent exposure.

INTERVIEWER: And you feel similarly?

LAUGHLIN: Yes. I feel I'm exposing myself, perhaps because so much of it is love poetry. I wonder what impression people get of what my life has been, writing so many poems about girls. I'm very romantic.

INTERVIEWER: I like the poem called "The Trout." The image in there, the "blue blonde trout."

LAUGHLIN: Trout, the way it's cooked in Europe in those funny pans, comes out blue. The girl in the poem was very blonde, and I just put the two together.

INTERVIEWER: Do you have to do anything to provoke the mood in which images come up from the subconscious?

LAUGHLIN: I think they come at a moment when I'm emotionally exhilarated, exalted by something.

INTERVIEWER: In a poem called "The Empty Day" you talk about needing to clear the deck of everything before you can start. Did it have to do with getting ready to write poetry?

LAUGHLIN: I don't think so. Perhaps it was a reaction to overwork, being continually under pressure to get out the correspondence or to read the New Directions manuscripts. It was a complaint. I remember that Rexroth placed great importance on giving himself empty days for meditation. He and I were skiing once up at Mineral King, a very remote place in the Sierras. You have to walk in about twenty miles. We made camp there and pitched a tent. Next day I climbed up the mountain on my skis. But Rexroth spent the entire day sitting on a stump in the sun meditating. I could see him from up on the mountain. He never moved all day. He just sat on that stump and meditated. He was taking an "empty day" to think. To contemplate. He was a Buddhist, you know, as well as being an anarchist, though he converted to Catholicism on his death-bed. It was his way of purging himself of surface preoccupations.

INTERVIEWER: You wrote a poem called "Step on His Head," in which children step on the shadow of their father's head. Had your children started stepping on your head when you wrote that poem?

LAUGHLIN: No, not at all. They were very little—I don't remember how old they were—maybe four and six. Though the battle between the generations is something that happens in almost every family, even those with the best of intentions to avoid it. I think that's the poem most people like best because it does mean something to them. They've experienced it themselves. Of course, it goes back to that passage in Gertrude Stein, which you probably know, where she begins *The Making of Americans.* A son is dragging his father through the orchard by the feet. The father is getting pretty beat up. They come to a certain tree and he says to the son, "Stop. This is as far as I dragged *my* father." It's a marvelous opening to a book.

INTERVIEWER: Your demeanor is so gentle, yet a poem such as "The Summons" offers a scathing indictment of war. It's simply not a gentle statement. Do you reserve your anger for special causes or moments?

LAUGHLIN: Perhaps my hatred of war came largely from Pound. That was something he was always talking about—the causes of war and how to stop it. That became deeply rooted in my consciousness. I am enraged by these stupid, useless wars that we keep getting into. There may have been something tolerable about war in Provence when the troubadour knights would ride out in armor—it was like a game—but our recent

wars have just been dirty. It's pure destruction. It's everything
that Ezra was against. He ends the *Cantos:* "To be men not
destroyers." I'm angry, also again from Ezra, at our economic
system, which I think is ridiculous. It's becoming worse every
day because the bankers and politicians continue to pile up
debt. That's in my poem "What the Animals Did," the poem
against the conglomerators.

INTERVIEWER: Your poetry, then, seems to involve a mix of
Pound's drive for the Roman keystone and Williams's drive
toward the unique American idiom. Is that a fair statement of
where you're headed?

LAUGHLIN: Absolutely. They were the two big influences.

INTERVIEWER: In one of your poems you described a plant
as so fragile-looking, yet strong and solid. What's the meaning
of that poem?

LAUGHLIN: That would be "The Wild Anemone." It was the
one written to my wife. The wild anemone resists the wind. In
the wind the anemone sways so gracefully, but the wind can't
blow it over.

INTERVIEWER: What prompted "The Mountain Afterglow"?

LAUGHLIN: I was out at Alta, feeling very depressed about
World War II. I watched the mountain afterglow, and the idea
came to me. That poem has something I like in the way I used
hard consonants for the ending to give the feeling of the rock
mountain. "Bright / rock and snow fade into / night and night
clouds / fold dark on the stars." That particular evening the
afterglow was very red, which made me think of blood. That
made me think of war, and then that made me think of Christ's
blood, and it all pulled together just from that redness.

INTERVIEWER: You have mentioned elsewhere that you
showed up in Saul Bellow's *Humboldt's Gift.*

LAUGHLIN: Bellow was writing about Delmore Schwartz. It's
a very accurate portrait. Delmore was always inventing fantastic schemes. One of them was that he would persuade Bob

Hutchins, whom he had met through me, to have the Ford Foundation endow a chair of poetry for him at Princeton. Bellow handles this very nicely. Hutchins is called "Longstaff." There's a good portrait of Hutchins, who was a very debonair man as well as a brilliant one. And I was called "my playboy publisher."

INTERVIEWER: Why "playboy" publisher?

LAUGHLIN: That came out of the fact that once Delmore sent a manuscript to me at Alta which got lost in the bottom of the mailman's truck coming up the canyon. It was some time before it was recovered. Delmore was very agitated. He said that I would have to decide whether I was going to be a playboy or a publisher.

INTERVIEWER: Are you amused by that portrait in there?

LAUGHLIN: Very much. I think it's funny and very well done.

INTERVIEWER: Hayden Carruth has said that he suspects you have a lot of unpublished poetry and stories hidden away in a file drawer somewhere. Is he correct?

LAUGHLIN: No. I've thrown away the poems that didn't work out, and most of the others are either embalmed in my little early books or have been in magazines. As for stories, I haven't written any since college days, so most of them are in the *Harvard Advocate* or *Story* magazine. That's a long way back. But recently something strange has happened. At my age one doesn't normally branch out in new directions. I have begun to try two, for me, new kinds of writing. First there are poems in the tradition of the macaronic. These are poems written in, or quoting from, more than one language—English and Latin, English and Italian or French, or all four mixed—where the intention is to have the languages "work" on each other. Obviously, this comes from Pound's polylingualism and his ideogramic method of incongruous (or congruent) juxtaposition. Then, from both Pound and Williams, I have been writing "collages," abandoning my old short, visual-pattern lines for a long, prose-cadence line. These sometimes come out as verse and sometimes as little prose-poetry paragraphs. The idiom is a mixture of colloquial and more elevated language. Again, the two tones "working" on each other. These are memory poems: my memories of others and memories of how their lives affected mine. And they are heavily studded with quotations from the work of earlier poets which comment on and illuminate the relationships. I hope these writings are not parodies; I don't so intend them. I mean them to be tributes, and, more than that, expressions of my gratitude to the poets who have done so much for me: Pound, Williams, Eliot, and many others.

—RICHARD ZIEGFELD
July 19–20, 1982

6. Cynthia Ozick

Born in New York City's Yorkville on April 17, 1928, and raised in the Pelham Bay section of the Bronx, Cynthia Ozick attended P.S. 71 and Hunter College High School. She received her B.A. from New York University, where she was inducted into Phi Beta Kappa, and her M.A. from Ohio State University, where her master's thesis was "Parable in the Later Novels of Henry James."

Ozick is the author of three novels, *Trust* (1966), *The Cannibal Galaxy* (1983), and, most recently, *The Messiah of Stockholm* (1987); three collections of short stories, *The Pagan Rabbi and Other Stories* (1971), *Bloodshed and Three Novellas* (1976), and *Levitation: Five Fictions* (1982); and a collection of essays, *Art & Ardor* (1983). In 1986, she was named the first recipient of the Rea Award for the short story, given annually to a living American writer whose short stories have made a significant contribution to the form. Her other awards include the American Academy of Arts and Letters Award for Literature, three O. Henry First Prizes for the short story, a Guggenheim fellowship, and, in 1983, the National Institute of Arts and Letters Mildred and Harold Strauss Living Award.

Ozick lives in New Rochelle, New York.

A manuscript page from Cynthia Ozick's essay "Good Novelists, Bad Citizens," published in The New York Times Book Review.

Cynthia Ozick

A few words about the collaborative process that yielded the text that follows: initially, Ozick was concerned that her spoken words would later betray her in print. "Conversation is air," she said, and asked whether I might submit questions to be answered in writing. I made an acceptable counterproposal: I would ask questions, Ozick would type out her answers.

I sent no questions beforehand. Instead, we sat down at the dining room table of her [New Rochelle] home on a June day in 1985. I turned on my tape recorder, she turned on her electric typewriter. I asked a question, she typed out her answer and then read it to me. Ozick is a rapid typist and the exchange flowed quickly. It was a conversation, with the typing giving pause for thought. We drank tea and I munched on cookies. Occasionally we would drift into conversation lost to the typescript but cap-

tured on tape. The end product was a manuscript which when amended by her oral comments doubled in length. At a later date, Ozick reviewed and revised her spoken comments. Her changes, true to our intent, were more of a copyedit than a rewrite. "Whoever thinks the taped voice is 'true to life' is in error," she wrote me later. "It is false to life. But I am satisfied with the interview."

I had feared that the rigorous intellect evidenced in Cynthia Ozick's essays and stories would be matched in person by a severe manner. But what is most disarming about Ozick in person is her gentleness, sensitiveness, and directness, which put the visitor at ease. At as great a length as I interviewed Ozick, or more, she later interviewed me, with interest, sympathy, and encouragement.

INTERVIEWER: You write all night. Have you always done so?

OZICK: [*Speaking, not yet typing*] Always. I've written in daylight too, but mainly I go through the night.

INTERVIEWER: How does this affect your interaction with the rest of society?

OZICK: It's terrible. Most social life begins in the evening, when I'm just starting. So when I do go out at night, it means I lose a whole day's work.

INTERVIEWER: You don't just start at midnight or whenever you get home?

OZICK: I almost never get home at midnight. I'm always the last to leave a party.

INTERVIEWER: What are your regular working hours?

OZICK: You're talking as if there's some sort of predictable schedule. I don't have working hours. I wake up late. I read the mail, which sometimes is a very complex procedure. Then I eat breakfast with the *Times.* Then I start priming the pump, which is to read. I answer the letters.

INTERVIEWER: You answer every letter you get?

OZICK: I am compulsive. I take care of everything.

INTERVIEWER: You are also known as a letter writer.

OZICK: No, I don't feel that. I feel that what I'm doing is conscientiously and responsibly replying. Occasionally, though, an urgent spontaneous letter will fly out—love, polemics, passion.

INTERVIEWER: One of the footnotes in your Forster essay mentions a correspondence you had with Lionel Trilling.

OZICK: Lionel Trilling wrote in response to something I had published about Forster a long time ago. It was an astonishing letter. He said that he realized E. M. Forster was homosexual only years after he had completed his book on Forster's work. It wasn't an issue in the society at the time he was writing. The atmosphere didn't lead anyone to think along those lines, and Trilling himself was unaware. I met Leon Edel at the Academy in May and he's doing . . . That thing [the tape recorder] is going! I just realized that. I thought I was just talking. Hmmm. [*turns on typewriter, starts typing*] Leon Edel is doing a one-volume reissue of his magnificent biography and he said he's putting in a lot of new matter about James and the issue of his possible homosexuality because when he was writing that part of the biography it was the fifties and one didn't talk about such things.

INTERVIEWER: I take it that you're reading even when you're working on a piece of fiction.

OZICK: I read in order to write. I read out of obsession with writing.

INTERVIEWER: So, for example, does what you're reading influence what you write?

OZICK: Not precisely. I read in order to find out what I need to know: to illuminate the riddle.

INTERVIEWER: When you were writing *The Cannibal Galaxy*, what were you reading then?

OZICK: For that? Nothing at all. Oh, yes, street maps of Paris. Guidebooks about Paris. Anything I could find on the Marais, on the rue des Rosiers, for instance: the Jewish quarter.

INTERVIEWER: What are you reading now, for the novella you're working on?

OZICK: Swedish stuff! A book with pictures of the Swedish landscape, a book about the Swedish royal family; a Swedish-English dictionary. But the dictionary is dangerous. Looking up how to say a simple (and immaculate) "Goddamn," I came up (some Swedish friends later wrote me) with a super-four-letter-stinger. The novella will be called, I think, "The Messiah of Stockholm." It takes place in Stockholm. I'd better say no more, or the Muse will wipe it out.

INTERVIEWER: Do you really believe that? Has that happened before?

OZICK: I have lost stories and many starts of novels before. Not always as punishment for "telling," but more often as a result of something having gone cold and dead because of a hiatus. Telling, you see, is the same as a hiatus. It means you're not *doing* it.

INTERVIEWER: When you first graduated from college you undertook a long novel.

OZICK: Immediately after graduate school . . . ah, here I should stop to explain that there was a very short period in the early fifties when would-be writers were ASHAMED to go on to get a Ph.D. A very short period! But that was when one tried out teaching for a while after college—as a teaching assistant on a stipend—and then fled homeward to begin the Novel. Mine, typically, was immensely ambitious. I thought of it as a "philosophical" novel, and was going to pit the Liberal-Modernists against the Neo-Thomists. I wrote about 300,000 words of it.

INTERVIEWER: What possessed you to want to write a novel at all?

OZICK: I never conceived of not writing a novel. I believed—oh, God, I "believed," it was an article of Faith!—I was born to write a novel.

INTERVIEWER: You believed that since childhood.

OZICK: Yes, since my first moments of sentience.

INTERVIEWER: Is deciding to be a writer a question of "personality" or of "content," of what the person has to say?

OZICK: That's an interesting question. I think it's a condition, a given; content comes later. You're born into the condition of being an amphora; whether it's wine or water that fills it afterward belongs to afterward. Lately I think of this given condition as a kind of curse, because there is no way out of it. What a relief it would be to have the freedom of other people! Any inborn condition of this sort is, after all, a kind of slavery. There is no choice. Nor can one choose to stop: although now that I'm no longer young, I talk to writers of my own age about this. About the relief of being allowed to stop. But I know I will never stop until the lip of limitation: that is, disability or the grave. But you ask about the beginning. The beginning was almost physiological in its ecstatic pursuits. I'm embarrassed as I say this—"ecstatic pursuits"!—but I am thinking back to the delectable excitement, the *waiting-to-be-born* excitement, of longing to write. I suppose it is a kind of parallel Eros.

INTERVIEWER: But to return to after graduate school—you took the plunge into a long novel.

OZICK: Yes. I was working on the novel I called, from Blake, *Mercy, Pity, Peace, and Love.* I abbreviated it: Mippel, I called it, deriving that from MPPL. And I developed a little self-mocking joke about that. I referred to it as the Mippel on which I sucked for so long. Somewhere in the middle of it, I read of a paperback company that was doing collections of novellas—a sort of "contest." The editor, I seem to recall, was named Oscar De Liso. I thought I would polish off a novella in, say, six weeks, and then return to Mippel. As it turned out, the novella grew longer and longer and took nearly seven years, and became *Trust.* I had already spent about seven years with Mippel. This is a part of my life that pains me desperately to recall. Such waste, so many eggs in one basket, such life ~~~~~ such foolish concentration, such goddamned stupid "p

In the middle of *Trust*, as it happened, I stopped to write a shorter novel, which I *did* write in six sustained nonstop weeks. It was called *The Conversion of John Andersmall.* I conceived of it as a relief, a kind of virtuoso joke: a comic novel. It was turned down by, among others, the agent Candida Donadio, and by E. L. Doctorow, then an editor at Dial. I believe there is a carbon of it somewhere up in the attic. It was finally lost somewhere in a London publisher's office.

INTERVIEWER: Were you writing full-time then?

OZICK: Yes. Full-time.

INTERVIEWER: And how were you supporting yourself?

OZICK: I had gotten married and my husband, Bernard Hallote, supported me. I used to say that I was on a "Hallote"; some people are on a Guggenheim, I was on a Hallote.

INTERVIEWER: What sustained you without publication during that period?

OZICK: Belief. Not precisely self-belief, because that faltered profoundly again and again. Belief in Art, in Literature: I was a worshipper of Literature. I had a youthful arrogance about my "powers," and at the same time a terrible feeling of humiliation, of total shame and defeat. When I think about that time—and I've spent each decade as it comes regretting the decade before, it seems—I wish I had done what I see the current generation doing: I wish I had scurried around for reviews to do, for articles to write. I wish I had written short stories. I wish I had not been sunk in an immense dream of immense achievement. For most of this time, I was living at home in my parents' house, already married. But my outer life was unchanged from childhood. And my inner life was also unchanged. I was fixed, transfixed. It was Literature every breathing moment. I had no "ordinary" life. I despised ordinary life; I had contempt for it. What a *meshuggas!*

INTERVIEWER: Can you describe the feeling of first publication?

OZICK: I was thirty-seven years old. I had the baby and the galleys together, and I sat at my desk—the same desk I use now, the same desk I inherited from my brother when I was eight years old—correcting the galleys with my right hand, and rocking the baby carriage with my left. I felt stung when the review in *Time*, which had a big feature on first novels that season, got my age wrong and added a year. I hated being so old; beginning when I thought I'd be so far along. I've had age-sorrow all my life. I had it on publication, but for the next ten years or so the child was so distracting that I hardly noticed what publication "felt" like.

INTERVIEWER: How did you go about getting *Trust* published?

OZICK: Oh! What a story. I mustn't defame the dead. It was a long, hopeless process. I finished it on the day John Kennedy was assassinated, in November 1963. Publication wasn't until three years later. Those were three hellish years. It began when an agent, Theron Raines, wrote me a letter after a poem of mine had appeared in the *Virginia Quarterly Review:* in those days I was writing poems all the time. The biographical note at the back of the magazine said I was writing a novel, and this interested Raines, who got in touch. He has been my representative ever since. At first an option was taken on the novel by the late Hal Scharlatt, who procrastinated over a year, and just let the manuscript sit there. He was busy, he told me, with the big long manuscript of someone called Henry Kissinger. An unknown name. A political writer of some kind. Scharlatt asked for revisions and said he would tell me what they ought to be; but he never called me in to talk about this. Finally, after a year and a half, I appealed to him to see me. He was sitting at his desk in his office at New American Library with a yellow sheet in the typewriter; he was just making his first notes on the famous "revisions." I saw he was making them up on the spot. And he had kept me dangling and suffering, for a year and a half, over nothing at all! The important editorial ideas he had promised me and for which I'd waited so long turned out not to exist. Vapor. The manuscript was finally taken over by his colleague, David Segal, a remarkable editor who became my friend. His wife, Lore Segal, the novelist, is one of my closest friends now. David Segal sent me a hundred pages with red-pencil marks all over them, and asked for cuts. I had known all along that I would never have accepted any cuts from Scharlatt; and I could not bring myself to accept any from David, whom I respected. I had a dilemma: accept the cuts, and be published; refuse, and languish forever unpublished. I declined David Segal's cuts. He, amazing man, went ahead and published the novel anyhow.

INTERVIEWER: You then turned to shorter fiction.

OZICK: I was afraid of ever again falling into hugeness. It had been a time of extended darkness, and I was afraid.

INTERVIEWER: Now, so much time after that, more than twenty years, almost thirty years later, are you still consciously avoiding length? Avoiding, or in fear of, the large novel?

OZICK: [*starts typing—stops suddenly*] Is it usually part of your interview technique that your subjects end up delivering long confessions? I have a truth-telling syndrome and I wish to God I didn't. . . .

INTERVIEWER: Why?

OZICK: We're strangers and it leaves me utterly un-protected—I don't know what I need protection from, but I can't believe that when you interviewed Isaac Bashevis Singer he told you all about his life-hurts—he didn't. Jerzy Kosinski, whom you also interviewed, is certainly a protected person. Have you ever run into the completely unprotected—or as the psychoanalysts say—undefended?

INTERVIEWER: It's true that Kosinski is very adept at press interaction. But I was conscious of that and . . .

OZICK: You can never second-guess him. You can never penetrate beyond his penetration of you. It's impossible.

He's—he's a genius. Your question was about avoiding the longer forms.

INTERVIEWER: The large novel.

OZICK: [*Resumes typing*] The Modernist Dream. I recently did a review of William Gaddis and talked about his ambition—his coming on the scene when it was already too late to be ambitious in that huge way with a vast modernist novel. But I was ambitious that way too. I no longer believe in Literature, capital-*L*, with the same fervor I used to. I've learned to respect living, perhaps. I think I have gotten over my fear of largeness as well, because I have gotten over my awe—my idolatrous awe. Literature is not all there is in the world, I now recognize. It is, I admit, still my All, but it isn't *the* All. And that is a difference I can finally see.

INTERVIEWER: But what about your literary ambitions in terms of subject matter and length?

OZICK: I see it as a simple matter of choosing a subject, or having the subject choose itself, and letting the subject dictate the length. It's not my "ambition" that dictates the size of the enterprise. I am not interested in ego, if that's what this question is about. "The Pagan Rabbi," for instance, a short story written so long ago, touches on a large theme: the aesthetic versus the moral commitment. Profound subject matter can be encompassed in small space—for proof, look at any sonnet by Shakespeare! *Multum in parvo.* I am not avoiding length these days—not consciously. But perhaps there's some truth in the speculation that I may be living my life backwards! Doing the short forms now, having begun with a "Great Work," a long ambitious "modernist" novel of the old swollen kind.

INTERVIEWER: Can one write and avoid ambition?

OZICK: One *must* avoid ambition *in order to* write. Otherwise something else is the goal: some kind of power beyond the power of language. And the power of language, it seems to me, is the only kind of power a writer is entitled to.

INTERVIEWER: But is writing idolatry?

OZICK: Until quite recently I held a rather conventional view about all this. I thought of the imagination as what its name suggests, as image-making, and I thought of the writer's undertaking as a sovereignty set up in competition with the sovereignty of—well, the Creator of the Universe. I thought of imagination as that which sets up idols, as a rival of monotheism. I've since reconsidered this view. I now see that the idol-making capacity of imagination is its lower form, and that one *cannot* be a monotheist without putting the imagination under the greatest pressure of all. To imagine the unimaginable is the highest use of the imagination. I no longer think of imagination as a thing to be dreaded. Once you come to regard imagination as ineluctably linked with monotheism, you can no longer think of imagination as competing with monotheism. Only a very strong imagination can rise to the idea of a noncorporeal God. The lower imagination, the weaker, falls into the proliferation of images. My hope is someday to be able to figure out a connection between the work of monotheism-imagining and the work of story-imagining. Until now I have thought of these as enemies.

INTERVIEWER: What do you attribute your change of mind to?

OZICK: Somebody gave me this idea. I had a conversation with a good thinker.

INTERVIEWER: Who's that?

OZICK: [*Stops typing*] I don't want to give him the attribution here, because I did once before in print and he was embarrassed by it. So the alternative is to plagiarize. Either embarrass or plagiarize. He's put me in that position.

INTERVIEWER: But in any case, you're still in the storytelling business.

OZICK: I'm in the storytelling business, but I no longer feel I'm making idols. The insight that the largest, deepest, widest imaginative faculty of all is what you need to be a monotheist teaches me that you simply cannot be a Jew if you repudiate the imagination. This is a major shift for me.

INTERVIEWER: And now you feel better about it. But neither of the two positions . . .

OZICK: . . . will stop me from doing it. Exactly. I can't stop. Right, that's true. I'd better write that down. [*Starts typing again*] In any case, whether I were ultimately to regard story-telling as idol-making or not, whether I might some day discover the living tissue that connects the capacity for imagery with the capacity to drive beyond imagery—whatever my theoretical condition, I would go on writing fiction.

INTERVIEWER: How come?

OZICK: Because I will do it. Whether it is God's work or Satan's work, I will do it.

INTERVIEWER: Why?

OZICK: Willfulness.

INTERVIEWER: In your critical articles on the Edith Wharton and Virginia Woolf biographies, you say "the writer is missing."

OZICK: That's true. It's quite true.

INTERVIEWER: What is "the writer" that is missing?

OZICK: Quentin Bell's biography told the story of his aunt, who happened to be the famous writer Virginia Woolf. But it was a family story really, about a woman with psychotic episodes, her husband's coping with this, her sister's distress. It had, as I said, the smell of a household. It was not about the sentences in Virginia Woolf's books. The Wharton biography, though more a "literary" biography, dealt with status, not with the writer's private heart. What do I mean by "private heart"? It's probably impossible to define, but it's not what the writer does—breakfast, schedule, social outings—but what the writer *is*. The secret contemplative self. An inner recess wherein insights occur. This writer's self is perhaps coextensive with one of the writer's sentences. It seems to me that more can be found about a writer in any single sentence in a work of fiction, say, than in five or ten full-scale biographies. Or interviews!

INTERVIEWER: So which sentence of yours shall we take? Shall I pick one out? *(begins rummaging through books)*

OZICK: *[Stops typing]* Oh my God!

INTERVIEWER: I'm calling you on this one.

OZICK: Yes, you are. Good God. Okay. Let's see where this takes us.

INTERVIEWER: We can start with the opening sentence of *The Cannibal Galaxy:* "The Principal of the Edmond Fleg Primary School was originally (in a manner of speaking) a Frenchman, Paris-born—but whenever he quoted his long-dead father and mother, he quoted them in Yiddish."

OZICK: There is a piece of autobiography in that sentence. It may need a parenthetical explanation. I was taking a course with Lionel Trilling and wrote a paper for him with an opening sentence that contained a parenthesis. He returned the paper with a wounding reprimand: "Never, never begin an essay with a parenthesis in the first sentence." Ever since then, I've made a point of starting out with a parenthesis in the first sentence. Years later, Trilling was cordial and very kind to me, and I felt redeemed, though it took two decades to earn his approval. But you can see how the sentence you've chosen for this crafty experiment may not be to the purpose—there's too much secret mischief in it.

INTERVIEWER: What else does it reveal?

OZICK: Nothing.

INTERVIEWER: Shall we turn to *Puttermesser?* "Puttermesser, an unmarried lawyer and civil servant of forty-six, felt attacked on all sides."

OZICK: Cadence. Cadence is the fingerprint, isn't it? Suppose *you* were going to write that sentence with that precise content. How would it come out? It's short enough for you to give it a try just like that, on the spot.

INTERVIEWER: I might just write "Puttermesser felt attacked on all sides."

OZICK: Yes. That's interesting. It's minimali.
away. You are a Hemingwayesque writer, then?

INTERVIEWER: A Hemingwayesque rewriter. But to get ⌐
to my question: is the heart of Ozick, the writer, cadence?

OZICK: It's one element, not the only one. Idea counts too.

INTERVIEWER: But you must have a notion of what a writer
is. You have criticized the biographies of Wharton and Woolf
as "missing the writer," and you have written about the writer
as being genderless and living in the world of "as if" rather than
being restrained by her own biographical . . .

OZICK: Parochial temporary commitments.

INTERVIEWER: So then how would you define this writer?
And how would you define the "Ozick" writer that stems from
your written work and stands independent of your biographical
data and which otherwise might be missing from this interview?

OZICK: But I worry about any Platonic notion of "a writer."
I now *must* (perhaps in defiance of my own old record) believe
that a writer is simply another citizen with a profession. I don't
want to cling to any pretensions of the writer as that inspired
mystical Byronic shaman or special select ideal holy person. I
don't want to live in the world with such mystical figures; I
don't like self-appointed gurus, and even less the kind that's
divinely appointed. A writer is someone born with a gift. An
athlete can run. A painter can paint. A writer has a facility with
words. A good writer can also think. Isn't that enough to define
a writer by? The rest is idiosyncrasy—what I meant earlier
when I spoke of the cadence of any single sentence. And what
is idiosyncrasy except minute individual difference? In the
human species, individual differences *are* minute. Think how
we all come equipped with all the parts that make up a face,
and how every face is different from every other face, even as,
simultaneously, every face is equal to every other face.

INTERVIEWER: How does your Jewishness fit in here? Don't
we have to speak about that?

OZICK: To be Jewish is to be a member of a civilization—a civilization with a long, long history, a history that is, in one way of viewing it, a procession of ideas. Jewish history is intellectual history. And all this can become the content of a writer's mind; but it isn't equal to a writer's mind. To be a writer is one thing; to be a Jew is another thing. To combine them is a third thing.

INTERVIEWER: In those writers' classes where one is always told, "Write about what you know."

OZICK: Ah! When I've taught those classes, I always say, "Forget about 'Write about what you know.' Write about what you don't know." The point is that the self is limiting. The self—subjectivity—is narrow and bound to be repetitive. We are, after all, a species. When you write about what you don't know, this means you begin to think about the world at large. You begin to think beyond the home-thoughts. You enter dream and imagination.

INTERVIEWER: Where is the vanishing point? What do you mean by these limits of subjectivity? The limits of our gray cells?

OZICK: Our gray cells aren't our limitations. It's our will to enter the world: by the world I mean history, including the history of thought, which is the history of human experience. This isn't an intellectual viewpoint. In fact, it asks for the widening of the senses and of all experience.

INTERVIEWER: But how far do you intend to go?

OZICK: As far as I can. As far as is necessary.

INTERVIEWER: In the kingdom of As-If, there are some writers who never leave the house, and some writers who are explorers of the Universe.

OZICK: And some who do both at the same time. Emily Dickinson.

INTERVIEWER: Philip Roth stays close to home, Doris Lessing goes out. In terms of content, some are homebodies, some are astronauts, some are chameleons. Which are you?

OZICK: None of the above. An archaeologist, maybe. I stay home, but I'm not a homebody. I go out, but only to dig down. I don't try to take on the coloration of the environment; I'm not an assimilationist. I say "archaeologist," because I like to think about civilizations. They are illuminated in comparison. Stories are splinters of larger ideas about culture. I'm aware that there are writers who deny idea completely, who begin from what-happens, from pure experience. But for me ideas are emotions.

INTERVIEWER: Have you ever rejected a story, or character, or idea, because you've felt you couldn't "do" it, or didn't know it?

OZICK: Yes, once. I began a novel meant to trap Freud. I read the Jones biography, read *Civilization and Its Discontents* and some other things, and then quit. I saw it would take a lifetime of study.

INTERVIEWER: Do you have a notion of having created a writer "Cynthia Ozick" whose nose might be *Levitation,* eyes *Cannibal Galaxy,* and mouth *Bloodshed?*

OZICK: I once was asked to draw a self-portrait. [*starts drawing*] It came out something like this:

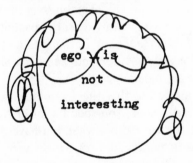

What is the true import of this metaphorical question?

INTERVIEWER: Again, I'm trying to get you to define the writer "Ozick."

OZICK: I honest-to-God don't know. Can one say what one

is? How does one define one's own sense of being alive? I think it is this hum, or buzz, blablablablabla, that keeps on talking inside one's head. A stream of babble. The inner voice that never, never, never shuts up. Never. What is it saying? One can't listen; if one listened, it would be, I think, the moment just before death.

INTERVIEWER: Again this points out how difficult it is for any biographer to seize the inner self of a writer.

OZICK: You've really backed me to the wall—you're saying I was unfair, unreasonable, in criticizing those biographers.

INTERVIEWER: It's not where I started out at—I imagined that if you found something lacking you might yourself have a sense of what belongs there.

OZICK: I've never tried to write a biography and I have no idea if it's doable. But . . . [*starts typing*] I have kept a diary since 1953. Maybe the self-definition of a writer is there, cumulatively, and not on purpose. Maybe the only biography is the writer's diary. And yet that too is partial; mine is a bloodletting, and moans more than feels elation.

INTERVIEWER: On a lighter note . . . I wanted to ask you about the pictures that appear on the back covers of the paperback editions of your works. The pictures on the back . . . three different pictures have been used on the paperbacks. One for *Trust* and *The Pagan Rabbi* and *Levitation,* another for *Bloodshed,* a third for *Art & Ardor* and *The Cannibal Galaxy.*

OZICK: They get older!

INTERVIEWER: It's not that they get older. It's that—when you buy and read a book, you spend a lot of time looking at that picture of the writer. It's what you have of them.

OZICK: I look at photographs of writers very closely too.

INTERVIEWER: Did you have any say in all this: that your pictures are the entire back cover, and did you have any say over which pictures they chose? In the picture on the back of *Art & Ardor* you look like you're scowling.

OZICK: Using photographs was the publisher's idea. But I like the photographer and I like where I was standing and I like the bleak day. Bleak days are introspective, evocative. They smell of childhood reading.

INTERVIEWER: What is it you like about the place? Why do you feel it represents you?

OZICK: Well, it's up the shore a way from Pelham Bay Park where I grew up. I felt at home, inside my own landscape, on my own ground. My sense of that photo is a kind of pensiveness. Anxiety at worst but not a scowl. I hope not a scowl! Especially since after a certain number of years our faces become our biographies. We get to be responsible for our faces. I do the same—draw conclusions about writers from their photos. But when I see you doing that with my photograph I think: it's only a snapshot, it's not a soul. If it *were* soul, you would read tremble rather than scowl. Or so I imagine.

INTERVIEWER: You have dedicated many of your books to your editors. What part have they played in your life?

OZICK: Norman Podhoretz was the first cause of my getting invited to Jerusalem for the first time. That is a large thing to owe someone. He published my short story "Envy; or, Yiddish in America," and that led to a conference in Israel, for which I composed an essay called "Toward a New Yiddish." Gordon Lish was fiction editor at *Esquire* and wrote me out of the blue asking for a story. I took "An Education" out of a drawer and sent it to him along with the letter of rejection I thought he would write back to me. To my amazement, he published that story—which was the first thing I wrote after *Trust,* "in the manner of" Frank O'Connor, and even borrowing one of O'Connor's names for his heroines: Una. My editor at Knopf for many years has been Robert Gottlieb. The day he telephoned me—just after the tragic early death of David Segal—to tell me he would keep me on at Knopf, and publish *The Pagan Rabbi and Other Stories,* which had been accepted by David Segal, was also the day his little daughter was born; he telephoned from the hospital. About once every half-decade I go to see him for two or more hours. I live on what happens in those two hours all the rest of the time. Editors are parental figures, even when they are much younger than oneself; or else they are a kind of Muse. Frances Kiernan at *The New Yorker* is another one of my distant Muses.

INTERVIEWER: In "Envy" you portray a character who many see as I. B. Singer. In "Usurpation" some see Shmuel Agnon and Bernard Malamud. Kosinski is seen in "A Mercenary." Why do you do that?

OZICK: Infatuation perhaps. But I don't do it anymore, and never will again. Even when one invents, invents absolutely, one is blamed for stealing real people. You remind me of something I haven't thought of for a long, long time. One of my first short stories, written for a creative writing class in college, was about plagiarism. Apparently the idea of "usurpation" has intrigued me for most of my life. When I was a small child I remember upsetting my father; I had recently learned, from a fairy tale, the word "impostor" and I made him prove he wasn't an impostor by demanding that he open the pharmacy safe, which had a combination lock. Since only my real father, the pharmacist, knew the combination, his opening it would prove he was my father. I felt both theatrical and anxious at the same time; both real and unreal. I envied orphans; they were romantic. One of my favorite childhood books was called *Nobody's Boy,* and there was a companion volume called *Nobody's Girl.* These were, I believe, translated from the French; who reads them now? I don't know the origin of these fascinations; fairy tales, perhaps, and their extreme sadnesses. Princesses and princes trapped in the bodies of beasts, human souls looking for release.

INTERVIEWER: What about the chutzpah involved?

Chutzpah? I never thought of that. I think of the ⊃n as a place of utter freedom. There one can do one wants.

INTERVIEWER: Aren't you tossing stones at literary houses of glass, bringing these writers to the mat . . . ?

OZICK: No. Such a thought never occurred to me. On the contrary, it was their great fame I was playing with—an act of homage, in fact.

INTERVIEWER: Did "Envy" create an uproar?

OZICK: There was a vast brouhaha over this story. A meeting was called by the Yiddish writers, I learned later. The question was whether or not to condemn me publicly. Privately, they all furiously condemned me. Simon Weber, editor of the *Forward*, wrote an article—he's since apologized—in which he compared me to the "commissars of Warsaw and Moscow," anti-Semites of the first order. I was astonished and unbelievably hurt. I wrote a letter exclaiming that I felt my mother and father had broken my skull. What I had intended was a great lamentation for the murder of Yiddish, the mother-tongue of a thousand years, by the Nazis. Instead, here were all these writers angry at me.

INTERVIEWER: More recently, my far-flung sources informed me, you gave a reading at the Yale Medical School.

OZICK: Oh God. What sources?

INTERVIEWER: I never reveal sources. But I understand you read "The Sewing Harems" there and they didn't get it.

OZICK: No, but out of that, out of their not "getting it," out of this resistance to parable and metaphor, came an essay called "Metaphor and Memory," which I delivered at Harvard recently as the Phi Beta Kappa oration. The incident with the Yale doctors—it was hard on me—inspired whole discoveries about the nature and meaning of metaphor. I owe all this to the Yale doctors' impatience with me. They wanted plain language. Is that what you heard?

INTERVIEWER: I heard you read; they didn't get it. And then you told them that they didn't get it.

OZICK: Yes. I made a mistake. It was I who was obtuse. I was taken by surprise. I was embarrassed at Yale—but also considerably educated. It is possible to profit from being misunderstood.

INTERVIEWER: What about being misunderstood in general? What about audience?

OZICK: I don't want to be the Platonic cow in the forest—if you remember the opening of E. M. Forster's *The Longest Journey.* Or the tree that may or may not fall, depending on if there are any human ears around to hear its thud. Like any writer, I want to be read. I know I can't be "popular," and I regard this as a major failing. There *are* writers who are artists of language—everyone knows who they are!—who can also be read by large numbers of readers, who are accessible. In our own time, Nabokov and Updike, intricate embroiderers.

INTERVIEWER: Major failing?

OZICK: Yes. There is the first consummation, and then there is the second consummation. One can't live without the first; luckily one can live without the second. The first is getting into print. The second is getting read. I have been writing for years and years, without ever being read.

INTERVIEWER: Do you really believe that?

OZICK: It's not a matter of belief. It's a matter of knowing.

INTERVIEWER: Of knowing that very few people who read you are getting it?

OZICK: [*Stops typing*] Very few people read me.

INTERVIEWER: Very few people read you? You're in paperback.

OZICK: That's a small miracle. I have no idea whether any of those paperbacks are finding readers. I'm sure not. I'm sure *Trust* isn't. Those paperbacks represent an act of philanthropy on the part of one person, Bill Whitehead, who originated Obelisk. A publisher willing to lose money.

INTERVIEWER: Really? I don't think that Obelisk or anyone is in the business of publishing to lose money. There are people being read less than you, as well.

OZICK: Given the literary situation in our country, there are always people being read less. Not only young newcomers. I know an established writer with three unpublished novels going the rounds. Finding people who are read less is no trick. Finding out that one is read at all *is* a trick. For a long time I didn't feel I could honorably call myself a writer because I didn't have any of the accoutrements. Readers, mainly.

INTERVIEWER: When did you start feeling you could say you were a writer?

OZICK: Pretty recently.

INTERVIEWER: Things like the Harold and Mildred Strauss Living Award must help.

OZICK: That certainly was a validation. But I always need validation. A major, marvelous, unbelievable event. I was in Italy when the letter arrived and my husband opened it because he had a sense it was important. I came home from the airport and he put the letter in front of me on the kitchen table and said open it. And I did and I simply wept and wept and said I cannot possibly accept this. Why me? There are so many others with the same track record who could use this just as much as I. And I had such a wallow of guilt. I think it took more than a year before I felt that I could receive it with pure—I should say purified—joy without the guilt of having won a lottery and feeling undeserving and unmerited. That's why I don't see that photo as a scowl, I see it as expressing all these things about someone who feels unsure, unvalidated, un-, un-, un-, any word that begins with *un-*.

INTERVIEWER: Do you have a certain amount of bitterness about that?

OZICK: No, not at all. That picture must strike you as a bitter scowl. No, I'm not bitter.

INTERVIEWER: I used the word bitter because I thought *The Cannibal Galaxy* had an edge of bitterness to it.

OZICK: I am still hurt by P.S. 71. The effect of childhood hurt continues to the grave. I had teachers who hurt me, who made me believe I was stupid and inferior.

INTERVIEWER: Yes. You've written about that. Is your validation your revenge?

OZICK: I've discussed "revenge" with other writers, and discovered I'm not alone in facing the Medusalike truth that one reason writers write—the pressure toward language aside; and language is always the first reason, and most of the time the only reason—one reason writers write is out of revenge. Life hurts; certain ideas and experiences hurt; one wants to clarify, to set out illuminations, to replay the old bad scenes and get the *Treppenworte* said—the words one didn't have the strength or the ripeness to say when those words were necessary for one's dignity or survival.

INTERVIEWER: Have you achieved it?

OZICK: Revenge? On P.S. 71? Who knows? Where now are the snows of yesteryear? Where is Mrs. Florence O'Brien? Where is Mr. Dougherty? Alas, I think not. In the end, there *is* no revenge to be had. "Too late" is the same as not-at-all. And that's a good thing, isn't it? So that in the end one is left with a story instead of with spite. Any story is worth any amount of vindictiveness.

INTERVIEWER: "Too late." Is there really such a thing as too late?

OZICK: I am ashamed to confess this. It's ungrateful and wrong. But I am one—how full of shame I feel as I confess this—who expected to achieve—can I dare to get this out of my throat?—something like—impossible to say the words—Literary Fame by the age of twenty-five. By the age of twenty-seven I saw that Holy and Anointed Youth was over, and even then it was already too late. The decades passed. I'm afraid I think—deeply think—that if it didn't come at the right time, at the burnished crest of youth, then it doesn't matter. And I am not even sure what you or I mean by "it." I will not now know how to say what "it" is. So I have put all that away. It is now completely, completely beside the point. One does what one needs to do; that's all there is. It's wrong, bad, stupid, senseless to think about anything else. I think *only* of what it is I want to write about, and then about the problems in the doing of it. I don't think of anything else at all.

INTERVIEWER: The Holocaust figures in many of your stories. Is the Holocaust a subject you feel you must confront in your writing?

OZICK: I write about it. I can't not. But I don't think I ought to. I have powerful feelings about this. In our generation, it seems to me, we ought to absorb the documents, the endless, endless data, the endless, endless what-happened. Inevitably it will spiral into forms of history that are myth, legend: other kinds of truth. For instance, I believed in my childhood—I got it straight from my grandmother—that since the Inquisition there has been a *cherem* around Spain: a ban, a Jewish ban that prohibits Jews from entering Spain ever again. Of course this is pure myth; and yet it tells a great truth about the inheritance of the Inquisition in the hearts of Jews. Probably this sort of thing, in new forms, will happen concerning the destruction of European Jews and their civilization. It *is* inevitable, and it's not going to be a historical mistake. But for now? Now we, each one of us, Jew and Gentile, born during or after that time, we, all of us, forever after are witnesses to it. We know it happened: we are the generations that come after. I *want* the documents to be enough; I don't want to tamper or invent or imagine. And yet I have done it. I can't not do it. It comes, it invades.

INTERVIEWER: I read that you have formed a writer's group. Can you tell me about it?

OZICK: Nothing so official as a "group." Writers who are friends—three novelists, one critic, who meet not very often to talk informally. We meet in a Manhattan restaurant, or sometimes in New Rochelle; one of us lives in the midwest. Lore Segal and Norma Rosen and Helen Weinberg; Helen is the only Ph.D.—the critic.

INTERVIEWER: Are these meetings related in any way to "validation" of oneself as a writer?

OZICK: No! A thousand times no. We talk about our lives. We are very amusing. We are amusing even about our sadnesses. We are amusing about being "smart," and we enjoy one another's minds. We learn from each other in subtle and indirect ways. Nothing is validated except the sense of being fully and beautifully human.

INTERVIEWER: Would this meeting be in existence if you weren't all writers of a certain level of success?

OZICK: We talk about the children. It's no coincidence, though, that we like to be together because we are writers. I believe unashamedly that writers are the most (maybe the only) interesting people.

INTERVIEWER: You began your literary career by writing poetry. What happened to the poetry in your life?

OZICK: Well, I still do it in a sort of indirect and undercover way: through the infinite bliss of translation. But there the initial work is done! Still, the pleasure of fashioning a new poem in English . . . but I stopped writing my own poetry at around age thirty-six. This fits exactly the dictum—whose? was it T. S. Eliot's?—that all writers write poetry in their youth, but that it's only the real poets who continue writing poetry after the middle thirties. But also, you know, I got discouraged. I sent my manuscript—a book—of poetry to the Yale Younger Poets series year after year, and finally I turned forty, and wasn't eligible any more. So I stopped. But nowadays when I read Amy Clampitt, I think: ah, *she* is myself continued! I hope this admission is not entirely outrageous. It's something I imagine.

INTERVIEWER: I wanted, for the record, to ask you how you've felt about our use of the typewriter.

OZICK: Replying to your questions by typewriter has been an experiment for both of us. It was your idea, and I thought it was wonderful and just right. It has not interfered one iota with spontaneity, because I have been typing extremely fast. It has been a form of speech. The difference is that the sentences are somewhat more coherent than speech allows. At least I can put the punctuation in! At least I can be responsible for the *sound*, in the way I can't be responsible for the looseness and even wildness of talk. Not that this way of talking has been without its wildness! In fact, there may be something excessively open here: a sinister kind of telling-too-much. One thing I've learned. Speech is far more guarded than talking through one's fingers.

INTERVIEWER: You said earlier that you envy my being thirty and having published articles. What I envy in your personal history is your Hallote fellowship.

OZICK: I was waiting for your comment on my being a woman. Is this it? A wife can support a husband quite as capably as the reverse.

INTERVIEWER: That may well be your reaction to my comment, but what I had in mind is more an envy of the financial freedom to write, of having someone willing to support you.

OZICK: Then let me be a kind of sibyl for you, or Cassandra, and with a not-so-bony finger warn you away from what you most desire. You know the old fairy-tale theme: don't wish for something, or you may get it. And then what? Youth is for running around in the great world, not for sitting in a hollow cell, turning into an unnatural writing-beast. There one sits, reading and writing, month after month, year after year. There one sits, envying other young writers who have achieved a grain more than oneself. Without the rush and brush and crush of the world, one becomes hollowed out. The cavity fills with envy. A wasting disease that takes years and years to recover from. Youth-envy, on the other hand, one can never recover from. Or at least I haven't so far. I suffered from it at seventeen. I suffered from it at five, when on a certain midsummer midafternoon I looked at an infant asleep in its pram and felt a terrible and unforgettable pang.

INTERVIEWER: But isn't there anything to be said about what seems to be a luxury—the ability to write full-time?

OZICK: Time to write isn't a luxury, that goes without saying. It's what a writer needs to write. But to have it coextensive with one's whole youth isn't absolutely a good thing. It's unnatural to do anything too much. "Nothing in excess," especially when everything else in the case *must* be in excess: the reading-hunger, language-hunger, all the high literary fevers and seizures. That kind of "excess" is what defines a writer. An image of the writer came to me the other day: a beast howling inside a coal-furnace, heaping the coals on itself to increase the fire. The only thing more tormenting than writing is not writing. If I could do it again, I would step out of the furnace now and then. I'd run around and find reviews to write, articles, I'd scurry and scrounge. I'd try to build a little platform from which to send out a voice. I'd do, in short, what I see so many writers of your generation doing: chasing a bit of work here, a bit there, publishing, getting acquainted. What *you* do, in fact. Churning around in the New York magazine world. What *I* did, a child crazed by literature, was to go like an eremite into a cavern and spin; I imagined that I would emerge with a masterpiece. Instead I emerged as an unnatural writing-beast, sooty with coal dust, my fingers burned and my heart burning up. Have you read *Lost Illusions*?

INTERVIEWER: Oh my God, yes!

OZICK: Eve Ottenberg, a young writer in New York who lives the kind of life I've described—an admirable life, I think—put me on to it.

INTERVIEWER: When you talk about the pain of having read Henry James at too early an age—well, that is nothing compared to reading *Lost Illusions* at the right age.

OZICK: It's understandable. I read *Lost Illusions* only recently. It was so painful it lasted me a whole year, and I never got to the very end. I intend to finish it. But I take it not so much for a warning as for a model and a marvel. Not a model for myself—it's too late for that. What's necessary above all is to publish while young. All those roilings happening at once, the speed, the trajectory! All that activity, all that being-in-the-world, all those plots and devisings, all that early variation, a spoon in every pot! Interchange, intercourse, inter-inter-. You know. If only someone had given me *Lost Illusions* in my cradle! Would I have been saved? There I was, at twenty-five, reading eighteen hours a day, novels, philosophy, criticism, poetry, Jewish history, Gibbon. . . . I read and read and it made me into some kind of monster. I'm still that monster.

INTERVIEWER: But you got some work done then . . .

OZICK: Nothing came of it. Great tracts of words without consummation. All the years I gave to *Mercy, Pity, Peace, and Love,* and nothing left of it but the title, and the title all Blake. Remorse and vacuum.

INTERVIEWER: You don't think your writing is richer for that, and for what you learned from your reading?

OZICK: So what? I still have plenty of gaps in my reading. I'm not Faust, and never was.

INTERVIEWER: But isn't your writing—aren't the ideas in your writing—richer?

OZICK: How can I tell? Living in one's own time is an obligation, isn't it? The isolation and profound apartness of my twenties and early thirties probably crazed me for life. And yet even as I declare my remorse, I'm not certain I believe what I say. Even as I tell you how I would do it otherwise if I had it to do over, I'm feeling the flanks of these words all up and down to see if I detect the lump of a lie in them. I was too fixed, too single-minded, too much drawn by some strange huge Illumination, too saturated in some arcane passion of Ideal Purity . . . Am I normal now? I don't feel so. But I am absolutely on the side of normality. I believe in citizenship.

—TOM TEICHOLZ
June 1985

7. Elie Wiesel

Elie Wiesel is one of the most honored writers of his generation. Andre Schwarz-Bart has called him "this generation's only prophet," and S. N. Behrman has described him as "a writer on a plane almost entirely uninhabited except by him." He has won many prizes and awards, including the International Literary Prize for Peace from the Royal Academy of Belgium, the Congressional Gold Medal of Achievement, the French Prix Medicis, the Eleanor Roosevelt Award, the Martin Luther King Medallion, the Jewish Book Council Literary Award, the Grand Prix de la Litterature de la Ville de Paris, and, in 1986, the Nobel Peace Prize. Wiesel has written more than twenty-five books, including *Night, The Gates of the Forest, A Beggar in Jerusalem, Souls on Fire, Messengers of God, A Jew Today, The Testament, Somewhere a Master, The Fifth Son, Signes d'Exode,* and, most recently, *Le Crepuscule, au Loin,* which is currently being translated into English. Since 1976, Wiesel has been Andrew W. Mellon Professor in the Humanities at Boston University.

Wiesel was born on September 30, 1928, in the town of Sighet in Transylvania, and was transported to Auschwitz sixteen years later. There, his mother and sister were gassed to death. In 1945 Wiesel was sent to Buchenwald, where his father died of starvation and dysentery. After the war, Wiesel was educated at the Sorbonne in Paris, and in 1956 he published his first book. The novel appeared in English two years later, in condensed form, as *Night.* In 1956 he moved to New York, and in 1963 he became a United States citizen. He and his wife Marion, who translates much of his work from its original French into English, live with their son in New York City.

Parti enfant, je me réveille vieillard

10.000 exécutions sommaires après libération —
torture, toutes etc —
devant 5.000 personnes...
Pas en Israël.

Michovei: Inquisition inconcevable en histoire juive

monde de violence la vrit' en nous

Notes for an essay by Elie Wiesel on the literature of memory.

© Jill Krementz

Elie Wiesel

Elie Wiesel grants few interviews. This conversation took place in 1978, during two sessions at his apartment a few months before his fiftieth birthday. Through the open windows of his book-filled study, breezes carried the sounds of Manhattan spring afternoons. It was a rare privilege to converse with him. His dark, deep-set eyes were like the eyes of one of his characters in which "joy and despair wage a silent, implacable, eternal battle."

INTERVIEWER: I would like to begin by asking about the subject matter of your books. You have written about the

Holocaust, about the Bible, about Hasidism. Why haven't you written about your years here in New York?

WIESEL: I have lived here for some twenty years, more than anywhere in the world, and yet I have devoted only a few pages to New York in *The Accident* and one chapter in *The Gates of the Forest.* Why? Because I have not yet exhausted my childhood. Words grow, age, die, and I am still interested in that metamorphosis. And the words that I use are still those that relate to my childhood.

INTERVIEWER: Yet in *Messengers of God* and *Souls on Fire* you have departed from the earlier themes of childhood.

WIESEL: I have, but, again, not entirely. In *Souls on Fire,* my childhood is present through my grandfather, the Hasid, and the stories I tell. The tone may be different, the treatment may be different because now it's no longer a child speaking. In *Messengers of God,* again, it's the Bible. When did I learn the Bible? When I was four or five years old. It's still the pull of my childhood, a fascination with the vanished world, and I can find everything *except* that world.

INTERVIEWER: What is it you are trying to find?

WIESEL: Many things. First, what we all find in childhood: innocence, trust. Children are trusting. And in my case, order. There was a certain order in creation. I once believed that children are young and old men are old. Now I know that some children are very old. Also, I know that the secret to all the other enigmas is rooted in that childhood. If ever I find an answer to my questions, it will be there, in that period, in that place.

INTERVIEWER: Any particular aspect of your childhood?

WIESEL: Sighet, my little town, all the characters that I am inventing or reinventing, all the tunes that I have heard. It is always, whatever its name, that little town Sighet. The very existence of that town in the midst of so much hostility was a miracle then and is a miracle now.

INTERVIEWER: For ten years you waited until you were ready to write about the Holocaust in your first book, *Night.*

WIESEL: I didn't want to use the wrong words. I was afraid that words might betray it. I waited. I'm still not sure that it was the wrong move, or the right move, that is, whether to choose language or silence.

INTERVIEWER: Why do you say that?

WIESEL: Maybe if we had kept quiet then—this is what I try to say in *The Oath*—maybe we wouldn't have this fashionable phenomenon. The Holocaust would not have become a fashionable subject which I find as offensive, if not more so, than what we had before: ignorance of the subject.

INTERVIEWER: But then you no longer would have been a messenger.

WIESEL: Sometimes you don't have to speak in order to be heard, not when the message is so powerful. It used to be said that when the Baal Shem Tov came into a town his impact was so strong, he didn't have to speak. His disciples had to dance or to sing or to preach to have the same effect. I think a real messenger, myself or anyone, by the very fact that he is there as a person, as a symbol, could have the same impact.

INTERVIEWER: But often by remaining silent we lose communication.

WIESEL: That's a danger. That's why I did not keep silent. If I had thought that by my silence, or rather by our silence, we could have achieved something, I think I would have kept silent. I didn't want to write those books. I wrote them against myself. But I realize that if we do not use words, the whole period will be forgotten. Therefore, we had to use them, *faute de mieux.*

INTERVIEWER: What do you mean you didn't want to write those books?

WIESEL: I didn't want to write a book on the Holocaust. To write such a book, to be responsible for such experiences, for such words—I didn't want that. I wanted to write a commentary on the Bible, to write about the Talmud, about celebration, about the great eternal subjects: love and happiness.

INTERVIEWER: But you had no choice?

WIESEL: Exactly. I had to. It wasn't voluntary. None of us wanted to write. Therefore when you read a book on the Holocaust, written by a survivor, you always feel this ambivalence. On one hand, he feels he must. On the other hand, he feels . . . if only I didn't have to.

INTERVIEWER: What happens when this conflict occurs inside of you? Does it change the nature of the work?

WIESEL: No, because the work itself then reflects the conflict. I incorporate it. Take *The Oath,* a novel set at the beginning of the century, about a village and ritual murder, nothing about the Holocaust. But then on another level, it is the Holocaust—not of the Jews but of the world. That's why I called the village Kolvillàg. Villàg in Hungarian means world, and Kol in Hebrew means all—the entire world.

INTERVIEWER: On one hand there is the almost elemental force to write about something you don't want to write about; on the other, there are the celebrations, which you enjoy writing about.

WIESEL: Oh, that I love to do.

INTERVIEWER: What about the process of each? Is it a struggle, for instance, to get up each morning to write about something you would prefer not to write about?

WIESEL: It depends. I don't have many examples of writing about the Holocaust because I haven't written that much about it. But there is never a struggle in the morning. It's a pleasant agony. I am myself only when I work. I work for four hours without interruption. Then I stop for my studies. But these four hours are really mine. It is a struggle when I have to cut. I reduce nine hundred pages to one hundred sixty pages. I also enjoy cutting. I do it with a masochistic pleasure although even when you cut, you don't. Writing is not like painting where you add. It is not what you put on the canvas that the reader sees. Writing is more like a sculpture where you remove, you eliminate in order to make the work visible. Even those pages you remove somehow remain. There is a difference between a book of two hundred pages from the very beginning, and a book of two hundred pages which is the result of an original eight hundred pages. The six hundred pages are there. Only you don't see them.

INTERVIEWER: Have you destroyed the original nine hundred pages of *Night*?

WIESEL: No, I have them. Others I destroy; *Night* is not a novel, it's an autobiography. It's a memoir. It's testimony. Therefore I believe it should be kept and one day I may publish it because I have no right not to. It's not mine.

INTERVIEWER: After *Night*, why did you move away from the Holocaust?

WIESEL: If I moved away from the theme of the Holocaust it was to protect it. I didn't want to abuse words; I didn't want to repeat words. I want to surround the subject with a fence of *kedushah*, of sacredness. To me the sanctuary of Jewish history is there; therefore I wrote other things in order not to write about that. I wrote all kinds of novels and books on all kinds of subjects in order not to write about the Holocaust. I wrote about the Bible, Hasidism, Russian Jews. Somehow it was almost a conscious effort to go as far away as possible from the subject, to keep it as a block of silence.

INTERVIEWER: You wrote on the subject of asceticism in your doctoral dissertation. Why has that never been published?

WIESEL: It wasn't that urgent. I write under pressure. Every book that I have written corresponds to a certain immediacy. *The Accident* is about suicide; *Dawn* is urgent, political action; *The Jews of Silence*, Russian Jewry; *Beggar in Jerusalem*, war, isolation, survival. The dissertation on asceticism—Christianity, Judaism, Buddhism—can wait. Also, I never finished the degree. I didn't really want to become a teacher. I became a journalist. In order to go on with my studies I needed an income from somewhere to pay my tuition. So I continued writing for newspapers. Later on, when I did become a teacher, whether I had a Ph.D. or not was superfluous. I received Ph.D.'s without asking for them.

INTERVIEWER: What attracted you to the subject of asceticism?

WIESEL: I have always been attracted to mysticism, cabbala. Of course I didn't know any aspect but the Jewish one. I had a teacher who was a mystic. We tried all kinds of things together in mysticism. Later, I discovered that what all the religions had in common was suffering. Suffering is a basic problem in history or antihistory—how we deal with suffering. After I began exploring the subject, all kinds of avenues opened. I realized that Christianity is almost solely based on suffering. Then I wondered about the Oriental religions.

INTERVIEWER: During this period when you were studying in Paris, I know that you were greatly influenced by the existentialists. Was your exposure to them through books or in more personal ways?

WIESEL: First through books and then personally. I had never read novels before. The Talmud, but not novels. I discovered novels in Paris. And the novels then were existential ones. Kafka on one hand, Dostoyevsky on the other. And Malraux, Camus, Sartre. In those times a new Camus was an event in your life. People were waiting. I was waiting for the new Camus, the new Malraux, the new Mauriac, the new Montherlant. But I also met some of them. I was a student and they came to the university. Camus at that time was an editor of *Combat.* I was already, so to speak, a journalist. He was accessible; I saw him. Mauriac became a friend of mine; Gabriel Marcel, a Christian version of Buber, I knew. But the influence was really books.

INTERVIEWER: In books such as *Souls on Fire* you describe Hasidism in an almost existential way. Hasidism was existential, you seem to be saying.

WIESEL: More or less. Born in the eighteenth century in Eastern Europe, Hasidism gave hope to hopeless Jews while emphasizing the notion that the way to God is through one's fellowman. Hasidism then was an existential experience. And that's why it was so great and so sudden. It wasn't philosophically clear to the Hasidim: the Hasid of Pshiskhe didn't know that he was living a philosophical event, or engaged in a philosophical debate, yet *we* know that he was.

INTERVIEWER: But there are differences. You imply in your writings that there is more joy, more mystical involvement in Hasidism than in existentialism.

WIESEL: Not in Hasidism but in my own work. I couldn't add to Hasidism. It doesn't need me to be enriched, but in my work—certainly. My characters are Hasidim who are unwittingly influenced by existentialism; or the other way around, existentialists, young people, often not knowing what they are, who are influenced by Hasidism.

INTERVIEWER: Your characters seem a step beyond the existential characters.

WIESEL: Because they are Hasidim. My characters express themselves that way even if they aren't Jewish. In *The Town Beyond the Wall*, Pedro, who is not Jewish, is an existentialist Hasid. Or Gregor in *The Gates of the Forest.* Most of my characters have this mixture of both.

INTERVIEWER: Are all the characters in your books imaginary?

WIESEL: In my novels, but not in my nonfiction. I don't want to mislead. If I say it's a memoir, it's a memoir. If it's a novel, it's a novel. If I write about Rav Mordechai Shushani, I must make it clear he existed. That's why I added another chapter about him in *One Generation After.*

INTERVIEWER: Have any of your women characters been real?

WIESEL: Not in my novels. I am too personal, too private. I don't talk about things that really happened to me. I like to be discreet about others, about myself.

INTERVIEWER: Did Pedro exist in any form?

WIESEL: No, Pedro is the ideal friend or the friend idealized. You write only about people you don't have, people you want to have.

INTERVIEWER: What about Moshe the Madman who reappears in your novels?

WIESEL: He represents the ultimate mystical madness of man. He is an archetypal character in my books. I have very few types in my novels. I build a world and people it with strange characters and they are always the same. Sometimes I take a projector, a flashlight, and illuminate one, and then the others are secondary characters. Other times I do the opposite.

INTERVIEWER: Your characters frequently assist other people when they need help. But in *The Oath* Moshe didn't help at the very time he could have. Why?

WIESEL: We are impotent; we are helpless. There is not much we can do. So we speak and we get mad. But madness can be anger, or madness can be clinical insanity, in which case it is destructive, or mystical madness, which is helpful. Moshe in my books is always mystical. Mystical madness is by nature a redemptive madness. It becomes a vehicle for redemption, while clinical madness is destructive.

INTERVIEWER: Doesn't mystical madness contain the possibility of man isolating himself?

WIESEL: It means solitude and isolation. But instead of becoming less sensitive to others, the person becomes more sensitive.

INTERVIEWER: If a man withdraws for twenty years, and sees only a few disciples, is that becoming more or less sensitive?

WIESEL: That's an exception. The Kotzker Rebbe was an

exception. Most Hasidic Rebbes moved together with their disciples. They became saintlier and more mystical too, profoundly mystical, together with the community, not outside of it.

INTERVIEWER: Do you try to approach the state of mystical madness when you write?

WIESEL: No, it would be presumptuous to say that. Of course, I try to enter my characters; they enter me. When I write about Moshe the Madman, I try to see him. Very often I do. But he was a real man. I move him around. I hear his voice, and I see his eyes. I am burned by his madness.

INTERVIEWER: What do you think about the question of the madness of the artist?

WIESEL: What is good for me is not necessarily good for someone else. Writing is so personal, so profoundly and terribly personal. Your entire personality goes into every word. The hesitation between one word and another is filled with many centuries, much space. And you deal with it one way, because of what you are, and somebody else deals with it another way. There are no rules. Even technically, some writers need all kinds of idiosyncrasies. One took a wet cloth to his forehead; another had to get drunk; a third had to take drugs; Hemingway stood, another was sitting, another was lying. Would you say there are precepts that you have to sit or lie?

INTERVIEWER: And you?

WIESEL: I am disciplined, hardworking. I have no superstitions. I conjure the perils.

INTERVIEWER: When you begin a book, is there a particular approach you use?

WIESEL: Literature is a tone. It is a melody. If I find the melody of the book, the book is written. I remember *The Town Beyond the Wall*: I wrote one page—I remember exactly what time it was—I wrote one page and I knew the book was finished. I didn't know what I was going to say—I never do—but I knew the book was done, or waiting to be done.

INTERVIEWER: You speak of melody. How would you describe it?

WIESEL: Every book has its own. It's more than simple rhythm. It's like a musical key, major or minor, but more so. If you have that key, you know you can go on—the book is there. It's a matter of time. Before I begin to know more or less what I want to say: the ideas, the characters, the opinions. But the profound meaning of the book is within me; I still don't know what it is. And then, suddenly, at the corner of a sentence, an astonishing discovery: *this* is where I was trying to go.

INTERVIEWER: Do you choose the epigraphs before you begin or after?

WIESEL: Sometimes before, but usually after. At one point I understand what I am doing. Sometimes I stop in the middle of a book, sometimes at the end when I see something that strikes me, and that becomes the epigraph.

INTERVIEWER: I remember the epigraph from *The Gates of the Forest*:

When the great Rabbi Israel Baal Shem-Tov saw misfortune threatening the Jews it was his custom to go into a certain part of the forest to meditate. There he would light a fire, say a special prayer, and the miracle would be accomplished and the misfortune averted.

Later, when his disciple, the celebrated Magid of Mezritch, had occasion, for the same reason, to intercede with heaven, he would go to the same place in the forest and say: "Master of the Universe, listen! I do not know how to light the fire, but I am still able to say the prayer." And again the miracle would be accomplished.

Still later, Rabbi Moshe-Leib of Sasov, in order to save his people once more, would go into the forest and say: "I do not know how to light the fire, I do not know the prayer, but I know the place and this must be sufficient." It was sufficient and the miracle was accomplished.

Then it fell to Rabbi Israel of Rizhyn to overcome misfortune.

Sitting in his armchair, his head in his hands, he spoke to God: "I am unable to light the fire and I do not know the prayer; I cannot even find the place in the forest. All I can do is to tell the story, and this must be sufficient." And it was sufficient.

God made man because he loves stories.

It troubled me that when you repeated this epigraph in *Souls on Fire*, you added that it was no longer enough: "The proof is that the threat has not been averted. Perhaps we are no longer able to tell the story. Could all of us be guilty? Even the survivors? Especially the survivors?" What accounts for this revision?

WIESEL: In *The Gates of the Forest* I tried to transmit a story. In *Souls on Fire* I changed the story. The context was different. In other words, I tried to do something more and it wasn't enough.

INTERVIEWER: You have said elsewhere that you write only when "the pillow is on fire." Does that mean that every time you write you feel obsessed?

WIESEL: Not always. I force myself to write. And often what I write is not good. I destroy it. Very, very often. But sometimes in the middle of writing, suddenly I feel it is there. Words are burning. Then I know it's good. But at times I can rewrite a page ten times without changing a word. I feel I have to do something. And I write and write and write.

INTERVIEWER: It must be very frustrating to rewrite a page ten times and not make any changes.

WIESEL: No, I did not come into this world in order to write a thousand pages. If I write one good page, it's enough. If I write the same page ten times in order to find in the eleventh time, the real page, I'm more than happy.

INTERVIEWER: What happens when you are blocked?

WIESEL: Usually the block occurs after the first book. In my case it didn't. But if it had I would not have been unhappy. I have never felt blocked.

INTERVIEWER: I imagine that your experience as a journalist helped.

WIESEL: Yes, the craft helped me to write anywhere—on a plane, in a café, while waiting.

INTERVIEWER: Unlike a Hemingway, your tools weren't so much the craft, as much as . . .

WIESEL: Knowledge. I needed knowledge. I knew that I needed ten years to start writing, and I was collecting all kinds of materials. That's why I studied mysticism, that's why I went to India, that's why I studied languages and literature—all these were tools. Psychology too. In France in those times if you studied philosophy, one of the components was psychology. So I took a course in psychopathology for two years, and the courses were given at the St. Anne Psychiatric hospital. It was a mental institution.

INTERVIEWER: And you are still developing your tools?

WIESEL: Of course, I study every day.

INTERVIEWER: I am intrigued by the fact that you still write in French.

WIESEL: It's my best medium. At this age—I don't think it's worthwhile to acquire another language or to perfect my English or abandon French which, after all, I mastered. It became my language. My constant challenge. The French language is Cartesian; it must be clear and concise. And yet I try to communicate something which is not precise or clear. I like that challenge. I also acquired French at a certain time of my life, after the war. If I had gone then, let us say, to England, I probably would have acquired English.

Before the war, I didn't even know that French existed. I knew simply that there were foreign words. After the war, I had a psychological need to acquire a new vehicle, a new tool—everything new, as though now I would start living again. And that's why French became so important. I can write an article in Yiddish but not a book. I have written one book in Yiddish, out of sentimental duty. I have written hundreds of articles in

Hebrew. But I would not be able to write a book in Hebrew. I may feel inhibited. Isaiah wrote in Hebrew . . . and *I* write in Hebrew? In French I don't have such inhibitions. True, Racine wrote French and I write French, but I am not saying what Racine is saying. While as a Jew of my generation, I am probably trying to say what Jeremiah tried to say. And yet, if I had gone to Israel in 1945 instead of France, I would probably have written in Hebrew.

INTERVIEWER: Do you write in any other forms, such as poetry?

WIESEL: Not really, though I like to experiment in literature. That's why I wrote *Ani Maamim* as a poem. First I wrote the poem, then I gave it to Darius Milhaud. I wrote the words and he wrote the music. I went to Geneva once to see him. He was an old man and couldn't move. I sang the Hasidic *Ani Maamim.* I wanted him to hear it. He comes from a Sephardic family where they never sang this kind of *Ani Maamim.* That was the only contact. He worked alone; I worked alone. In *One Generation After,* I develop another genre: the dialogue. I bring the dialogue back in *A Jew Today.* What are these dialogues? They are dialogues with the dead. Nobody else listens, nobody else hears.

INTERVIEWER: I want to pursue the subject of the dialogues, but for the moment I want to discuss other experiments you have made in literature. For instance, why did you write a play about Russian Jews instead of a novel?

WIESEL: Desperation. I had written the book, *The Jews of Silence.* It appeared in some ten languages and had no impact. The Jewish establishment didn't move. I went from one convention to another trying to alert people, in vain. I became desperate. I wanted to try something that no one else had tried. A report did not help Russian Jewry, a nonfiction book did not help, so I wrote a play—same results.

INTERVIEWER: I know you had some problems with the play in Israel.

WIESEL: The Habima Theatre produced it. They shortened it and added material from other books I have written. They changed the name to *The Jews of Silence*—they didn't know that I had written a book with the same title. They had promised a certain actor, a certain director, and suddenly they put before me a *fait accompli*. . . . They wrote me a letter which said, "Except for a few parts which we omitted and a few parts which we added, and except for a different director, and a different name, the play is the same." I wanted to stop it. It wasn't easy because I cannot hurt Israel. The play became a great commercial success in Israel. But it wasn't my play. I went on television and appealed to the public not to see it.

INTERVIEWER: As a result of the experience, have you decided not to write any more plays?

WIESEL: I just finished one! It's a kind of Purimschpiel, a play that was customarily performed on Purim, the annual day of fools, children, and beggars. Its title is *The Trial of God,* and it takes place somewhere in Russia in the year 1649. When I had written *Zalmen,* which deals with the plight of contemporary Russian Jewry, I thought it would be my only play. But you don't really decide. At one point, the subject comes and seizes you and imposes upon you its own rhythm, its own mode. I hinted in some of my books at a scene I had witnessed in the camp: God being judged by three rabbis. One day I decided that since I was the one who had witnessed it, I had to do justice to the theme. I wrote almost a full novel. It didn't work. I wrote a poem. It didn't work. I wrote a kind of dialogue, not a play, but a dialogue. It didn't work. Then I decided I would move the same theme back to the sixteenth century. And it worked. It's no longer in a camp, it's somewhere else. And it's no longer a tragedy but a comedy. It's a Purimschpiel. And the only way to do such a Purimschpiel, as a Purimschpiel, is a play. You can indict God on Yom Kippur; it's a tragedy. But indict God on Purim, it's not even a tragedy. It's much more. It goes one step beyond. It's laughter, philosophical laughter, meta-physical farce.

INTERVIEWER: You said that you tried different forms before you were satisfied with the Purimschpiel. I wonder why you have never written a film based on one of your novels and why they have never been made into films.

WIESEL: I have always resisted. I don't think it can be done. In one way I have no rights over my books. They all belong to my French publisher, Le Seuil. It's the general practice in France. Therefore options were often bought, even for *Night.* I didn't want that. I tried to sabotage the process. Usually it ends when the producer asks, "Would you like to write a script? Or would you like to advise?" Then I start explaining it's impossible.

INTERVIEWER: It is very difficult to express mysticism on film.

WIESEL: It's not only mysticism. My books are either mystical books or, in the beginning, they were about the Holocaust. I don't believe either can be done on film. I don't believe they should be.

INTERVIEWER: Yet you participated in making the film *Sighet, Sighet.*

WIESEL: That was a documentary. The producer went to my town and took stills. I simply narrated it in New York. This is a story I had written for *Legends of Our Time.* I simply took the text that had been published in *Commentary* and read it in a studio. The story describes my return to my hometown, which I did not recognize. Not because it had changed so much, but quite the opposite: because it had *not* changed. Everything remained the same: the streets, gardens, houses, schools, shops . . . Only—the Jews were no longer there. They had all been driven out twenty years earlier, in 1944. And yet, the town seemed to get along without them.

INTERVIEWER: Would you ever make another documentary?

WIESEL: I would, but I wouldn't be involved in any other type of film.

INTERVIEWER: I have always thought *The Gates of the Forest* would make a superb movie—the descriptions of the "clouds which weighed upon the night."

WIESEL: It was just bought again. But I don't think they will make it.

INTERVIEWER: If you were giving advice to a young writer, what would you tell him?

WIESEL: First, to read. I never taught creative writing courses. I believe in creative reading. That's what I am trying to teach—creative reading. I'd assign the Scripture and Midrash, Ovid and Kafka, Thomas Mann and Camus, Plato and André Schwarz-Bart. A writer must first know how to read. You can see whether a person is a writer by the way he reads a text, by the way he deciphers a text. I'd also say to a young writer, if you can choose not to write, don't. Nothing is as painful. From the outside, people think it's good; it's easy; it's romantic. Not at all. It's much easier not to write than to write. Except if you are a writer. Then you have no choice.

INTERVIEWER: What is your present routine? Do you spend most of your time in New York?

WIESEL: We live in New York. I teach in Boston. Once a week I go to Boston for a whole day. I teach and see my students. The rest of the time I work here, except when I go out of town to lecture, which I am doing less and less. Once a year I go to France. I used to go more often. I also go to Jerusalem once a year.

INTERVIEWER: Why do you live in New York?

WIESEL: We almost moved to Boston. But the few friends we have live in New York, and friends are important. Otherwise, I don't participate in a social life.

INTERVIEWER: What about your activities besides teaching and writing? For instance, are you still involved in helping Russian Jewry?

WIESEL: In the beginning my activities were more visible because no one else did anything. I published *The Jews of Silence* in 1965. And I returned to Moscow in 1966. As I said earlier, in those years it was impossible to make the Jewish organizations do anything. Until 1970, they refused even to establish an American Conference on Soviet Jewry. Now it's a *cause célèbre*. What do I do? I speak with senators and people who have power; I send friends to Russia to create contacts. Whatever can be done, I try to do.

INTERVIEWER: Why after the war did you not go on to Palestine from France?

WIESEL: I had no certificate. In 1946 when the Irgun blew up the King David Hotel, I decided I would like to join the underground. Very naïvely I went to the Jewish Agency in Paris. I got no further than the janitor who asked: "What do you want?" I said, "I would like to join the underground." He threw me out. About 1948 I was a journalist and helped one of the Yiddish underground papers with articles, but I was never a member of the underground.

INTERVIEWER: I am surprised to hear you say you wanted to join since the notion of killing is so foreign to you.

WIESEL: Still, at that point, I felt I had to do something. I could only hope that if I had become a member I would not have had to kill. In 1946 I wanted to do something. The Jewish people were awakening, and my place was with the Jewish people. Whatever the Jews were doing, I had to be with them. Everything about the underground was alien to me. I was against killing, against violence.

INTERVIEWER: A Christian friend of mine recently told me that by being in Israel in the wars of 1967 and 1973, I was indirectly helping to kill. . . .

WIESEL: I was there in 1967 and in 1973 too. But I didn't have a gun. I came to help the Israelis. To say that they were killers is not true. They were being killed as well. They were fighting. It's a paradox. I don't pretend to be able to solve the paradoxes in me. There are many paradoxes which are part of my life. I am absolutely a pacifist, against violence, surely against killing, and yet I am totally for Israel. Maybe because I believe that they really don't want to fight. And whenever they do, they don't fight as others do. They never celebrate their military heroes. In 1967, when they won, and it was a just war, they were sad. All the generals were sad. In 1973, they were so sad they didn't talk. I remember that when I came back from a one-day visit to the Golan Heights, I couldn't talk.

INTERVIEWER: Several people who have known you for a long time said that you have changed since your marriage and the birth of your son.

WIESEL: Of course. My son changed me. Once you bring life into the world, you must protect it. We must protect it by changing the world. There was more anger in me before. There still is, but now it's a different kind of anger. It's more positive.

INTERVIEWER: At whom was the anger directed?

WIESEL: Everything. At history, at the world, at God, at myself, at whatever surrounded me.

INTERVIEWER: How did you express it?

WIESEL: I didn't, I contained it. All my writing was born out of anger. In order to contain it, I had to write. If I had not written, I would have exploded.

INTERVIEWER: The anger didn't have a particular focus? You weren't angry at the Germans or the past?

WIESEL: There was accumulated anger but not personal anger at Germans, or Poles, or Hungarians, or at the silent witnesses, at the silent onlookers. During those years, all that happened day after day and minute after minute intensified my anger. But I didn't show it. I didn't express it. I sublimated it by writing about something else, by writing about the glory of Jewish life, by writing about the joy of Hasidism, by writing about the Bible.

INTERVIEWER: Then you were aware that the anger disappeared once your son was born?

WIESEL: It didn't disappear. It is still present. Except now it's on a different level. Today I occasionally let it burst out. I speak up and fight for Israel, for Russian Jews and so forth. I'm angrier now than then.

INTERVIEWER: Has your son enabled you to see a joyous side of life?

WIESEL: Both joyous and not. When I see my son, I am full of joy, full of fear. I realize how vulnerable life is, how vulnerable Jewish life is. The past has never disappeared. I imagine other fathers look at their children the way I look at mine. I feel real fear. Whenever he is not at home, I am afraid. I am sure this fear is rooted in a deeper fear. At the same time, nothing gives me as much joy as my son.

INTERVIEWER: You have said that you wrote *The Accident* with a sense of urgency because of the question of suicide. Did you ever contemplate suicide?

WIESEL: I did, but not that way. After the war, there was a point when I felt I could have slid into death. I was sick. It was a strange moment. I haven't written about it yet. I felt on the edge. I was seeing the land of the dead, and I was no longer alive. It was strong, dark, powerful. I knew I was dying, and if I had not resisted, I would have died. The resistance itself was a conscious decision.

INTERVIEWER: Was that in Paris?

WIESEL: First, in Germany. I was sick for some ten days. I was in a coma. I had blood poisoning. Out of twenty thousand people who were liberated, at least five thousand died in those days. We all had blood poisoning. After five or six days of total starvation, we were given the wrong food by Americans who liberated the camp. In my case, it was even worse. They distributed ham or some kind of pork. If anyone had given me pork during the war, I would have eaten it. After, when I was already free, I brought the pork, or ham, or spam, whatever it was, to my lips, and I got blood poisoning. But other people who didn't have these problems or these inhibitions, or the psychosomatic reactions that I had, also died of blood poisoning, stomach trouble, and so forth.

INTERVIEWER: You also had a near-fatal accident in New York.

WIESEL: Yes. When I was hit by a taxi in New York, I was brought to Roosevelt Hospital, which didn't want to accept me. I was in a coma. I didn't have any money. I didn't have anything. They sent me away in an ambulance, and we went to New York Hospital. A surgeon named Paul Braunstein saved my life. *The Accident* is dedicated to him.

INTERVIEWER: Do you still have difficulty walking for more than five minutes?

WIESEL: Yes. That's why I sit when I lecture, instead of standing. I can walk a maximum of ten minutes. After ten minutes, I am tired.

INTERVIEWER: I want to return to an earlier subject. You spoke of your dialogues with the dead and of being on the edge of life. Are you still near the abyss?

WIESEL: I haven't left it. I don't think anyone can, once you have been there. There isn't a day, there simply isn't a day without my thinking of death or of looking into death, darkness, or seeing that fire or trying to understand what happened. There isn't a day. I don't write about it. I don't speak about it. I try not to touch the subject at all, but it is present.

INTERVIEWER: It is like carrying around a nightmare.

WIESEL: I believe that all the survivors are mad. One time or another their madness will explode. You cannot absorb that much madness and not be influenced by it. That is why the children of survivors are so tragic. I see them in school. They don't know how to handle their parents. They see that their parents are traumatized: they scream and don't react normally.

At Stanford, a boy came up to me crying and sobbing. He took me aside and told me his father was a survivor. "Will he ever stop being a survivor?" he asked me. The children are now more tragic than their parents.

INTERVIEWER: I wonder if your struggle also involves melancholy, as in the title of your book: *Four Hasidic Masters and Their Struggle Against Melancholy.*

WIESEL: That's mainly the Hasidic struggle. I identify with the Hasidic experience. When I lecture, I don't speak about subjects that make people cry. I don't want people to cry; I want them to laugh. I want them to sing. They cried enough. Also, it's too easy to cry—instant catharsis. Nothing is easier than that. I want them to laugh.

INTERVIEWER: That seems outside your character. I don't see you expressing laughter.

WIESEL: You don't express laughter, you communicate it. You cannot express it because once you do, it is no longer laughter. Bergson said the joke you explain is no longer a joke. Philosophical laughter may be a response.

INTERVIEWER: Do you try to communicate philosophical laughter when you appear before audiences?

WIESEL: No, I try to teach. I am a teacher. My main objective in lecturing is to teach. I like to teach. I don't like to give one lecture and go away. At the YM-YWHA in New York the same people come year after year. Part of my knowledge is invested in them. If you ask what I want to achieve, it's to create an awareness, which is already the beginning of teaching.

INTERVIEWER: What is the connection between your teaching and your writing?

WIESEL: Teaching helps me. If it were to entertain, I would stop because my first commitment is to writing. Teaching forces me to prepare. I prepare a lot. Fortunately, I always use my lectures later in my books. I can't afford to waste research, so I use it.

INTERVIEWER: Earlier you spoke of the Hasid in you. What is your relationship today with the Hasidic community?

WIESEL: Obviously not what it was when I was very young. Then it was simple. I had a Rebbe which, of course, is Hasidic for "rabbi," and he was my teacher, my master, my guide. That Rebbe died, his son died, and his children I no longer know. But still, in my memory, I am faithful to the first Rebbe I knew as a child. Now I feel at home within every Hasidic community. Not all accept me. The Satmarer, very fanatic, were close to me when I was a child. The Satmar Rebbe comes from my town. His assistants are childhood friends. Still they don't accept me. They don't accept any Jew who is not part of their sect. For them, the Jewish people number maybe ten or twenty thousand souls. I feel at home with the others. I feel more at home among Hasidim than among secular Jews because of my childhood experiences.

INTERVIEWER: Do you spend much time with the Hasidic community?

WIESEL: I stay in close touch with Hasidim, but I go less to their synagogues. I go to the Lubavitch "evenings" because they are so colorful. The Lubavitch community is in Brooklyn; its head is Rebbe Menahem-Mendel Schneerson. Thousands of followers gather there on those festive occasions to listen to their Master—and sing with him. I used to go more often. Now I'm more involved in books, Hasidic books.

INTERVIEWER: There seems to be an irreconcilable split between Hasidic Jews and secular Jews.

WIESEL: There always was. The opponents of the Hasidic movement were strong. Hasidism won because of its fervor. Also its sense of history: Hasidism came at a certain time in a certain place. Today, Hasidism is gaining, especially among young people. I dislike the extremists of either side though. I dislike all fanatics. They exist within the Hasidic community but at least they are a small minority. The majority is tolerant, and its attitude toward secular Jews is kinder than it was in the beginning.

Now, being almost fifty years old and without the innocence I had when I was really a Hasid, I would make the tradition stricter. I would like the Hasid to start by learning. Learning is more important to Judaism than anything I know. To learn and to learn and to learn; then to find himself or herself in the Hasidic framework. It should not be at the expense of learning. In other words, what I don't like today is, to put it coarsely, the phony Hasidism, the phony mysticism. Many students say, "Teach me mysticism." It's a joke. If you want to study mysticism, start by studying the Bible, then the prophets, then Midrash, and then the Talmud, and then and then and then, and finally at a certain age, you enter mysticism. Today they don't even know how to read Hebrew. And they come and say, teach me mysticism. Some of them think it's easy to be a Hasid because they don't know what it means; to them it's a mystical movement. Of course, not all. Some are enlightened and learned.

INTERVIEWER: Can one learn mysticism?

WIESEL: No, and yet there is no other way. By that I mean if you don't learn, you cannot. That doesn't mean if you learn you are a mystic. But if you don't, you are not.

INTERVIEWER: Aren't there people like Kazantzakis who have been spontaneous mystics?

WIESEL: Kazantzakis was a great scholar. You can have a mystical temperament, an inclination. If, on the strength of that, you go on studying, fine. But if you don't study, you never will. Mysticism without study is impossible.

INTERVIEWER: I suppose I was thinking of some of the simpler forms of mysticism, the peasants of Europe, for instance, who have a mystical experience and the Church declares it a miracle.

WIESEL: That's a passing thing. Mysticism is more serious than that. Miracles in mysticism don't occupy such an important place. It's a metaphor, for the peasants, for the crowds, to impress people. What does mysticism really mean? It means the way to attain knowledge. It's close to philosophy, except in philosophy you go horizontally while in mysticism you go vertically. You plunge into it. Philosophy is a slow process of logic and logical discourse: A bringing B bringing C and so forth. In mysticism you can jump from A to Z. But the ultimate objective is the same. It's knowledge. It's truth.

INTERVIEWER: Is Indian or eastern mysticism different?

WIESEL: Yes, but even there it's study. They study the *Ghitas* and the *Upanishads* and we study our texts, the *Zohar* and other mystical works. Their relationship between student and teacher is more strenuous and also more intense than ours. In our case, one teacher may have many students, many disciples. There it's one to one. The real guru has one student. And their secret is one secret. The ritual is different.

INTERVIEWER: You once said you don't write *about* God. What do you mean?

WIESEL: God comes in here and there in my books. I oppose Him. I fight Him. I quarrel with Him. Some of my characters pray to Him. But when I say I don't speak *about* God, it means theologically, the whole theological art, which is a way of reaching the attributes of God: What is He doing? Who is He?

INTERVIEWER: Are these questions often unsaid, unwritten in your books?

WIESEL: Yes. I am very concerned, even obsessed, with God.

INTERVIEWER: So by implication you are doing what you don't want to be doing?

WIESEL: Again yes, but not with words. I rarely speak about God. To God, yes. I protest against Him. I shout at Him. But to open a discourse about the qualities of God, about the problems that God imposes, theodicy, no. And yet He is there, in silence, in filigree.

INTERVIEWER: In *Night*, you wrote, "Never shall I forget those flames which consumed my Faith forever." Yet faith permeates your work.

WIESEL: This may sound like a contradiction but it is not. I had to include those words in *Night* and I had to write the later books. If it were the other way around, it would be a contradiction. But *Night* was a beginning and an end. Furthermore, the problem of faith is never solved. In *Night,* only those who did not believe in God did not deny Him. I could say now too—only those who do not believe in God have easy faith in Him.

INTERVIEWER: If each character in *Messengers of God* were compared with God, each character would come out ahead.

WIESEL: Of course. If I have to choose between God and man, I will choose man because God wins. So what's the point? To help God win? He will win anyway. We are all His victims. But before being His victims, we are His associates.

INTERVIEWER: Do you praise Him?

WIESEL: I have great difficulties praying, even the simple prayers. To read a prayer book, especially today, in English translation, makes me feel uneasy. I have great difficulties. . . .

INTERVIEWER: Wouldn't a Rebbe consider that a blasphemy?

WIESEL: No, I think a real Rebbe would say the same thing. But then he would pray. The Pshiskhe Rebbe used to say that he was angry at God all the time. But afterwards, he would pray. I am angry too, and I say that I have difficulties praying, but I go to the synagogue with Hasidim, and I stay with them and occasionally pray with them.

INTERVIEWER: Is that a Kierkegaardian leap of faith?

WIESEL: Kierkegaard stresses God. I stress the Hasidim, the Jews with whom I pray. Sometimes I go to the synagogue not to be with God, but to be with the Jews.

INTERVIEWER: What is there in Judaism that has enabled so many to accept on blind faith the continual record of God's "inhumanity" to man?

WIESEL: At the very beginning of our history we suffered. We began in suffering, and the suffering continued into our history. Second, as a challenge, a strange defiance, a mutual defiance. God and the people of Israel somehow try to see who will tire the other out first.

INTERVIEWER: But God always wins, as you said earlier.

WIESEL: Not always. God does not always win because God says in the Talmud I want to lose; I want to be defeated by my own children. In all kinds of legends He loses. But in history He wins because we all die. Malraux said something beautiful: At the end, death is the victor, but as long as I live, with every breath I take, death is defeated. In our tradition, I would phrase it differently: Man, as long as he lives, is immortal. One minute before his death he shall be immortal. But one minute later, God wins.

INTERVIEWER: Doesn't God also win if man is alive, but barely alive; if he is suffering?

WIESEL: No. If man suffers he can still speak up. Job did. Jeremiah did. However, when God's unfair practices enter, God may always say that He wanted them. There is no superiority in any independent rebellion against God.

INTERVIEWER: So man loses again?

WIESEL: Of course he loses again. He cannot win.

INTERVIEWER: Then what is the point of rebellion?

WIESEL: Here we come to the existential rebellion. I lose and still I rebel—for my own dignity. Although I know I will never defeat God, I still fight Him. Suddenly the role of man is greatly enhanced. Therefore his defeat is not really a defeat.

INTERVIEWER: Is art too a form of rebellion against God?

WIESEL: Absolutely. Not only against God. Art means rebellion. Art means to say no.

INTERVIEWER: In what way?

WIESEL: A painter would say, that's not the way I see nature. I will show you how I see nature. Furthermore, your Nature, God, dies. Mine will stay. If it's Picasso, he will say, man doesn't have two eyes but three; if it's Braque, he will say, man doesn't have these kinds of lines, he has different kinds of lines; Goya will say man is cruel, but not the way you think he is; if it's in poetry, the poet will say no to prose, life is poetry. I say to God, you want me to do this, I will not. You want me to forget my village, I will not. Art means for man to say no to death, too.

INTERVIEWER: So the artist is able to defeat God through the immortality of his art?

WIESEL: Yes, if you confound God and death, which is quite plausible. The *Malaach Ha Mavet,* the Angel of Death, and God together because both, so to say, are immortal. Except in *Had Ga Ya* on Pesach [Passover], when we say that God killed the Angel of Death. Still, I have doubts. Let me give an example. I write books because there *was* a tragedy. I try to bring some characters back and defeat death, defeat the killer, defeat God. But one day of one child weighs more than all the books that I could ever write. So what kind of a victory is it? Beckett once told me he found a manuscript of *Quand Malone meurt.* On the manuscript he found an epigraph, which is not printed in the book: *"En désespoir de cause,"* which means that's the only thing I can do—write.

INTERVIEWER: Do you mean to say that because God sets the parameters we have no choice? The only way we can defeat Him is through something beyond the self—art?

WIESEL: If there were a domain then it would be art. But why defeat Him in that case?

INTERVIEWER: Not for its own sake, certainly not for His sake, but for our sake.

WIESEL: Why should that be a goal?

INTERVIEWER: Perhaps to show that we can create in life something that can live beyond us.

WIESEL: But why against God? Why not life-centered? Man-centered?

INTERVIEWER: To elevate man?

WIESEL: Must we take on God to elevate man? Why don't we take on man to elevate man? Unless you accept a religious exigency in man, God is much less important in art. God is important in the Bible, in life, but not in art. Unless you admit that there is some religious aspect to art, which is possible. Or unless you yourself are religiously motivated.

INTERVIEWER: Do you consider your art a religion?

WIESEL: My writing may be a response to a religious need, not a religion.

INTERVIEWER: I have thought that you and Joyce have many parallels. Even your words are often similar. At the end of *A Portrait of the Artist*, he writes of silence and cunning. Would you say that in some ways his transposition of Catholicism to art is similar to your transposition of Judaism to art?

WIESEL: Not entirely. My preoccupations are not his preoccupations. My preoccupation—it depends whether in the novels, the memoirs, or the nonfiction—is memory. God being the source of memory, I'm preoccupied with God. Why the good are punished and the wicked rewarded is the second question. The first question is, How can I achieve a situation in which the victims, all the victims, can enter memory? That is my major preoccupation—memory, the kingdom of memory. I want to protect and enrich that kingdom, glorify that kingdom and serve it. God from the religious point of view is part of that kingdom. But my concerns go far beyond it.

INTERVIEWER: Memory is really the uncreated memory of the race?

WIESEL: Of the species. If I could remember, what would I remember? What would I dare to remember? The fact that we have selective memories may be bad or may be good. I would lose my mind if I remembered everything. Every child, every old man, every sick man, every victim. I would go insane. Here again we have a dichotomy, the ambivalent attitude. On one hand, I want to preserve every single aspect, every gesture, every look, every word; and on the other hand, I would fail.

INTERVIEWER: Why do you want to preserve the past?

WIESEL: For them and for me. If I am here and they are not, they must be in me.

INTERVIEWER: And why for you?

WIESEL: Because without them what would I be?

INTERVIEWER: If it's the memory of the species, how do you know where to begin?

WIESEL: In the beginning, in my own mind, in my memory—that's why I go back to childhood. Strangely enough, I have always been attracted to beginnings: the beginning of the world, the beginning of the Hasidic movement, the beginning of the cabalistic movement, the beginning of the war, the beginning of my life in my shtetl. . . .

INTERVIEWER: Then you are similar in some ways to Proust.

WIESEL: Oh, I love Proust. We all learned from him how to go back in time. The difference is that Proust stayed in his room, and he observed himself. He was Proust lying in his bed looking at Proust at the window who was looking at Proust in bed. In our generation's case, we are always in the middle. We are never on the outside. Whatever happens, happens to us.

INTERVIEWER: How do you differ from a chronicler?

WIESEL: I don't. To be a chronicler would be a great honor.

INTERVIEWER: Similar to the character of your father, in *The Oath?*

WIESEL: Yes. I want to recreate. I want to record.

INTERVIEWER: Why not journalism?

WIESEL: It's a different kind of recording. Journalism is too immediate, too monotonous and superficial. A chronicler is alone in his room and writes. A journalist is rarely alone. He writes about other people, and the essential is always missed. I was a journalist long enough to know. You write only of the fleeting moment—the most dramatic, the most visible, not the underlying reasons.

INTERVIEWER: Do you think in some way you will be able to recapture the past?

WIESEL: I am trying, like Sisyphus. He knows he will not succeed, but he is trying. I know I will never recapture the past in its entirety because no matter what, the past is richer than the future.

INTERVIEWER: It has been said that you write in an eternal present, but it seems that you are really writing in an eternal past.

WIESEL: An eternal past expressed in the present. To me time, as an element of art, is the most challenging concept, and therefore I play with it. I run from the present to the past, especially in French where there are so many pasts—*passé défini, passé composé,* and so forth. I run from tense to tense to show this vertical approach to the past.

INTERVIEWER: Are you waiting for the Messiah?

WIESEL: Not for a personal one. But I am waiting for something. It may be forever, but I would not want to stop waiting.

INTERVIEWER: Why?

WIESEL: Life would be empty. If everything were concentrated in the present, there would be no possibility of transcending the present. We are suspended between the absolute past and the absolute future over which we have no control. It's a creeping flame. Sometimes it bends one way, sometimes the other way. Sometimes it brings light and sometimes fire—life or destruction. Take away the waiting, what remains? I think the Messianic concept, which is the Jewish offering to mankind, is a great victory. What does it mean? It means that history has a sense, a meaning, a direction; it goes somewhere, and necessarily in a good direction—the Messiah. At least we would like to think that history is going in that direction. But I think it's going in the wrong direction. We are heading towards catastrophe. I think the world is going to pieces. I am very pessimistic. Why? Because the world hasn't been punished yet, and the only punishment that could be adequate is the nuclear destruction of the world.

INTERVIEWER: The Jews have been punished.

WIESEL: The Jews, but not the world. And if the world were punished now we would be punished as well. I don't want the world to be punished, anything but that. Yet logically there must be punishment, the signs point to a terrible catastrophe. Cambodia can happen today. A million people liquidated there, and nobody cares, nobody shouts. The Cambodians stopped all telephone communications with the outside world. They uprooted everybody from the cities. People died of starvation and hunger. They broke up families. They broke up communities. It was genocide, and nobody paid any attention. It doesn't stand to reason. It cannot go without punishment. If you think of the Holocaust, of course there must be punishment. And think of all the other things that happen—pollution. In two villages of New Jersey, people suddenly develop cancer. Why there? A friend of mine in New York told me he has hundreds of people working for him and in the last seven months, five families were struck with cancer. We create and produce many nuclear weapons. Can we continue with impunity? Tomorrow a man may push a button in the Kremlin or Washington; or worse, Idi Amin, for five hundred million dollars, may buy an atomic bomb. And he would push the button. He is crazy. Or Quadaffi, who is a fanatic and crazy. Imagine Ahmad Shukairy, Yasir Arafat's predecessor and the chief of a group that was a forerunner of the PLO, having the bomb in 1967. Don't you think he would have used it? Nobody thinks of these possibilities. There is an apathy born out of fear. People don't want to face these things. People prefer not to think.

INTERVIEWER: Is the punishment going to come from God or from man?

WIESEL: From man. Ourselves. I don't think that God will intervene. It will be mankind. It's almost the logical outgrowth of the situation. Strangely enough, the only thing that can save mankind would be a real awareness of the Holocaust. I don't believe anything else has the moral power. That's why I reacted so strongly towards the television dramatization of the Holocaust. You don't take such an event and reduce it. The Holocaust was a shield. We were protected. The Jewish people were shielded, as was the world, because of that event, for forty years. Demystify it or banalize it, it loses its power. If it's something you can't imagine, something that you can't reproduce, it has power.

INTERVIEWER: Can we do anything?

WIESEL: Even if we cannot, we must. That's why I am teaching; that's why I am writing. It's not only because I am near the abyss and I see the dead. It is also because I see the living.

INTERVIEWER: Is there anyone who is doing what should be done and saying what should be said?

WIESEL: Nobody possesses the total truth. We all have fragments, sparks. The problem is that truth has become something that doesn't interest people. I come from a tradition where truth mattered more than anything in the world. Today truth is not a commodity. What matters is image, efficiency, rapidity . . . truth has disappeared. After my review of the television program about the Holocaust appeared in *The New York Times,* I received a very moving letter from one of the most important judges in the country. He said that he agreed with everything I wrote, but also understood that the program did some good. But what about truth? Truth becomes something we can do without. Let me push it to the limits: If truth were bad for the Jews but half-truth good for the Jews, these people would say better half-truth than truth. I can't accept that. People don't have convictions anymore. I don't know what kind of a generation this is . . . maybe it is still the result of my generation. Policy is being made in Washington in response to polls. The same thing is true of our Jewish leadership—no convictions. It's only what's favorable or favorably received that influences policy decisions. Yet here and there are people—Sartre in France, for instance. When he was old and blind, I had respect for the man. I don't agree with everything he said, but he had convictions. He knew what he was saying. Camus was another. Absolute convictions. I respected him throughout. There are people in this category. Some are less known, writers and scholars. Yet the sum of their fragments is still not the truth. And that is tragic.

INTERVIEWER: Isn't that always going to be the case?

WIESEL: That's why life is not a happy event in the absolute sense of the word. It's always a tragedy, by definition. It's short. We come from nowhere; we go nowhere. And in the eyes of the pyramids, as Napoleon would say, what are we? Rebbe Nahman of Bratzlav once saw a man running. His name was Haim. He called him and said: "Haim, look outside, what do you see?" He said, "I see the clouds in the sky." "What else do you see?" "I see horses and wagons and people running." "Haim, Haim, a hundred years from now there will be clouds and people will run and horses will run and I will not be here and you will not be here, then why are you running?"

INTERVIEWER: I think that people allow themselves to be fooled because if they accepted the truth, in some cases, they wouldn't be able to go on living.

WIESEL: Truth is a tremendous passion. It can become a positive passion. I can understand why people fight in the name of truth and do anything in the name of truth—even things I wouldn't do. But when they act in the name of something that is not truth, that is the problem.

INTERVIEWER: Why would somebody passionately seek out such a horror as the truth of Cambodia?

WIESEL: Because it happens, because it's true, because I am a contemporary of the victims and of the killers. It's a small planet. How can I not know? The same thing happened during the Holocaust. An Israeli army major wrote a Ph.D. dissertation on the Holocaust; he went through the newspapers, and he lost his mind—literally. He had to be institutionalized. He had read the American Jewish papers, the *Forward*, and other publications. On the front pages he read reports of the ghettos being liquidated, communities being massacred, and on the inside pages he found ads—Go and enjoy your summer in the Catskills . . . See the comedian Mr. So and So. . . . A student at City College went through all the bulletins of one particular synagogue, one of the most famous in New York. The Warsaw Ghetto uprising began on April 19th, it was the eve of Pesach; two days later on the 21st, *The New York Times* had a full story. Not one mention was made in the bulletin in subsequent weeks of the Warsaw Ghetto. The sermon a week later did not include the Warsaw Ghetto. I don't understand it. How could they go on? The same thing I don't understand today. How can we go on knowing of Cambodia?

INTERVIEWER: Somewhere people listen and in their own ways will try to do something.

WIESEL: I wish. I ask Moynihan, Kissinger, others. It's become my obsession, whomever I meet. No matter what we talk about, at one point I must come back to Cambodia. The United Nations didn't even take up the subject. It's like a sealed wagon in the time of the Holocaust, and I don't like to use images, just like that, from the Holocaust. The country has become a sealed wagon and nobody cares. But then why should they? If the world was indifferent a generation ago, why should it care now?

INTERVIEWER: Maybe that's why we are going to be punished.

WIESEL: It's already the beginning of the punishment.

INTERVIEWER: You have written that every generation has its own prophet. Who is our prophet?

WIESEL: He is a dead prophet and a living prophet. As a Jew I would say that our prophets are in the past. Jeremiah is my prophet. To me he is still alive. And my prophet is also someone whom I knew during the war. He was a child. I never knew his name. I never knew where he came from, but we were together in the camp. I can see him walking. I can hear him talking. He uses simple words. He says, "Are we going to have soup tonight? Are we going to have potatoes? Are we going to have bread tonight? Are we going to live tomorrow?" He is the prophet of my generation.

INTERVIEWER: He is dead?

WIESEL: Yes.

INTERVIEWER: And the prophet of the Gentiles?

WIESEL: The same. Except the problems that I have to face in regard to this boy are not the same as the ones they have to face in regard to him. When I think of him, I feel compassion and love but no remorse. When they think of him, they feel remorse as well. It's not because of me that he was there but because of them.

INTERVIEWER: So we are lost, truly lost.

WIESEL: Unless we accept small measures of victory. There is Israel, for us at least. What no other generation had, we have. We have Israel in spite of all the dangers, the threats and the wars, we have Israel. We can go to Jerusalem. Generations and generations could not and we can. In my time, anyone could beat up a Jew with impunity. We were beaten up twice a year. If a Jew was killed in a pogrom, who cared? Today it's not that easy. Again the paradox. We never had better conditions, not even two thousand years ago in the time of the Temple. At the same time, we have the weight of memories—visions of horror.

INTERVIEWER: What can we do?

WIESEL: My favorite expression, the most Jewish of all Jewish expressions is "and yet, and yet." It's bad, and yet; it's good, and yet. I choose for myself the role of teacher, storyteller, witness, sometimes they overlap. And you hope that the abyss will not grow. You don't try to reduce it; it would be unfair to the dead. But at least you hope that the abyss will not grow larger.

INTERVIEWER: Walking close to the abyss, your dialogues with the dead, what price have you paid for what you once referred to as "messianic experiments"?

WIESEL: I as a person? That is irrelevant. For some of us, survivors, death is a constant measurement. I am trying to look for simplicity, for simple joys and small miracles. I am looking for them but once they are there, I discard them. If you are a survivor, you are in a way invulnerable. At the same time, you are more vulnerable because you are more fragile, more sensitive. Wounds hurt more. That is the price. It is high. There is a paradox: nobody is stronger, nobody is weaker than someone who came back. There is nothing you can do to such a person because whatever you could do is less than what has already been done to him. We have already paid the price.

INTERVIEWER: How do you know you are not going to fall?

WIESEL: You can't know. That is the danger. The rate of suicides among survivors is very high, especially those who wrote. Terrible things happened to these people. For them every moment is a victory. At the same time despair is a temptation. And it is powerful. In French there is a word for it: *le vertige,* dizziness. You are strong and at the same time open to pain. The slightest wound opens a thousand others.

INTERVIEWER: Does walking on the edge give you a vision?

WIESEL: It provides a vision but not a normal vision. You know the truth, but as I said through one of my characters, it's the truth of a madman. What else is there beyond that knowledge?

INTERVIEWER: Ultimate knowledge?

WIESEL: That is why I am seeking mystical experiences. In mysticism there is always a beyond. It's infinite. In philosophy you stop with a wall, not in mysticism. I know, we know, that knowledge is there. When you see the abyss, and we have looked into it, then what? There isn't much room at the edge— one person, another, not many. If you are there, others cannot be there. If you are there, you become a protective wall. What happens? You become part of the abyss. But the word may be misleading. It means many things. Fear. Fear of forgetting. And of remembering. Fear of madness.

INTERVIEWER: You become a wall protecting others from the abyss?

WIESEL: Certainly. Then you become, in the best sense, part of the abyss. You push them away. They don't come too close for the danger is in being immunized. I have some immunity. The madness in me is immunity. It's bad and good. Whatever I could say, the opposite is as true a statement.

INTERVIEWER: Has anyone protected you from the abyss?

WIESEL: In a beautiful way, my son. I can't afford tumbling. If things go badly, I think of my son. Strange, if things go badly or well, I think of two people—my father and my son. Sometimes I see the same gestures in my son. I have protection—my son, my wife, my close friends. I could count them on five fingers.

INTERVIEWER: What about Rav Mordechai Shushani? Where did you and he meet?

WIESEL: We met in Paris and I stayed with him for several years. He was a strange man. A genius who looked like a bum, or a clown. He pushed me to the abyss. But he believed in that. One day I am going to write a monograph about him. His concept was to shock, to shake you up, to push you further and further. If you don't succeed, too bad. But you must risk it. If I had stayed with him longer, I don't know what would have happened.

INTERVIEWER: Did he push anybody over the abyss?

WIESEL: He did. I heard stories later when I began picking up pieces looking for him. He did it with the best of intentions. Few people have had such an influence on my life as he did.

INTERVIEWER: Who were the others?

WIESEL: Here and there a teacher, a friend. But he is probably the strongest. He's the opposite of Professor Saul Lieberman, who is no longer alive, but whom I considered to be the greatest Jewish scholar of his day. One cannot study the Talmud without the help of his commentaries. He was my friend and my teacher. Shushani, on the other hand, was not my friend. Surely he possessed a certain strength and power; so did Professor Lieberman—but his was not frightening.

INTERVIEWER: Where is your quest leading you?

WIESEL: I don't know. I know two things. One, I am going in a concentric circle. That I set out to do. I came from the outside and I am going deeper and deeper. I don't know what I will find there. I know the moment I find the last point, I will stop. Maybe I will never find it. I also know that I haven't begun. It's a strange feeling. I say to myself, you have written this and this and this, and you haven't even begun. That doesn't mean that I deny my work. On the contrary, I stand behind every word I have written. There isn't a book I would not write the same way today. There isn't a story I would disown, not a word. My entire life and entire work are behind every line. At the same time, on the edge you see so much. I haven't even begun to communicate what I have seen.

—JOHN S. FRIEDMAN
Spring 1978

8. Derek Walcott

Derek Walcott was born on the Caribbean island of St. Lucia in 1930. He was educated at St. Mary's College in St. Lucia and at the University of the West Indies in Jamaica. For many years he lived in Trinidad—he still spends most of his summers there—where from 1959 to 1976 he directed the Trinidad Theater Workshop. Since then he has spent much of his time in the United States, living first in New York City and more recently in Boston.

Walcott's first three booklets—*25 Poems* (1948), *Epitaph for the Young* (1949), and *Poems* (1951)—were privately printed in the West Indies. His mature work begins with *In a Green Night: Poems 1948–1960* (1962) and *Selected Poems* (1964). Since then he has published nine books of poetry: *The Castaway* (1965), the book-length autobiographical poem *Another Life* (1973), *Sea Grapes* (1976), *The Star-Apple Kingdom* (1979), *The Fortunate Traveller* (1981), *Midsummer* (1984), *Collected Poems* (1986), and *The Arkansas Testament* (1987).

Considering himself equally a poet and a playwright, Walcott has also published three books of plays in America: *Dream on Monkey Mountain and Other Plays* (1970), *The Joker of Seville and O Babylon* (1978), and *Remembrance and Pantomime: Two Plays* (1980). Currently, he holds a MacArthur Fellowship and teaches in the writing program at Boston University.

Brown , *goose-step*

The camps hold their distance—brown chestnuts and gray smoke
that coils like barbed wire. The profit in guilt continues.
Wild pigeons gurgle, squirrels pile up acorns like little shoes,
and moss, voiceless as smoke, hushes the peeled bodies
like abandoned kindling. In the clear pools, fat
trout rising to lures bubble in umlauts.
Forty years gone, in my island childhood, I felt that
the gift of poetry had made me one of the chosen,
that all experience was kindling to the fire of the Muse.
Now I see her in autumn on that pine bench where she sits,
their nut-brown ideal, in gold plaits and *lederhosen*,
the blood drops of poppies embroidered on her white bodice,
the spirit of autumn to every Hans and Fritz *when*
whose gaze raked the stubble fields where the smoky cries
of rooks were nearly human. They placed their cause in
her cornsilk crown, her cornflower iris,
winnower of chaff for whom the swastikas flash
in skeletal harvests. But had I known then *would*
that the fronds of my island were harrows, its sand the ash
of the distant camps, should I have broken my pen *being*
because this century's pastorals were written
by the chimneys of Dachau, Auschwitz, and Sachsenhausen?
of *of*

*A galley of Derek Walcott's poem "Midsummer XLI," showing revisions by
the author.*

Derek Walcott

I went to visit Derek Walcott on his home island of St. Lucia in mid-June 1985. St. Lucia is one of the four Windward Islands in the eastern Caribbean, a small mountainous island which faces the Atlantic Ocean on one side and the Caribbean Sea on the other. For a week Walcott and I stayed in adjacent bungalows, called "Hunt's Beach Cottages," just a few miles from the harbor city of Castries, where he was born and raised. Outside of our large, mildly ramshackle cottages, a few stone tables and chairs were cemented into a strip of grass; beyond was a row of coconut trees and then, just a few yards away, what Walcott has called "the theater of the sea," the Caribbean. One is always aware of the sea in St. Lucia—an inescapable natural presence which has deeply affected Walcott's sense of being an islander, a New World poet.

To live next door to Walcott, even for a week, is to under-

stand how he has managed to be so productive over the years. *A prodigious worker, he often starts at about 4:30 in the morning and continues until he has done a four- or five-hour stint— by the time most people are getting up for the day. On a small easel next to a small blue portable typewriter, he had recently done a pencil drawing of his wife, Norline, and a couple of new watercolors to serve as storyboards for a film version of* Pantomime *(he is doing the film script); he had also just finished the draft of an original screenplay about a steel band, as well as an extended essay about the Grenada invasion (to be called "Good Old Heart of Darkness"), and a new manuscript of poems,* The Arkansas Testament. *At the time of this interview the cuttings for two more films were all but complete: a film version of his play,* Haitian Earth *(which he had produced in St. Lucia the previous year), and a documentary film about Hart Crane for public television. At times one gets the impression that the poetry for which he is primarily known has had to be squeezed between all his other projects.*

Our conversation took place over three days—beginning in the late afternoon or early evening and continuing until dark. We talked at the table and chairs outside our cottages, where we could hear the wind in the coconut trees and the waves breaking on the shore. A compact man in his mid-fifties, Walcott was still dressed from his afternoon on the beach—barefoot, a pair of brown beach trunks and a thin cotton shirt. Often he kept a striped beach towel draped around his shoulders, a white flour-sack beach hat pushed forward jauntily on his head. He seemed always to be either smoking or about to start.

INTERVIEWER: I'd like to begin by asking you to talk about your family background. In many ways it was atypical for St. Lucia. For example, you were raised as a Methodist on a primarily Catholic island. Your family also seems to have been unusually oriented toward the arts.

WALCOTT: My family background really only consists of my mother. She was a widow. My father died quite young; he must have been thirty-one. Then there was my twin brother and my sister. We had two aunts as well, my father's sisters. But the immediate family consisted of my mother, my brother, my sister, and me. I remember from very early childhood my mother, who was a teacher, reciting a lot around the house. I remember coming across drawings that my father had done, poems that he had written, watercolors that were hanging in our living room—his original watercolors—and a terrific series of books: a lot of Dickens, Scott, quite a lot of poetry. There was also an old Victrola with a lot of classical records. And so my family always had this interest in the arts. Coming from a Methodist minority in a French Catholic island, we also felt a little beleaguered. The Catholicism propounded by the French provincial priests in St. Lucia was a very hidebound, prejudiced, medieval, almost hounding kind of Catholicism. The doctrine that was taught assigned all Protestants to limbo. So we felt defensive about our position. This never came to a head, but we did feel we had to stay close together. It was good for me too, to be able to ask questions as a Protestant, to question large authority. Nobody in my generation at my age would dare question the complete and absolute authority of the church. Even into sixth form, my school friends and I used to have some terrific arguments about religious doctrine. It was a good thing. I think young writers ought to be heretical.

INTERVIEWER: In an essay called "Leaving School" you suggest that the artifacts of your father's twin avocations, poetry and painting, made your own sense of vocation seem inevitable. Would you describe his creative work and how it affected you?

WALCOTT: My mother, who is nearly ninety now, still talks continually about my father. All my life I've been aware of her grief about his absence and her strong pride in his conduct. He was very young when he died of mastoiditis, which is an ear infection. Medicine in St. Lucia in those days was crude or very minimal; I know he had to go to Barbados for operations. I don't remember the death or anything like that, but I always felt his presence because of the paintings that he did. He had a self-portrait in watercolor in an oval frame next to a portrait of my mother, an oil that was very good for an amateur painter. I remember once coming across a backcloth of a very ordinary kind of moonlight scene that he had painted for some number that was going to be done by a group of people who did concerts and recitations and stuff like that. So that was always there. Now that didn't make me a morose, morbid child. Rather, in a sense, it gave me a kind of impetus and a strong sense of continuity. I felt that what had been cut off in him somehow was an extension that I was continuing.

INTERVIEWER: When did you first discover his poems?

WALCOTT: The poems I'm talking about are not a collection. I remember a couple of funny lyrics that were done in a southern American dialect for some show he was probably presenting. They were witty little satirical things. I can't remember any poems of a serious nature. I remember more of his art work. I remember a fine watercolor copy of Millet's "The Gleaners" which we had in the living room. The original is an oil painting and even now I am aware of the delicacy of that copy. He had a delicate sense of watercolor. Later on I discovered that my friend Harold Simmons, who was a professional painter, evidently was encouraged by my father to be a painter. So there's always this continuity in my association with people who knew him and people who were very proud to be his friend. My mother would tell us that, and that's what I felt.

INTERVIEWER: Your book-length autobiographical poem, *Another Life,* makes it clear that two painters were crucial to your development: your mentor Harold Simmons, called Harry in the poem, and your friend Dunstan St. Omer, renamed Gregorias. Would you talk about their importance to you?

WALCOTT: Harry taught us. He had paints, he had music in his studio, and he was evidently a good friend of my father's. When he found out that we liked painting, he invited about four or five of us to come up to his studio and sit out on his veranda. He gave us equipment and told us to draw. Now that may seem very ordinary in a city, in another place, but in a very small, poor country like St. Lucia it was extraordinary. He encouraged us to spend our Saturday afternoons painting; he surrounded us with examples of his own painting. Just to let us be there and to have the ambience of his books, his music, his own supervision, and the stillness and dedication that his life meant in that studio was a terrific example. The influence was not so much technical. Of course, I picked up a few things from him in terms of technique: how to do a good sky, how to water the paper, how to circle it, how to draw properly and concentrate on it, and all of that. But there were other things apart from the drawing. Mostly, it was the model of the man as a professional artist that was the example. After a while, the younger guys dropped out of the drawing thing and Dunstan St. Omer and I were left. We used to go out and paint together. We discovered it at the same time.

INTERVIEWER: Did you have a favorite painter then?

WALCOTT: The painter I really thought I could learn from was Cézanne—some sort of resemblance to oranges and greens and browns of the dry season in St. Lucia. I used to look across from the roof towards Vigie—the barracks were there and I'd see the pale orange roofs and the brickwork and the screen of trees and the cliff and the very flat blue and think a lot of Cézanne. Maybe because of the rigidity of the cubes and the verticals and so on. It's as if he knew the St. Lucian landscape—you could see his painting happening there. There were other painters of course, like Giorgione, but I think it gave me a lot of strength to think of Cézanne when I was painting.

INTERVIEWER: What would you say about the epiphanic experience described in *Another Life,* which seems to have confirmed your destiny as a poet and sealed a bond to your native island?

WALCOTT: There are some things people avoid saying in interviews because they sound pompous or sentimental or too mystical. I have never separated the writing of poetry from prayer. I have grown up believing it is a vocation, a religious vocation. What I described in *Another Life*—about being on the hill and feeling the sort of dissolution that happened—is a frequent experience in a younger writer. I felt this sweetness of melancholy, of a sense of mortality, or rather of immortality, a sense of gratitude both for what you feel is a gift and for the beauty of the earth, the beauty of life around us. When that's forceful in a young writer, it can make you cry. It's just clear tears; it's not grimacing or being contorted, it's just a flow that happens. The body feels it is melting into what it has seen. This continues in the poet. It may be repressed in some way, but I think we continue in all our lives to have that sense of melting, of the "I" not being important. That is the ecstasy. It doesn't happen as much when you get older. There's that wonderful passage in Traherne where he talks about seeing the children as moving jewels until they learn the dirty devices of the world. It's not *that* mystic. Ultimately, it's what Yeats says: "Such a sweetness flows into the breast that we laugh at everything and everything we look upon is blessed." That's always there. It's a benediction, a transference. It's gratitude, really. The more of that a poet keeps, the more genuine his nature. I've always felt that sense of gratitude. I've never felt equal to it in terms of my writing, but I've never felt that I was ever less than that. And so in that particular passage in *Another Life* I was recording a particular moment.

INTERVIEWER: How do you write? In regard to your equation of poetry and prayer, is the writing ritualized in any way?

WALCOTT: I don't know how many writers are willing to confess to their private preparatory rituals before they get down to putting something on paper. But I imagine that all artists and all writers in that moment before they begin their working day or working night have that area between beginning and preparation, and however brief it is, there is something about it votive and humble and in a sense ritualistic. Individual writers have different postures, different stances, even different physical attitudes as they stand or sit over their blank paper, and in a sense, without doing it, they are crossing themselves; I mean, it's like the habit of Catholics going into water: you cross yourself before you go in. Any serious attempt to try to do something worthwhile is ritualistic. I haven't noticed what my own devices are. But I do know that if one thinks a poem is coming on—in spite of the noise of the typewriter, or the traffic outside the window, or whatever—you do make a retreat, a withdrawal into some kind of silence that cuts out everything around you. What you're taking on is really not a renewal of your identity but actually a renewal of your *anonymity*, so that what's in front of you becomes more important than what you are. Equally—and it may be a little pretentious-sounding to say it—sometimes if I feel that I have done good work I do pray, I do say thanks. It isn't often, of course. I don't do it every day. I'm not a monk, but if something does happen I say thanks because I feel that it is really a piece of luck, a kind of fleeting grace that has happened to one. Between the beginning and the ending and the actual composition that goes on, there is a kind of trance that you hope to enter where every aspect of your intellect is functioning simultaneously for the progress of the composition. But there is no way you can induce that trance.

Lately, I find myself getting up earlier, which may be a sign of late middle age. It worries me a bit. I guess this is part of the ritual: I go and make a cup of coffee, put on the kettle, and have a cigarette. By now I'm not too sure if out of habit I'm getting up for the coffee rather than to write. I may be getting up that early to smoke, not really to write.

INTERVIEWER: What time is this?

WALCOTT: It can vary. Sometimes it's as early as half-past three, which is, you know, not too nice. The average time would be about five. It depends on how well I'm sleeping. But that hour, that whole time of day, is wonderful in the Caribbean. I love the cool darkness and the joy and splendor of the sunrise coming up. I guess I would say, especially in the location of where I am, the early dark and the sunrise, and being up with the coffee and with whatever you're working on, is a very ritualistic thing. I'd even go further and say it's a religious thing. It has its instruments and its surroundings. And you can feel your own spirit waking.

INTERVIEWER: Recently, I heard you say that you were deeply formed by Methodism. How?

WALCOTT: In a private way, I think I still have a very simple, straightforward foursquare Methodism in me. I admire the quiet, pragmatic reason that is there in a faith like Methodism, which is a very practical thing of conduct. I'm not talking about a fanatical fundamentalism. I suppose the best word for it is "decency." Decency and understanding are what I've learned from being a Methodist. Always, one was responsible to God for one's inner conduct and not to any immense hierarchy of angels and saints. In a way I think I tried to say that in some earlier poems. There's also a very strong sense of carpentry in Protestantism, in making things simply and in a utilitarian way. At this period of my life and work, I think of myself in a way as a carpenter, as one making frames, simply and well. I'm working a lot in quatrains, or I have been, and I feel that there is something in that that is very ordinary, you know, without any mystique. I'm trying to get rid of the mystique as much as possible. And so I find myself wanting to write very simply cut, very contracted, very speakable, and very challenging quatrains in rhymes. Any other shape seems ornate, an elaboration on that essential cube that really is the poem. So we can then say the craft is as ritualistic as that of a carpenter putting down his plane and measuring his stanzas and setting them squarely. And the frame becomes more important than the carpenter.

INTERVIEWER: *Another Life* suggests that eventually you gave up painting as a vocation and decided to concentrate on poetry. Recently, though, you seem to be at work on your watercolors again. What happened?

WALCOTT: What I tried to say in *Another Life* is that the act of painting is not an intellectual act dictated by reason. It is an act that is swept very physically by the sensuality of the brushstroke. I've always felt that some kind of intellect, some kind of preordering, some kind of criticism of the thing before it is done, has always interfered with my ability to do a painting. I am in fairly continual practice. I think I'm getting adept at watercolor. I'm less mucky. I think I could do a reasonable oil painting. I could probably, if I really set out, be a fairly good painter. I can approach the sensuality. I know how it feels, but for me there is just no completion. I'm content to be a moderately good watercolorist. But I'm not content to be a moderately good poet. That's a very different thing.

INTERVIEWER: Am I correct that you published your first poem, "The Voice of St. Lucia," at the precocious age of fourteen? I've read that the poem stirred up a considerable local controversy.

WALCOTT: I wrote a poem talking about learning about God through nature and not through the church. The poem was Miltonic and posed nature as a way to learn. I sent it to the local papers and it was printed. Of course, to see your work in print for any younger writer is a great kick. And then the paper printed a letter in which a priest replied (in verse!) stating that what I was saying was blasphemous and that the proper place to find God was in church. For a young boy to get that sort of response from a mature older man, a priest who was an Englishman, and to be accused of blasphemy was a shock. What was a more chastising thing was that the response was in verse. The point of course was to show me that he was also capable of writing verse. He did his in couplets and mine was in blank verse. I would imagine if I looked at both now that mine was better.

INTERVIEWER: Most American and English readers think of *In a Green Night* as your first book. Before you published abroad, however, you had already printed three booklets at your own expense in the West Indies. How did you come to publish the first one, *25 Poems?*

WALCOTT: I used to write every day in an exercise book, and when I first wrote I wrote with great originality. I just wrote as hard and as well as I felt. I remember the great elation and release I felt, a sort of hooking on to a thing, when I read Auden, Eliot, and everyone. One day I would write like Spender, another day I would write like Dylan Thomas. When I felt I had enough poems that I liked, I wanted to see them in print. We had no publishing house in St. Lucia or in the Caribbean. There was a Faber collection of books that had come out with poets like Eliot and Auden, and I liked the typeface and how the books looked. I thought, "I want to have a book like that." So I selected a collection of twenty-five of them and thought, "Well, these will look good because they'll look like they came from abroad; they'll look like a published book." I went to my mother and said, "I'd like to publish a book of poems, and I think it's going to cost me two hundred dollars." She was just a seamstress and a schoolteacher, and I remember her being very upset because she wanted to do it. Somehow she got it—a lot of money for a woman to have found on her salary. She gave it to me, and I sent off to Trinidad and had the book printed. When the books came back I would sell them to friends. I made the money back. In terms of seeing a book in print, the only way I could have done it was to publish it myself.

INTERVIEWER: Frank Collymore wrote a very appreciative essay about your early poetry. That must have been a heady experience for a nineteen-year-old. After all, he was the editor of the ground-breaking Caribbean literary magazine, *Bim,* a man that Edward Braithwaite once called "the greatest of West Indian literary godfathers."

WALCOTT: Frank Collymore was an absolute saint. I got to know him through Harry Simmons. I have never met a more benign, gentle, considerate, selfless person. I'll never forget the whole experience of going over to Barbados and meeting him. To be treated at that age by a much older man with such care and love and so on was wonderful. He treated George Lamming the same way. There are people like that, people who love other people, love them for their work and what it is. He was not by any means a patronizing man. He never treated you as if he were a schoolmaster doing you good. I had great fortune when I was young in being treated like that by people, by people much older than I was who treated me, who treated my mind, as if I were equal to them. He was the best example of that.

INTERVIEWER: You once described yourself at nineteen as "an elated, exuberant poet madly in love with English" and said that as a young writer you viewed yourself as legitimately prolonging "the mighty line" of Marlowe and Milton. Will you talk about that sense of yourself?

WALCOTT: I come from a place that likes grandeur; it likes large gestures; it is not inhibited by flourish; it is a rhetorical society; it is a society of physical performance; it is a society of style. The highest achievement of style is rhetoric, as it is in speech and performance. It isn't a modest society. A performer in the Caribbean has to perform with the right flourish. A Calypsonian performer is equivalent to a bullfighter in the ring. He has to come over. He can write the wittiest Calypso, but if he's going to deliver it, he has to deliver it well, and he has to hit the audience with whatever technique he has. Modesty is not possible in performance in the Caribbean, and that's wonderful. It's better to be large and to make huge gestures than to be modest and do tiptoeing types of presentations of oneself. Even if it's a private platform, it is a platform. The voice does go up in a poem. It is an address, even if it is to oneself. And the greatest address is in the rhetoric. I grew up in a place in which if you learned poetry, you shouted it out. Boys would scream it out and perform it and do it and flourish it. If you wanted to approximate that thunder or that power of speech, it couldn't be done by a little modest voice in which you muttered something to someone else. I came out of that society of the huge gesture. And literature is like that, I mean *theatrical* literature is like that, whether it's Greek or whatever. The recitation element in poetry is one I hope I never lose because it's an essential part of the voice being asked to perform. If we have poets we're really asking them, "Okay, tell me a poem." Generally the implication is, "Mutter me a poem." I'm not in that group.

INTERVIEWER: There is a confident, fiery sense of privilege in your early work. In a recent poem, *Midsummer,* you write "Forty years gone, in my island childhood, I felt that / the gift of poetry had made me one of the chosen, / that all experience was kindling to the fire of the Muse."

WALCOTT: I never thought of my gift—I have to say "my gift" because I believe it is a gift—as anything that I did completely on my own. I have felt from my boyhood that I had one function and that was somehow to articulate, not my own experience, but what I saw around me. From the time I was a child I knew it was beautiful. If you go to a peak anywhere in St. Lucia, you feel a simultaneous newness and sense of timelessness at the same time—the presence of where you are. It's a primal thing and it has always been that way. At the same time I knew that the poor people around me were not beautiful in the romantic sense of being colorful people to paint or to write about. I lived, I have seen them and I have seen things that I don't need to go far to see. I felt that that was what I would write about. That's what I felt my job was. It's something that other writers have said in their own way, even if it sounds arrogant. Yeats has said it; Joyce has said it. It's amazing Joyce could say that he wants to write for his race, meaning the Irish. You'd think that Joyce would have a larger, more continental kind of mind, but Joyce continued insisting on his provinciality at the same time he had the most universal mind since Shakespeare. What we can do as poets in terms of our honesty is simply to write within the immediate perimeter of not more than twenty miles really.

INTERVIEWER: How does your sense of discovery of new subject matter integrate with the formal elements in your work?

WALCOTT: One of the things that people have to look at in West Indian literature is this: that what we were deprived of was also our privilege. There was a great joy in making a world which so far, up to then, had been undefined. And yet the imagination wants its limits and delights in its limits. It finds its freedom in the definition of those limits. In a sense, you want to give more symmetry to lives that have been undefined. My generation of West Indian writers has felt such a powerful elation at having the privilege of writing about places and people for the first time and, simultaneously, having behind them the tradition of knowing how well it can be done—by a Defoe, a Dickens, a Richardson. Our world made us yearn for structure, as opposed to wishing to break away from it, because there was no burden, no excess of literature in our heads. It was all new.

INTERVIEWER: Well, then how do you see yourself in terms of the great tradition of poetry in the English language?

WALCOTT: I don't. I am primarily, absolutely a Caribbean writer. The English language is nobody's special property. It is the property of the imagination: it is the property of the language itself. I have never felt inhibited in trying to write as well as the greatest English poets. Now that has led to a lot of provincial criticism: the Caribbean critic may say, "You are trying to be English," and the English critic may say, "Welcome to the club." These are two provincial statements at either end of the spectrum. It's not a matter of trying to be English. I am obviously a Caribbean poet. I yearn for the company of better Caribbean poets, quite frankly. I feel a little lonely. I don't see what I thought might have happened—a stronger energy, a stronger discipline, and a stronger drive in Caribbean poetry. That may be because the Caribbean is more musical: every culture has its particular emphasis and obviously the Caribbean's poetry, talent, and genius is in its music. But then again the modern Caribbean is a very young thing. I consider myself at the beginning, rather than at the end, of a tradition.

INTERVIEWER: Would you say that your relationship to English poetry has changed over the years? As your work has progressed you seem to have increasingly affiliated yourself with a line of New World poets from Whitman through St. John Perse to Aimé Césaire and Pablo Neruda.

WALCOTT: Carlos Fuentes talked in a *Paris Review* interview about the essential Central American experience, which includes the whole basin of the Caribbean—that it is already a place of tremendous fertility. The whole New World experience here is shared by Márquez as it is by Borges, as it is still by American writers. In fact, too many American poets don't take on the scale of America. Not because we should write epics but because it seems to be our place to try to understand. In places that are yet undefined the energy comes with the knowledge that this has not yet been described, this has not yet been painted. This means that I'm standing here like a pioneer. I'm the first person to look at this mountain and try to write about it. I'm the first person to see this lagoon, this piece of land. Here I am with this enormous privilege of just being someone who can take up a brush. My generation of West Indian writers, following after C. L. R. James, all felt the thrill of the absolute sense of discovery. That energy is concomitant with being where we are; it's part of the whole idea of America. And by America, I mean from Alaska right down to Curaçao.

INTERVIEWER: How do you respond to V. S. Naipaul's repeated assertion—borrowed from Trollope—that "Nothing was created in the British West Indies"?

WALCOTT: Perhaps it should read that "Nothing was created *by the British* in the West Indies." Maybe that's the answer. The departure of the British required and still requires a great deal of endeavor, of repairing the psychological damage done by their laziness and by their indifference. The desolation of poverty that exists in the Caribbean can be very depressing. The only way that one can look at it and draw anything of value from it is to have a fantastic depth of strength and belief, not in the past but in the immediate future. And I think that whenever I come back here, however desolate and however despairing I see the conditions around me to be, I know that I have to draw on terrible reserves of conviction. To abandon that conviction is to betray your origins; it's to feel superior to your family, to your past. And I'm not capable of that.

INTERVIEWER: Why is the figure of Robinson Crusoe so important to you?

WALCOTT: There was a time, both in terms of my own life and in terms of the society, when I had an image of the West Indian artist as someone who was in a shipwrecked position. He was someone who would have to build (again) from the concept of being wrecked on these islands. I wrote a poem called "The Castaway." I told my wife I was going to stay by myself for a weekend somewhere down in Trinidad. My wife agreed. I stayed in a beach house by myself and I wrote the poem there. I'm not saying that's the origin of my Crusoe idea. But it's possible. The beaches around here are generally very empty— just you, the sea, and the vegetation around you, and you're very much by yourself. The poems I have written around the Crusoe theme vary. One of the more positive aspects of the

Crusoe idea is that in a sense every race that has come to the Caribbean has been brought here under situations of servitude or rejection, and that is the metaphor of the shipwreck, I think. Then you look around you and you have to make your own tools. Whether that tool is a pen or a hammer, you are building in a situation that's Adamic; you are rebuilding not only from necessity but also with some idea that you will be here for a long time and with a sense of proprietorship as well. Very broadly that is what has interested me in it. There are other ironies, like the position of Friday as the one who is being civilized. Actually, the reverse happens. People who come out to the Caribbean from the cities and the continents go through a process of being recultured. What they encounter here, if they surrender to their seeing, has a lot to teach them, first of all the proven adaptability of races living next to each other, particularly in places like Trinidad and Jamaica. And then also in the erasure of the idea of history. To me there are always images of erasure in the Caribbean—in the surf which continually wipes the sand clean, in the fact that those huge clouds change so quickly. There is a continual sense of motion in the Caribbean—caused by the sea and the feeling that one is almost traveling through water and not stationary. The size of time is larger—a very different thing in the islands than in the cities. We don't live so much by the clock. If you have to be in a place where you create your own time, what you learn, I think, is a patience, a tolerance, how to make an artisan of yourself rather than being an artist.

INTERVIEWER: Your recent play *Pantomime* explores the racial and economic side of the relationship between Crusoe and Friday. In the play, a white English hotel owner in Tobago proposes that he and his black handyman work up a satire on the Crusoe story for the entertainment of the guests. Is the play a parable about colonialism?

WALCOTT: The point of the play is very simple. There are two types. The prototypical Englishman is not supposed to show his grief publicly. He keeps a stiff upper lip. Emotion and passion are supposed to be things that a trueblood Englishman avoids. What the West Indian character does is to try to wear him down into confessing that he is capable of such emotion and there's nothing wrong in showing it. Some sort of catharsis is possible. That is the main point of the play. It's to take two types and put them together, put them in one arena and have that happen. I have never thought of it really as a play about racial conflict. When it's done in America, it becomes a very tense play because of the racial situation there. When it's done here, it doesn't have those deep historical overtones of real bitterness. I meant it to be basically a farce that might instruct. And the instruction is that we can't just contain our grief, that there's purgation in tears, that tears can renew. Of course, inside the play there's a point in which both characters have to confront the fact that one is white and one is black. They have to confront their history. But once that peak is passed, once the ritual of confrontation is over, then that's the beginning of the play. I've had people say they think the ending is corny, but generally that criticism has come when I'm in America. The idea of some reconciliation or some adaptability of being able to live together, that is sometimes rejected by people as being a facile solution. But I believe it's possible.

INTERVIEWER: How would you differentiate your work of the middle and late sixties, *The Castaway* and *The Gulf,* from your previous writing?

WALCOTT: There's a vague period in any poet's life between thirty and forty that is crucial because you can either keep working in one direction, or you can look back on your earlier work as juvenilia, a nice thing to look at from a distance. You have to head toward being forty with a certain kind of mindset to try to recreate chaos so you can learn from it. Yet you also have the fear that your work really has been basically mediocre, a failure, predictable. You find yourself at a point at which you say, ah, so you have become exactly what you were afraid of becoming: this person, this writer, with a certain name and a certain thing expected of you, and you are fulfilling that mold. The later books attempt to work against the given identity. At this point I don't think they're deep enough in terms of their sense of sin. Their sense of guilt could be more profound. In a way a lot of these poems smooth over while seething underneath the surface. One can always put a sort of poster over the rough, you know. A smoothness of attitude over something that's basically quite null and chaotic and unsettling. A lot of the roughness is missing in these books, but then that dissatisfaction continues all one's life.

INTERVIEWER: Would you talk about your experience in the Trinidad Theater Workshop, which you founded in 1959 and finally left in 1976? You once stated that you wanted to create a theater where someone could produce Shakespeare and sing Calypso with equal conviction. Did the idea succeed?

WALCOTT: Yes, I think I made that happen. The best West Indian actors are phenomenal. Most West Indian actors have gone to West Indian secondary schools. The classical training and reading they get there is pretty wide and impressive—a lot of Shakespeare, and all the great English writers. Once that happens people read much more widely than if they hadn't done the great poets. So most West Indian actors have a familiarity with the classic theater of the English language. They also have an accent, not an affected accent, but a speech that is good diction. Some of the finest Shakespeare I have ever heard was spoken by West Indian actors. The sound of Shakespeare is certainly not the sound we now hear in Shakespeare, that androgynous BBC-type, high-tone thing. It's a coarse thing—a great range between a wonderful vulgarity and a great refinement, and we have that here. We have that vulgarity and we also have that refinement in terms of the diction. The West Indian actor has a great rhetorical interest in language. In addition to that, the actor is like the West Indian writer in that he is a new person: what he is articulating has just begun to be defined. There's a sense of pioneering. For me writing plays was even more exciting than working on poems because it was a communal effort, people getting together and trying to find things. When I won a fellowship to go to America in 1958, I wanted to have, much as the Actors Studio did, a place where West Indian actors, without belonging to any company, could just come together and try and find out simple things such as how to talk like ourselves without being affected or without being incoherent, how to treat dialect as respectfully as if we were doing Shakespeare or Chekhov, and what was our own inner psychology as individuals, in a people, as part of a people. The first couple of years we had a very tough time. Very few people would come. We didn't know what we were doing; we just improvised and explored and tried things. I was determined not to do a production until I thought we had some kind of ensemble. I had no intention of forming a company. At that time, all I wanted to do was to have the actors come and begin to work together. It took a very long time. But eventually we did put on a play and for about seventeen years I had a terrific company. It also began to involve dancers and some great actors. I remember Terry Hands came once (he is now one of the associate directors of the Royal Shakespeare Company) for a performance of *The Joker of Seville* that Margaret, my then wife, suggested we do. We had this little arena, like a bullfight ring, or a cockfight ring, and we served sandwiches and coffee and oranges and so on, and the crowd by that time had begun to know the songs and they were singing along with the actors. Terry said to me, "Derek, you're doing what Brecht tried to do." Well, I felt terrific because I knew what he meant. Brecht's idea of the participation of the audience, the whole idea of the boxing ring as a stage or the stage as an arena, had happened. But after several years of falling out and fighting and coming back together, eventually, for all sorts of reasons, the thing wore down. Although I still use actors from the company singly, I no longer run the company. But seventeen years is a long time to run a theater company.

INTERVIEWER: You've written that you first began writing drama "in the faith that one was creating not merely a play, but a theater, and not merely a theater, but its environment." But by the time you came to write the prologue to *Dream on Monkey Mountain* in 1970, the feeling of pride was replaced mainly by exhaustion and the sense of innocence seems to have given way to despair. What happened?

WALCOTT: Well, right now I'm writing a play called *A Branch of the Blue Nile*—about actors, a small company of actors and how they fall apart. I don't know up to now—and I'll have to decide pretty quickly—if it's going to end badly. The epiphany of the whole thing, the end of it, is a question that remains.

INTERVIEWER: Is the problem at all related to questions of whether the state should support the arts?

WALCOTT: I'm fifty-five now and all my life I've tried to fight and write and jeer and encourage the idea that the state owes its artists a lot. When I was young it looked like a romance; now that I'm older and I pay taxes, it is a fact. But not only do I want roads, I want pleasure, I want art. This is the terrible thing in the Caribbean. The middle class in the Caribbean is a venal, self-centered, indifferent, self-satisfied, smug society. It enjoys its philistinism. It pays very short lip service to its own writers and artists. This is a reality every artist knows. The point is whether you say that and then turn your back on it and say to hell with it for life. I haven't done that and I don't think I'm capable of doing it. What's wrong is this: a legacy has been left by the British empire of amateurism. What we still have as an inheritance is that art is an amateur occupation. That attitude is combined with some of the worst aspects of bour-geois mercantilism, whether it is French, Danish, British, or Spanish bourgeois. The whole of the Caribbean that I can think of has this stubborn, clog-headed indifference to things around them. The philanthropy that exists in the Caribbean is negligible. Money is here—you just have to see the houses and the cars, and to look at the scale of living in any one of these islands—but nobody gives anything. If they do, I don't know what they give to, but that penny-pinching thing is typical of the petty-bourgeois merchant, the hoarder of money. Without any bitterness I can say that anything that I have gotten, whether earned or not, has been from America and not from the Caribbean.

INTERVIEWER: What constitutes an artistic generation in the Caribbean?

WALCOTT: An artistic generation in this part of the world is about five years. Five years of endurance. After that, I think people give up. I see five years of humanity and boredom and futility. I keep looking at younger writers, and I begin to see the same kind of despair forming and the same wish to say the hell with it, I'm getting out of here. There's also a problem with government support. We have come to a kind of mechanistic thinking that says, a government concerns itself with housing, food, and whatever. There will always be priorities in terms of sewage and electricity. If only a government could form the idea that any sensible human being wants not only to have running water, but a book in hand and a picture on the wall. That is the kind of government I had envisaged in the Caribbean when I was eighteen or nineteen. At fifty-five, I have only seen an increase in venality, an increase in selfishness, and worse than that, a shallow kind of service paid to the arts. I'm very bitter about the philistinism of the Caribbean. It is tough to see a people who have only one strength and that is their culture. Trinidad is perhaps the most concentrated example of a culture that has produced so many thousands and thousands of artisans at Carnival. Now Carnival is supported by the government, but that's a seasonal kind of thinking. I'm talking about something more endemic, more rooted, more organic to the idea of the Caribbean. Because we have been colonies, we have inherited everything and the very thing we used to think was imperial has been repeated by our own stubbornness, stupidity, and blindness.

INTERVIEWER: Your prologue to *Dream on Monkey Mountain* also blasts the crass, state-sponsored commercialization of folk culture. One of your subjects in both poetry and essays has been how negatively tourism has affected the West Indies. Would you discuss that?

WALCOTT: Once I saw tourism as a terrible danger to a culture. Now I don't, maybe because I come down here so often that perhaps literally I'm a tourist *myself* coming from America. But a culture is only in danger if it allows itself to be. Everybody has a right to come down in the winter and enjoy the sun. Nobody has a right to abuse anybody, and so I don't think that if I'm an American anybody should tell me, please don't come here because this beach is ours, or whatever. During the period I'm talking about, certainly, servility was a part of the whole deal—the waiters had to smile, and we had to do this and so forth. In tourism, it was just an extension really of master/servant. I don't think it's so anymore. Here we have a generation that has strengthened itself beyond that. As a matter of fact, it can go beyond a balance and there's sullenness and a hostility toward people who are your guests. It can swing too far as well. But again, it's not enough to put on steel bands and to have people in the hotels entertaining and maybe to have a little show somewhere to keep them what they think is light-minded and happy and indifferent and so on. If that's the opinion that the government or culture has of itself, then it deserves to be insulted. But if it were doing something more rooted in terms of the arts, in terms of its writers, its painters, and its performers, and if there were more pride in that and not the kind of thing you see of guys walking around town totally bored and hoping that something can happen. . . . I'm not one to say that you can't do things for yourself because certainly having spent all my life in the Caribbean theater and certainly seventeen very exacting years in the workshop, I do say, yes—get up and do it yourself and stop depending on the government. But there is a point where you have to turn to the state and say, "Look man, this is ridiculous. I pay my taxes. I'm a citizen. I don't have a museum. I don't have a good library. I don't have a place where I can perform. I don't have a place where I can dance." That's criminal. It's a carryover of the same thing I said about the West Indies being seized and atrophied by a petty-bourgeois mentality from the metropolis that has been adopted by the Creole idea of life, which is simply to have a damn good time and that's it, basically. I mean that's the worst aspect of West Indian life: have a good time, period.

INTERVIEWER: What do you have against folklorists and anthropologists? Some people think of them as an intellectually respectable lot.

WALCOTT: I don't trust them. They either embarrass or elevate too much. They can do a good service if they are reticent and keep out of the way. But when they begin to tell people who they are and what they are, they are terrifying. I've gone to seminars in which people in the audience who are the people the folklorists are talking about, are totally baffled by their theories.

INTERVIEWER: One of your most well-known early poems, "A Far Cry from Africa," ends with the question, "How can I turn from Africa and live?" However, by 1970 you could write that "The African revival is escape to another dignity," and that "Once we have lost our wish to be white, we develop a longing to become black, and those two may be different, but are still careers." You also assert that the claim to be African is not an inheritance but a bequest, "a bill for the condition of our arrival as slaves." These are controversial statements. What is your current sense of the West Indian writer's relationship to Africa?

WALCOTT: There is a duty in every son to become his own man. The son severs himself from the father. The Caribbean very often refuses to cut that umbilical cord to confront its own stature. So a lot of people exploit an idea of Africa out of both the wrong kind of pride and the wrong kind of heroic idealism. At great cost and a lot of criticism, what I used to try to point out was that there is a great danger in historical sentimentality. We are most prone to this because of suffering, of slavery. There's a sense of skipping the part about slavery, and going straight back to a kind of Eden-like grandeur, hunting lions, that sort of thing. Whereas what I'm saying is to take in the fact of slavery, if you're capable of it, without bitterness, because bitterness is going to lead to the fatality of thinking in terms of revenge. A lot of the apathy in the Caribbean is based on this historical sullenness. It is based on the feeling of "Look what you did to me." Well, "Look what you did to me," is juvenile, right? And also, "Look what I'm going to do to you," is wrong. Think about illegitimacy in the Caribbean! Few people can claim to find their ancestry in the linear way. The whole situation in the Caribbean is an illegitimate situation. If we admit that from the beginning that there is no shame in that historical bastardy, then we can be men. But if we continue to sulk and say, "Look at what the slave-owner did," and so forth, we will never mature. While we sit moping or writing morose poems and novels that glorify a nonexistent past, then time passes us by. We continue in one mood, which is in too much of Caribbean writing: that sort of chafing and rubbing of an old sore. It is not because one wishes to forget; on the contrary, you accept it as much as anybody accepts a wound as being a part of his body. But this doesn't mean that you nurse it all your life.

INTERVIEWER: *The Fortunate Traveller* is filled with poems set in a wide variety of places. The title poem itself elaborates the crisis of a fortunate traveller who goes from one underdeveloped country to another. And in "North and South" you write that "I accept my function / as a colonial upstart at the end of an empire, / a single, circling, homeless satellite." Has the Castaway given way to the Traveller? Do you still feel the old tugs between home and abroad?

WALCOTT: I've never felt that I belong anywhere else but in St. Lucia. The geographical and spiritual fixity is there. However, there's a reality here as well. This afternoon I asked myself if I would stay here for the rest of my life if I had the chance of leaving. The answer really is, I suppose, no. I don't know if I'm distressed by that. One is bound to feel the difference between these poor, dark, very small houses, the people in the streets, and yourself because you always have the chance of taking a plane out. Basically you are a fortunate traveller, a visitor; your luck is that you can always leave. And it's hard to imagine that there are people around you unable, incapable of leaving either because of money or because of any number of ties. And yet the more I come back here the less I feel that I'm a prodigal or a castaway returning. And it may be that as it deepens with age, you get more locked into what your life is and where you've come from and what you misunderstand and what you should have understood and what you're trying to reunderstand and so on. I'll continue to come back to see if what I write is not beyond the true experience of the person next to me on the bus—not in terms of talking down to that person, but of sharing that person's pain and strength necessary in those pathetically cruel circumstances in which people have found themselves following the devastations of colonialism.

INTERVIEWER: What led you to assert, as you do in *Midsummer,* that "to curse your birthplace is the final evil"?

WALCOTT: I think it is. I think the earth that you come from is your mother and if you turn around and curse it, you've cursed your mother.

INTERVIEWER: You've written a number of poems about New York City, Boston, old New England, and the southern United States. I'm thinking in particular of the first section of

The Fortunate Traveller where one of the poems is entitled "American Muse" and another asserts "I'm falling in love with America." What are your feelings about living in the United States? Do you think you've been Americanized in any way?

WALCOTT: If so, voluntarily. I don't think I've been brainwashed. I don't think I have been seduced by all the prizes and rewards. America has been extremely generous to me—not in a strictly philanthropical sense; I've earned that generosity. But it has given me a lot of help. The real thing that counts is whether that line is true about falling in love with America. That came about because I was traveling on a bus from one place to another, on a long ride looking at the American landscape. If you fall in love with the landscape of a place the next thing that comes is the people, right? The average American is not like the average Roman or British citizen. The average American doesn't think that the world belongs to him or her; Americans don't have imperialist designs in their heads. I find a gentleness and a courtesy in them. And they have ideals. I've traveled widely across America and I see things in America that I still believe in, that I like a lot.

INTERVIEWER: What are your feelings about Boston, which you have called the "city of my exile"?

WALCOTT: I've always told myself that I've got to stop using the word "exile." Real exile means a complete loss of the home. Joseph Brodsky is an exile; I'm not really an exile. I have access to my home. Given enough stress and longing I can always get enough money to get back home and refresh myself with the sea, the sky, whatever. I was very hostile about Boston in the beginning, perhaps because I love New York. In jokes, I've always said that Boston should be the capital of Canada. But it's a city that grows on you gradually. And where I live is very comfortable. It's close to the university. I work well there, and I very much enjoy teaching. I don't think of myself as having two homes; I have one home, but two places.

INTERVIEWER: Robert Lowell had a powerful influence on

you. I'm thinking of your memorial poem "RTSL" as well as the poem in *Midsummer* where you assert that "Cal's bulk haunts my classes." Would you discuss your relationship to Lowell?

WALCOTT: Lowell and Elizabeth Hardwick were on a tour going to Brazil and they stopped off in Trinidad. I remember meeting them at Queen's Park Hotel and being so flustered that I called Elizabeth Hardwick, Edna St. Vincent Millay. She said, "I'm not that old yet." I was just flabbergasted. And then we became very friendly. My wife Margaret and I took them up to the beach. Their daughter, Harriet, was there. I remember being up at this beach house with Lowell. His daughter and his wife, I think, must have gone to bed. We had gas lanterns. *Imitations* had just come out and I remember that he showed me his imitations of Hugo and Rilke and asked me what I thought about them. I asked him if two of the stanzas were from Rilke, and he said, "No, these are mine." It was a very flattering and warm feeling to have this fine man with this great reputation really asking me what I thought. He did that with a lot of people, very honestly, humbly, and directly. I cherish that memory a lot. When we went back to New York, Cal and Lizzie had a big party for us with a lot of people there, and we became very close. Cal was a big man in bulk but an extremely gentle, poignant person, and very funny. I don't think any of the biographies have caught the sort of gentle, amused, benign beauty of him when he was calm. He kept a picture of Peter, my son, and Harriet for a long time in his wallet, and he'd take it out and show it to me. He was sweetly impulsive. Once I went to visit him and he said, "Let's call up Allen Ginsberg and ask him to come over." That's so cherishable that it's a very hard thing for me to think of him as not being around. In a way, I can't separate my affection for Lowell from his influence on me. I think of his character and gentleness, the immediacy that was part of knowing him. I loved his openness to receive influences. He was not a poet who said,

"I'm an American poet, I'm going to be peculiar, and I'm going to have my own voice which is going to be different from anybody's voice." He was a poet who said, "I'm going to take in everything." He had a kind of multifaceted imagination; he was not embarrassed to admit that he was influenced even in his middle age by William Carlos Williams, or by François Villon, or by Boris Pasternak, all at the same time. That was wonderful.

INTERVIEWER: What about specific poetic influence?

WALCOTT: One of the things he said to me was, "You must put more of yourself in your poems." Also he suggested that I drop the capital letters at the top of the line, use the lower-case. I did it and felt very refreshed; it made me relax. It was a simple suggestion, but it's one of those things that a great poet can tell you that can be phenomenal—a little opening. The influence of Lowell on everyone, I think, is in his brutal honesty, his trying to get into the poetry a fictional power that wasn't there before, as if your life was a section of a novel—not because you are the hero, but because some of the things that were not in poems, some of the very ordinary banal details, can be illumined. Lowell emphasized the banality. In a sense to keep the banality banal and still make it poetic is a great achievement. I think that's one of the greatest things that he did in terms of his directness, his confrontation of ordinariness.

INTERVIEWER: Would you tell the story of your first poetry reading in the States? It must have been rewarding to hear Lowell's extravagant introduction.

WALCOTT: Well, I didn't know what he said because I was in back of the curtain, I think it was at the Guggenheim. I was staying at the Chelsea Hotel, and that day I felt I needed a haircut, so, foolishly, I went around the corner and sat down. The barber took the electric razor and gave me one of the wildest haircuts I think I've ever had. It infuriated me, but you can't put your hair back on. I even thought of wearing a hat. But I went on anyway, my head looked like hell. I had gotten some distance into the reading—I was reading "A Far Cry from Africa"—when suddenly there was the sound of applause from the auditorium. Now I had never heard applause at a poetry reading before. I don't think I'd ever given a formal poetry reading, and I thought for some reason that the applause was saying it was time to stop, that they thought it was over. So I walked off the stage. I felt in a state of shock. I actually walked off feeling the clapping was their way of saying, "Well, thank you, it's been nice." Someone in charge asked me to go back and finish the reading, but I said no. I must have sounded extremely arrogant, but I felt that if I went back out there it would have been conceited. I went back to Trinidad. Since I hadn't heard Lowell's introduction, I asked someone for it at the Federal Building, which had archives of radio tapes from the Voice of America. I said I would like to hear the Lowell tape, and the guy said, "I think we erased that." It was only years later that I really heard what Cal said, and it was very flattering.

INTERVIEWER: How did you become friends with Joseph Brodsky?

WALCOTT: Well, ironically enough, I met Brodsky at Lowell's funeral. Roger Straus, Susan Sontag, and I went up to Boston for the funeral. We waited somewhere for Joseph, probably at the airport, but for some reason he was delayed. At the service I was in this pew when a man sat down next to me. I didn't know him. When I stood up as the service was being said, I looked at him and I thought, if this man is not going to cry then *I'm* not going to cry, either. I kept stealing glances at him to see if anything was happening, but he was very stern looking. That helped me to contain my own tears. Of course it was Brodsky. Later, we met. We went to Elizabeth Bishop's house, and I got to know him a little better. The affection that developed after that was very quick and, I think, permanent—to be specific about it is hard. I admire Joseph for his industry, his valor, and his intelligence. He's a terrific example of someone who is a complete poet, who doesn't treat poetry as anything else but a very hard job that he does as well as he can. Lowell worked very hard too, but you feel in Joseph that that is all he lives for. In a sense that's all any of us lives for or can hope to live for. Joseph's industry is an example that I cherish a great deal.

INTERVIEWER: When did you first become friends with Seamus Heaney?

WALCOTT: There was a review by A. Alvarez of Seamus's book, a very upsetting review—to put it mildly—in which he was describing Heaney as a sort of blue-eyed boy. English literature always has a sort of blue-eyed boy. I got very angry over the review and sent Seamus a note via my editor with a little obscenity in it. Just for some encouragement. Later, in New York we had a drink at someone's house. From then on, the friendship has developed. I see him a lot when he is in Boston at Harvard. I just feel very lucky to have friends like Joseph and Seamus. The three of us are outside of the American experience. Seamus is Irish, Joseph is Russian, I'm West Indian. We don't get embroiled in the controversies about who's a soft poet, who's a hard poet, who's a free verse poet, who's not a poet, and all of that. It's good to be on the rim of that quarreling. We're on the perimeter of the American literary scene. We can float out here happily not really committed to any kind of particular school or body of enthusiasm or criticism.

INTERVIEWER: Over the years your style seems to have gotten increasingly plainer and more direct, less gnarled, more casual, somehow both quieter and fiercer at the same time. Is that an accurate assessment of the poetic style of your middle age? I can't imagine a book like *Midsummer* from the young Derek Walcott.

WALCOTT: It varies, of course. When I finished *Another Life*, I felt like writing short poems, more essential, to the point, things that were contracted. They didn't have the scale of the large book and so on. It goes in that kind of swing, in that kind of pendulum. In the case of *Midsummer,* I felt that for the time being I didn't want to write any more poems, although that sounds arrogant. I just felt perhaps I was overworking myself. I was going to concentrate purely on trying to develop my painting. While painting, I would find lines coming into my head. I would almost self-destruct them; I'd say, all right, I'll put them down . . . but with antipoetic vehemence. If they don't work, then I'll just forget it. What kept happening is that the lines would come anyway, perhaps out of that very irritation, and then I would make a very arbitrary collage of them and find they would take some sort of loose shape. Inevitably, of course, you try to join the seams. I was trying to do something, I think, that was against the imagination, that was not dictated in a sort of linear, lyrical, smooth, melodic—but rather something that was antimelodic. For a poem, if you give a poem personality, that's the most exciting thing—to feel that it is becoming antimelodic. The vocabulary becomes even more challenging, the meter more interesting, and so on. So what happened was that by the very wish not to write, or to write a poem that was against the idea of writing poems, it all became more fertile and more contradictory and more complex. Gradually a book began to emerge. Inevitably you can't leave things lying around with unjoined shapes, little fragments and so on. I began to weld everything together—to keep everything that I felt worthwhile. I thought, well, whether this is just an ordinary thing or not, it has as much a right to be considered as something a little more grandiose. That's what I think happened in *Midsummer.*

INTERVIEWER: How do you feel about publishing your *Collected Poems*?

WALCOTT: You're aware of the fact that you have reached a certain stage in your life. You're also aware that you have failed your imagination to some degree, your ambitions. This is an amazingly difficult time for me. I'm absolutely terrified. It's not because I have a kind of J. D. Salinger thing about running away from publicity. It's really not wanting to see myself reflected in that way. I don't think that that's what the boy I knew—the boy who started to write poetry—wanted at all, not praise, not publicity. But it's troubling. I remember Dylan Thomas saying somewhere that he liked it better when he was not famous. All I can say is this: I do have another book about ready, and I hope it will be a compensation for all the deficiencies in the *Collected Poems,* something that will redeem the *Collected Poems.*

—EDWARD HIRSCH
June 1985

9. E. L. Doctorow

E. L. Doctorow was born in New York City in 1931 and grew up in the Bronx. At Kenyon College (from which he graduated in 1952) he studied under the poet and critic John Crowe Ransom. He attended graduate school at Columbia University for a year, where he met his wife, Helen, and afterward spent two years in the U.S. Army in Germany (1953–55). Before his literary career started, he worked as a reservations clerk at LaGuardia Airport, and then as a reader for a motion-picture company.

His first two novels were *Welcome to Hard Times* (1960) and *Big as Life* (1966)—the first a western, the second a science fiction, both engendered from Doctorow's desire, at that stage, to write seriously in "disreputable genres." During this time he took an editorial position at the New American Library (1959–64), moving from associate to senior editor. In 1964 he became editor-in-chief of the Dial Press, going on to become its publisher. Among his charges during his editorial years were James Baldwin, Thomas Berger, Vance Bourjaily, William Kennedy, and Norman Mailer.

With *The Book of Daniel*, published in 1971, Doctorow gave up his publishing career and devoted himself entirely to writing books, all of which have either been nominated for, or won, the most prestigious literary awards offered in this country. He is the author of *Ragtime* (1975), *Loon Lake* (1980), *Lives of the Poets* (1984), and his most recent novel, *World's Fair*, which won the 1986 American Book Award for fiction. He has written a play, *Drinks Before Dinner*, which was produced in 1978 by Joseph Papp. Doctorow lives with his wife in New Rochelle and Sag Harbor, New York. They have three children.

fourteen lane highways, real little cars moving on them at different
speeds, the center lanes for the higer speeds, the lanes on the edge for
the lower; and this was all regulated by radio controls, the drivers
didnt even do the driving!   Higways and HOrizons, was the name of
this ~~maxingxfarxmay~~ and it showed how everything could be planned,
people lived in these modern streamlined buildings, each of them
accomodating the populationof a small town and holding all the things
~~schools~~ and they wouldnt have even to go out of the
might need , just as if 174th Street and all the neighborhood around
was packed into one giant building. And we passed bridges and streams,
and electrified farms and airports which brought up airliners on
elevators from underground hangars. And there werefactories with
lights and smoke, and lakes and forests and mountains, and it was all
real, which is to say bult to scale, the forests had real tiny
trees, and the water in the lakes was real, and around it all we went,
at different levels, seeing everything in more and more detail, and
thousands of tiny cars zipping right along on their tracks as if
carrying their small beings about their business. And out in the
coutry side were these tiny houses with people sitting in them and
reading the paper and listening to the radio. In the cities of the
future, pedestrian streets connected the buildings and the highways wer
sunken on tracks below them, no one would get run over in a futuristic
world like this, everything made sense, people didnt have to travel
except to see the ~~parklands, the wilderness areas~~, everything else,
their schools, beir jobs were right where they lived. I was very impressed:
All the small moving parts, all the lights and shadows, the animation
of ~~zzhiszexbibiz~~, as if u was looking at the largest most complicated
toy every made. And there was music ~~~~ the announcer who told
us about all these wonderful things, these raindrop cars, these
airconditioned cities. This is what really thrilled me; my delight in
small things, bginging the world ~~~~ ~~~~ be confirmed in your own secret feeling
of ~~~~

Ah what a day this was. We ran out when the show was over and
were ready to stand on lne to see it all over ggain. Norma laughed and
understanding what about it had so fascinated us, its tinyness, took
us to the consolidated Edison exhibit, which ~~gave us the same feelings~~
because it was a diaorama of the entire city of New York, showing the
life in the city from morning till night, the great stone skyscrapers,
th ers and busses in the street,s the subways and elevated trains, all
of it working, all of it spraking with life, and when afternoon came,
there was even a thunderstorm, and all the lights of the ~~city~~ came up
to deal with the darkness.

Everywhere atheWworld' Fair the world was reduced to manageable size
by the cunning and ingenuity of is builders and engineers. But anything
that distorted the scale of things delighted me. In the Public Health
building there was an exhibit showing the functions of different parts
f the body, each of them portrayed in an enormous model. An enormous
ear, or nose, with their canais and valves and bone marrow, big pink
plastic things, bigger than I was. ~~And then an enormous man in~~ his
enitrety, made of plexiglass I suppose, with all his giant
organs visible, but is visible a mistake in
rperesnetation whichx about which I said nothing to Betsy and Norma,
but thinking it was not polite. And everywhere outside were enormous
statues of naked men and women in various poses, wrestling dogs,
or swimming with dolphins or ~~~~
carrying farm tools. All these statues were made of stone, and you could
see the muscles in their legs, or arms, and the ribs and spinal columns,
you you count the bones, the stood or lay about in pools or atop
pylons or rose up from shrubbery. Some of them were pressed into the
sides of buildings, so only the front halves of them showed, sculputres
of concrete pressed in like sandmolds. I was made lightheaded by the

A manuscript page from E. L. Doctorow's novel World's Fair.

E. L. Doctorow

*This interview on the craft of writing with E. L. Doctorow is one
of the first in this series conducted in public—which it was,
under the auspices of The Poetry Center, in the main auditorium of New York City's famed cultural spa, the 92nd Street
YMHA. An audience of about five hundred was on hand. After
a short introduction Doctorow and his interviewer came out and
sat facing each other in two chairs at center stage. The audience
was invited to ask questions at the end of the formal interview.
Actually, the first question from the floor suggested that the
public forum might not be the best place for such an interview.
A befuddled lady in the fifth row asked, "What made you write
about the firestorm in Dresden?" With the patience of one who
has taught at a number of institutions (Sarah Lawrence, Princeton, Yale Drama School, and New York University, among
others), Doctorow informed his questioner politely that she*

probably had Kurt Vonnegut's Slaughterhouse-Five *in mind, and that the Dresden firestorm had been done "so beautifully" there was little reason for anyone else to try. After the flurry caused by this exchange had died down, the questions from the audience were more germane. They are included with their answers at the end of this interview.*

At first meeting, Doctorow gives the impression of being somewhat retiring in manner. Yet, though his voice is soft, it is distinctive and demands attention. His expression is perhaps quizzical (described by The New York Times *as "elfin"), yet it is instantly apparent that a great deal of thought has been put into what he is about to say. The fact that a large audience was listening during the interview seemed not to discomfit him in the slightest.*

INTERVIEWER: You once told me that the most difficult thing for a writer to write was a simple household note to someone coming to collect the laundry, or instructions to a cook.

DOCTOROW: What I was thinking of was a note I had to write to the teacher when one of my children missed a day of school. It was my daughter, Caroline, who was then in the second or third grade. I was having my breakfast one morning when she appeared with her lunch box, her rain slicker, and everything, and she said, "I need an absence note for the teacher and the bus is coming in a few minutes." She gave me a pad and a pencil; even as a child she was very thoughtful. So I wrote down the date and I started, "Dear Mrs. So and So, my daughter Caroline . . . " and then I thought, No, that's not right, obviously it's my daughter Caroline. I tore that sheet off, and started again. "Yesterday, my child . . . " No, that wasn't right either. Too much like a deposition. This went on until I heard a horn blowing outside. The child was in a state of panic. There was a pile of crumpled pages on the floor, and my wife was saying, "I can't believe this. I can't believe this." She took the pad and pencil and dashed something off. I had been trying to write the perfect absence note. It was a very illuminating experience. Writing is immensely difficult. The short forms especially.

INTERVIEWER: How much tinkering do you actually do when you get down to nonhousehold work—a novel, say?

DOCTOROW: I don't think anything I've written has been done in under six or eight drafts. Usually it takes me a few years to write a book. *World's Fair* was an exception. It seemed to be a particularly fluent book as it came. I did it in seven months. I think what happened in that case is that God gave me a bonus book.

INTERVIEWER: Did you feel as though He were speaking to you as you wrote things down?

DOCTOROW: No, no. I imagine He just decided, Well, this one's been paying his dues, so let's give him a bonus book. But Faulkner wrote *As I Lay Dying* in six weeks. Stendhal wrote *Charterhouse of Parma* in twelve days. That's proof God spoke to them—if proof is needed. Twelve days! If it wasn't God it was crass exhibitionism.

INTERVIEWER: In *World's Fair* you make a very interesting shift—writing from the points of view of Rose and Donald and Aunt Frances and then the protagonist. So you have several voices, really. Is it difficult to shift from one to the other?

DOCTOROW: In the past few years I've been interested in the work of the so-called oral historians. The statements people make about their own lives to oral historians have a certain form which I think I have figured out. Now the basic convention of *World's Fair* is that it is memoir. That is what it pretends to be in the voice of the protagonist. My idea was to lend that voice verisimilitude by dropping in some oral-historic statements by other members of the family. I composed these to read as if they were spoken into a tape recorder. You always try to find ways to break down the distinction between fiction and actuality. Another advantage of those voiced intrusions is to provide a kind of beat or a caesura in the ongoing narrative. I thought that was a good thing to do.

INTERVIEWER: So there is an ongoing change and shift in the forms of voice.

DOCTOROW: To me the more interesting change has to do with the voice of the major narrator, the protagonist, Edgar, who as he recalls more and more of his childhood, as he passes from infancy to youth, takes on the voice of an articulate child. The diction changes, the tone changes, as if Edgar is gradually possessed by his memory. So there's a kind of two-voiced effect, I think, the man recalling, but in the boy's higher pitch. I really like that. I didn't know I was going to do that.

INTERVIEWER: You didn't? Well, how calculated is all this?

DOCTOROW: Do you mind if I loosen my tie?

INTERVIEWER: Allowable.

DOCTOROW: It's not calculated at all. It never has been. One of the things I had to learn as a writer was to trust the act of writing. To put myself in the position of writing to find out what I was writing. I did that with *World's Fair,* as with all of them. The inventions of the book come as discoveries. At a certain point, of course, you figure out what your premises are and what you're doing. But certainly, with the beginnings of the work, you really don't know what's going to happen.

INTERVIEWER: What comes first? Is it a character? You say a premise. What does that mean? Is it a theme?

DOCTOROW: Well, it can be anything. It can be a voice, an image; it can be a deep moment of personal desperation. For instance, with *Ragtime* I was so desperate to write something, I was facing the wall of my study in my house in New Rochelle and so I started to write about the wall. That's the kind of day we sometimes have, as writers. Then I wrote about the house that was attached to the wall. It was built in 1906, you see, so I thought about the era and what Broadview Avenue looked like then: trolley cars ran along the avenue down at the bottom of the hill; people wore white clothes in the summer to stay cool. Teddy Roosevelt was President. One thing led to another and that's the way that book began, through desperation to those few images. With *Loon Lake,* in contrast, it was just a very strong sense of place, a heightened emotion when I found myself in the Adirondacks after many, many years of being away . . . and all this came to a point when I saw a sign, a road sign: Loon Lake. So it can be anything.

INTERVIEWER: Do you have any idea how a project is going to end?

DOCTOROW: Not at that point, no. It's not a terribly rational way to work. It's hard to explain. I have found one explanation that seems to satisfy people. I tell them it's like driving a car at night. You never see further than your headlights, but you can make the whole trip that way.

INTERVIEWER: How many times do you come to a dead end?

DOCTOROW: Well if it's a dead end, there's no book. That happens too. You start again. But if you're truly underway you may wander into culverts, through fences into fields, and so on. When you're off the road you don't always know it immediately. If you feel a bump on page one hundred, it may be you went off on page fifty. So you have to trace your way back, you see. It sounds like a hazardous way of working—and it is—but there is one terrific advantage to it: each book tends to have its own identity rather than the author's. It speaks from itself rather than you. Each book is unlike the others because you are not bringing the same voice to every book. I think that keeps you alive as a writer. I've just read the latest Ernest Hemingway publication, *The Garden of Eden*—it's actually a fragment of a work he never completed—and in this as in the others he spoke with the Hemingway voice. He applied the same strategies to every book, strategies as it happens that he came upon and invented quite early on in his career. They were his triumph in the early days. But by the last decade or two of his working life they trapped him, restricted him, and defeated him. He was always Hemingway writing, you see. Of course at his best that wasn't such a bad thing, was it? But if we're speaking of entry to the larger mind, his was not the way to find it.

INTERVIEWER: Does that change you at all? The voice, for example, in *Loon Lake* is very different from the voice in *Ragtime.* Do you change as a character yourself?

DOCTOROW: Well, you do participate, I suppose, as an actor does in a role. As the roles change, the actor's voice and deportment, his physique, even his makeup, everything changes.

INTERVIEWER: But sitting around the house you don't behave like Joe of Paterson, for example, the hobo in *Loon Lake.*

DOCTOROW: Well, how do you know?

INTERVIEWER: I don't know!

DOCTOROW: Writing is a socially acceptable form of schizophrenia. You can get away with an awful lot. One of my children once said—it was a terrible truth, too, and, of course, it had to be a young child who said this: "Dad is always hiding in his book."

INTERVIEWER: But aren't you very evident in your books? I mean, *Lives of the Poets,* who is that?

DOCTOROW: I don't know. It's somebody who might be me. Or part of me. Certainly in the past two books, I've used my own memory as a resource. But that does not mean I've written autobiographically. I recognize Jonathan, the narrator of *Lives of the Poets,* as a character, but he is not me. Not the fellow I see in the mirror. In *World's Fair* I gave the young hero my name, Edgar, but I don't think he's me either. You use found materials as you use anything else from your own life. Books are acts of composition. You compose them. You make music. The music is called fiction.

INTERVIEWER: Is that to suggest that *Ragtime,* for example, with all those extraordinary historical reminiscences and facts is in fact stretched truth?

DOCTOROW: Oh no, not stretched: the appropriate word is *discovered* or *revealed*. Everything in that book is absolutely true.

INTERVIEWER: Where did you ever find out, for example, that Theodore Dreiser, after *Sister Carrie* was published, was so upset that he rented a room and spent a great deal of time realigning a chair? That's an extraordinary detail.

DOCTOROW: I know a lot about the sufferings of writers. It's a subject that interests me. Dreiser wrote this magnificent novel. It was published in 1900; it was then and is still the best first novel ever written by an American. It's an amazing work. He found a voice, speaking of voice, for that book, of the wise septuagenarian. I don't know how he found it—he was twenty-eight when he began writing. Nevertheless it is the voice of a world-weary man who has seen it all. The book was a magnificent achievement but the publisher, Doubleday, didn't like it, they were afraid of it. So they buried it. And naturally it did nothing; I think it sold four copies. I would go crazy too in that situation. Dreiser rented a furnished room in Brooklyn. He put a chair in the middle of this room and sat in it. The chair didn't seem to be in the right position so he turned it a few degrees, and he sat in it again. Still it was not right. He kept turning the chair around and around, trying to align it to what—trying to correct his own relation to the universe? He never could do it, so he kept going around in circles and circles. He did that for quite a while, and ended up in a sanitarium in Westchester, in White Plains. But the trip to the sanitarium didn't interest me. Only the man turning the chair. So that's where Dreiser is in *Ragtime,* in that room, trying forever to align himself.

INTERVIEWER: For describing J. P. Morgan, for an example, did you spend a great deal of time in libraries?

DOCTOROW: The main research for Morgan was looking at the great photograph of him by Edward Steichen.

INTERVIEWER: That's all?

DOCTOROW: Well, I needed the names of the various companies he took over, railroads and so on, so I suppose I must have looked that up. But my research is idiosyncratic. Very often in *Ragtime* it involved finding a responsible source for the lie I was about to create, and discovering that it was not a lie, which is to say someone else had thought of it first.

INTERVIEWER: Isn't there an enormous temptation as a fiction writer to take scenes out of history, since you do rely on that so much, and fiddle with them just a little bit?

DOCTOROW: Well, it's nothing new, you know. I myself like the way Shakespeare fiddles with history. And Tolstoy. In this country we tend to be naïve about history. We think it's Newton's perfect mechanical universe, out there predictably for everyone to see and set their watches by. But it's more like curved space, and infinitely compressible and expandable time. It's constant subatomic chaos. When President Reagan says the Nazi S.S. were as much victims as the Jews they murdered—wouldn't you call that fiddling? Or the Japanese educators who've been rewriting their textbooks to eliminate the embarrassing facts of their invasion of China, the atrocities they committed in Manchuria in 1937? Orwell told us about this. History is a battlefield. It's constantly being fought over because the past controls the present. History is the present. That's why every generation writes it anew. But what most people think of as history is its end product, myth. So to be irreverent to myth, to play with it, let in some light and air, to try to combust it back into history, is to risk being seen as someone who distorts truth. I meant it when I said everything in *Ragtime* is true. It is as true as I could make it. I think my vision of J. P. Morgan, for instance, is more accurate to the soul of that man than his authorized biography. . . . Actually, if you want a confession, Morgan never existed. Morgan, Emma Goldman, Henry Ford, Evelyn Nesbit. All of them are made up. The historical characters in the book are Mother, Father, Tateh, The Little Boy, The Little Girl.

INTERVIEWER: Do you have a reader in mind as you write?

DOCTOROW: No, it's just a matter of being in language, of living in the sentences. With *The Book of Daniel,* for example, I obviously had an idea I thought I could do something with. But beyond that I couldn't have had any reader in mind, because I didn't even know what I was doing for the first several months. In fact, with Daniel I wrote a hundred and fifty pages and threw them away because they were so bad. The realization that I was doing a really bad book created the desperation that allowed me to find its true voice. I sat down rather recklessly and started to type something almost in mockery of my pretensions as a writer—and it turned out to be the first page of *The Book of Daniel.* What I had figured out in that tormented way was that Daniel should write the book, not me. Once I had his voice I was able to go on. That's the kind of struggle writing is. There's no room for a reader in your mind: you don't think of anything but the language you're in. Your mind is the language of the book.

INTERVIEWER: When did you come by this? When did you get into the language, as you put it. At college? You speak of Kenyon as a place where people think about writing the way they think about football at Ohio State.

DOCTOROW: What I actually said was that Kenyon was a place where we did literary criticism the way they played football at Ohio State. We did textual criticism. I studied poetry with John Crowe Ransom. I could write twenty-page papers on an eight-line lyric of Wordsworth. Of course it was invaluable training. You learned the powers of precision of the English language. The effect, for instance, of juxtaposing Latinate and Anglo-Saxon words. But criticism is a different conduct of the brain. That kind of analytical action of the mind is not the way you work when you write. You bring things together, you synthesize, you connect things that have had no previous connection when you write. So all in all as valuable as my training was, it took me through language in the wrong direction. It cost me a few years of writing time to recover my ignorance, the way I felt about writing as a child. I really started to think of myself as a writer when I was about nine.

INTERVIEWER: At nine? How did this feeling manifest itself?

DOCTOROW: Whenever I read anything I seemed to identify as much with the act of composition as with the story. I seemed to have two minds: I would love the story and want to know what happened next, but at the same time I would somehow be aware of what was being done on the page. I identified myself as a kind of younger brother of the writer. I was on hand to help him figure things out. So you see I didn't actually have to write a thing because the act of reading was my writing. I thought of myself as a writer for years before I got around to writing anything. It's not a bad way to begin. It's to blur that distinction between reader and writer. If you think about it, any book that you pick up as a reader, if it's good, is a printed circuit for your own life to flow through—so when you read a book you are engaged in the events of the mind of the writer. You are bringing your creative faculties into sync. You're imagining the words, the sounds of the words, and you're thinking of the various characters in terms of people you've known—not in terms of the writer's experience but your own. So it's very hard to make any distinction between reader and writer at this ontological level. As a child I somehow drifted into this region where you are both reader and writer: I declared to myself that I was the writer. I wrote a lot of good books. I wrote *Captain Blood* by Rafael Sabatini. That was one of my better efforts.

INTERVIEWER: It's amazing how many people have been affected by *Captain Blood*—Norman Mailer talks at length about it.

DOCTOROW: Does he really? I'm flattered. Did he ever read *Smoky* by Will James? That was one of my best.

INTERVIEWER: Does this twin-barreled construction mean that you are constantly an observer? That is, do you spend your day noticing things and saying to yourself, "Ah, that will work in a book"?

DOCTOROW: No, not at all. I don't think of myself as an observer. I feel things and have to work back from my feelings, my intuitions, to what must have caused them. I'm like most people: I don't usually understand what's happening to me while it's happening. I have to reconstruct it later, like a detective.

INTERVIEWER: But I mean if you went to a dinner party one night and there was an extraordinary argument between a husband and wife, would that not be something you would store away?

DOCTOROW: Well I might store it away. Of course, I might have walked out of the room first. You do see things. But I'm trying to say you can't turn around and move too quickly on them. As a matter of fact, anything that you want to use too quickly is suspect. You need time. I had heard a story, for instance, that a housekeeper in a suburb in New Jersey had secretly had a child and abandoned the child in the garden of another home in the neighborhood—swaddled the newborn infant and buried it in the garden bed. The child was discovered alive and the woman was found out—a very sad story. Well, about twenty years after I heard it I gave it to Sarah to do in *Ragtime,* a novel set in the 1900s in New Rochelle. That's the way it works. You collect all these things without knowing really what if anything you're going to do with them—old rags and scraps.

INTERVIEWER: How much experience do you think a writer should have? Would you ever suggest journalism, for example, as a career to begin with? Or send a writer to a war, or whatever.

DOCTOROW: You seem to think the writer has a choice—whether to work here or there or run off to a war. Maybe it's an American middle-class question, because in most places writers don't have a choice. If they grow up in the *barrio,* or get sent to the *gulag,* their experience is given to them whether they want it or not. Even here we respond to what's given: I seem to be of a generation that has somehow missed the crucial collective experiences of our time. I was too young to understand the Depression or fight in World War II. But I was past draft age for Vietnam. I've always been a loner. Perhaps for that reason I subscribe to what Henry James tries to indicate when he gives that wonderful example of a young woman who has led a sheltered life walking along beside an army barracks and hearing a snatch of soldier's conversation coming through the window. On the basis of that, said James, if she's a novelist she's capable of going home and writing a perfectly accurate novel about army life. I've always subscribed to that idea. We're supposed to be able to get into other skins. We're supposed to be able to render experiences not our own and warrant times and places we haven't seen. That's one justification for art, isn't it—to distribute the suffering? Writing teachers invariably tell students, Write about what you know. That's, of course, what you have to do, but on the other hand, how do you know what you know until you've written it? Writing is knowing. What did Kafka know? The insurance business? So that kind of advice is foolish, because it presumes that you have to go out to a war to be able to do war. Well, some do and some don't. I've had very little experience in my life. In fact, I try to avoid experience if I can. Most experience is bad.

INTERVIEWER: Could you describe the genesis of *Loon Lake?* A poem runs through the book.

DOCTOROW: What you call the poem was the very first writing I did on that book. I never thought of it as a poem, I thought of it as lines that just didn't happen to go all the way across the page. I broke the lines according to the rhythm in which they could be read aloud. I didn't know it at the time, but I was writing something to be read aloud—I think because

I liked the sound of the two words together—loon lake. I had these opening images of a private railroad train on a single track at night going up through the Adirondacks with a bunch of gangsters on board, and a beautiful girl standing, naked, holding a white dress up in front of a mirror to see if she should put it on. I didn't know where these gangsters came from. I knew where they were going—to this rich man's camp. Many years ago the very wealthy discovered the wilderness in the American eastern mountains. They built these extraordinary camps—C.W. Post, Harriman, Morgan—they made the wilderness their personal luxury. So I imagined a camp like this, with these gangsters, these lowdown people going up there on a private railroad train. That's what got me started. I published this material in the *Kenyon Review,* but I wasn't through. I kept thinking about the images and wondering where they'd come from. The time was in the 1930s, really the last era a man would have had his own railroad car, as some people today have their own jetliners. There was a Depression then, so the person to see this amazing train was obviously a hobo, a tramp. So then I had my character, Joe, out there in this chill, this darkness, seeing the headlamp of the engine coming round the bend and blinding him, and then as the train goes by seeing these people at green baize tables being served drinks and this girl standing in a bedroom compartment holding the dress. And at dawn he follows the track in the direction the train has gone. And he's off and running and so am I.

INTERVIEWER: Given this method of yours, how do you know when to stop?

DOCTOROW: As the book goes on it becomes inevitable. Your choices narrow, the thing picks up speed. And there's the exhilaration of a free ride—like a downhill ski run. You know before you get there what the last scene is. Sometimes what the last line is. But even if none of that happens, even if you find yourself at the end before you expected to, a kind of joy breaks over you, spills out of your eyes. And you realize you've finished. And then you want to be sure, you see. You need confirmation. You ask somebody you love to read it and see if it works. I remember when I finished *The Book of Daniel.* We were living in a house on the beach in Southern California. One of those houses with sliding glass doors for windows. I asked my wife if she would read the manuscript. She said she would be pleased to. And I left her sitting and reading with the sun coming through those big windows, and I went for a walk on the beach. It was a Sunday and the beach was crowded; they really use their beaches in California, every inch of them. Back toward the road were the volleyball players and the kite flyers. Boys throwing footballs or frisbees. Then the sunbathers, the children with their sandpails, the families. Then the runners splashing along at the edge of the surf. Or the people looking for little shells in the tide pools in the rocks. Then the swimmers. Beyond them the surfers in their wet suits waiting on their boards. Further out snorkelers' flags bobbing in the water. Out past the buoys the water skiers tearing along. Or rising into the air in their parachutes. And beyond that sailboats, flotillas of them, to the horizon. And all in this light. It was like a Brueghel, a Southern Californian Brueghel. I walked for several hours and thought about my book, and worried in my mind, in that California light worrying about this dark book, very much a New York City book. Was it done? Was it any good? And I came back to the house in the late afternoon, the house in shadows now, and there was Helen sitting in the same chair and the manuscript was all piled upside down on the table and she couldn't speak; she was crying, there were these enormous tears running down her cheeks, and it was the most incredible moment—never before had I known such happiness.

INTERVIEWER: How much confidence do you have when you finish? I would guess a wife's tears would help.

DOCTOROW: Well, at that point you've made an extraordinary investment of time and emotion, and you're just grateful to be there. Then the rest of the world rushes in, everything you've been holding off: your mind becomes ordinary. You worry if anyone's going to buy the book; if your publisher is going to publish it properly; you fret about the jacket, the typography, and the copyright, that it be correctly drawn; you worry about everything. But no matter what kind of reaction the book receives, whether people like the book or don't like it, nothing comes up to the experience of writing the book. That's what drives you back.

INTERVIEWER: How much time a day do you spend on this pleasure?

DOCTOROW: I would say I'm at work six hours a day, although the actual writing might take fifteen minutes or an hour, or three hours. You never know what kind of a day it's going to be; you just want to do whatever you set out to do. I type single space, to get as much of the landscape of the book as possible on one page. So if I do a single-space page with small margins, that's about six hundred words. If I do one page I'm very happy; that's my day's work. If I do two, that's extraordinary. But there's always a danger to doing two, which is you can't come up with anything the next day.

INTERVIEWER: What are the destroyers of this pleasure? Not for you, necessarily, but for writers? I remember we had a dinner once with John Irving and we started talking about how alcohol had diminished so many American writers.

DOCTOROW: A writer's life is so hazardous that anything he does is bad for him. Anything that happens to him is bad: failure's bad, success is bad; impoverishment is bad, money is very, very bad. Nothing good can happen.

INTERVIEWER: Except the act of writing itself.

DOCTOROW: Except the act of writing. So if he shoots birds and animals and anything else he can find, you've got to give him that. And if he/she drinks, you give him/her that too, unless the work is affected. For all of us, there's an intimate connection between the struggle to write and the ability to survive on a daily basis as a human being. So we have a high rate of self-destruction. Do we mean to punish ourselves for writing? For the transgression? I don't know.

INTERVIEWER: But this is not applicable in your own case, obviously.

DOCTOROW: Well, time will tell. I have a few vices, but one of them is moderation.

INTERVIEWER: Do you enjoy the company of other writers?

DOCTOROW: Yes, when they're my friends.

INTERVIEWER: Does anybody see anything you've written until it's finished?

DOCTOROW: Usually nobody sees anything until at least a draft is done. Sometimes I will read from it in public just to see how it sounds. To get a feeling back from the audience. But I tend to clutch it to myself as long as possible.

INTERVIEWER: You were an editor for a long time, weren't you? What is the relationship between that and the craft of writing?

DOCTOROW: Editing taught me how to break books down and put them back together. You learn values—the value of tension, of keeping tension on the page and how that's done, and you learn how to spot self-indulgence, how you don't need it. You learn how to become very free and easy about moving things around, which a reader would never do. A reader sees a printed book and that's it. But when you see a manuscript as an editor, you say, Well this is chapter twenty, but it should be chapter three. You're at ease in the book the way a surgeon is at ease in a human chest, with all the blood and the guts and everything. You're familiar with the material and you can toss it around and say dirty things to the nurse.

INTERVIEWER: Do you accept advice ever?

DOCTOROW: No, none.

INTERVIEWER: Well, on that decisive note perhaps some of

you in the audience have some questions to put to Mr. Doctorow.

AUDIENCE *(gentleman wearing dark glasses):* What responsibilities do you think writers or artists should have to those who can't be heard—like Andrei Sakharov? Do you consider yourself to be someone who should be speaking out?

DOCTOROW: Well, yes. Modernism made us think of writing as an act of ultimate individualism. But, in fact, every writer speaks for a community. If you read Mark Twain, for instance, you know that there's a whole people behind that voice. I don't mean necessarily ethnically or geographically, but as a writer you get that feeling once you get going that you're not just speaking for yourself. You remember the way people waited at New York docks for the ship bringing in the latest Dickens installment? They called up to the crew, "Is little Nell dead?" Or how when Victor Hugo died all of France went into mourning. That's what I mean. There's a profound relationship. The writer isn't made in a vacuum. Writers are witnesses. The reason we need writers is because we need witnesses to this terrifying century. Novelists have always written about intimacies, about personal relationships. Since in the twentieth century one of the most personal relationships to have developed is that of the person and the state, we have to write about it, and some of us have. It's become a fact of life that governments have become very intimate with people, most always to their detriment.

AUDIENCE *(a young student):* Do you see a danger in the proliferation of creative writing graduate programs around the country?

DOCTOROW: Are you a writing student?

AUDIENCE: Actually, I'm trying to decide whether or not to become one. . . .

DOCTOROW: Well, there is a danger. Since World War II the university has become the great patron of writers. Originally the poets worked out this scheme for staying alive. Robert Frost was drawing big audiences for his readings. Dylan Thomas came and read from this very stage at the 92nd Street Y. Suddenly there was this whole new possibility: it was like the poet's equivalent of the invention of the computer chip. Poets got university jobs teaching poetry. Then they invited other poets to come and read. A network sprang up. Writing programs came into being. The poets built up this alternate communication system of poetry. We novelists never paid much attention. Poets are much better friends to each other than we are. We are always relating to our publishers. So we came to this kind of late. Nevertheless we are in it now. There are writing programs all over the country. The great danger is that you are creating and training not just writers but teachers of writing. In other words, someone goes into a graduate writing program, gets an MFA in writing, and immediately gets a job on another campus teaching other young people to get their MFA's in writing. So you have this whole other thing—teachers of writing begetting teachers of writing, and that's bad. On one hand you see the results of that, generally speaking, which is that the writing of young people today is much more technically assured than it's ever been. You'll see what I mean if you read Faulkner's first novel. It's a terrible, clumsy book. Most first novelists who come out of university training are craftier than he was. On the other hand the horizon of the university-trained writers is diminished; the field for their work and attention is generally the bedroom, the living room, the family. The doors are closed, the shades are pulled down, and it's as if there were no streets outside, and no town, no highway, no society. So that's the danger. But then you start thinking of all the good writers who have come out of the university writing programs, and how valuable they are and how fortunate we are to have them, and you can't condemn the system totally. [*To the student in the audience*] Why don't you just consult the I Ching before you make your decision?

AUDIENCE *(gentleman in back):* Have you ever consciously set out to develop a style, or have your books been more organic?

DOCTOROW: I don't want a style. This was something that I was trying to explain earlier, that I want the book to invent itself. I think that the minute a writer knows what his style is, he's finished. Because then you see your own limits, and you hear your own voice in your head. At that point you might as well close up shop. So I like to think that I don't have a style, I have books that work themselves out and find their own voice—their voice, not mine. So I'll have that illusion, I think—I hope—till the very end.

AUDIENCE *(same gentleman):* Isn't it true that there are many writers who have a definite style, like Henry James?

DOCTOROW: Yes! And look at the botch he made of things.

AUDIENCE *(lady in sixth row):* How was your experience writing a play different from writing a book? Would you write another?

DOCTOROW: That play happened roughly the way the books happen. I happened to be reading a translation of a speech that Mao Tse-tung made to his troops in the field in 1935. It had an extraordinarily familiar sound. I thought that he wrote just like Gertrude Stein. To test that proposition I went to my copy of Stein's essays, opened it at random. They both repeated nouns instead of using pronouns. In fact they repeated everything—nothing was ever stated just once. Pieces of the sentences changed during each repetition, and it turned out the unit of sense was not the sentence but the paragraph. So I reasoned that any rhetoric common to the leader of a billion people and Gertrude Stein was worth trying. It turned out, of course, that, as a Sinologist told me, not just Mao's prose, but all transliteration from the Chinese sounds like Gertrude Stein. Nevertheless I was on my way. I found myself writing a monologue. The speaker was angry at everything and everybody—a real sorehead. Then I began to hear opposition in the same rhetoric to all his assertions and claims. I wrote these down, and to keep everything straight I started giving the positions in this argument names. The sorehead, I thought it was only fair to give my own name. One thing led to another and these dialogues became a play in which a man pulls a gun at a dinner party; he sort of hijacks the dinner party and then ties up the honored guests, their children, and so on. This is not the way plays are usually written. Nor is it a typical American play. It's not a domestic biography. It doesn't have pathos in it. People don't talk about their childhoods. They take their characters from their ideas. They speak in this ceremonial way. It ran down at the Public Theater for six weeks. I had a wonderful cast. Christopher Plummer was in it, Mike Nichols directed it, and it was terrific. The critics—or what pass for critics in New York theater—hated it. It is now a kind of cult play in university and regional theaters, and I like to see it when I can. All in all it was a wonderful experience, and I hope never to do it again.

AUDIENCE *(gentleman waving hand):* What's the name of it?

DOCTOROW: *Drinks Before Dinner* is what it's called.

AUDIENCE *(woman in red scarf):* Have you ever had the experience of losing a story because you talked about it to somebody before you've written it?

DOCTOROW: Yes. When you're talking about a story you're writing it. You're sending it out into the air, it's finished, it's gone.

INTERVIEWER: Is that actually so? You couldn't tell a story at a dinner party that you thought you could use?

DOCTOROW: Occasionally, you want to show off. The moment's too good, and you want to impress somebody. So you take one of these secret, private things, and present it to the table. It's over, it's done, you'll never be able to use it. It's a very reckless thing to do. Maybe you've made a decision that you don't really want it, you don't really need it. Because there are certain stories that we all have that we never use, that are more valuable to us not being used. But by and large it's better to restrain yourself.

INTERVIEWER: The discipline must be extraordinary, because so many of the stories are so wonderful, very much the sort that should be told at dinner parties. I'm thinking of the story you have of the robbery on the Long Island Expressway, of the Chevrolet that bumps the Mercedes. It's in the monologue in *Lives of the Poets.*

DOCTOROW: But I didn't tell that story before I wrote it, because if I did I could not have written it.

INTERVIEWER: You must be very poor at dinner parties, holding on to those stories.

DOCTOROW: On the other hand, you never know when I might pull a gun.

—GEORGE PLIMPTON
May 1986

10. Anita Brookner

Anita Brookner was born in London to Polish-Jewish parents. Her father changed his name from Bruckner to Brookner ("Like calling yourself Batehoven!"). She studied French literature at the University of London and, later, art history at the Courtauld Institute of Art. After earning her doctorate, she became a reader in the history of art at the Courtauld Institute, where she still teaches, and in 1967 she became Slade Professor at Cambridge University, the first woman ever to hold that position. An international authority on eighteenth- and nineteenth-century French art, Brookner gained recognition with her studies of David, Greuze, and Watteau, and for *The Genius of the Future*, her collection of essays on poets and writers as art critics, from Diderot to Baudelaire.

Brookner was in her mid-forties before she started writing novels. In 1981, her first, *A Start In Life*, entitled *The Debut* in its American edition, was published to great critical and popular success. Two subsequent novels, *Providence* and *Look At Me*, followed in quick succession. Their mixture of feminine sensibility and intellectual vigor, elegant classical style and modern psychological complexity consolidated her reputation as an original and accomplished novelist. In 1984, she won the Booker-McConnell Prize for her fourth novel, *Hotel du Lac*, and later the same year her *Family and Friends* became a best-seller on both sides of the Atlantic. *The Misalliance* was published in 1986, and *A Friend from England* in 1988. Brookner is now working on another novel, and, she says, "taking it slowly." She plans to stop teaching soon, to devote herself entirely to her fiction and critical writing.

Max, grunting slightly, smiles at the television, shakes out his cigarette, & sits with an outstretched hand to his chest. Lunchperhaps or sometime also often finds him in this position. Betty at such moments wakes him to cups of tea and reminds him that they [downstairs] were invited to meet some people for dinner & that when he has drunk his tea he had better think & shower & change. Fortunately Betty is not one of those wives who make a fuss. It would not occur to her to call a doctor & in this way he is prevented from an invalid's regimen, but will continue to lead his intense & cynical & say this shape with undrawn existence. He is grateful to his wife for not noticing that anything is amiss, grateful too that she is tough enough to take whatever may come, grateful that their love is not of the overwhelming variety that makes such thoughts unbearable.

When Betty finds Max sitting on the bed, staring yet again at the wedding photographs, she tells him quite sharply that if he does not stop mooning around in this unchivalrous he way they will soon be late. When he says that he does not feel like going out she reproaches him for being selfish. When, with a sigh, he gets up, in hanging unopened on the bottle since the way first options open to him, Betty exclaims, 'And about time too'. When he slowly topples forward Betty is at her dressing table, trying on & discarding various pairs of earrings. In that way, when she looks in the mirror, she sees behind her reflection only absence.

A manuscript page from Anita Brookner's novel Family and Friends.

Anita Brookner

Anita Brookner works in an office at the Courtauld Institute filled with books and pictures of French paintings, a desk strewn with papers, and an old typewriter. She also works in her Chelsea home, where this interview took place. She lives in a small but sunny and quiet apartment, furnished in light colors and overlooking a large, pleasant communal garden. When asked how it felt to work in the male-dominated atmosphere of Cambridge University in the sixties, she answered, "Nobody looked all that male and I didn't look all that female." In fact, though, she does look very feminine: petite, slim, and casually but most elegantly dressed. Reddish well-cut hair frames her pale, striking face, which is dominated by large beautiful blue eyes. Her exquisite manners disarm and put visitors at ease, and at the same time secure a reasonable distance. She speaks in a deep, gentle

voice, with fluency and deliberation in equal measure, and some-
times in "short, military sentences," as she once said of Sten-
dhal. Occasionally she smokes a very slim cigarette.

INTERVIEWER: Let us start at the beginning. Did anything in your background lead you to believe that one day you would become a scholar and a novelist?

BROOKNER: Oh no! Anything but! I was brought up to look after my parents. My family were Polish Jews and we lived with my grandmother, with uncles and aunts and cousins all around, and I thought everybody lived like that. They were transplanted and fragile people, an unhappy brood, and I felt that I had to protect them. Indeed that is what they expected. As a result I became an adult too soon and paradoxically never grew up. My mother had been a concert singer but had given up to marry. She was inclined to melancholy and when she sang at home my father used to get angry, with good reason—it was only in her singing that she showed passion. I would start to cry and be taken out of the room by the Nanny. She, not I, should have been the liberated woman. My father, who didn't really understand the English, loved Dickens; he thought Dickens gave a true picture of England, where right always triumphed. I still read a Dickens novel every year and I am still looking for a Nicholas Nickleby!

INTERVIEWER: Is that why all your heroines have a "displaced person" quality, and the family backgrounds are very Jewish, even though not explicitly? Were you brought up Jewish?

BROOKNER: Yes, very much so. I never learnt Hebrew because my health was fragile and it was thought that learning Hebrew would be an added burden. I regret it, because I would like to be able to join in fully. Not that I am a believer, but I would like to be. As for the "displaced person" aspect, perhaps it is because although I was born and raised here I have never been at home, completely. People say that I am always serious and depressing, but it seems to me that the English are *never* serious—they are flippant, complacent, ineffable, but never serious, which is sometimes maddening.

INTERVIEWER: The foreignness of your heroines is emphasized by the contrast between them and the very solidly English, Protestant men they are attracted to.

BROOKNER: I think the contrast is more between damaged people and those who are undamaged.

INTERVIEWER: Your first books were on artists and art history. What made you decide to try your hand at the novel?

BROOKNER: It was literally trying my hand, as you put it. I wondered how it was done and the only way to find out seemed to be to try and do it.

INTERVIEWER: You took the title, *A Start in Life,* from an obscure novel by Balzac, *Un Début dans la vie.* Was it autobiographical?

BROOKNER: It was. I wrote it in a moment of sadness and desperation. My life seemed to be drifting in predictable channels and I wanted to know how I deserved such a fate. I thought if I could write about it I would be able to impose some structure on my experience. It gave me a feeling of being at least in control. It was an exercise in self-analysis, and I tried to make it as objective as possible—no self-pity and no self-justification. But what is interesting about self-analysis is that it leads nowhere—it is an art form in itself.

INTERVIEWER: In your two subsequent novels you give different reasons for wanting to write. In *Look At Me* you say that writing is your penance for not being lucky.

BROOKNER: I meant that writing is a very lonely activity. You go for days without seeing or talking to anyone. And all the time out there people are living happy, fulfilled lives—or you think they are. If I were happy, married with six children, I wouldn't be writing. And I doubt if I should want to. But since I wrote that sentence I have changed. Now I write because I enjoy it. Writing has freed me from the despair of living. I feel well when I am writing; I even put on a little weight!

INTERVIEWER: You also said that you write to be hard, to remind people that you are there.

BROOKNER: I have changed my mind about that too. Far from making me hard, writing has made me softer, more understanding, more observant, and perhaps more passive in the sense that other people and their opinion of me seems to matter less.

INTERVIEWER: It seems that writers wish to find a reason for their activity: Paul Eluard called it *"le dur désir de durer."* And lately E. M. Cioran said, *"L'écriture est la revanche de l'homme contre une Creation baclée."* And you say, in *Providence,* that you write to tell the truth, what you call the Cassandra complex.

BROOKNER: I agree with Cioran, in so far as we all try to put some order into chaos. The truth I'm trying to convey is not a startling one, it is simply a peeling away of affectation. I use whatever gift I have to get behind the facade. But I hope I am not an aggressive writer, and that I see through people with compassion and humor. My own life was disappointing—I was *mal partie,* started on the wrong footing; so I am trying to edit the whole thing. It was the need for order in my own life that made me start. And once the floodgates are open, you must go all the way.

INTERVIEWER: Your first three novels seem to be variations on the same theme. The basic argument is that we are deceived by literature into believing that virtue is rewarded, that good will win in the end, and that Cinderella will always get the Prince. Whereas, in reality, honest, disciplined, and principled people lose to the beautiful and the selfish.

BROOKNER: Not selfish—plausible. My new novel goes further: I now feel that all good fortune is a gift of the gods, and that you don't win the favor of the ancient gods by being good, but by being *bold.*

INTERVIEWER: Sometimes the beautiful and the bold lose to lesser people because they don't use the right stratagems. For example, Anna Karenina: Tolstoy very cleverly shows that all around her people are having love affairs which everyone knows about and condones because it is all a game and does not threaten the accepted order. Anna, too honest, wants to go all the way and rock the boat, divorce her husband, and marry her lover; she creates a scandal and so she is condemned.

BROOKNER: Anna loses because, for all her boldness, she can't commit herself morally to her actions. She feels guilty about her son and misjudges her Vronsky. She can't accept that men can't keep up the same pitch of passion as women can—that they cool off. With men passion is all at the beginning and with women it is all along.

INTERVIEWER: In your fourth novel, *Hotel du Lac,* you expose the falsehood of another myth, "The Tortoise and the Hare," and you say that in real life the hare wins every time, never the slow, patient tortoise.

BROOKNER: Every time! Look around you. It is my contention that Aesop was writing for the tortoise market. Anyway, hares have no time to read—they are too busy winning the game!

INTERVIEWER: All your heroines follow "an inexorable progress toward further loneliness," as you say of Kitty Maule in *Providence.* It seems to me very deterministic. Is there nothing we can do to alter our fate?

BROOKNER: I think one's character and predisposition determine one's fate, I'm afraid. But *Providence* seems deterministic because it is a *novel,* and a novel follows its own organic structure.

INTERVIEWER: At the same time you say that existentialism is the only philosophy you can endorse. Now existentialism with its emphasis on personal freedom seems the opposite of determinism.

BROOKNER: I don't believe that anyone is free. What I meant was that existentialism is about being a saint without God; being your own hero, without all the sanction and support of religion or society. Freedom in existentialist terms breeds anxiety, and you have to accept that anxiety as the price to pay. I think choice is a luxury most people can't afford. I mean when you make a break for freedom you don't necessarily find company on the way, you find loneliness. Life is a pilgrimage and if you don't play by the rules you don't find the Road to Damascus, you find the Crown of Thorns. In *Hotel du Lac* the heroine, Edith Hope, twice nearly marries. She balks at the last minute and decides to stay in a hopeless relationship with a married man. As I wrote it I felt very sorry for her and at the same time very angry: she should have married one of them— they were interchangeable anyway—and at least gained some worldly success, some social respectability. I have a good mind to let her do it in some other novel and see how she will cope!

INTERVIEWER: You also said that existentialism is a Romantic creed. How so?

BROOKNER: Because Romanticism doesn't make sense unless you realize that it grew out of the French Revolution in which human behavior sank to such terrible depths that it became obvious no supernatural power, if it existed, could possibly countenance it. For the first time Europeans felt that God was dead. Since then we have had Hitler, Stalin, Pol Pot, whose activities make the French Revolution seem like a picnic. The Romantics tried to compensate the absence of God with furious creative activity. If you do not have the gift of faith which wraps everything up in a foolproof system and which is predicated on the belief that there is a loving Father who will do the best for you, then, as Sartre said, you have to live out of that system completely, and become your own father. This is a terrible decision, and, as I said, in existential terms freedom is not desirable, it is a woeful curse. You have to live with absence. Nowadays I wonder if it is really possible to live without God, maybe we should dare to hope . . . I don't know. I'm not there yet.

INTERVIEWER: Perhaps this is the reason some people convert to religion at the last minute. Even Voltaire called a priest just before he died!

BROOKNER: Ah, but Voltaire accepted the priest on *his* terms: when the priest asked him, *"Monsieur* de Voltaire, do you believe in the divinity of Jesus Christ?"* he replied, "Don't talk to me about that *man!"* He rejected the divinity of Christ but accepted him as the Perfect Man. But not everyone is as brave as Voltaire.

INTERVIEWER: In your study of French art you started with the eighteenth century and switched to the nineteenth. It was the latter century that influenced you in your novels. What is the difference between the two, for you?

BROOKNER: I think the acquisition of greater experience and the loss of a certain innocence. The eighteenth century believed that Reason could change things for the better, and that all would have the vote in the Republic of Virtue. After the Revolution, people realized that Reason could not change anything, that man is moved not by Reason but by darker forces. Despotism, tyranny, even cannibalism—informing on one's neighbors—became quite routine. After 1793 it was no longer possible to close one's eyes to the base aspect of human nature—God really was dead. It opened the floodgates to self-examination. "Where does it all come from?" they asked. And it was discovered that once you no longer were constrained to be good, either by Christianity or by a secular philosophy which for a time was even stronger, namely the Enlightenment, there was no limit to bad behavior. But also to inventive, creative, autobiographical behavior.

INTERVIEWER: It produced alienation or separation anxiety, as they call it.

BROOKNER: Exactly. Because to find yourself in a world without beginning or end is a Romantic discovery.

INTERVIEWER: Did you read the German Romantics?

BROOKNER: Kleist, yes. He seems to be the really tragic figure. But I don't know them well.

INTERVIEWER: I asked the question because what you said tallies with what Isaiah Berlin says—that all the problems of our age can be traced back to Romanticism, especially the Germans who were the true Romantics and invented the whole thing, so to speak—nihilism, Marxism, existentialism, etc. . . .

BROOKNER: He is absolutely right. It was hearing him lecture on the subject that impressed me so much and made me decide to take it up and teach it myself.

INTERVIEWER: What about Goethe? He started life as a Romantic and changed his heart: "Classicism is health, Romanticism is sickness," he said.

BROOKNER: He did turn his coat, didn't he? He precipitated the discovery of Romanticism-as-sickness with *Werther,* where he appears to condone a Romantic suicide. But *Elective Affinities* is a very difficult book. It has no moral center. It is about the mechanistic behavior of people in society and goes like clockwork. I find it an enigmatic, and rather a disgusting, book.

INTERVIEWER: You once said that Zola was your favorite writer when you were young. Do you think your determinism is due to Zola's influence?

BROOKNER: No. Zola's determinism is too crude and mechanistic. He is talking about heredity in genetic terms; for example, if your father was an alcoholic you will become one too. I don't believe that. When I said that Zola was my favorite writer, I meant that I loved his courage, his indignation. Like Dickens he was an angry writer—angry at the unfairness of things, and the burden transmitted by ancestors for which we are not responsible and to which we have to succumb.

INTERVIEWER: Apart from Zola and Dickens, who were your early influences?

BROOKNER: When I was studying French at the university I read an enormous number of French novelists. I never thought that one day I would write a novel myself, because I thought that these people were telling me something very important which could not be duplicated. My influences were Balzac, Stendhal, and to a much lesser degree Flaubert. I think Flaubert colludes too much—he *wants* his characters to be defeated. Stendhal was the one I loved most. He was the true Romantic: "I walk in the street marvelling at the stars and I'm run over by a cab," he said. That sums it up! I also read English Victorian novels: Trollope for decent feelings, George Eliot for moral seriousness. And of course the great Russians.

INTERVIEWER: What about Proust?

BROOKNER: He is an exceptional case and very precious to me. He kept himself in a state of mind so hypnotic and dangerous that one approaches rereading him almost with fear. He remained always marginal, observing. The cost was too high, when all is said and done. The periods of remaining in that childlike state of receptivity are terrifying. The awful thing is that he got it *right all the time.* It is all true!

INTERVIEWER: In *A Start in Life* there is a critique of Balzac's *Eugénie Grandet* and in *Providence* one of Benjamin Constant's *Adolphe.* Did you mean that although literature can mislead one, it can also provide moral models?

BROOKNER: Yes, *Adolphe* is a deeply serious and moral novel: it asks what do you do when you are the author of a disaster? Ellénore in *Adolphe* and Kitty in *Providence* are victims of disasters because they misjudge their men.

INTERVIEWER: You seem to insist on great moral rectitude in your characters. Do you think all great novelists have been moralists, from Tolstoy to Camus?

BROOKNER: Indeed I do. And some lesser ones too. In my case it comes from a grounding in the nineteenth century novel and because my own family were very strict in that respect. I have never unlearnt the lesson. I would love to be more plausible, flattering, frivolous, but I am handicapped by my expectations. Isn't it sad?

INTERVIEWER: Hence your recent passion for Henry James and Edith Wharton, whom you said you would most wish to resemble.

BROOKNER: Henry James seems to me to have all the moral conscience that everybody should have. He writes basically about scruples, and his hesitations are so valid that they are the secular equivalent of religious obligations.

INTERVIEWER: Yet Henry James's duality—innocent American versus wily European—seems less relevant today, while Edith Wharton's overall complexity is more universal.

BROOKNER: That is true, and for that reason Wharton has worn better and reads more easily. Someone said that Edith Wharton's novels are what Henry James would have written if he had been a man! She is Henry James without the duality of innocence versus experience. But she does not have the lamb-to-the-slaughter quality which Henry James invests in his heroines and which is almost Greek. It is a very potent theme in fiction: innocence betrayed. Isabel Archer in *Portrait of a Lady* is completely innocent of other people's plans. But I don't believe that, past a certain age, anyone is innocent, except in fiction! But no one can get near Lily Bart of Wharton's *The House of Mirth*, because she is innocent yet has no conscience. She wants someone to pay her way through life but balks at the horrible men who are willing to do it for her. Of the two, Henry James is more of a giant, simply because Wharton didn't write as many great novels—perhaps four—while James's sheer bulk and Balzacian fecundity is overwhelming. I am now reading his short stories: there are hundreds of them and mostly wonderful.

INTERVIEWER: One original and interesting aspect of Edith Wharton is that in her great novels the moral option is nearly always taken by the women; just as the men are about to succumb to temptation and cause havoc, the women pull them back from the brink.

BROOKNER: Yes, they are much braver and less divided than the men. I am afraid my heroines do the same, according to their own, contemporary, light.

INTERVIEWER: Do you read contemporary novelists?

BROOKNER: Constantly! And everything that comes out. At present I am rereading Philip Roth, and I *adore* him! I buy hardback books, which I am told is rather extravagant, but I feel I owe it to my fellow writers.

INTERVIEWER: What about women novelists?

BROOKNER: The women novelists I admire in the English tradition are Rosamond Lehmann, Elizabeth Taylor, and Storm Jameson. Much less Ivy Compton-Burnett—she is brilliantly clever but too cruel. I admire Jean Rhys, especially *Wide Sargasso Sea*, but she is too limited by her pathology. Outside the English tradition the Czech novelist Edith Templeton, who writes in impeccable English, is marvelously restrained. She tells strong stories about life in old-style Central Europe, with recognizable passions and follies. The Canadians Mavis Gallant and Edith de Born I very much enjoy too. These are all much more stoical and less sentimental than English writers.

INTERVIEWER: In *Hotel du Lac* Edith Hope is a writer of "romance" novels, of the Barbara Cartland, Mills & Boon type. She says, "I believe every word I write." What is the difference between that kind of romantic novel and the genuine article? Is it just the invariably happy ending? Or simply the quality of writing and the mind behind it?

BROOKNER: Both. Romance novels are formula novels. I have read some and they seem to be writing about a different species. The true Romantic novel is about delayed happiness. The pilgrimage you go through to get that imagined happiness. In the genuine Romantic novel there is confrontation with truth and in the "romance" novel a similar confrontation with a surrogate, plastic version of the truth. Romantic writers are characterized by absolute longing—perhaps for something that is not there and cannot be there. And they go along with all the hurt and embarrassment of identifying the real thing and wanting it. In that sense Edith Hope is not a twentieth-century heroine, she belongs to the nineteenth century. What I can't understand is the radical inauthenticity of some women's novels which are written to a formula: from the peatbogs of Killarney to the penthouses of Manhattan, orgasms all the way! Pornography for ladies. It is not only impure artistically, it is untrue and unfeminine. To remain pure a novel has to cast a moral puzzle. Anything else is mere negotiation.

INTERVIEWER: In *Hotel du Lac* you say that you prefer the company of men to that of women. Which brings me to ask you about your relation to feminism.

BROOKNER: I prefer the company of men because they teach me things I don't know.

INTERVIEWER: One might say, to paraphrase Sartre, *"L'homme c'est l'autre"*?

BROOKNER: Exactly. It is the otherness that fascinates me. As for feminism, I think it is good for women to earn their living and thereby control their own destinies to some extent. They pay a heavy price for independence though. I marvel at the energy of women who combine husbands, children, and a profession. Anyone who thinks she will fulfill herself in that way can't be realistic. The self-fulfilled woman is far from reality—it is a sort of Shavian fantasy that you can be a complete woman. Besides, a complete woman is probably not a very admirable creature. She is manipulative, uses other people to get her own way, and works within whatever system she is in. The *ideal* woman, on the other hand, is quite different: She lives according to a set of principles and is somehow very rare and always has been. As for the radical feminism of today, the rejection of the male, I find it absurd. It leads to sterility. They say it is a reasoned alternative, but an alternative to what? To continuity?

INTERVIEWER: But if feminism has not succeeded in dispelling mistrust between men and women, or in making their relationship any easier, it seems to have enhanced friendship between women. Don't you think so?

BROOKNER: I believe that is true. There was a time when if a woman went to the theater with a girlfriend it was considered an admission of failure. Not so anymore. Sometimes one prefers going with a friend, because it is less of a production. It is casual and relaxed, an evening's entertainment, not a prelude to something else.

INTERVIEWER: I would like to talk about your style, which has rightly been praised as exceptionally elegant, lucid, and original. You explain it somewhat in *Providence* by saying, "A novel is not simply confession, it is about the author's choice of words." What does style mean to you?

BROOKNER: Very little. I am not conscious of having a style. I write quite easily, without thinking about the words much but rather about what they want to say. I do think that respect for form is absolutely necessary in any art form—painting, writing, anything. I try to write as lucidly as possible. You might say that lucidity is a conscious preoccupation. I am glad people seem to like it.

INTERVIEWER: Where do you write?

BROOKNER: Anywhere. In my flat, or in my office at the Courtauld. I have even written on a bus. When you live in a small flat you write on the edge of things—there is no great setup. I type what I have written at the office. I prefer working there because I like the interruptions—telephone calls, visitors. I am completely schizophrenic, as I can carry on a conversation in my head while another, apparently sensible conversation, is taking place with someone who has just come into the room. At home the isolation weighs on me. It is a terrible strain.

INTERVIEWER: Do you keep regular hours?

BROOKNER: I only write in the summer holidays when the Institute is closed. Each novel has been written during a summer, over three or four months. Then I work every day all day and stop in the evening. I try to switch off completely and not think about it till the next day.

INTERVIEWER: What do you do when the day's work is finished?

BROOKNER: I go for very long walks and wind down. I am grateful for the life in the streets—the people, the shop windows . . .

INTERVIEWER: With success must have come a certain amount of lionization: invitations to parties, literary gatherings, lectures. Are you good at saying no?

BROOKNER: Very good! Much too good! I ration myself strictly with regard to social life. I try not to give offense and I am never brutal, but I do say no.

INTERVIEWER: Don't you feel lonely sometimes?

BROOKNER: Often. I have said that I am one of the loneliest women in London. People have resented it—it is not done to confess to loneliness, but there it is.

INTERVIEWER: Do you ever rewrite what you have written?

BROOKNER: Never. It is always the first draft. I may alter the last chapter; I may lengthen it. Only because I get very tired at the end of a book and tend to rush and go too quickly, so when I have finished it I go over the last chapter.

INTERVIEWER: Do you know exactly how a novel would develop and end when you start, or do you let its organic growth take over?

BROOKNER: The latter. I have an idea, but I don't know exactly what will happen. As I said, in *Hotel du Lac* I wanted to let Edith Hope marry Mr. Neville, but like her I balked at the last minute! I am not really an imaginative writer.

INTERVIEWER: What do you mean by that? And who do you think is an imaginative writer?

BROOKNER: I mean that I am not very inventive. Some contemporary American novelists are imaginative. Peter Ackroyd's *Hawksmoor* is a marvelously imaginative novel. So is Yann

Quéffelec's *Noces Barbares,* because it cannot be verified. Whereas I like to examine the behavior of characters, the possibilities: why this way and not that way?

INTERVIEWER: So far all your novels have been the same length, around two hundred pages, with the same group of characters and more or less the same circumstances producing the same results. (Although *Family and Friends* has a bigger cast of characters.) Are you not afraid of being accused of writing to a formula, even though of your own creation?

BROOKNER: I have been so accused! But the latest book, *The Misalliance,* is much longer and has a broader canvas. It is quite different from the others, not at all deterministic, and rather sentimental. It has had excellent notices in the States but here the reviews were mixed, ranging from good to hostile, even abusive.

INTERVIEWER: Do you think English critics thought it was not "fair" that you should go around collecting dithyrambs for every novel?

BROOKNER: No, I think they had made the initial mistake of identifying me with my female protagonists, so that the criticism that comes my way, particularly in *The Misalliance,* is a semipersonal kind which does not rank as real criticism: I can't learn from it, I can only feel hurt by it. Also it wasn't a very good book, but it wasn't *that* bad either. I have written it off. I didn't like it even as I was writing it.

INTERVIEWER: Was it because the heroine, Blanche Vernon, is somewhat irritating, even boring?

BROOKNER: Well, she was a very aseptic character. The book has quite an interesting theme, which is that even good behavior can go wrong, if it is based on a fallacy or a misconception, that you can't take anything for granted, and that you are walking on eggshells every time you make a choice.

INTERVIEWER: But what emerged was that here was yet another "good woman," who behaves honorably but gets abandoned for someone more frivolous and jolly.

BROOKNER: There is a personal dislike directed against Blanche Vernon, because you can't blame her for anything, except perhaps for being a prig. Now that is a very minor vice in my book. The point is that there are a lot of women like her: nice, innocent, but boring. Nobody likes them and as a result they lead very miserable lives. They are not fun to be with and in England you've got to be *fun;* you must be a *fun* person, having fun all the time! It is very superficial, but there it is. The bad reviews were partly a dislike of Blanche, and of me since I'm supposed to be all these women I create. In America they liked it because they thought it was Jamesian, which I would not have dared to presume. Yet it *is* about a moral problem; so is the next one, which is coming out in the autumn and is called *A Friend from England.* It is a very old-fashioned moral tale.

INTERVIEWER: Can you tell me a bit about it—without giving it away?

BROOKNER: It is about an extremely emancipated young woman—whom they will *not* be able to think is me!—who is drawn into a family of blameless innocence whom she feels called upon to protect, but by whose innocence she finds herself finally vanquished. She can't measure up to it. It is quite complicated, not only because it has a larger cast but because it is about men.

INTERVIEWER: Is it difficult because a woman can't get into the skin of a man, to understand what makes him tick?

BROOKNER: I am finding it surprisingly easy!

INTERVIEWER: It is often said that the greatest female heroines have been created by male novelists—Anna Karenina, Madame Bovary, *et al.*—but that the reverse has not yet happened. The only exceptions might be a couple of George Eliot's heroes.

BROOKNER: I was thinking of George Eliot, too. I think it can be done, but only at the end of a very long process. When you start to write a novel you have to learn to internalize your characters, not to describe them from the outside—that doesn't work. And this process of internalizing goes on through life. In the case of a male protagonist gradually you begin to internalize him too—if you are lucky—and this is more difficult for a woman and takes longer. Somehow it is more difficult for a woman to get inside a man than for a man to get inside a woman. Men are better at this, let us face it. I think women have an inborn fear of men, which of course they could never confess to. Instinctively they will cower from a man if he shows some kind of energy or violence. So to reconcile your instinct as a woman with a man's instinct takes a long time. A long time. But I'm trying!

INTERVIEWER: You review books for *The Spectator* and before writing novels you wrote excellent art history books. Your book on David is considered a model of the genre, combining as it does biography, history, and criticism. Do you see a radical difference between the two genres—criticism versus creative writing? I ask this because some distinguished critics have found it difficult, if not impossible, to write fiction. I am thinking of Edmund Wilson and George Steiner, to mention but two who have tried.

BROOKNER: Wilson's novel is a very good and disturbing book. But I know what they mean: perhaps because in fiction you give too much away while in criticism you can hide behind another writer's personality and work. For me both are ways of working through a problem. I liken the whole process to writing an examination paper—you have a certain amount of time and space and you have to do your best. It is nerve-racking but not particularly difficult.

INTERVIEWER: What about teaching? Are you leaving the Courtauld Institute because you can now make a living as a writer?

BROOKNER: Not really, because I have loved teaching, and I've loved my students. Indeed, I'm having the happiest year of my teaching life—perhaps because it is the last! It is just that

I have taught for twenty-five years and the thought of having to go through the syllabus for the twenty-sixth year was more than I could take.

INTERVIEWER: Will you ever write on art history again?

BROOKNER: No. That particular career is over. Once you have let it go you can't go back. I shall not give up studying, but I might do it with words rather than pictures, although pictures will come into it. At present I am working on a new novel and doing it more slowly than before.

INTERVIEWER: Despite their subtlety and variations, all your books so far have been basically about love. Do you think you will go on writing about love?

BROOKNER: What else is there? All the rest is mere literature!

—SHUSHA GUPPY
Winter 1987

11. Robert Stone

Robert Stone was born in Brooklyn in 1937. He left high school in his senior year to join the U.S. Navy. Upon discharge from the Navy, he worked for the *New York Daily News* and traveled extensively.

In 1962 he went to Stanford on a Stegner Fellowship and lived near Perry Lane, where he "took to hanging around with Ken Kesey which was richly rewarding in many ways" but which delayed his first novel considerably. In August of 1967 his first novel, *A Hall of Mirrors,* appeared as the Houghton Mifflin literary fellowship novel for that year, and won the William Faulkner Award. Before his second book came out, Stone had received both an award from the American Academy of Arts and Letters and a Guggenheim Fellowship. He and his wife Janice spent the years between 1968 and 1971 in London; in May of 1971, Stone went to Vietnam for two months as a representative of various English publications. His reports from Vietnam appeared in *The Guardian.*

Each of Stone's four long novels, *A Hall of Mirrors* (1967), *Dog Soldiers* (1974), *A Flag For Sunrise* (1981), and *Children of Light* (1986) has met with critical acclaim; *Dog Soldiers* won the 1975 National Book Award.

Ten miles to the south, the road on which they drove turned inland, crossed the mountains on the spine of Baja, and ran for thirty miles within sight of the Sea of Cortez. At the final curve of its eastward loop, a dirt track led from the highway toward the shore, ending at a well appointed fishing resort called Benson's Marina. At Benson's there was a large comfortable ranchhouse in the Sonoran style, a few fast powerboats rigged for big game fishing and a small air strip. Benson ran a pair of light aircraft for long distance transportation and fish spotting.

Early on during production, Lu Anne had been told about Benson's by Frank Carnehan; she and Lionel had hired Benson's son to fly them to San Lucas for a long weekend. The flight had produced much corporate anxiety after the fact because the film's insurance coverage did not apply to impromptu charter flights in unauthorized carriers. Charlie Freitag had been cross and Axelrod had been upbraided.

In the early hours of the morning, their car turned into Benson's and pulled up beside his dock. Walker had slept; a light cokey sleep, full of theatrical nightmares that had his sons in them.

Lu Anne walked straight to the lighted pier and stood next to the fuel pumps, looking out across the gulf. Walker climbed from the car and asked the driver to park it out of the way. In the shadow of the boat house, he had some more cocaine. The drug made him feel jittery and cold in the stiff ocean wind. Lu Anne had Lowndes' bottle of scotch in her tote bag, so he had a drink from it.

A Robert Stone manuscript page, from his most recent novel, Children of Light; *an indication of how barren the word processor has made examples of a work-in-progress.*

© Jerry Boyer

Robert Stone

Robert Stone lives in a small frame house on the Connecticut coast. Inside, a long white living room with curving walls suggests Oriental calm, and a pocket kitchen like a ship's galley offers the comic sight of tame ducks feeding on the water just below. The hesitant phrases of the Modern Jazz Quartet chime from a battered stereo flanked by bookshelves filled with fiction, philosophy, and church history. Over a built-in sofa hangs an unframed poster for Who'll Stop The Rain?, *the film Stone coauthored from his second novel,* Dog Soldiers. *Stone and his wife Janice moved into this house in the fall of 1981; they have a son and daughter, grown and gone.*

The novelist works in an attic room crowded with cardboard boxes and manuscripts and decorated with several brightly colored samples of Spanish religious art. At one end of the long room, a wide window affords a view of a gray October sea; another looks down on the gravel parking lot of a clam bar. Stone writes at a table only a little larger than the word processor it supports. When his office phone rings, it may be an editor on the line begging him to cover a story, a director seeking to interest him in a new part (in the summer of 1982, Stone played Kent in a professional production of King Lear in California), or an interviewer plaguing him with yet another question that he will answer with care and unfailing courtesy.

Although the Stones have lived in many parts of the country, and for four years in London, changes of locale have rarely altered the writer's routine: "I get up very early, drink a pot of tea, and go for as long as I can." Stone says he stops only when he has left himself a clear starting point for the following day. For weeks on end he will take few days off if his work is going well. "My imagination will still be functioning," he says with a laugh, "twelve hours after my brain is dead."

He lives more quietly now than in his years in the California counterculture as one of Ken Kesey's "Merry Pranksters"; his free time is given over to milder pleasures, such as the exploration by canoe of the salt lagoon behind his house. But even this quiet coast has its threat: the past summer, Stone told me, a large shark was spotted in the lagoon, just off the docks, importing a frisson of fear into the neighborhood.

Stone is in his late forties, a trim man whose thinning hair and well-barbered beard frame a ruddy, pensive face yet to be done justice by his book jacket photos. His voice, branded by years of Scotch and smoke, was deep and serene as we began our two days of talk.

INTERVIEWER: Was there one book that started you writing?
STONE: It was a rereading of *The Great Gatsby* that made me think about writing a novel. I was living on St. Mark's Place in New York; it was a different world in those days. I was in

my twenties. I decided I knew a few meanings; I understood patterns in life. I figured, I can't sell this understanding, or smoke it, so I will write a novel. I then started to write *A Hall of Mirrors*. It must have taken me six years, a dreadful amount of time. I really began work on the novel during my Stegner Fellowship at Stanford, which brought me out to California just about the time that everything was going slightly crazy. So I spent a lot of my time, when I should have been writing, experiencing death and transfiguration and rebirth on LSD in Palo Alto. It wasn't an atmosphere that was conducive to getting a whole lot of work done.

INTERVIEWER: You once described writing your first novel as a process that paralleled your life.

STONE: *A Hall of Mirrors* was something I shattered my youth against. All my youth went into it. I put everything I knew into that book. It was written through years of dramatic change, not only for me, but for the country. It covers the sixties from the Kennedy assassination through the civil rights movement to the beginning of acid, the hippies, the war . . .

INTERVIEWER: Does that mean you changed your conception of the book as you were writing it, that you tried to respond to those changes?

STONE: Yes. And to things that were happening with me. One way or another, it all went into the book. And of course it all went very slowly because once my Stegner Fellowship was over, my wife, Janice, and I had to take turns working. I'd work for twenty weeks and then be on unemployment for twenty weeks and so on. So it took me a long, long time to finish it.

INTERVIEWER: You mention responding to national as well as personal change. Do you consciously try to write about America?

STONE: Yes, I do. That is my subject. America and Americans.

INTERVIEWER: You have been cited as a writer who addresses

larger social issues. Do you start with those in mind, or do you simply start out with the characters and because you have political concerns these issues naturally come out?

STONE: It is very natural. You construct characters and set them going in their own interior landscape, and what they find to talk about and what confronts them are, of course, things that concern you most.

INTERVIEWER: Is writing easy for you? Does it flow smoothly?

STONE: It's goddamn hard. Nobody really cares whether you do it or not. You have to make yourself do it. I'm very lazy and I suffer as a result. Of course, when it's going well there's nothing in the world like it. But it's also very lonely. If you do something you're really pleased with, you're in the crazy position of being exhilarated all by yourself. I remember finishing one section of *Dog Soldiers*—the end of Hicks's walk—in the basement of a college library, working at night, while the rest of the place was closed down, and I staggered out in tears, talking to myself, and ran into a security guard. It's hard to come down from a high in your work—it's one of the reasons writers drink. The exhilaration of your work turns into the daily depression of the aftermath. But if you heal that with a lot of Scotch you're not fit for duty the next day. When I was younger I was able to use hangovers, but now I have to go to bed early.

INTERVIEWER: You really think of yourself as lazy?

STONE: Well, my books aren't lazy books, but I have a lazy way of working. I do a very rough first draft and then a second and sometimes I have to do a third because I didn't take the trouble to really organize the first. And I take breaks between drafts. And I do altogether too much traveling.

INTERVIEWER: You have gone for relatively long periods of time between books. Seven years between *A Hall of Mirrors* and *Dog Soldiers*, and then another seven before *A Flag For Sunrise*. Are you writing all that time?

STONE: It seems to me that I am. I was working all those years on *A Flag For Sunrise*. I could probably have gotten six books out of my three if I'd wanted to do smaller themes. Twice as many books and they would have been half as good. Six so-so books. I don't need that. I like big novels; I really admire the grand slam.

INTERVIEWER: Do you have any special requirements, conditions necessary for your working environment?

STONE: Well, of course, I find ways to delay the day as much as possible, but there are no particular rituals connected with that for me, like having a special coffee cup or sharpening six pencils. I do need physical order, because I'm addressing the insubstantiality of structures—that's where the blank page starts. No top, no bottom, no sides. I find it hard to sit still. I pace a lot. I've got to have a pen in my hand when I'm not actually typing.

INTERVIEWER: You mostly type?

STONE: Yes, until something becomes elusive. Then I write in longhand in order to be precise. On a typewriter or word processor you can rush something that shouldn't be rushed—you can lose nuance, richness, lucidity. The pen compels lucidity.

INTERVIEWER: Do you read work aloud to yourself?

STONE: No. My inner ear is very accurate. I know what the writing sounds like.

INTERVIEWER: Your prose is very rich in sensual detail—imagery intensified by the cadence of the sentence.

STONE: I use the white space. I'm interested in precise meaning and in reverberation, in associative levels. What you're trying to do when you write is to crowd the reader out of his own space and occupy it with yours, in a good cause. You're trying to take over his sensibility and deliver an experience that moves from mere information.

INTERVIEWER: I see that. But one of the things I respond to

most in your writing is the tremendous particularity, your way of relating language to reality. It seems to me that there's a danger, if language takes the reader too far into cosmic preoccupations, of losing that immediacy.

STONE: The object is to make a connection between your characters and the contour of things as they are. The danger is of becoming pretentious. And yet it's necessary that a given dramatized scene have a richness of reference. Take a basic philosophical question: why is there something rather than nothing? Two people in love, two people in a battle to the death, refer to that question. To say so directly is preposterous; you have to get there along the path of your art. How do you relate events to that basic question? You choose words that open up deeper and deeper levels of existence by sustaining a sound which perfectly serves the narrative and which at the same time relates through a series of associations to the larger questions.

INTERVIEWER: That would account for the shifting levels of your rhetoric, which plays the colloquial against high ornamentation. The effect is a constant tone of irony.

STONE: Irony is my friend and brother. "To know true things by what their mockeries be." There's only one subject for fiction or poetry or even a joke: *how it is.* In all the arts, the payoff is always the same: recognition. If it works, you say that's real, that's truth, that's life, that's the way things are. "There it is."

INTERVIEWER: The classic aphorism of the Vietnam war.

STONE: Exactly.

INTERVIEWER: I understand one article you filed from Vietnam was about a Saigon rock festival. That certainly puts two worlds of the time together.

STONE: That was a funny scene. Stoned rear-echelon GIs and a Vietnamese band that was a phonocopy of The Grateful Dead. Meanwhile, a light plane kept circling overhead streaming a Christian banner attacking rock as the devil's music.

There was an oncoming monsoon and the banner kept threatening to foul the guy's propeller. Finally he fell out of sight and everybody waited for the crash, which didn't come. I remember one very stoned GI saying to another, "There it is."

INTERVIEWER: You were a correspondent in Vietnam in 1971. . . .

STONE: Well, I was there less than two months, but every day was different. It was the kind of place where anything could have happened. There's nothing that couldn't have happened there. If you encountered choirs of seraphim up the river or if somebody said he'd just seen a vision of St. George on Hill 51, you'd just say, "There it is. . . ." I was in Saigon a lot of the time. I did get deeper into I Corps, and I was in Cam Rahn Bay. But in Saigon I picked up with a guy who was involved in the dope trade there and in a very short time I had found out more than I really wanted to know. It was very frightening. I should also say that this period—1971—was a time when, in the line, there was not a lot of combat involving American troops. There was rocketing up around Phu Bai, there were some bombs going off in Saigon, but nobody was quite sure who was responsible for them. American troops were not heavily engaged. It was the time of Vietnamization. The talks were going on in Paris, and American troops were being kept out of the line to keep the casualty rates down.

INTERVIEWER: Was Vietnam your first experience of war?

STONE: No, I first saw war when I was in the Navy, in the Mediterranean, in 1956. I saw the French air attack on Port Said—jets from the carrier *Lafayette* coming in right on top of our radar mast and shelling. Those multicolored tracers in the night that I saw again in Vietnam I saw with something like nostalgia. But it was quite horrible. You could look through the glasses and see donkeys and people flying through the air, chewed up by 7.62s and rockets. It was a slaughter of civilians. But it always is.

INTERVIEWER: Are you interested in observing future wars, or have you had enough?

STONE: I don't know. There was a wonderful expression soldiers had in the American Civil War that captures the strangeness of combat, the charm—they called it "going to see the elephant." There are times when I feel that once you've seen war, you want to see it again.

INTERVIEWER: It seems to me that your work is in the tradition of twentieth-century fiction that takes war as its principal metaphor for our lives. Would you say that war is the most complete description of our situation?

STONE: It's literally true that the world is seen by the superpowers as a grid of specific targets. We're all on military maps. There happens to be no action in those zones at present, but they're there. And then there are the wars we fight with ourselves in our own cities. It is the simple truth that, wherever you are, there is an armed enemy present, not far away.

INTERVIEWER: I'd like to ask a little about your evolution as a writer.

STONE: My early life was very strange. I was a solitary; radio fashioned my imagination. Radio narrative always has to embody a full account of both action and scene. I began to do that myself. When I was seven or eight, I'd walk through Central Park like Sam Spade, describing aloud what I was doing, becoming both the actor and the writer setting him into the scene. That was where I developed an inner ear.

INTERVIEWER: So you grew up in New York?

STONE: For the most part we were in New York, my mother and I. It was just the two of us. My mother was, I now realize, schizophrenic, and sometimes she was better than at other times. She lost a job as a schoolteacher in New York for medical reasons; she had a very small pension, and when she was very ill, there was really no place for me to go. Except this place that was, well, it functioned partly as a day school. My mother was in and out of hospitals. I was in an orphanage run by the Marist brothers from the age of six until just before I was ten.

INTERVIEWER: I wonder how her schizophrenia influenced your imagination.

STONE: I wonder that too. I am not really sure. One thing I know is that I usually can recognize schizophrenics when I see them. There is a certain way of speaking. I am talking about functioning schizophrenics, professional people; there are a lot of them around. It is very hard to talk about it in the abstract. In California, years ago, I had a doctor who would tell me these rather askew anecdotes that didn't seem to have any point. What it reminded me of was my mother's disconnection. Their associative patterns seemed to be similar. I finally realized what his problem was. He was about halfway into another kind of reality, but at the same time he was a doctor, functioning as a GP.

INTERVIEWER: Lu Anne, the heroine of *Children of Light,* is schizophrenic.

STONE: Lu Anne's condition is based on what I have experienced with people. There are people who have delusional systems they are really quite aware of and treat as nemeses. That is Lu Anne's condition; she has a lot of insight into her own delusional systems. Actually, many people have that, and I have been waiting a long time to write about it. It seems to be part of how I see things. I think that is partly because of my mother, whom I liked very much, but who was very difficult for me to understand. When she was my contact person for reality, for information about the world, I got some confusing signals.

INTERVIEWER: Have you ever written about your childhood?

STONE: I don't write about my childhood or New York; I have hardly any references to it at all. In a way, that's because I always used my imagination as a kind of alternative life when I wanted to be in another place than the one I was in. I just didn't want to write about that stuff. I wanted to enjoy myself.

I wasn't ready to write about it; perhaps I'm not ready to write about it yet.

INTERVIEWER: Did you read in the Navy?

STONE: Yes. Everybody on a ship reads, whether it's comic books, or Westerns, or the Bible, or whatever. They always read a lot. I was reading *Moby Dick,* which sounds terribly precious, but I thought if you can't read *Moby Dick* in the roaring forties, you'll never read *Moby Dick.* So I brought it along. I also read *Ulysses* on the same trip. I seem to have imprinted the ocean in a very strong way because I end up with all these marine images that just seem so readily at hand for me.

INTERVIEWER: Many people think of you as having a considerable grasp on the major shift in American culture from the Beats in the fifties to the sixties' counterculture.

STONE: I was in the right place at the right time to see that. It started out with Jack Kerouac's *On the Road* while I was still in the Navy. My mother recommended the book to me. I am probably the only person who had *On the Road* recommended to him by his mother. It is very hard to go back and think about what *On the Road* was saying to me. I pick it up now and all I can see is Neal Cassady. I got to know him. It was a wonderful rendering of him, but I don't see much else in it. Now it just reminds me of somebody writing on speed. That may be uncharitable, but frankly I find it very sentimental. As I say, I am not sure what it was that moved me. I suppose there was that tradition of the American road. I can almost remember what that was like. Thinking about the great continent out there and the city intersections, that myth of the roadside traveler. It reminded me of how every once in a while my mother and I would take off on some migration to where things were going to be better, like Chicago or wherever. We went all the way to New Mexico. I can't remember what we were in quest of. We were in quest of something though. We usually ended up on welfare, then trying to get out of wherever we were. One time we went to Chicago and ended up in a Salvation Army shelter on the North Side because we ran out of money. We stayed for as long as the Salvation Army would keep us, and then somehow my mother scraped together money to get back to New York. When we got back, we spent two nights sleeping on a roof. It was wild, you know. It was useful. On the one hand, it gave me a fear of chaos, and on the other hand, it was a romance with the world and bus stations and things like that.

INTERVIEWER: You didn't finish college, did you?

STONE: No, I started at New York University and hung on for about a year, but I couldn't stay with it. I was working at the *Daily News* at night and trying to go to classes in the daytime and I just couldn't do it, so I dropped out. In Greenwich Village, a lot of stuff was happening then. Janice worked in the Figaro and she also worked at the Seven Arts on Forty-third and Ninth Avenue. The Seven Arts, of course, was where Kerouac and Allen Ginsberg and Ray Bremser and all those other guys with droopy expressions were regulars. I kind of hung out smoking lots of cigarettes, looking very cool, listening to Coltrane. Janice and I were both at NYU until I quit. She had another job as a guidette in the RCA Building. We both got out about one o'clock, I from the *Daily News.* She took off her guidette uniform and put on her black stockings and was a waitress in the Seven Arts where I'd go to hang out.

INTERVIEWER: Were you writing poetry at that time?

STONE: Yes, I was writing it, and reading, and hanging out, though I didn't have too much time to hang out. I had to assume a languid posture in a hurry because I had to be up early in the morning. I really felt that hanging out was the price I had to pay, whether I wrote anything or not; these were the people who were more like me or what I wanted to be. One had the sense in those days that it was a relatively small thing, not mass bohemia like you had in the sixties. There was a lot of marijuana and you could really go to jail for years; we all thought it was very decadent and terrific of us. There was an espresso place on Sixth Street between First and Second avenues run by a guy named Baron, who was a follower of Ayn Rand—he had a dollar sign outside his café. Baron sold peyote buttons. It was very hard to eat peyote; you had to put it into a Waring blender and do all sorts of things to get enough down. I remember being on peyote and seeing a wrestling match for the *Daily News* in Madison Square Garden; seeing this on peyote may have changed my life. Once I got my Stegner and got out to California, I happened to collide with Ken Kesey; he lived just a couple of streets away. That whole scene was just ready to take off. And I thought I knew all about peyote and drugs and such. It didn't bother me to experiment. Kesey had a job as an orderly in the Veteran's Hospital and he was involved in the first experiments that were being conducted in psychedelic drugs. He was a volunteer and so was his friend Vic Lovell, who is a psychologist now. They were doing all these crazy drugs on an experimental basis. Some of them worked, some of them did not. I can remember really off-the-wall things called IT290s; they didn't even have names they were so arcane. Whatever IT290 was, I remember walking through the woods and suddenly encountering this huge locomotive, a green locomotive with gold trim, a very detailed hallucination which I remember particularly well. I still have a lot of friends out there, people who I went through that stuff with.

INTERVIEWER: Were your friends important to your work at that point?

STONE: The whole scene probably set me back a year or two, but my friends were certainly important in my life. California in the early sixties was really quite wonderful. It seemed so civilized and so easygoing; really it was fun when the strangest thing around was us, and we were pretty harmless.

INTERVIEWER: *A Hall of Mirrors* is a cohesive book, considering the conditions under which it was written and the long span of time. . . .

STONE: It was necessary that it be cohesive. I was looking for a vision of America, for a statement about the American condition. I was after a book that would be as ambitious as possible. I wanted to be an American Gogol if I could, I wanted to write *Dead Souls.* All of the characters represent ideas about America, about an America in a period of extraordinary, vivid transition.

INTERVIEWER: In a way, it seems to me that the novel is a kind of counterpart to *On the Road.*

STONE: *On the Road* twenty years after. In a way. Yes.

INTERVIEWER: Certainly Ray Hicks in *Dog Soldiers* has some biographical touches drawn from the same Neal Cassady who appeared as Dean Moriarty in *On the Road.* Did you know Kerouac when you were hanging out with Kesey—"on the bus"?

STONE: I didn't know him well. And I didn't travel on the bus. I saw the bus off and greeted the bus when it arrived on Riverside Drive. We went to a party where Kerouac and Ginsberg and Orlovsky and those guys were, and Kerouac was at his drunken worst. He was also very jealous of Neal, who had shifted his allegiance to Kesey. But Neal was pretty exhausted, too. I saw some films taken on the bus—Neal looked like he was tired from trying to keep up with the limitless energy of all those kids. Anyway . . . Kerouac at that party was drunk and pissed off, a situation I understand very well. The first thing I ever said to him was, "Hey, Jack, have you got a cigarette?" And he said, "I ain't gonna give you no fucking cigarette, man, there's a drugstore on the corner, you can go down there and buy a fucking pack of cigarettes, don't ask me for cigarettes." That's my Kerouac story.

INTERVIEWER: That's a sad story. The passing of the torch. Is Tom Wolfe's book on Kesey, *The Electric Kool-Aid Acid Test,* a pretty good picture of that whole scene?

STONE: It's amazingly good. It also forces a coherence on

that scene that it didn't necessarily have. I mean that stuff was all so ephemeral, there was no philosophical core to it, particularly, it was all just goofiness.

INTERVIEWER: Well, the Wolfe book on Kesey does convey—or impose—the notion of religious quest.

STONE: It's hard to stay away from religion when you mess with acid.

INTERVIEWER: Neal Cassady as a figure on that scene does more than form a historical link between the Beat Generation and the counterculture. He also carries on the image of the affectless sociopath as a major American cultural type, a figure of particular interest to you in your fiction.

STONE: Well, Cassady was a benign version of that figure. Gary Gilmore may be closer to what I mean, a vicious drifter of the kind America seems to produce in greater quantity than does any other country, probably because there is no moral center to our middle class. This society is so fractured. It never really had that period of high bourgeois cultural development that most European countries had. The American underclass has never had the tradition and stability of a European peasantry so it could never develop feudal loyalties. Instead we get these institutionalized personalities whose arrested emotions oblige them to mimic mood, feeling, love. This is the origin of their violence.

INTERVIEWER: Such people will always constitute the night side of a counterculture. Charles Manson. Gilmore. Figures like Kesey and Kerouac draw forth its princes and saints.

STONE: I think cultural undergrounds develop in the void left by the abdication of the official culture. During the sixties, so many august institutions seemed to have no self-confidence. The universities, corporations, the very fabric of the state. Everything you pushed just seemed to fall over. Everything was up for grabs. For me, the counterculture was like a party that spilled out into the world until one had the odd feeling in society that one was walking around looking at the results of a party that had ended a few years before—a big experiment. But there was no program, everybody wanted different things. I think Kesey wanted a cultural revolution, the nature of which was uncertain; he was just making it up as he went along. Other people were into political reform. Others thought the drugs would fix it all. Peace and love and dope.

INTERVIEWER: There's a lot of dope, and an epic amount of drinking in your books—

STONE: I can't stop them from doing it. I just can't. It's getting ridiculous. I get laughed at for the volume of chemicals that gets consumed, the amount of dope and booze. And now this guy's doing it again in my new book.

INTERVIEWER: Whom do you consider your literary forebears?

STONE: My "forebears" are unsurprising. The great masters, the late Victorians; more Hemingway and Fitzgerald than Faulkner. I like Céline and Nathanael West and Dos Passos. I can't really begin to characterize my own style beyond saying that it closely reflects my thinking, my world view. But in my first novel, I felt pretty free—I was all over the lot. And I did try as forcefully as I could to invent a voice. It's filled with influences and echoes, but it's mine, as nearly as I can make it so. I began *A Hall of Mirrors* as a realistic novel, but my life changed and the world changed and when I thought about it I realized that "realism" was a fallacy. It's simply not tenable. You have to write a poem about what you're describing. You can't render, can't dissect. Zola was deluded.

INTERVIEWER: Those remarks suggest an affinity with writers like John Barth and William Gass and Donald Barthelme. But I don't really see you in that camp.

STONE: My difference with those writers is that they take realism too seriously and so have to react against it. I don't feel the necessity of reacting against it. I don't believe in it to start with. Realism as a theory of literature is meaningless. I can start with it as a mode precisely because I don't believe in it. I *know* it's all a world of words—what else could it be? I had the curious luck to be raised by a schizophrenic, which gives one a tremendous advantage in understanding the relationship of language to reality. I had to develop a model of reality in the face of being conditioned to a schizophrenic world. I had to sort out causality for myself. My mother's world was pure magic. And because I had no father I eventually went into a sort of orphanage when my mother could no longer cope. So at the age of six I went into an institution, which taught me to be a listener. I had to deal with all the ways people were coming on to me, had to listen to all their trips and sort them out. Realism wasn't an issue because there wasn't any. I always had a vaguely dreamlike sense of things. There was no strong distinction for me between objective and imaginative worlds.

INTERVIEWER: Life was failing to provide you with coherent narrative.

STONE: That's right. Life wasn't providing narrative so I had to. I had very little personal mythology of my own.

INTERVIEWER: All this suggests some intricate connections among living and writing and acting. Many of your characters seem preoccupied with the shifting roles in their lives: who am I here?

STONE: Yes. And my becoming a writer was my answer to that question. It was an absolute necessity. I had to create somebody significant or I would have been swept away. I've been known to say, not altogether facetiously, that life is a means of extracting fiction. If I start out with the claim that I tell stories to serve life, it's easy enough to reverse the terms.

INTERVIEWER: The characters in your books are often writers, but of forms other than fiction. Can you speak a bit about your own work in other forms?

STONE: I intend to write a play. I'd direct a film if the chance came my way. But with those forms too many other people get their hands on your work. The joy of fiction is its autonomy. You take the risks, you take the rap.

INTERVIEWER: Has your work as a screenwriter taught you anything about writing novels?

STONE: No. My screenplays have had no influence on my fiction. But many writers of my generation, which was spared television in its youth, grew up with their sense of narrative influenced by the structure of film. And you can go back much earlier to see that. Joyce, for example. Interestingly, Dickens seems to have anticipated the shape of the movies—look at the first few pages of *Great Expectations.*

INTERVIEWER: When you think of the writers of your generation, do you find a special constellation of contemporaries where you locate yourself?

STONE: Not really. I think more of generations of readers— for me, people who had some intense experience of the sixties. That's a generation I address. I share their concerns, their history. I get a certain amount of mail that reflects that. But there are no writers I'm aware of who are doing the same sort of thing I'm doing because I take seriously questions that the culture has largely obviated. In a sense, I'm a theologian. And so far as I know I'm the only one.

INTERVIEWER: Does this connect in a way to what you've called the fractured state of American letters?

STONE: You have famous writers, but there's no center. There are the best-seller writers, who are anonymous, almost industrial figures. You have writers who write primarily for other writers. And you have writers with their separate and different constituencies. But American fiction is not in a state of high health. This has something to do with the economic exigencies of publishing, of course. There's a lot of pressure on the noncommercial novel, on what publishers call marginal fiction. Fewer first novels are published, fewer books of any real quality that don't seem immediately bankable. This has to show itself in a kind of reduced, duller national literature, at least for the near future.

INTERVIEWER: As far as best-selling fiction is concerned—

STONE: The best-seller list has always for the most part been the work of hacks, but in the past there seems to have been more space for serious writers. The pressure that's squeezing them out is dangerous and worrying. At the same time there are all these academic writing programs turning out the new second lieutenants of literature, and some of them somehow do manage to get published.

INTERVIEWER: All of your books offer the same general structure: multiple characters, introduced at disparate points woven slowly together until the principals collide. How is that done in the writing? Is one figure followed nearly to the end, or is each scene treated in what will be its final sequence?

STONE: The latter. To run all those lines out one at a time would quickly turn stale. You have to be able to surprise yourself. In *Dog Soldiers,* for example, I didn't know Hicks was going to shoot Dieter until the day I wrote it. I just began writing their dialogue until it became inevitable. I was always attracted to the idea of bringing different elements together. One of my favorite radio programs was "Tell Me A Story," in which people were presented with three things to weave into one.

INTERVIEWER: As material emerges, do you control it with an outline? Charts, notebooks, things like that?

STONE: The only thing I do is make a short list that indicates sequence, very loosely. And then I sometimes jumble the stuff once I've got it written.

INTERVIEWER: You juxtapose sequences in ways you hadn't planned on?

STONE: Yes. Literally juggle them. But I don't use charts or notes.

INTERVIEWER: You don't plot through to a conclusion?

STONE: I know the beginning and usually the end. My problem is the middle—the second act, so to speak.

INTERVIEWER: At what point in the process of a book is your

consciousness of technique strongest, as opposed to times when the sheer energy of invention carries you along?

STONE: There are always certain metaphorical events that have to carry special weight. My stress on technique will be strongest when I encounter them. But there's no point at which the pleasure of invention justifies you in self-indulgence. You can never give yourself a break, you always have to make the hardest decisions. That means, for example, writing a brilliant passage and then throwing it away if there's no use for it in terms of the total design. It means scorning to find a clever way around problems that must be grappled with. There are times you have to take the chance that you may derail the structure of your book.

INTERVIEWER: Can you give an example?

STONE: Well, the meeting of the revolutionaries in *A Flag For Sunrise* broke some rules of structure. They invaded the order of the book—for good reason—and then were never seen again. That scene was tough, I had to rewrite it a lot. The scene of Naftali's suicide—I must have rewritten that eight times. And cut it to the bone. In the book, it's only a fourth as long as it was in earlier drafts. All kinds of great lines—they had to go. It took forever. I couldn't get it right for the longest time. And when I reread it in the finished book, I thought it was awful. I was desolate. But Janice persuaded me that the scene was good. I always feel desolate when I finish a book. I thought that *A Flag For Sunrise* had some good scenes, but it troubled me overall. I fell into a great depression.

INTERVIEWER: Has there ever been a negative criticism of your work that you found useful?

STONE: Well, I've seen negative positions I could respect. But I don't know that I learned anything from them. Negative criticism of my work tends to be very vitriolic.

INTERVIEWER: The religious element in your work often asserts itself in classic existential form—for example, Hicks's ideal of ideas embodied in action, or Holliwell's remark in *A Flag For Sunrise,* "There's always a place for God—there's some question as to whether he's in it." This seems a near reflection of Heidegger's assertion that he is neither theistic nor atheistic but adrift in a world from which God is absent.

STONE: I feel a very deep connection to the existentialist tradition of God as an absence—not a meaningless void, but a negative presence we live in terms of. I do have the sense of a transcendent plane from which I'm barred and I want to play off of it. If it's there, I'll get one sound. If it's not, I'll get a different sound.

INTERVIEWER: Was the Catholic orphanage the start of your religious opinions?

STONE: Yes. I felt very rebellious. Every once in a while I would get very angry at the whole structure, although I guess I believed it. I was in that very difficult position you get in when you really believe in God, and at the same time you are very angry: God is this huge creature who we must know, love, and serve, though actually you feel like you want to kick the son of a bitch. The effect on me was I felt I was just doing things wrong.

INTERVIEWER: Do you have a fully articulated theory of fiction? In the sense, say, that Conrad framed his in the preface to *The Nigger of the Narcissus*?

STONE: "Fiction must justify itself in every line." Yes. I'm beginning to frame one—and along rather Conradian lines. Prose fiction must first of all perform the traditional functions of storytelling. We *need* stories. We can't identify ourselves without them. We're always telling ourselves stories about who we are: that's what history is, what the idea of a nation or an individual is. The purpose of fiction is to help us answer the question we must constantly be asking ourselves: who do we think we are and what do we think we're doing?

INTERVIEWER: This quest can, on the part of some of your characters, particularly the more blighted or thwarted, take very brutal forms. Think of Rheinhardt, in *A Hall of Mirrors,* who can't seem to make America deliver on the American dream.

STONE: What I'm always trying to do is define that process in American life that puts people in a state of anomie, of frustration. The national promise is so great that a tremendous bitterness is evoked by its elusiveness. That was Fitzgerald's subject, and it's mine. So many people go bonkers in this country—I mean, they're doing all the right things and they're still not getting off.

INTERVIEWER: Do you think those expectations will be changed by the economic fact that most Americans will probably live in somewhat more straitened circumstances for some years to come?

STONE: I'm not sure. I think even the poorest people, partly for purely commercial reasons, are still encouraged to think of themselves as candidates for participation in the big American payoff. And of course the nature of the payoff has changed—no more white picket fences. The mass media has taught everybody the glamour of crime. When you're a crook, you're on the side of the chaos; how can you lose? If you're the guy that walks home from the felt factory after twenty years on the job and gets blown away by a freak on angel dust for the pay in your pockets, you're a chump.

INTERVIEWER: This touches on a condition central to your work—what you've called everybody's "diminishing margin of protection." Thus in *Dog Soldiers* you replay Vietnam in Southern California. And in the other books people are always falling prey to some form of planned or random violence—

STONE: We live in a time of ongoing war and the threat of violence is very close to all of us. It's not an exotic thing. You have to be pretty lucky to get through a year without witnessing it.

INTERVIEWER: If a writer explores violence at length in his work, is there a sense in which he inevitably celebrates it?

STONE: I would call it a coming to terms. There is a catharsis. For me, it's a way of dealing with the violence in myself. I think it can do that for the reader as well. Violence *is* a preoccupation of mine. It occurs in my books perhaps disproportionately. But it's been my fortune to see rather a lot of it and to have to think about it. I try to curb my fears in what I write. There's a sense in which I use my characters as scapegoats to pay my dues for me, to ward with their flesh danger away from mine. You know, when some drama intrudes on your life your first impulse is to recount it—to turn disaster into anecdote or art. I deal with much that's negative and gruesome, but I don't write to dispirit people. I write to give them courage, to make them confront things as they are in a more courageous way.

INTERVIEWER: Let me return to Conrad, with whom you've claimed some affinity. I've seen it suggested that Freud and Conrad provide polar notions of reality and thus suggest a continuum along which we may locate ourselves. In Freud there's the faith that psychic reality is knowable once we strip away the skins of neurotic fiction that conceal it. In Conrad, we find reality numinous, and indeed composed of all our fictions about it.

STONE: Well, Freud created a mythology out of a nineteenth-century scientific optimism; he said that the glow in the haunted house was just phosphorescence from the swamp—a comforting high bourgeois myth. Conrad was a man of the world and a skeptic who worked not on the basis of ideology but of common sense. He saw things as they are without wanting to reduce them to theory. In that respect he's closer to the temper of our own time and certainly closer to my own ideas about reality and about how to explore it in fiction.

INTERVIEWER: Conrad provided you with a powerful epigraph for *Dog Soldiers*. And Robert Lowell one for *A Hall of Mirrors*. There's no epigraph for *A Flag For Sunrise*.

STONE: It's in the book. The Emily Dickinson poem Justin quotes. "A wife—at daybreak—shall I be—"

INTERVIEWER: Of course. "Sunrise, hast thou a flag for me?" That throws a lot of the weight of the book on Justin.

STONE: It gives many of her scenes the quality of metaphorical event I mentioned. It links religious themes with erotic encounter. But it also summarizes a larger idea, the question of what awaits us all on the morning after the battle, so to speak. What will be there to claim our allegiance—the red banner of revolution, or some emblem we can't recognize but that we've somehow created? And of course I intend an ironic reference to the American flag.

INTERVIEWER: Do you have your own ways, like Hicks, of "endeavoring to lead a spiritual life"? I mean, distinct from your work.

STONE: I attempt to. I'm always looking for a spiritual discipline I can live with. When I stopped being religious, being a Catholic, it was—as I did not realize at the time, but have come to since—devastating to me. It was a spiritual and moral devastation—shattering. And yet there was no trauma at the time; it seemed painless, it felt like ordinary maturation. But it left a great hunger.

INTERVIEWER: Is Catholicism still important to you?

STONE: Somebody has said that it's almost as hard to stop being a Catholic as it is to stop being a black. But I greatly admire the Protestant spirit, the Protestant heroes—Luther, Kierkegaard. And I admire the great skeptics—Erasmus and Montaigne, that cast of mind. It's very valuable. And, ironically, it's built into the kind of rigorous training in language and logic that I received.

INTERVIEWER: Catholic reason enabled you to cast off Catholic faith?

STONE: Well, it surely wasn't intended to. But I did learn the lucid analysis of rhetorical argument and thus became more immune to propaganda. And yet the skepticism that led me out of religious belief also leads me out of secular complacency.

INTERVIEWER: Aside from that childhood training in rhetoric, did you learn anything about writing in other academic programs? Anything useful or valuable about creative writing?

STONE: Not really. But a creative writing class can at least be good for morale. When I teach writing, I do things like take classes to bars and race tracks to listen to dialogue. But that kind of thing has limited usefulness. There's no body of technology to impart. But that doesn't mean classes can't help. The idea that young writers ought to be out slinging hash or covering the fights or whatever is bullshit. There's a point where a class can do a lot of good. You know, you throw the rock and you get the splash.

INTERVIEWER: Your own experience in a way represents a synthesis of available models for American novelists: some academic background and connection, and an active life in a varied world.

STONE: I think writers at present can pass fairly easily between these worlds. I have no academic credentials aside from my work, but I've been able to teach and I sometimes enjoy it.

INTERVIEWER: Do you have any interest in writers' conferences and colonies, that kind of thing?

STONE: I've been several times to a wonderful conference in Alaska that's filled with trappers and fishermen and people who spend a lot of time alone. Every year, on the winter solstice, they get together to talk books and writing and party.

INTERVIEWER: You've been accorded from the beginning a handsome ration of prizes, awards, literary recognition of that kind. Has that had an effect on your work—given you an image you had to live in terms of?

STONE: I've kept my edge, stayed hungry, I think. I never sold so many copies that I got overfed. It's less things like prizes than the simple fact of your first publication that changes everything forever. The minute you appear in print you lose some freedom and innocence and accept a degree of responsibility.

INTERVIEWER: Are there things you'd like to attempt in fiction that you haven't done yet?

STONE: I'd like to write more comic stuff. I mean, there's always some humor in all the awfulness I write about, but sometimes I think of writing—well, I don't know that I could write a purely humorous book that wouldn't have some sort of ghastliness in it. It would have to be a weird kind of humor.

INTERVIEWER: Are there areas of weakness in your work so far that you can identify, things that dissatisfy you?

STONE: Ken Kesey once told me I use too many commas.

INTERVIEWER: Do you ever have writer's block?

STONE: I have a lot of depressed periods during which I'm incapable of working. But I'm not blocked by material or anything when I'm actually writing. I turn up more stuff I want to do than I have room or time to do it in.

INTERVIEWER: That must be in part because you don't stay in your study numbed by an inward gaze, but return repeatedly to the world of experience—to Central America, for example. It's that fact that gives your work its political dimension and lets your readers encounter realized characters in a recognizable world. Incidentally, I'm interested in a remark of yours I encountered somewhere to the effect that Central America is a "due bill coming up for payment."

STONE: No mystery there. That's been a sphere of influence we've exploited economically and dominated politically and militarily very much the way the French, with a bit more success, continue to dominate their former colonies in Africa. We've run that part of the world without a lot of respect for the people who live down there; we've looked down on them as racial inferiors. I have a copy of the *Navy Times* from around 1913 that carries an ad for Shinola shoe polish that says, "Whether you're going on the beach for a party or storming ashore to teach the greasers a lesson, you want to look sharp!" We saw these places as banana republics peopled by gooks who somehow were not quite real people. Nobody thought it compromised American virtue to kick their ass if they got out of line. It was, you know, the white man's burden. And we have to remember that when Kipling passed that duty on to the United States there was no cynicism or irony intended. I don't believe this country has simply been some horror story of racism and murder. But we have incurred a blood debt and it *is* coming up for payment. The end of empire comes for everybody and it's coming for us. So now we're faced with this area close to our southern sea frontier where people have it in for us and are only too eager to collaborate with our enemies. I mean, if there was an invasion of the United States and whoever it was wanted to have a Central American legion, they'd get plenty of volunteers.

INTERVIEWER: You've remarked in your own voice, as has Holliwell in *A Flag For Sunrise,* that we've exported what's worst in our culture, while what's best doesn't export. What is best? What have we got at home that keeps us going?

STONE: Idealism. A tradition of rectitude that genuinely does exist in American society and that sometimes has been translated into government. Enlightenment ideas written into the Constitution. Emerson and Thoreau. The whole tradition so wonderfully mythologized in John Ford's Westerns—the Boston schoolmarm seeking service on the frontier. We've tried to export that in the form of, say, missions to China, but it hasn't really worked because we were more a commercial than a military or cultural empire, so it was our appetites that we exported, along with the relevant parts of our popular culture. The French at least attempted to include their artistic traditions in their *mission civiliatrice;* they and the British, to a lesser extent, did have something to offer their colonials. All we wanted was to do business. The point is that so much that is best in America is a state of mind that you can't export.

INTERVIEWER: But, as you say, we do export shoddy aspects of our culture along with our commerce. Holliwell argues this in his speech in Compostella.

STONE: Low-level pop culture, yes. Because America has managed to create a working class with the leisure and money to command the resources of the society but without the taste to enhance those resources. From that derived the pop culture we've exported. Now that isn't evil but it is a form of pollution. It's why you get Central American Indians with transistor radios glued to their skulls. I don't mean to make a reactionary argument about the purity of the noble savage. But there is such a thing as authenticity. You'll recall that Holliwell's speech attacks American culture but also America's enemies. He sees, as I see, contradictions that simply have to be faced and that possibly cannot be solved. There's a shared Marxist and American attitude that where there's a problem there must be a solution. What about the problem that doesn't have a solution?

INTERVIEWER: There it is.

STONE: There it is. That aphorism may not be the least significant link between Central America and Vietnam.

INTERVIEWER: You've raised the specter that haunts all of your work—as an aspect of American culture that fuels Rheinhardt's spite in *A Hall of Mirrors,* as the heart of the darkness of *Dog Soldiers,* and as a dreadful nostalgia in *A Flag For Sunrise.* Do you think the war will persist as a background for your work for some time?

STONE: I'm constantly drawn back to it. I had to keep myself from doing that in my new book, *Children of Light,* which is about the personal lives of some fucked-up people, unhappy writers and actors in the movie business. But even here I try to refer those lives to the American condition, my usual subject. And the war, as you say, continues to haunt us.

—WILLIAM CRAWFORD WOODS
Winter 1985

12. Joseph Brodsky

Joseph Brodsky was born in 1940 in Leningrad, the only son of a photographer and a translator. At fifteen, he left school; he writes about his decision to leave in *Less Than One* (1986), a book of essays: "I simply couldn't stand certain faces in my classes . . . mostly of my teachers." In the late fifties Brodsky came to know a small circle of poets—later referred to as "the Petersburg circle"—and concentrated increasingly on his own writing.

It was his trial in 1964, for "social parasitism," that made Brodsky known to the West. He had held, in the preceding nine years, a series of thirteen jobs that included working as an assistant at a hospital morgue, as a laborer on a geological expedition, and as a metalworker. When the judge asked him his occupation, Brodsky responded, famously, that he wrote poetry. He served twenty months of a five-year hard labor sentence in the Arkhangelsk region. In 1972 the authorities "asked" him to leave. Brodsky emigrated to Austria, where he sought out W. H. Auden at his summer home in Kirchstetten, bearing a gift of a bottle of vodka. Auden took immediate care of him; he introduced Brodsky to other writers and later wrote the introduction to his first major collection of poems in English, *Selected Poems* (1973).

From 1972 until 1980, Brodsky was poet-in-residence at the University of Michigan in Ann Arbor. He has taught also at Columbia University and New York University. His books of poetry include *Elegy to John Donne and Other Poems* (1967), *A Stop in the Desert* (1970), *A Part of Speech* (1980), and, most recently, *Homage to Urania* (1987). At present Brodsky divides his time between his home in New York City and Mount Holyoke College, where he teaches. He was awarded the Nobel Prize for Literature in 1987.

A Joseph Brodsky manuscript page: Sonnet No. 14 from the cycle "Twenty Sonnets to Mary Queen of Scots" which was included in the Russian version of A Part of Speech.

© Willem Diepraam

Joseph Brodsky

Joseph Brodsky was interviewed in his Greenwich Village apartment in December, 1979. He was unshaven and looked harried. He was in the midst of correcting the galley proofs for his book—A Part of Speech—*and he said that he had already missed every conceivable deadline. The floor of his living room was cluttered with papers. It was offered to do the interview at a more convenient time, but Brodsky would not hear of it.*

The walls and free surfaces of his apartment were almost entirely obscured by books, post cards, and photographs. There were a number of pictures of a younger Brodsky, with Auden and Spender, with Octavio Paz, with various friends. Over the fireplace were two framed photographs, one of Anna Akhmatova, another of Brodsky with his son, who remains in Russia.

Brodsky made two cups of strong instant coffee. He sat in a chair stationed beside the fireplace and kept the same basic pose for three hours—head tilted, legs crossed, the fingers of his right hand either holding a cigarette or resting on his chest. The fireplace was littered with cigarette butts. Whenever he was tired of smoking he would fling his cigarette in that direction.

His answer to the first question did not please him. Several times he said: "Let's start again." But about five minutes into the interview he seemed to have forgotten that there was a tape recorder, or for that matter, an interviewer. He picked up speed and enthusiasm.

Brodsky's voice, which Nadezhda Mandelstam once described as a "remarkable instrument," is nasal and very resonant.

During a break Brodsky asked what kind of beer the interviewer would like and set out for the corner store. As he was returning through the back courtyard one of his neighbors called out: "How are you, Joseph? You look like you're losing weight." "I don't know," answered Brodsky's voice. "Certainly I'm losing my hair." A moment later he added: "And my mind."

When the interview was finished Brodsky looked relaxed, not at all the same man who had opened the door four hours before. He seemed reluctant to stop talking. But then the papers on the floor began to claim his attention. "I'm awfully glad we did this," he said. He saw the interviewer out the door with his favorite exclamation: "Kisses!"

INTERVIEWER: I wanted to start with a quotation from Nadezhda Mandelstam's book, *Hope Abandoned*. She says of you, "He is . . . a remarkable young man who will come to a bad end, I fear."

BRODSKY: In a way I *have* come to a bad end. In terms of Russian literature—in terms of being published in Russia. However, I think she had in mind something of a worse denomination—namely, physical harm. Still, for a writer not to be published in his mother tongue is as bad as a bad end.

INTERVIEWER: Did Akhmatova have any predictions?

BRODSKY: Perhaps she did, but they were nicer, I presume, and therefore I don't remember them. Because you only remember bad things—you pay attention to them because they have more to do with you than your work. On the other hand, good things are originated by a kind of divine intervention. And there's no point in worrying about divine intervention because it's either going to happen or it's not. Those things are out of your control. What's under your control is the possibility of the bad.

INTERVIEWER: To what extent are you using divine intervention as a kind of psychic metaphor?

BRODSKY: Actually to a large extent. What I mean actually is the intervention of language upon you or into you. That famous line of Auden's about Yeats: "Mad Ireland hurt you into poetry—" What "hurts" you into poetry or literature is language, your sense of language. Not your private philosophy or your politics, nor even the creative urge, or youth.

INTERVIEWER: So, if you're making a cosmology you're putting language at the apex?

BRODSKY: Well, it's no small thing—it's pretty grand. When they say "the poet hears the voice of the Muse," it's nonsense if the nature of the Muse is unspecified. But if you take a closer look, the voice of the Muse is the voice of the language. It's a lot more mundane than the way I'm putting it. Basically, it's one's reaction to what one hears, what one reads.

INTERVIEWER: Your use of that language—it seems to me—is to relate a vision of history running down, coming to a dead end.

BRODSKY: That might be. Basically, it's hard for me to assess myself, a hardship not only prompted by the immodesty of the enterprise, but because one is not capable of assessing himself, let alone his work. However, if I were to summarize, my main interest is the nature of time. That's what interests me most of all. What time can do to a man. That's one of the closest insights into the nature of time that we're allowed to have.

INTERVIEWER: In your piece on St. Petersburg you speak of water as "collected time."

BRODSKY: Ya, it's another form of time . . . it was kind of nice, that piece, except that I never got proofs to read and quite a lot of mistakes crept in, misspellings and all those things. It matters to me. Not because I'm a perfectionist, but because of my love affair with the English language.

INTERVIEWER: How do you think you fare as your own translator? Do you translate or rewrite?

BRODSKY: No, I certainly don't rewrite. I may redo certain translations, which causes a lot of bad blood with translators, because I try to restore in translation even those things which I regard as weaknesses. It's a maddening thing in itself to look at an old poem of yours. To translate it is even more maddening. So, before doing that you have to cool off a great deal, and when you start you are looking upon your work as the soul looks from its abode upon the abandoned body. The only thing the soul perceives is the slow smoking of decay.

So, you don't really have any attachment to it. When you're translating, you try to preserve the sheen, the paleness of those leaves. And you accept how some of them look ugly, but then perhaps when you were doing the original that was because of some kind of strategy. Weaknesses have a certain function in a poem . . . some strategy in order to pave the reader's way to the impact of this or that line.

INTERVIEWER: Do you get very sensitive about the way someone renders you into English?

BRODSKY: My main argument with translators is that I care for accuracy and they're very often inaccurate—which is perfectly understandable. It's awfully hard to get these people to render the accuracy as you would want them to. So rather than brooding about it, I thought perhaps I would try to do it myself.

Besides, I have the poem in the original, that's enough. I've done it and for better or worse it stays there. My Russian laurels—or lack of them—satisfy me enough. I'm not after a good seat on the American Parnassus. The thing that bothers me about many of those translations is that they are not very good English. It may have to do with the fact that my affair with the English language is fairly fresh, fairly new, and therefore perhaps I'm subject to some extra sensitivity. So what bothers me is not so much that the line of mine is bad—what bothers me is the bad line in English.

Some translators espouse certain poetics of their own. In many cases their understanding of modernism is extremely simple. Their idea, if I reduce it to the basics, is "staying loose." I, for one, would rather sound trite than slack or loose. I would prefer to sound like a cliché . . . an ordered cliché, rather than a clever slackness.

INTERVIEWER: You've been translated by some impeccable craftsmen—

BRODSKY: I was quite lucky on several occasions. I was translated by both Richard Wilbur and Anthony Hecht—

INTERVIEWER: Well, I was at a reading recently where Wilbur was describing to the audience—quite tartly, I thought—how you and Derek Walcott were flying in a plane over Iowa, re-correcting his translation of one of your poems—which did not make him happy. . . .

BRODSKY: True. The poem only profited out of that. I respect him enormously. Having asked him to do certain passages three, four, or more times, I merely felt that I had no human right to bother him with that one more time. I just didn't have the guts. Even that uncorrected version was excellent. It's more or less the same thing when I said no to Wystan Auden when he volunteered to translate some poems. I thought, "Who the hell am I to be translated by Wystan?"

INTERVIEWER: That's an interesting reversal—the poet feeling inadequate to his translator.

BRODSKY: Ya, well, that's the point. I had the same sentiment with respect to Dick Wilbur.

INTERVIEWER: When did you begin to write?

BRODSKY: I started to write when I was eighteen or nineteen. However, until I was about twenty-three, I didn't take it that seriously. Sometimes people say, "the best things you have written were when you were nineteen." But I don't think I'm a Rimbaud.

INTERVIEWER: What was your poetic horizon then? Did you know of Frost, or Lowell?

BRODSKY: No. But eventually, I got to all of them, first in translation, then in the original. My first acquaintance with Robert Frost was when I was twenty-two. I got some of his translations, not in a book, again, from some friends of mine—well, this is the way you get things—and I was absolutely astonished at the sensibility, that kind of restraint, that hidden, controlled terror. I couldn't believe what I'd read. I thought I ought to look into the matter closely, ought to check whether the translator was really translating, or whether we had on our hands a kind of genius in Russian. And so I did, and it was all there, as much as I could detect it. And with Frost it all started.

INTERVIEWER: What were you getting in school up until then—Goethe, Schiller?

BRODSKY: We got the whole thing. The English poets would be Byron and Longfellow, nineteenth century-oriented. Classics, so to speak. You wouldn't hear anything about Emily Dickinson, or Gerard Manley Hopkins or anyone else. They give you two or three foreign figures and that's about it.

INTERVIEWER: Did you even know the name "Eliot"?

BRODSKY: We all knew the name Eliot. *(laughs)* For any Eastern European, Eliot is a kind of Anglo-Saxon brand name.

INTERVIEWER: Like Levi's?

BRODSKY: Ya, like Levi's. We all knew there was a poet Eliot, but it was very hard to get any stuff of his. The first attempt to translate him was made in 1936, 1937, in an anthology of English poetry; the translation was quite hapless. But since we knew his reputation we read more into the lines than there ever was—at least in Russian. So . . . immediately after the accomplishment the translators got executed or imprisoned, of course, and the book was out of circulation.

However, I managed to make my way through it gradually, picking up English by arming myself with a dictionary. I went through it line by line because, basically, at the age of twenty, twenty-three, I knew more or less all of the Russian poetry and had to look somewhere else. Not because Russian poetry ceased to satisfy me, but once you've read the texts you know them. . . .

INTERVIEWER: Then you were translating too?

BRODSKY: That was the way of making a living. I was translating all kinds of nonsense. I was translating Poles, Czechs, brother Slavs, but then I ventured across the borders; I began to translate Spanish poetry. I was not doing it alone. In Russia there is a huge translating industry, and lots of things weren't yet translated. In introductions or critical essays you would encounter the name of an obscure poet who had not been translated and you would begin to hunt for him.

Then I began to translate English poetry, Donne especially. When I was sent to that internal exile in the north, a friend of mine sent me two or three anthologies of American poetry . . . Oscar Williams, with the pictures, which would fire my imagination. With a foreign culture, a foreign realm that you think you are never going to see, your love affair is a lot more intense.

So I was doing those things, reading, translating, approximating rather than translating . . . until finally I came here to join the original *(laughs)* . . . came *too* close to the original.

INTERVIEWER: Have you lost any of the admirations you had? Do you still feel the same way about Donne, Frost?

BRODSKY: About Donne and Frost I feel the same way. I feel slightly less about Eliot, much less about e. e. cummings. . . .

INTERVIEWER: There was a point, then, when cummings was a very impressive figure?

BRODSKY: Ya, because modernism is very high, the avant-garde thing, trickery and all that. And I used to think about it as a most desirable goal to achieve.

I lost a lot of idols, say, Lindsay, Edgar Lee Masters. However, some things got reinforced, like Marvell, Donne . . . I'm naming just a few but it deserves a much more thorough conversation . . . and Edwin Arlington Robinson, for instance. Not to speak of Thomas Hardy.

INTERVIEWER: When did you first run into an Auden poem?

BRODSKY: In 1965. I was in that village, in that internal exile I had been sent to. I'd written several poems, a couple of which I sent to the man who did the translations of Frost that had impressed me so much—I regard his opinion as the highest judgment, even though there is very little communication—and he told me, "This poem of yours"—he was talking about "Two Hours in the Empty Tank"—"really resembles Auden in its sense of humor." I said, "Ya?" *(laughs)* The next thing, I was trying to get hold of Auden. And then I did and I began to read.

INTERVIEWER: What part of Auden's work did you first encounter?

BRODSKY: I don't really remember—certainly "In Memory of Yeats." In the village I came across that poem . . . I kind of liked it, especially the third part, ya? That "earth receive an honored guest" kind of ballad-cum-Salvation Army hymn. And short meter. I showed it to a friend of mine and he said, "Is it possible that they write better than ourselves?" I said, "Looks like."

The next thing, I decided to write a poem, largely aped from Auden's structure in "In Memory of W. B. Yeats." However, I didn't look into Auden any closer at that point. And then I came to Moscow and showed that friend of mine, the translator, these poems. Once more, he said, "This resembles Auden." So I went out and found Auden's poems and began to read him more thoroughly.

What interests me is his symptomatic technique of description. He never gives you the real . . . ulcer . . . he talks about its symptoms, ya? He keeps his eye all the time on civilization, on the human condition. But he doesn't give you the direct description of it, he gives you the oblique way. And then when you read a line like "The mercury sank in the mouth of the dying day"—well, things begin to change. *(laughs)*

INTERVIEWER: What about your younger years? How did you first come to think about writing poetry?

BRODSKY: At the ages of fifteen, sixteen, seventeen, I didn't write much, not at all, actually. I was drifting from job to job, working. At sixteen I did a lot of traveling. I was working with a geological expedition. And those years were when Russians were extremely interested in finding uranium. So, every geological team was given some sort of Geiger device. I walked a lot. The whole thing was done on foot. So you'd cover about thirty kilometers daily through pretty thick swamps.

INTERVIEWER: Which part of Russia?

BRODSKY: Well, all parts, actually. I spent quite a lot of time in Irkutsk, north of the Amur River on the border of China. Once during a flood I even went to China. It's not that I wanted to, but the raft with all our things on it drifted to the right bank of the Amur River. So I found myself in China briefly. And then I was in Central Asia, in deserts, as well as in the mountains—the Tien Shan mountains are pretty tall mountains, the northwest branch of the Hindu Kush. And, also, in the northern part of European Russia, that is, by the White Sea, near Arkhangelsk. Swamps, dreadful swamps. Not that the swamps themselves were dreadful, but the mosquitoes! So, I've done that. Also, in Central Asia I was doing a little bit of mountain climbing. I was pretty good at that, I must say. Well, I was young . . . so, I had covered a good deal of territory, with those geological teams and mountain climbing groups. When they first arrested me, in 1959, I think, they tried to threaten me by saying, "We're going to send you far away, where no human foot ever trod." Well, I wasn't terribly impressed because I had already been to many of the regions they were talking about. When they indeed sent me to one of those places, it turned out to be an area which I knew somewhat well, climatically anyhow. That was near the polar circle, near the same White Sea. So, to me it was some sort of déjà vu.

INTERVIEWER: Still, there must be a pretty strong thread leading from the top of the mountain to your meeting Akhmatova.

BRODSKY: In my third or fourth year doing geology I got into writing poems. I started because I saw a book of poems a colleague of mine had. The subject matter was the romantic appeal of all those spaces. At least that's what it seemed to me. I thought that I could do better, so I started writing my own poetry. Which wasn't really terribly good . . . well, some people kind of liked it, but then again everybody who writes finds himself an audience. Oddly enough, ya? All the literati keep at least one imaginary friend—and once you start to write you're hooked. Still, all the same, at that time I had to make my living. So I kept partaking in those travels. It was not so much that they paid well, but in the field you spent much less; therefore your salary was just waiting for you.

I would get this money and return home and live on it for a while. Usually by Christmas time or New Year's the money would run out and I would start to look for a job. A normal operation, I think. And in one of my last travels, which was again to the far eastern part of the country, I got a volume of a poet of Pushkin's circle, though in ways much better than Pushkin—his name is Baratynsky. Reading him forced me to abandon the whole silly traveling thing and to get more seriously into writing. So this is what I started to do. I returned home prematurely and started to write a really quite good poem, the way I remember it.

INTERVIEWER: I read once in a book about Leningrad poets

a description of your lair, the lampshade covered with Camel
cigarette packs. . . .

BRODSKY: That was the place where I lived with my parents.
We had one big, huge room in the communal apartment,
partitioned by two arches. I simply stuffed those arches with
all kinds of bookshelves, furniture, in order to separate myself
from my parents. I had my desk, my couch. To a stranger, to
a foreigner especially, it looked really like a cave; you had to
walk through a wooden wardrobe with no back, like a kind of
a gate. I lived there quite a lot. However, I used every bit of
money that I made to try to rent or sublet a place for myself,
merely because at that age you would rather live someplace
other than with your parents, ya? Girls, and so forth.

INTERVIEWER: How was it that you finally came to meet
Akhmatova?

BRODSKY: It was in 1961, I think. By that time I'd befriended
two or three people who later played a very big role in my
life—what later came to be known as "the Petersburg circle."
There were about four of us. One of them is still, I think, the
best poet Russia has today. His name is Evgeny Rein; the name
comes from the Rhine River. He taught me a lot in terms of
poetic know-how. Not that he *taught*. I would read his poems
and he would read mine and we would sit around and have
high-minded exchanges, pretending we knew a lot more than
we did; *he* knew something more because he was five years
senior to me. At that age it matters considerably. He once said
the thing which I would normally say to any poet—that if you
really want your poem to work, the usage of adjectives should
be minimal; but you should stuff it as much as you can with
nouns—even the verbs should suffer. If you cast over a poem
a certain magic veil that removes adjectives and verbs, when
you remove the veil the paper still should be dark with nouns.
To a point I have followed that advice, though not exactly
religiously. It did me a lot of good, I must say.

INTERVIEWER: You have a poem which starts "Evgeny mine . . ."

BRODSKY: Ya, it is addressed to him, within that cycle "Mexican Divertimento." But I've written several poems to him, and to a certain extent he remains . . . what's Pound's description: *"il miglior fabbro."* One summer, Rein said: "Would you like to meet Akhmatova?" I said: "Well, why not?" without thinking much. At that time I didn't care much for Akhmatova. I got a book and read through it, but at that time I was pretty much in my own idiotic world, wrapped up in my own kind of things. So . . . we went there, actually two or three times. I liked her very much. We talked about this and that, and I showed her some of my poems without really caring what she would say.

But I remember one evening returning from her place—it was in the outskirts of Leningrad—in a filled-up train. Suddenly—it was like the seven veils let down—I realized who it was I was dealing with. And after that I saw her quite often.

Then in 1964 I got behind bars and didn't see her; we exchanged some kind of correspondence. I got released because she was extremely active in trying to get me out. To a certain extent she had blamed herself for my arrest, basically because of the harassment; she was being followed, etcetera, etcetera. Everybody thinks that way about themselves; even I in my turn later on was trying to be kind of cautious with people, because my place was being watched.

INTERVIEWER: Does that phenomenon give you a strange sense of self-importance?

BRODSKY: It really doesn't. It either scares you or it is a nuisance. You can't derive any sense of self-importance because you understand a) how idiotic it is, and b) how dreadful it is. The dreadfulness dominates your thoughts. Once, I remember Akhmatova conversing with somebody, some naïve woman, or perhaps not so naïve, who asked, "Anna Andreyevna—how do you notice if you are being followed?" To which she replied: "My dear, it's impossible not to notice such a thing." It's done to intimidate you. You don't have to suffer persecution mania. You really *are* being followed.

INTERVIEWER: How long did it take you to get rid of that feeling once you landed in Austria?

BRODSKY: It's still around, you're cautious. In your writing, in your exchanges with people, meeting people who are in Russian affairs, Russian literature, etcetera. Because it's all penetrated, not necessarily by the direct agents of State Security, but by those people who can be used for that.

INTERVIEWER: Were you familiar with Solzhenitsyn at that time?

BRODSKY: I don't think at that time Solzhenitsyn was familiar with himself. No, later on. When *One Day in the Life of Ivan Denisovich* was put out, I read it instantly. I remember, speaking of Akhmatova, talking about *One Day,* and a friend of mine said "I don't like this book." Akhmatova said: "What kind of comment is that—'I like it' or 'I don't like it?' The point is that the book ought to be read by two hundred million of the Russian population." And that's it, ya?

I followed Solzhenitsyn's output in the late sixties quite steadily. By 1971, there were about five or six books floating around in manuscript. *Gulag* wasn't yet published. *August 1914* surfaced at that time. Also his prose poems, which I found absolutely no good. But we like him not for his poetry, ya?

INTERVIEWER: Have you ever met him?

BRODSKY: No. We had one exchange in the mail. . . . I really think that in him the Soviet rule got its Homer: what he managed to reveal, the way he kind of pulled the world a little bit around, ya?

INTERVIEWER: Insofar as any one person is able to do anything—

BRODSKY: That's about it, ya? But then you have the millions of dead behind him. The force of the individual who is alive grows proportionately—it's not him essentially, but them.

INTERVIEWER: When you were sent to the prison camp in 1965 . . .

BRODSKY: It was an internal exile, not a camp. It was a village, fourteen people, lost, completely lost in bogs up there in the north. With almost no access. First I went through transitory prisons: Crosses.* Then it was Vologda, then Arkhangelsk, and finally I ended up in that village. It was all under guard.

INTERVIEWER: Were you able to maintain an ongoing picture of yourself as someone who uses language?

BRODSKY: That's a funny thing, but I did. Even sitting there between those walls, locked up, then being moved from place to place, I was writing poems. One of them was a very presumptuous poem—precisely about that, being a carrier of the language—extremely presumptuous as I say, but I was in the height of the tragic mood and I could say something like that about myself, to myself even.

INTERVIEWER: Did you have any sense at that time that what had happened at the trial had already put you in the international spotlight?

BRODSKY: No, I knew nothing about the international echo of that trial, nothing at all. I realized that I got a great deal of shit on my palate—on my plate—on my palate as well *(laughs)*. I had to do my stretch. . . . What's more, that was the time which coincided in an unfortunate way—but then again it was fortunate for me—with my greatest personal trouble, with a girl, etcetera, etcetera . . . and a kind of triangle overlapped severely with the squares of the solitary confinements, ya? It was a kind of geometry—with vicious circles.

I was more fired up by that personal situation than by what

*Crosses is a prison in Leningrad.

was happening to my body. The displacement from one cell to another, one prison to another, interrogation, all that, I didn't really pay much attention to it.

INTERVIEWER: Were you able to stay in some sort of communication with the literati once you were sent into internal exile?

BRODSKY: I was trying. Mailing things in a kind of round-about fashion, or directly. Sometimes I even called. I was living in a "village." Fourteen little shacks. Certainly it was obvious that some letters were not read by my eyes alone. But, you know that you are up against it; you know who is the master of your house. It's not you. So therefore you're resigned to trying to ridicule the system—but that's about as much as can be done. You feel like a serf bitching about the gentry, which has its own entertaining aspects.

INTERVIEWER: But still a situation in which you must have been under extreme duress—

BRODSKY: No, I wasn't. In the first place I was young. Secondly, the work was agriculture. My old joke is that agriculture is like public transportation in the U.S. It's a sporadic operation, poorly organized. So therefore you have enough time, ya? Sometimes it was pretty taxing, physically, that is; and also, it was unpleasant. I didn't have the right to leave. I was confined. Perhaps because of some turn in my character, I decided to get the most out of it. I kind of liked it. I associated it with Robert Frost. You think about the environment, the surroundings, what you're doing: you start to play at being almost a gentleman farmer. Other Russian writers, I think, had it much harder than me, much harder.

INTERVIEWER: Did this life give you the rural sense that you have?

BRODSKY: I love it. It gives you more than the rural sense . . . because you get up in the morning in the village, or wherever, and you go to get your daily load, you walk through the field and you know that at the same time most of the nation is doing the same. It gives you some exhilarating sense of being with the rest. If you look from the height of a dove, or a hawk, across the nation you would see it. In that sense it was nice. It gives you a certain insight into the basics of life.

INTERVIEWER: Was there anyone with whom you could talk literature?

BRODSKY: No—but I didn't need it, really. You don't really need it, frankly. Or at least I'm not one of that kind of literary person. Although I love to talk about those things. But once shorn of that opportunity, it's okay. Your democratic traits get set in motion. You talk to the people and try to appreciate what they're saying, etcetera. It pays psychologically.

INTERVIEWER: Did you have many classics at that point?

BRODSKY: Not really. Nothing, in fact. When I needed references I had to write letters to ask people's help. But I operate on a very basic level with the classics. That is, there's nothing very esoteric. You can find all of it in Bullfinch, ya? I'd read Suetonius and somebody else—Tacitus. But I don't remember, frankly.

INTERVIEWER: At some point the classics must have been quite important. I don't mean specifically the classics, as much as the historical reach. . . .

BRODSKY: Whenever you get in trouble you're automatically forced to regard yourself—unless you are self-indulgent—as a kind of archetypal character. So, who else could I think of being but Ovid? That would be the most natural thing. . . .

Well, that was a wonderful time, I must say. I'd written quite a lot and I think I had written rather well. I remember one breakthrough I made with poetry. I wrote the line "here on the hills, under the empty sky, on the roads leading on into the woods, life steps aside from itself and peers at itself in a state of bewilderment." This is perhaps not much, but to me it was important . . . it's not exactly a new way of looking, but being able to say that unleashes certain other things. You are then invincible.

INTERVIEWER: You had no intimation that you would ever reach the West?

BRODSKY: Oh, no. No Russian has that intimation. You're born to a very confined realm. The rest of the world is just pure geography, an academic discipline, not the reality.

INTERVIEWER: When you left Russia you were going to Israel.

BRODSKY: I had to go to Israel! I was given the walking papers to Israel. But I had no intention to go anywhere. I landed in Vienna and Carl Proffer from the University of Michigan, from Ardis, met me there. The first thing I saw when I looked out of the plane was his tall figure on the balustrade. We waved to each other. And the first thing he asked me as I walked up was, "Well, Joseph, where would you like to go?"

I said: "Jesus, I haven't the slightest idea." And I really didn't. I knew I was leaving my country for good, but for where, I had no idea whatsoever. One thing which was quite clear was that I didn't want to go to Israel. I didn't know Hebrew, though I knew a little English.

Besides, I didn't have much time to think about that. I never even believed that they'd allow me to go. I never believed they would put me on a plane, and when they did I didn't know whether the plane would go east or west.

INTERVIEWER: Was Carl Proffer trying to get you to come to the U.S.?

BRODSKY: When I told him that I had no plans whatsoever, he asked, "Well, how would you like to come to the University of Michigan?" Other proposals came from London and from the Sorbonne, I believe. But I decided, "It's a big change, let's make it really big." At that time they had expelled about 150 spies from England and I thought, "That's not all of them, ya?" *(laughs)* I didn't want to be hounded by what was left of the Soviet Security Service in England. So I came to the States.

INTERVIEWER: Was Auden actually in Vienna at the time?

BRODSKY: Auden wasn't in Vienna, but I knew that he was in Austria. He usually spent his summertimes in Kirchstetten. I had a gift for him. All I took out of Russia was my typewriter, which they unscrewed bolt by bolt at the airport—that was their way of saying goodbye—a small Modern Library volume of Donne's poems, and a bottle of vodka, which I thought that if I got to Austria I'd give to Auden. If I didn't get to Austria I'd drink it myself. I also had a second bottle from a friend, a Lithuanian poet, Tomas Venclova—a remarkable poet, I think—who gave me a bottle of Lithuanian booze. He said, "Give this thing to Wystan if you see him." So, I had two bottles, that typewriter, and Donne, along with a change of clothes, that is, underwear, and that was it.

On the third or fourth day in Vienna I said to Carl, "Wystan Auden may be in Austria—why don't we try to find him?" Since we had nothing to do except go to the opera and restaurants, we hired an Avis car, a VW, got a map of Austria, and went to look for him. The trouble was there are three Kirchstettens. We went through all of them, I think—miles and miles between them—and finally we discovered the Auden-Strasse, and found him there.

He began to take immense care of me immediately. All of a sudden the telegrams in my name began to arrive in care of Auden, ya? He was trying to kind of set me up. He told me about whom to meet here and there, etcetera. He called Charles Osborne in London and got me invited to the Poetry International, 1972. I stayed two weeks in London, with Wystan at Stephen Spender's place.

In general, because in those eight years I was as well read in English poetry as in Russian, I knew the scene rather well. Except that, for instance, I didn't know that Wystan was gay. It somehow escaped me. Not that I care much about that. However, I was emerging from Russia and Russia being quite a Victorian country, that could have tinged my attitude toward Wystan. But I don't think it did.

I stayed two weeks in London, and then I flew to the States.

INTERVIEWER: Your connections in the world of poetry have proliferated. You're friends with Hecht, Wilbur, Walcott—

BRODSKY: I met Derek [Walcott] at Lowell's funeral. Lowell had told me about Derek and showed me some poems which impressed me a great deal. I read them and I thought, "Well, another good poet." Then his editor gave me that collection *Another Life.* That blew my mind completely. I realized that we have a giant on our hands. He is the figure in English poetry comparable to, well, should I say Milton? *(laughs)* Well, more accurately, I'd put him somewhere between Marlowe and Milton, especially because of his tendency to write verse plays, and his vigor. He's astonishing. The critics want to make him a regional poet from the West Indies, and it's a crime. Because he's the grandest thing around.

INTERVIEWER: How about Russian writers?

BRODSKY: I don't know really quite whom I react to most. I remember the great impact Mandelstam's poetry had on me when I was nineteen or twenty. He was unpublished. He's still largely unpublished and unheeded—in criticism and even in private conversations, except for the friends, except for my circle, so to speak. General knowledge of him is extremely limited, if any. I remember the impact of his poetry on me. It's still there. As I read it I'm sometimes flabbergasted. Another poet who really changed not only my idea of poetry, but also my perception of the world—which is what it's all about, ya?—is Tsvetayeva. I personally feel closer to Tsvetayeva—to her poetics, to her techniques, which I was never capable of. This is an extremely immodest thing to say, but, I always thought, "Can I do the Mandelstam thing?" I thought on several occasions that I succeeded at a kind of pastiche.

But Tsvetayeva. I don't think I ever managed to approximate her voice. She was the only poet—and if you're a professional that's what's going on in your mind—with whom I decided not to compete.

INTERVIEWER: What was the distinctive element that attracted you but also frustrated you?

BRODSKY: Well, it never frustrated me. She's a woman in the first place. But hers is the most tragic voice of all Russian poetry. It's impossible to say she's the greatest because other people create comparisons—Cavafy, Auden—but I personally feel tremendously attracted to her.

It is a very simple thing. Hers is extremely tragic poetry, not only in subject matter—this is not big news, especially in the Russian realm—but in her language, her prosody. Her voice, her poetry, gives you almost the idea or sense that the tragedy is within the language itself. The reason I decided—it was almost a conscious decision not to compete with her—well, for one thing, I knew I would fail. After all, I'm a different person, a man what's more, and it's almost unseemly for a man to speak at the highest pitch of his voice, by which I don't mean she was just a kind of romantic, raving . . . she was a very dark poet.

INTERVIEWER: She can hold more without breaking?

BRODSKY: Ya. Akhmatova used to say about her: "Marina starts her poem on the upper *do,* that edge of the octave." Well, it's awfully hard to sustain a poem on the highest possible pitch. She's capable of that. A human being has a very limited capacity for discomfort or tragedy. Limited, technically speaking, like a cow that can't produce more than two gallons of milk. You can't squeeze more tragedy out of a man. So, in that respect, her reading of the human drama, her inconsolable voice, her poetic technique, are absolutely astonishing. I think nobody wrote better, in Russian, anyway. The tone with which she was speaking, that kind of tragic vibrato, that tremolo.

INTERVIEWER: Did you have to come to her gradually or did you discover her overnight?

BRODSKY: No, it was from the very threshold. I was given her poems by a friend of mine. That was it.

INTERVIEWER: In your own poems the speaking voice is so terribly solitary, without benefit of a single human interaction.

BRODSKY: Ya, that's what it is. Akhmatova said this about the first batch of poems I brought her in 1962. That's exactly what she said, verbatim. I presume that's the characteristic of it.

INTERVIEWER: As poems emerge are you conscious of the extent to which—for someone looking at them from the outside—they have a discernible line of development and movement?

BRODSKY: No—the only thing I'm conscious of is that I'm trying to make them different from the previous stuff I've written. Because one reacts not only to what he's read, but what he wrote as well, ya? So every preceding thing is the point of departure. There should be a small surprise that there is some kind of detectable linear development.

INTERVIEWER: You seem to write about places that don't appear to be the places where you've spent most of your time. Has there been anything on New York, or Venice?

BRODSKY: I don't think I've written anything about New York. You can't do much about New York. Whereas Venice—I've done quite a lot. But places like New England or Mexico, or England, old England—basically when you find yourself in a strange place, and the stranger the place it is, to a certain extent, the better—it somehow sharpens your notion of your individuality, say a place like Brighton *(laughs)* or York in England. You see yourself better against a strange background. It's to be living outside your own context, like being in exile. One of the advantages is that you shed lots of illusions. Not illusions about the world, but illusions about yourself. You kind of winnow yourself. I never had as clear a notion of what I am than I acquired when I came to the States—the solitary situation. I like the idea of isolation. I like the reality of it. You realize what you are . . . not that the knowledge is inevitably rewarding. Nietzsche put it in so many words: "A man who's left by himself is left with his own pig."

INTERVIEWER: I'll pay you the compliment of saying my

immediate sensation of any place you've described in a poem is to never want to go there.

BRODSKY: Terrific! *(laughs)* If you put it in writing I'll never be hired for an advertising job.

INTERVIEWER: Is it deliberate that you've waited so long between books?

BRODSKY: Not really. I'm not very professional as a writer. I'm not really interested in book after book. There's something ignoble about it, ya?

INTERVIEWER: Does your family in the U.S.S.R. have any sense of what you're doing?

BRODSKY: They have the basic idea, that I'm teaching and that I'm, if not financially, somehow psychologically, well off. They appreciate that I'm a poet. They didn't like it at the very beginning. For a good fifteen years they hated every bit of it, ya? *(laughs)*—but then why shouldn't they have? I don't think I'm so excited about it myself. Akhmatova told me that when her father learned that she was about to publish a book, he said, "Well, do please one thing. Please take care to not malign my name. If you're going to be in this business, please assume a pen name."

Personally, I'd much prefer to fly small planes, to be a bush pilot somewhere in Africa, than do this.

INTERVIEWER: How do you feel about writing prose?

BRODSKY: I love it, in English. To me it's a challenge.

INTERVIEWER: Is it sweat?

BRODSKY: I don't regard it as sweat. It's certainly labor. Yet it's almost a labor of love. If asked to write prose in Russian I wouldn't be so keen. But in English it's a tremendous satisfaction. As I write I think about Auden, what he would say—would he find it rubbish, or kind of entertaining?

INTERVIEWER: Is he your invisible reader?

BRODSKY: Auden and Orwell.

INTERVIEWER: Have you ever tried writing fiction in any form?

BRODSKY: No. Well, when I was young, I tried to write a novel. I wrote what I considered one of the breakthroughs in modern Russian writing . . . I'm awfully glad I never saw it again.

INTERVIEWER: Does anything shock or surprise you? How do you face the world when you get up—with what idea in mind? "Here we go again," or what?

BRODSKY: It certainly doesn't surprise me. I think the world is capable of only one thing basically—proliferating its evils. That's what time seems to be for.

INTERVIEWER: You don't have a corresponding idea that at some point people will advance a quantum leap in consciousness?

BRODSKY: A quantum leap in consciousness is something I rule out.

INTERVIEWER: Just deterioration—is that the picture?

BRODSKY: Well, dilapidation rather than deterioration. Well, not exactly dilapidation. If we look at things in a linear fashion, it certainly doesn't look any good, ya? The only thing that surprises me is the frequency, under the present circumstances, of instances of human decency, of sophistication, if you will. Because basically the situation—on the whole—is extremely uncongenial for being decent or right.

INTERVIEWER: Are you, finally, a thoroughly Godless man? It seems contradictory. In some of your poetry I sense an opening.

BRODSKY: I don't believe in the infinite ability of the reason, or the rational. I believe in it only insofar as it takes me to the irrational—and this is what I need it for, to take me as far as I can get toward the irrational. There it abandons you. For a little while it creates a state of panic. But this is where the revelations are dwelling—not that you may fish them out. But at least I have been given two or three revelations, or at least they have landed on the edge of reason and left their mark.

This all has very little to do with any ordered religious enterprise. On the whole, I'd rather not resort to any formal religious rite or service. If I have any notion of a supreme being I invest it with absolutely arbitrary will. I'm a little bit opposed to that kind of grocery store psychology which underlies Christianity. You do this and you'll get that, ya? Or even better still: that God has infinite mercy. Well, it's basically anthropomorphism. I would go for the Old Testament God who punishes you—

INTERVIEWER: Irrationally—

BRODSKY: No, arbitrarily. Even more I would go for the Zoroastrian version of deity, which is perhaps the cruelest possible. I kind of like it better when we are dealing with arbitrariness. In that respect I think I'm more of a Jew than any Jew in Israel. Merely because I believe, if I believe in anything, in the arbitrary God.

INTERVIEWER: I suspect you've probably meditated a great deal about Eliot and Auden, the way they made these . . .

BRODSKY: Flings . . .

INTERVIEWER: Well, flings or final decisions.

BRODSKY: Yes, I certainly did. I must say I stand by Auden's more readily than Eliot's. Although it would take somebody much smarter than I am to explain the distinction between the two.

INTERVIEWER: From all the pictures you get, though, Eliot in his last days was a wonderfully happy man, whereas Auden . . .

BRODSKY: Certainly he wasn't. I don't know. It denotes a lot of things. Basically, to arrange your life in such a way that you arrive at a happy conclusion is—well, perhaps I'm too romantic, or too young to respect this kind of thing, or take it seriously. Again, I wasn't fortunate enough to have had the structure laid out for me in childhood, as was the case with the both of them. So I've been doing the whole thing essentially on my own. For instance, I read the Bible for the first time when I was twenty-three. It leaves me somewhat shepherdless, you see. I wouldn't really know what to return to. I don't have any notion of paradise. I don't have one that I derived from childhood which, first of all, is the happiest time, and is also the first time you hear about paradise. I went through the severe, antireligious schooling in Russia which doesn't leave any kind of notion about afterlife. So, what I'm trying to say, what interests me is the degree—the graspable degree of arbitrariness.

INTERVIEWER: What are your highest moments then—when you are working in the depths of language?

BRODSKY: This is what we begin with. Because if there is any deity to me, it's language.

INTERVIEWER: Are there moments when you are writing when you are almost an onlooker?

BRODSKY: It's awfully hard for me to answer. During the process of writing—I think these are the better hours—of deepening, of furthering the thing. You're kind of entitled to things you didn't know were out there. That's what language brings you to, perhaps.

INTERVIEWER: What's that Karl Kraus line: "Language is the divining rod that discovers wells of thought"?

BRODSKY: It's an incredible accelerator of the cognitive process. This is why I cherish it. It's kind of funny, because I feel in talking about language I sound like a bloody French structuralist. Since you mention Karl Kraus at least it gives it kind of a continental thing to reckon with. Well, they have culture, we have guts, we Russians and Americans.

INTERVIEWER: Tell me about your love affair with Venice.

BRODSKY: In many ways it resembles my hometown, St. Petersburg. But the main thing is that the place is so beautiful that you can live there without being in love. It's so beautiful that you know that nothing in your life you can come up with or produce—especially in terms of pure existence—would have a corresponding beauty. It's so superior. If I had to live a different incarnation, I'd rather live in Venice as a cat, or anything, but in Venice. Or even as a rat. By 1970 I had an *idée fixe* to get to Venice. I even had an idea of moving there and renting a ground floor in some palazzo on the water, and sit there and write, and drop my cigarette butts so they would hiss in the water. And when the money would be through, finished, I would go to the store and buy a Saturday special with what was left and blow my mind *(puts his finger to temple and gestures)*.

So, the first thing I did when I became free to travel, that is, in 1972, after teaching a semester in Ann Arbor, I got a round-trip ticket for Venice and went there for Christmas. It is interesting to watch the tourists who arrive there. The beauty is such that they get somewhat dumbfounded. What they do initially is to hit the stores to dress themselves—Venice has the best boutiques in Europe—but when they emerge with all those things on, still there is an unbearable incongruity between the people, the crowd, and what's around. Because no matter how well they're dressed and how well they're endowed by nature, they lack the dignity, which is partially the dignity of decay, of that artifice around them. It makes you realize that what people can make with their hands is a lot better than they are themselves.

INTERVIEWER: Do you have a sense when you're there of history winding down? Is that part of the ambience?

BRODSKY: Yes, more or less. What I like about it apart from the beauty is the decay. It's the beauty in decay. It's not going to be repeated, ever. As Dante said: "One of the primary traits of any work of art is that it is impossible to repeat."

INTERVIEWER: What do you think of Anthony Hecht's *Venetian Vespers*?

BRODSKY: It's an awfully good book. It's not so much about Venice—it's about the American sensibility. I think Hecht is a superb poet. I think there are three of them in America, Wilbur, Hecht, and—I don't really know how to allocate that third palm.

INTERVIEWER: I'm interested to know why you put Wilbur up as high as you do.

BRODSKY: I like perfection. It's true that you don't hear the throbbings of the spheres, or whatever. However, the magnificence with which he uses the material compensates. Because— there is poetry and poetry. There are poets and poets. And Dick performs his function better than anyone else.

I think that if I were born here I would end up with qualities similar to Hecht's. One thing I would like to be is as perfect as Hecht and Wilbur are. There should be something else, I presume, of my own, but insofar as the craftsmanship is concerned one couldn't wish for more.

INTERVIEWER: Is the communication between kindred spirits pretty close? Do you watch each other carefully? Walcott, Milosz, Herbert, yourself—poets sharing a certain terrain?

BRODSKY: Not exactly that I watch Derek, but, for instance, I got two poems of his quite recently, scheduled to appear in *The New Yorker*—an editor sent me the xeroxes—and I thought, "Well, Joseph—." I thought, "This is something to reckon with the next time you write a poem." *(laughs)*

INTERVIEWER: Who else is there to reckon with?

BRODSKY: Oh, there are lots of shadows and lots of real people. Eugenio Montale would be one of the living ones. There is a German, a very good German, Peter Huchel. Nobody in France, to my knowledge. I don't really take that poetry seriously. Akhmatova has remarked, very wisely, that in the twentieth century, French painting swallowed French poetry. As for England, I'm certainly a great fan of Philip Larkin. I like him very much. The only complaint is the usual one— that Larkin writes so little. Also, Douglas Dunn—and there is a magnificent man in Australia, Les Murray.

INTERVIEWER: What do you read?

BRODSKY: Some books on disciplines with which I wasn't well acquainted, like Orientalism. Encyclopedias. I almost don't have time for such things. Please don't detect snobbery in this; it's merely a very grand fatigue.

INTERVIEWER: And what do you teach? Does that affect your reading?

BRODSKY: Only insofar as I have to read the poem before the class does *(laughs)*. I'm teaching Hardy and Auden and Cavafy—those three: it rather reflects my tastes and attachments. And Mandelstam, a bit of Pasternak.

INTERVIEWER: Are you aware that you are on a required reading list at Boston University for a course entitled "Modern Jewish Writing"?

BRODSKY: Well, congratulations to Boston University! Very good. I don't really know. I'm a very bad Jew. I used to be reproached by Jewish circles for not supporting the cause, the Jewish cause, and for having a great deal of the New Testament themes in my writing. Which I find absolutely silly. It's nothing to do with the cultural heritage. It's merely on my part the effect paying homage to its cause. It's as simple as that.

INTERVIEWER: You are also listed in a book called *Famous Jews*—

BRODSKY: Boy! Oh, boy! Well, *Famous Jews*—so I'm a famous Jew—that's how I'm going to regard myself from now on—

INTERVIEWER: What about some of the people you most admire? We've touched on some of the ones who have died. How about the living, people whose existence is important to you, if only to know they are there.

BRODSKY: Dick Wilbur, Tony Hecht, Galway Kinnell, Mark Strand. Those are just a few whom I know personally, and I'm extremely lucky in that sense. Montale, as I mentioned, would certainly be one; Walcott is another. And there are other people I like very much personally, and as writers. Susan Sontag, for instance. She is the best mind there is. That is on both sides of the Atlantic. Because, for her, the argument starts precisely where it ends for everyone else. I can't think of anything in modern literature that can parallel the mental music of her essays. Somehow, I can't separate people and writing. It just hasn't happened as yet that I like the writing and not the person. I would say that even if I know a person is dreadful I would be the first to find justifications for that dreadfulness if the writing is good. After all, it is hard to master both life and work equally well. So if you are bound to fake one of them, it had better be life.

INTERVIEWER: Tell me what it was like to meet Lowell for the first time.

BRODSKY: I'd met Lowell in 1972 at the Poetry International. He simply volunteered to read my poems in English as I read them in Russian, an extremely kind and moving gesture. So we both went on stage.

He invited me to come to Kent. I was somewhat perplexed—my English wasn't good enough. Also, I was somewhat worried about the railroad system in England—I couldn't make heads nor tails out of it. And the third, perhaps the primary reason why I didn't go, was that I thought it would be an imposition. Because, well, who the hell am I? And so, I just didn't do it.

Then in 1975 I was in the Five Colleges in Massachusetts, living in Northampton, and he called and invited me to come to Brookline. By that time my English was somewhat better and I went. The time we spent was in many ways the best time I can recall having while here in the States. We talked about this and that, and finally we settled on Dante. It was the first conversation about Dante since Russia which really made sense to me. He knew Dante inside out, I think, in an absolutely obsessive way. He was especially good on *Inferno*. I think he had lived for a while in Florence, or stayed there, so he felt more about *Inferno* than the other parts; at least the conversation revolved around those things.

We spent about five or six hours, more, and then we went for dinner. He said some very pleasant things to me. The only thing casting a shadow was that I knew that during Auden's last years they had had a row, kind of a lasting row. Wystan didn't like Lowell's extramoral situation, whereas Lowell was thinking that it was none of his business and was quite caustic about him as a poet.

INTERVIEWER: That doesn't sound like something Auden would worry about very much—

BRODSKY: In the sense that Wystan was a proper son of England, he would mind someone else's morality. I remember a remark he made. I asked him "What do you think of Lowell?" It was on the first day I saw Wystan. I sat down and started to grill him in my absolutely mindless way. He said something like, "I don't like men who leave a smoking tail of weeping women behind them." Or maybe it was the other way around: "A weeping tail of smoking women"—

INTERVIEWER: Either way—

BRODSKY: Ya, either way. He didn't criticize Lowell as a poet. It was simply kind of a commonplace morality at which I think he, Auden, enjoyed playing.

INTERVIEWER: But it was Auden, after all, who would have God pardoning various people for writing well—

BRODSKY: Ya, but he said that in 1939. I think, in a sense, that the reason behind all of this was that he insisted on faithfulness—in his own affairs as well as in a broader sense. Besides, he tended to become less flexible. When you live long you see that little things end up in big damages. Therefore, you get more personalized in your attitudes. Again, I also think it was kind of a game with him. He wanted to play schoolmaster and for that, in this world, he was fully qualified.

INTERVIEWER: If you could get either or both of them back, what kinds of things do you think you'd talk about now?

BRODSKY: Lots of things. In the first place—well, it's an odd question—perhaps about the arbitrariness of God. Well, that conversation wouldn't go far with Auden, merely because I don't think he'd like to talk about that heavy Thomas Mannish stuff. And yet, he became a kind of formal churchgoer, so to speak. I'm somewhat worried about that—because the poetic notion of infinity is far greater than that which is sponsored by any creed—and I wonder about the way he would reconcile that. I'd like to ask him whether he believes in the church, or simply the creed's notion of infinity, or paradise, or church doctrine—which are normally points of one's spiritual arrival. For the poet they are springboards, or points of departure for metaphysical journeys. Well, things like that. But mostly I would like to find out certain things about the poems, what he meant here and there. Whether, for instance, in "In Praise of Limestone" he really lists the temptations, or kind of translates the temptations as they are found in the Holy Book, or if they simply came out like a poem, ya? *(long pause)* I wish he were here. More than anyone else. Well, that's kind of a cruel thing to say, but—I wish three or four people were alive to talk to. Him, Akhmatova, Tsvetayeva, Mandelstam—which already makes four. Thomas Hardy.

INTERVIEWER: Is there anyone you'd want to pull out from the ages?

BRODSKY: Oh, that would be a big crowd. This room wouldn't hold them.

INTERVIEWER: How did Lowell feel with respect to religion, finally?

BRODSKY: We never talked about it, except ironically, mentioning it en passant. He was absolutely astonishing talking about politics, or writers' weaknesses. Or human weaknesses. He was extremely generous, but what I liked in him was the viciousness of tongue. Both Lowell and Auden were monologists. In a sense, you shouldn't talk to people like them, you should listen to them—which is kind of an ultimate existential equivalent for reading poetry. It's a kind of spinoff. And I was all ears, partly because of my English.

He was a lovely man, really lovely—Lowell, that is. The age difference wasn't that big between us—well, some twenty years, so I felt in a sense somewhat more comfortable with him than with Auden. But then again, I felt most comfortable with Akhmatova.

INTERVIEWER: Did either one of them interrogate you in the way you wanted to be interrogated about yourself and your writing?

BRODSKY: Lowell did. Akhmatova asked me several questions. . . . But while they were alive, you see, I felt as a young boy. They were the elders, so to speak, the masters. Now that they are gone I think of myself as terribly old all of a sudden. And . . . this is what civilization means, carrying on. Well, I don't think Auden would like rock music, nor do I. Nor Lowell, I think.

INTERVIEWER: Do you have any close friends who are artists, painters, musicians, composers?

BRODSKY: Here I don't. In Russia I had. Here the only person close to that is Baryshnikov. Composers, none at all. No, it's empty. The category of people I used to like most of all were graphic artists and musicians.

INTERVIEWER: But you draw a lot of sustenance from those realms.

BRODSKY: From music, yes. I don't really know how it is reflected in what I'm doing, but I certainly do.

INTERVIEWER: What do you listen to? I notice that Billie Holliday is on the turntable now—

BRODSKY: Billie Holliday's "Sophisticated Lady" is a magnificent piece. I like Haydn. Music is actually the best teacher of composition, I think, even for literature. If only because— well, the principle, for instance, of the concerto grosso: three parts, one quick, two slow, or vice versa. You know that you have to pour whatever you have into this twenty-minute thing. Also, what can follow in music: the alternation of lyricism with mindless pizzicato, etcetera . . . they're like the shifts, counterpoints, the fluid character of an argument, a fluid montage. When I first began to listen to classical music, the thing that haunted me was the way it moves, the unpredictability. So in that sense Haydn is terrific stuff because he's so absolutely unpredictable. *(long pause)* It's so silly . . . I think how meaningless everything is, except for two or three things—writing itself, listening to music, perhaps a little bit of thinking. But the rest—

INTERVIEWER: How about friendship?

BRODSKY: Friendship is a nice thing. I'd include food then *(laughs)* . . . But other things that you're forced to do—paying taxes, counting the numbers, writing references, doing your chores—don't all those things strike you as utterly meaningless? It's like when we sat in that café. The girl was doing something with the pies, or whatever—they were in that refrigerator with the glass. And she stuck her head in and she was doing all those things, the rest of her out of the refrigerator. She was in that position for about two minutes. And once you see it there's no point in existing any more. *(laughs)* Simple point, ya?

INTERVIEWER: Except that the minute you translate that into an image or a thought you've already taken it out of uselessness.

BRODSKY: But once you've seen it the whole of existence is compromised.

INTERVIEWER: It's coming back to time again—here because you're seeing the container with nothing in it.

BRODSKY: More or less, ya. Actually I read in the front of Penn Warren's recent book *(gets up and rummages at his desk):* "Time is the dimension in which God strives to define his own being." Well, "strives" is a little bit kindergartenish. But there is another quote, this one from the encyclopedia: "There is, in short, no absolute time standard."

INTERVIEWER: The last time I talked with you two things hadn't happened. How much of your time is filled with being preoccupied with Afghanistan and the hostage situation?

BRODSKY: When I'm not writing or reading, I'm thinking

about both. Of the two I think the Afghan situation is the most—tragic. When I saw the first footage from Afghanistan on the TV screen a year ago, it was very short. It was tanks rolling on the plateau. For thirty-two hours nonstop I was climbing the walls. Well, it's not that I'm ashamed of being Russian. I have felt that already twice in my life: in 1956 because of Hungary and in 1968 because of Czechoslovakia. In those days my attitude was aggravated by immediate fear, for my friends if not for myself—merely because I knew that whenever the international situation worsens, it's automatically followed by the internal crackdown.

But this is not what really blew my mind in Afghanistan. What I saw was basically a violation of the elements—because that plateau never saw a plough before, let alone a tank. So, it was a kind of existential nightmare. And it still sits on my retina. Since then I have been thinking about soldiers who are, well, about twenty years younger than me, so that some of them could be, technically speaking, my children. I even wrote a poem that said "glory to those that in the Sixties went marching into the abortion clinics, thereby saving the Motherland the disgrace."

What drives me absolutely wild is not the pollution—it's something much more dreadful. It's something I think when they're breaking ground to the foundation of a building. It's usurpation of land, violation of the elements. It's not that I am of a pastoral bent. No, I think, on the contrary, the nuclear power stations should be there—it's cheaper than oil, in the end.

But a tank rolling onto the plateau demeans space. This is absolutely meaningless, like subtracting from zero. And it is vile in a primordial sense, partly because of tanks' resemblance to dinosaurs. It simply shouldn't be.

INTERVIEWER: Are your feelings about these things very separate from what you write?

BRODSKY: I don't believe in writing it—I believe in action. I think it's time to create some sort of International Brigade. It was done in 1936, why not now? Except that in 1936 the International Brigade was financed by the GPU—that is, Soviet State Security. I just wonder if there's anybody with the money . . . somebody in Texas who could financially back the thing.

INTERVIEWER: What would you imagine the International Brigade doing?

BRODSKY: Well, the International Brigade can do essentially what it did in 1936 in Spain, that is, fight back, help the locals. Or at least give some sort of medical assistance—food, shelter. If there is a noble cause, it is this—not some Amnesty International . . . I wouldn't mind driving a Red Cross jeep. . . .

INTERVIEWER: It's hard to identify clear moral sides sometimes—

BRODSKY: I don't really know what kind of moral sides you are looking for, especially in a place like Afghanistan. It's quite obvious. They've been invaded; they've been subjugated. They may be just backward tribesmen but slavery isn't my idea of revolution either.

INTERVIEWER: I'm talking more in terms of countries.

BRODSKY: Russia versus the U.S.? I don't think there is any question. If there were no other distinction between those two, it would be enough for me to have the system of a jury of twelve versus the system of one judge as a basis for preferring the U.S. to the Soviet Union. Or, to make it less complicated—because even that perplexes most people—I would prefer the country you can leave to the country you cannot.

INTERVIEWER: You've said that you are fairly satisfied with your Lowell poem which you wrote in English. Is there any reason why you didn't just continue writing in English?

BRODSKY: There are several reasons. In the first place, I have enough to do in Russian. And in English you have lots of terrific people alive. There is no point in my doing that. I wrote an elegy in English simply because I wanted to please the shadow. And when I finished *Lowell,* I had another poem coming in English. There were wonderful rhymes coming my way, and yet I told myself to stop. Because I don't want to create for myself an extra reality. Also, I would have to compete with the people for whom English is the mother tongue, ya? And, lastly, which is the most important, I don't have that aspiration. I'm pleased enough with what I'm doing in Russian, which sometimes goes and sometimes doesn't. When it doesn't, I can't think of trying it in English. I don't want to be penalized twice *(laughs).* And, as for English, I write my essays, which gives me enough sense of confidence. The thing is—I don't really know how to put it—technically speaking, English is the only interesting thing that's left in my life. It's not an exaggeration and not a brooding statement. That's what it is, ya?

INTERVIEWER: Did you read Updike's piece on Kundera in *The New York Times Book Review*? He finished by referring to you, citing you as one who has dealt with exile by becoming an American poet—

BRODSKY: That's flattering, but that's rubbish.

INTERVIEWER: I imagine that he was referring not only to the fact that you have written a few things in English, but also to the fact that you were beginning to deal with American landscapes, Cape Cod—

BRODSKY: Could be—in that case, what can I say? Certainly one becomes the land one lives in, especially at the end. In that sense I'm quite American.

INTERVIEWER: How do you feel about writing something full of American associations in the Russian language?

BRODSKY: In many cases you don't have the Russian word for that, or you have a Russian word which is kind of cumbersome; then you look for ways around the problem.

INTERVIEWER: Well, you're writing about squad cars and Ray Charles' jazz—

BRODSKY: Ya, that you can do—because Ray Charles is a name, and "squad car" has an expression in Russian, and so does the hoop on the basketball pole. But the most difficult thing I had to deal with in that poem had to do with Coca-Cola, to convey the sensation that it reminded me of *Mene Mene Tekel Upharsin,* that line Belshazzar sees on the wall that foretold the end of his kingdom. That's where the expression "writing on the wall" comes from. You can't say "Coca-Cola sign" because there's no idiom for that. So, I had to describe it in a rather roundabout way—because of which the image rather profited. I said not "a sign," but something to the effect of the cuneiform or the hieroglyphics of Coca-Cola, ya? So that it reinforced the image of "the writing on the wall."

INTERVIEWER: What do you think happens psychically when you've brought the poem to a sort of dead point, to get beyond which you would have to go in a direction that you can't yet imagine?

BRODSKY: The thing is that you can always go on, even when you have the most terrific ending. For the poet the credo or doctrine is not the point of arrival but is, on the contrary, the point of departure for the metaphysical journey. For instance, you write a poem about the crucifixion. You have decided to go ten stanzas—and yet it's the third stanza and you've already dealt with the crucifixion. You have to go beyond that and add something—to develop it into something which is not there yet. Basically what I'm saying is that the poetic notion of infinity is far greater, and it's almost self-propelled by the form. Once in a conversation with Tony Hecht at Breadloaf we were talking about the usage of the Bible, and he said, "Joseph, wouldn't you agree that what a poet does is to try to make more sense out of these things?" And that's what it is—there's more sense, ya? In the works of the better poets you get the sensation that they're not talking to people any more, or to some seraphical creature. What they're doing is simply talking back to the language itself—as beauty, sensuality, wisdom, irony—those aspects of language of which the poet is a clear mirror. Poetry is not an art or a branch of art, it's something more. If what distinguishes us from other species is speech, then poetry, which is the supreme linguistic operation, is our anthropological, indeed genetic, goal. Anyone who regards poetry as an entertainment, as a "read," commits an anthropological crime, in the first place, against himself.

—SVEN BIRKERTS
December 1979

13. John Irving

John Winslow Irving was born on March 2, 1942, in Exeter, New Hampshire. He grew up on the campus of Phillips Exeter Academy, where his stepfather taught Russian history. After graduating *cum laude* in English from the University of New Hampshire in 1965, Irving went on to the University of Iowa Writers' Workshop on a fellowship. His Master of Fine Arts thesis was *Setting Free the Bears,* a novel published in 1968. Sale of the movie rights to that book, and a job adapting it into a screenplay, allowed the Irvings to move into an Austrian castle. When they returned to the United States in 1972, Irving published *The Water-Method Man.* He then spent three years as writer-in-residence at Iowa, publishing *The 158-Pound Marriage* in 1974. In 1975, he joined the faculty of Mount Holyoke College, serving as an assistant professor of English and working, with the aid of a Guggenheim Fellowship, on his fourth novel. When *The World According to Garp* was released in 1978, it met with almost immediate success, both critical and financial, holding a place on the best-seller lists for six months and selling more than 115,000 copies. *Garp* was nominated for both the 1978 National Book Critics' Circle Award and the National Book Award, and won the 1980 American Book Award. Irving's next novels, *The Hotel New Hampshire* (1981) and *The Cider House Rules* (1985), also became number one best-sellers and putting him on the cover of *Time.* His seventh novel, *A Prayer for Owen Meany,* will be published next year.

Irving lives with his second wife, Janet Turnbull, in New York, splitting his time between an Upper East Side apartment and a restored eighteenth-century house that was moved from Vermont to eastern Long Island. A gym containing a wrestling mat is on the second floor of the barn.

177 ~~163~~ a

~~4. THE CHRIST CHILD THE BABY JESUS THE LITTLE LORD JESUS~~

THE LITTLE LORD JESUS

The first Christmas following my mother's death was the first Christmas
I didn't spend in Sawyer's Depot. My grandmother told Aunt Martha and Uncle Alfred
that if the family were altogether, my mother's absence would be too apparent --
and
if Dan and Grandmother and I were alone in Gravesend, if the Eastmans were alone
in Sawyer's Depot, my grandmother argued that we would all miss each other; then
~~maybe,~~ she reasoned, we wouldn't miss my mother so much. Ever since ~~that~~ The
of '53,
Chirstmas I have felt that the yuletide in America is a special hell for those
families who have suffered any loss or who must admit to any imperfection;
the so-called spirit of giving can be as greedy as receiving -- Christmas is
our time to be aware of what we lack, of who's not home.

Dividing my time between my grandmother's house on 80 Front Street and
the abandoned dormitory where Dan had his little apartment also gave me my first
boarders
impressions of Gravesend Academy at Christmas, when all the ~~students, of course,~~ &
and stone
had gone home. The bleak brick ~~buildings~~, the ivy frosted with snow,
the dormitories and classroom buildings with their windows all equally closed
-- with a penitentiary sameness -- gave the campus the aura of a prison enduring
a hunger strike; and without the students hurrying on the quadrangle paths,
in
the bare, bone -colored birches stood out ~~so~~ black-and-white against the snow,
The alumni o
like charcoal drawings of themselves, or skeletons of ~~former students,~~

The ringing of the chapel bell, and the bell for class-hours, was suspended;
and so my mother's absence was underlined by the absence of Gravesend's most
routine music, the academy chimes I'd taken for granted -- until I couldn't hear
them. There was only the solemn, hourly bonging of the great clock in the bell-
tower of Hurd's Church; especially on the most brittle-cold days of December,
To
and against the landscape of old snow -- thawed and refrozen ~~with~~ the silver-gray
s
sheen of a pearl -- the clock-bell of Hurd Church tolled the time like a death knell.

A manuscript page from John Irving's novel-in-progress, A Prayer for Owen
Meany.

John Irving

John Irving was interviewed in the cramped back room of his otherwise large and luxurious apartment in Manhattan. A jump rope hangs on the door, a heavy set of weights "is always in the way" on the floor, and by one window is a stationary bike that Irving uses on days he doesn't go to his private athletic club or jog in Central Park. He writes at a blue IBM typewriter beneath color photographs of his sons wrestling in prep-school competitions and black-and-white photographs of himself in prep-school and college matches. Among a great many books in the high bookcases are foreign editions of his novels in fifteen languages.

On the day of this interview, he wore a tweed coat, a green plaid flannel shirt, blue jeans, and running shoes. Irving is a vigorous, brawny man with brown hair that is increasingly gray. His height is probably five-feet-eight and he weighs only twenty-

five pounds more than the 136 1/2 pounds he wrestled at years ago. He's a storyteller and a generous teacher; when asked a question, Irving pauses for so long a time it nearly seems his inner works have stopped, but once his reply has been fully considered, he replies at length in a gentlemanly, New England voice.

INTERVIEWER: You're only forty-four and yet you've already published six big and important novels as well as a great many uncollected essays, stories, and reviews. How do you get so much work done?

IRVING: I don't give myself time off or make myself work; I have no work routine. I am compulsive about writing, I need to do it the way I need sleep and exercise and food and sex; I can go without it for a while, but then I need it. A novel is such a long involvement; when I'm beginning a book, I can't work more than two or three hours a day. I don't know more than two or three hours a day about a new novel. Then there's the middle of a book. I can work eight, nine, twelve hours then, seven days a week—if my children let me; they usually don't. One luxury of making enough money to support myself as a writer is that I can afford to have those eight-, nine-, and twelve-hour days. I resented having to teach and coach, not because I disliked teaching or coaching or wrestling but because I had no time to write. Ask a doctor to be a doctor two hours a day. An eight-hour day at the typewriter is easy; and two hours of reading over material in the evening, too. That's routine. Then when the time to finish the book comes, it's back to those two- and three-hour days. Finishing, like beginning, is more careful work. I write very quickly; I rewrite very slowly. It takes me nearly as long to rewrite a book as it does to get the first draft. I can write more quickly than I can read.

INTERVIEWER: How do you begin a book?

IRVING: Not until I know as much as I can stand to know without putting anything down on paper. Henry Robbins, my late editor at E. P. Dutton, called this my enema theory: keep from writing the book as long as you can, make yourself *not* begin, store it up. This is an advantage in historical novels. *Setting Free the Bears* and *The Cider House Rules*, for example. I had to learn so much before I could begin those books; I had to gather so much information, take so many notes, see, witness, observe, study—whatever—that when I finally was able to begin writing, I knew everything that was going to happen, in advance. That never hurts. I want to know how a book feels after the main events are over. The authority of the storyteller's voice—of mine, anyway—comes from knowing how it all comes out before you begin. It's very plodding work, really.

INTERVIEWER: Have any of your novels changed drastically as you created them?

IRVING: Along the way accidents happen, detours get taken—the accidents turn out to be some of the best things. But these are not "divine" accidents; I don't believe in those. I believe you have constructive accidents en route through a novel only because you have mapped a clear way. If you have confidence that you have a clear direction to take, you always have confidence to explore other ways; if they prove to be mere digressions, you'll recognize that and make the necessary revisions. The more you know about a book, the freer you can be to fool around. The less you know, the tighter you get.

INTERVIEWER: Could you give an example of one of those accidents?

IRVING: One such accident was Melony. I knew she was the force in *The Cider House Rules* that would get Homer Wells back to St. Cloud's; at first, of course, the reader is supposed to think that if Melony ever finds Homer, she'll kill him. And in a way, she does; she has the power to bring him up short. But what she kills is his illusion that he's living a good life. She's a moral force, not a lethal one; she's just as devastating to him as she would be if she were trying to kill him, really. She's the one who tells him his life is shabby and ordinary. She has the power to do that. I didn't know exactly what she would do, I mean physically, when she found him; then I thought of her frustrated rage in his bathroom, her very particular handling and dismantling of his things. I thought of that ugly, frightening weapon she constructs out of a toothbrush and a razor blade; she melts the toothbrush handle until it's soft enough to stick a blade in it; when the plastic hardens, she's got a lethal weapon. That's a frightening moment, but she just leaves it in his bathroom medicine cabinet; he cuts himself on it, by accident. "By accident," but it's no accident; it's a reminder to him of her potential for violence. That was a lucky discovery; it just fit perfectly.

INTERVIEWER: Except for *The Water-Method Man,* which you've said was called *Fucking Up* as you wrote it, you seem to know your novel's title very early in your conception of it. Is it crucial to you to have a working title before you begin a project?

IRVING: Titles *are* important; I have them before I have books that belong to them. I have last chapters in my mind before I see first chapters, too. I usually begin with endings, with a sense of aftermath, of dust settling, of epilogue. I love plot, and how can you plot a novel if you don't know the ending first? How do you know how to introduce a character if you don't know how he *ends up?* You might say I back into a novel. All the important discoveries—at the end of a book—those are the things I have to know before I know where to begin. I knew that Garp's mother would be killed by a stupid man who blindly hates women; I knew Garp would be killed by a stupid woman who blindly hates men. I didn't even know which of them would be killed first; I had to wait to see which of them was the main character. At first I thought Jenny was the main character; but she was too much of a saint for a main character—in the way that Wilbur Larch is too much of a saint to be the main character of *The Cider House Rules.* Garp and

Homer Wells are flawed; by comparison to Jenny and Dr.
Larch, they're weak. They're main characters. Actors know
how they end up—I mean how their *characters* end up—
before they speak the opening lines. Shouldn't writers know at
least as much about their characters as actors know? I think so.
But I'm a dinosaur.

INTERVIEWER: How do you mean?

IRVING: I'm not a twentieth-century novelist, I'm not modern, and certainly not postmodern. I follow the form of the
nineteenth-century novel; that was the century which produced the models of the form. I'm old-fashioned, a storyteller.
I'm not an analyst and I'm not an intellectual.

INTERVIEWER: How about the analysts and intellectuals?
Have you ever learned anything from reading criticism about
your work? Do reviews please or annoy you, or do you pay too
little attention to them for that?

IRVING: Reviews are only important when no one knows who
you are. In a perfect world all writers would be well-enough
known to not need reviewers. As Thomas Mann has written:
"Our receptivity to praise stands in no relationship to our
vulnerability to mean disdain and spiteful abuse. No matter
how stupid such abuse is, no matter how plainly impelled by
private rancors, as an expression of hostility it occupies us far
more deeply and lastingly than praise. Which is very foolish,
since enemies are, of course, the necessary concomitant of any
robust life, the very proof of its strength." I have a friend who
says that reviewers are the tickbirds of the literary rhinoceros—
but he is being kind. Tickbirds perform a valuable service to
the rhino and the rhino hardly notices the birds. Reviewers
perform no service to the writer and are noticed too much. I
like what Cocteau said about them. "Listen very carefully to
the first criticisms of your work. Note just what it is about your
work that the reviewers don't like; it may be the only thing in
your work that is original and worthwhile."

INTERVIEWER: And yet you review books yourself.

IRVING: I write only favorable reviews. A writer of fiction whose own fiction comes first is just too subjective a reader to allow himself to write a negative review. And there are already plenty of professional reviewers eager to be negative. If I get a book to review and I don't like it, I return it; I only review the book if I love it. Hence I've written very few reviews, and those are really just songs of praise or rather long, retrospective reviews of all the writer's works: of John Cheever, Kurt Vonnegut, and Günter Grass, for example. And then there is the occasional "younger" writer whom I introduce to readers, such as Jayne Anne Phillips and Craig Nova. Another thing about not writing negative reviews: grown-ups shouldn't finish books they're not enjoying. When you're no longer a child, and you no longer live at home, you don't have to finish everything on your plate. One reward of leaving school is that you don't have to finish books you don't like. You know, if I were a critic, I'd be angry and vicious, too; it *makes* poor critics angry and vicious—to have to *finish* all those books they're not enjoying. What a silly job criticism is! What unnatural work it is! It is certainly not work for a grown-up.

INTERVIEWER: And what about fiction?

IRVING: Of course. What I do, telling stories, is childish work, too. I've never been able to keep a diary, to write a memoir. I've tried; I begin by telling the truth, by remembering real people, relatives and friends. The landscape detail is pretty good, but the people aren't quite interesting enough— they don't have quite enough to do with one another; of course, what unsettles me and bores me is the absence of plot. There's no story to my life! And so I find a little something that I exaggerate, a little; gradually, I have an autobiography on its way to becoming a lie. The lie, of course, is more interesting. I become much more interested in the part of the story I'm making up, in the "relative" I never had. And then I begin to think of a novel; that's the end of the diary. I promise I'll start another one as soon as I finish the novel.

Then the same thing happens; the lies become much more interesting—always.

INTERVIEWER: Especially in your younger work, but even now, one gets the sense of a grown-up at play, of a very natural writer enjoying himself. Are you having as much fun writing now as when you began writing stories at Exeter?

IRVING: I can't say I have fun writing. My stories are sad to me, and comic too, but largely unhappy. I feel badly for the characters—that is, if the story's any good. Writing a novel is actually searching for victims. As I write I keep looking for casualties. The stories uncover the casualties.

INTERVIEWER: Some people say you write disaster fiction.

IRVING: Such things don't happen? Is that what they mean? You bet I write disaster fiction. We have compiled a disastrous record on this planet, a record of stupidity and absurdity and self-abuse and self-aggrandizement and self-deception and pompousness and self-righteousness and cruelty and indifference beyond what any other species has demonstrated the capacity for, which is the capacity for all the above. I am sick of secure and smugly conventional people telling me that my work is bizarre simply because they've found a safe little place to live out the chaos of the world—and who then deny that this chaos happens to other, less fortunate people. If you're rich, are you permitted to say there's no poverty, no starvation? If you're a calm, gentle soul, do you say there's no violence except in bad movies and bad books? I don't make much up. I mean that. I am not the inventor I've been given credit for being. I just witness a different news—it's still news, it still is just what happens, but more isolated and well-described so you might notice it a little more clearly. George Santayana wrote: "When people say that Dickens exaggerates, it seems to me that they can have no eyes or no ears. They probably have only *notions* of what things and people are; they accept them conventionally, at their diplomatic value."

INTERVIEWER: Your literary debts to Charles Dickens,

Günter Grass, and Kurt Vonnegut are pretty clear in your work, at least to some readers. How do you see their books contributing to your own?

IRVING: Well, yes, they're all fathers of my work, in a way. The polite world calls them extremists, but I think they are very truthful, very accurate. I am not attracted to writers by style. What style do Dickens, Grass, and Vonnegut have in common? How silly! I am attracted to what makes them angry, what makes them passionate, what outrages them, what they applaud and find sympathetic in human beings and what they detest about human beings, too. They are writers of great emotional range. They are all disturbed—both comically and tragically—by who the victims of a society (or of each other) are. You can't copy that; you can only agree with it.

INTERVIEWER: How did your stay in Vienna contribute to your growth as a writer?

IRVING: Living with Vienna's history helped me look for history in my own work, make history for my characters, respect the passage of time as a finite kind of truth. I never really learned much about Vienna but I was taught to think about the past there—about my past, New England's past, and my characters' pasts.

INTERVIEWER: Have you studied the psychology of Sigmund Freud? Do you feel any kinship with his theories?

IRVING: I think Freud was a great novelist. Period.

INTERVIEWER: Period.

IRVING: Well, all right—a little more about that. Sigmund Freud was a novelist with a scientific background. He just didn't know he was a novelist. All those damn psychiatrists after him, they didn't know he was a novelist, either. They made simply awful sense out of his intuitions. People say Carl Jung is better, but Jung can't write! Freud was a wonderful writer! And what a storyteller! I don't think about his theories very much; sometimes they work, sometimes they don't fit at all, but when people say Freud was "wrong" about this or that,

I have to laugh. Was Charles Dickens "wrong" about Fagin in *Oliver Twist*? I don't mean Fagin's Jewishness either—I mean, how could he have been "wrong" about Fagin as a character? What a great character! So I love reading Freud: the detail, the observations, the characters, the histories. The hell with the rest of it.

INTERVIEWER: You say your work is becoming increasingly political.

IRVING: You're right: I said I was becoming more political. I know I said that. I'm not, though. I am becoming more social; I care that the social abuses, the social evils and ills of this and every other time be exposed, vividly. I am interested in exposing wrongdoing, good and evil, injustice. That I am active in political causes has been well observed. I'm active, okay. But as a writer I am not interested so much in taking a political side as I am interested in exposing a corruption or an abuse (usually of an individual or group, but also by a law, or by a general indifference). Like Charles Dickens, I believe that society is a conditioning force, and often an evil force, but I also believe in absolutely good men and women, too. I read a critic of my work who found it ludicrous that I still wrote about "good" and "bad" people. Where has this man been? What has he seen? And I don't mean what literature has he read. I mean, what has he seen of the world? There *are* bad people in the world; and good ones, too. Society is responsible for much that is evil; but no one thing is responsible for everything. President Reagan would like the American people to believe that the liberals in this country, and the Communists outside this country, have made the world as bad as it is. He seems to be meeting with fair success with this lunatic proposition, too. A Marxist view of literature is offensive to me. Also, a feminist view of abortion: it is as offensive as a Catholic view, if you're not a Catholic.

INTERVIEWER: Do you think political considerations should be more important to American writers?

IRVING: Günter Grass and I were having dinner not long ago. He's a great hero of mine. And he said he wanted to keep his fiction pure, that is, free of politics; but when he was not writing fiction, he wanted to be as politically active as possible. A good way to live, but perhaps it is a more successful way for a West German novelist than for an American. Chancellor Willy Brandt had the wisdom to let Grass write for him. What American political figure would *dare* to have an American novelist write for him—write real details, real arguments, real right and wrong? I tell you, Kurt Vonnegut would be a better president than any president we've had since I've been voting. E. L. Doctorow would be pretty good too. And what would happen if Philip Roth volunteered to write campaign speeches for a presidential candidate? I doubt that the promise that the speeches would be more concrete and literate and wise and humane would much influence the people making the self-canceling political "statements" that pass for speeches today. I doubt that any politician would hire Philip Roth or William Styron or Arthur Miller or any good writer you could name.

INTERVIEWER: How do you explain the comparative indifference of American novelists to national politics?

IRVING: I told Grass that there was no way for American writers to *be* politically active in this country. What we do, mainly, is join a general protest movement. We speak for causes; we speak to our friends; we speak to audiences already predisposed to agree with us. We have *zero* effect, in my opinion. We do a lot of political good deeds that make us feel self-righteous and not a part of the awful mainstream when yet another completely stupid and dangerous thing happens in this country. We say, complacently, "Well, I'm not part of that"; or, "As I said in *The Nation*"; or, "As I told the students at Stanford"; or, "When I was on the 'Today Show'" (for two minutes)—and on and on. I think if we're going to be politically active, it *has* to start creeping into our novels. Günter Grass may feel he has an effect as a political activist in Germany, and maybe he does. He certainly has uncounted effect as a wonderful novelist. But what effect do we political activists have here? I'm impatient with what I see; more and more impatient. So I look for novels that will make people feel more and more uncomfortable about what's taken for granted in our society. Writers must describe the terrible. And one way to describe the terrible is to write comically, of course. George Bernard Shaw, who admitted to getting most of his satiric methods from Dickens, said that the thing to do is to find one true thing and exaggerate it, with levity, until it's obvious. I know it is not very postmodernist to be obvious, but politically one has to become more and more that way.

INTERVIEWER: Politically?

IRVING: Maybe I should stop using the word "political" and just claim that social observation is a writer's business; just to observe the society truthfully is, of course, being "political." I think New Englanders and Southerners have this in common, in their social observations, as writers: we recognize that America is a class society. People who differ from one another or draw lines between each other on matters of "taste" are a part of the class society, just as surely as wealth and power are parts of it. These are more than manners, in a society; these things politicize us. By demonstrating how Americans discriminate we are also being political, as writers. And as long as we have presidents who lie to us—who use language as irresponsibly as President Reagan uses it—we'll be political just by using language clearly. But I'm getting tired of blaming Reagan for being Reagan; the American people have to take responsibility for this man—they wanted him; they wanted him *twice.* He is never held accountable. His first reaction to Marcos' "victory" in the Philippines was to advise Mrs. Aquino to "respect the democratic process," to accept her defeat gracefully, in other words. And in the face of so much alarming evidence, to say, as he did, that there had been manipulations of the vote by both sides—it was ridiculous. Well, in one sense, he didn't get away with it; Marcos is out. But five minutes later we hear the Reagan Administration taking credit for "the democratic process" in the Philippines; do Americans simply forget what the man's first, terrible instincts were? They do appear to forget what he, literally, said. This is very troubling to writers; we couldn't have a president as irresponsible as this if the American people paid attention to language. The news is: language doesn't matter. But writers make language matter; we describe *exactly*. You see? Even caring about language becomes "political."

INTERVIEWER: Could you describe your involvement in the 1984 presidential campaign?

IRVING: I spoke for Walter Mondale and Geraldine Ferraro and for the good guys running against the bad guys in North Carolina, Texas, Iowa, and Michigan. Campaigning was especially depressing on college campuses. I cared more about abortion rights than my audience of students who were fucking each other day and night and taking for granted that they would never have any trouble getting an abortion. I cared more about whether their generation was going to suffer another Vietnam in Central America—although, as I told them, *I* wouldn't be one of the Americans sent to die there, those Americans would come from *their* generation. A lot of well-fed, well-dressed, career-oriented young people smiled back at me with a kind of what's-he-worried-about? look on their faces. At the New School once some wit in the audience hollered out to me when I was talking about *The Cider House Rules*. The subject was migrant workers and the period in the late 1950s when I worked in the orchards with black apple pickers from the South, and I was saying that not much had changed for the migrants since then and that I felt great sympathy for poor people as a kid and I always wanted to write about them as truthfully as I could. And this jerk in the audience pipes up: "Will the migrants read it?" And there's a small chant from about two or three of his pals saying "Yeah!" And raised fists;

shouts. I don't know exactly what their point was but they seemed to think they had made one—possibly, the migrants won't read it, therefore so what? Of course, if you know the book, you know that's one of my points about the migrants: they can't read! Anyway, I thought it was funny, and bewildering, and typical.

INTERVIEWER: How?

IRVING: People are angry—politically—and the last people they see as helping a political or just plain social situation are the artists and writers and intellectuals. And as a group we have been of next to no help in this country. Every administration thinks we're silly, not to be counted, and in the popular media, intellectuals and artists are always cast as totally unreliable and selfish people, as flakes and phonies and wimps altogether out of touch with the common man. Some problem, wouldn't you agree? I have an instinct for victims; that's all I can tell you. I see who gets hurt and I describe it. Do people like to see themselves as victims, or to hear about victims? In my experience, no.

INTERVIEWER: Probably no male writer has given as much serious attention as you have to the issues of adultery, rape, and now, with *The Cider House Rules,* abortion. Could you comment on that?

IRVING: I've been writing about one form or another of violence to women for years. And illegal abortion is simply a most sanctimonious form of violence against women. It is the most accepted form of violence in this country, violence against women. Rape is still funny, a wife is still the easiest person to beat up and get away with it, and the old line is still true: if men could get pregnant, don't imagine for a moment that anyone would be complaining about legalized abortion. Some conventionally smug people, eyes tightly closed, say that all this violence to women in my books—as if it happened only there!—is exploitative. Others, who think violence to women is perfectly okay, think I am just a man of quaint concerns, or one writing feminist tracts. The same idiot who called *The World According to Garp* a feminist tract, by the way, also called *The Cider House Rules* sadistic to women. Does he mean I've changed? Does he even know what he means?

INTERVIEWER: You worked on a screenplay of *Setting Free the Bears* and on the acknowledgments page of *The Water-Method Man* you thanked that project's director, Irvin Kershner, "for a valuable and exciting film experience"; and yet since then you've rejected every opportunity to become involved in screen adaptations of your novels. Why?

IRVING: Well, movies, movies, movies—they are our enemy, of course. Movies are the enemy of the novel because they are replacing novels. Novelists shouldn't write for the movies, unless, of course, they discover they're no good at writing novels. I learned a lot from Kershner, who's a dear friend of mine to this day, but I hated writing the script. I like people who make movies, and I'm glad some of them, who are terribly smart, are not writing novels. There are enough people writing novels, God knows. Anyway, the main thing I learned by writing a screenplay of *Setting Free the Bears* for Kershner was that screenwriting isn't really writing; it's carpentry. There's no language in it, and the writer is not in control of the pace of the story, or of the tone of the narration, and what else is there to be in control of? Tony Richardson told me that there *are* no screenwriters, so there is at least one director who agrees with me. It could be that it was the most valuable thing I ever did—to have my shot at writing a movie when I was so young, right after my first novel was published—because I was never tempted to do it again.

INTERVIEWER: Have you generally liked the films made of *The World According to Garp* and *The Hotel New Hampshire*?

IRVING: I helped George Roy Hill with *The World According to Garp;* that is, I commented to him on the Steve Tesich screenplay, and looked at some of the shooting and the rushes, and I even played a small part as a wrestling referee—that wasn't acting, by the way; for years I used to *be* a wrestling referee. My kids got in the movie, too; they had a ball. And George is one of my best friends now. He did a good job with *The World According to Garp;* he took it to the suburbs and gave all the characters haircuts and made them much nicer than they were in the book, but he was true to the domestic line, to the main, linear narrative. He's a good storyteller, George; witness what a good job he did with *Slaughterhouse-Five,* and look at *The Sting.* Good narrative. He was the right director for *The World According to Garp.* What's missing from that film is, of course, nine-tenths of the book, but George was faithful to what he could do. And that's another reason I'm not interested in writing for the movies, personally: the main job in making a movie out of a novel by me is to throw away nine-tenths of the novel. Why would that be any fun for me? Tony Richardson took a more difficult route with *The Hotel New Hampshire.* He was not as literal as George, and the storytelling is jumpier, but he tried to make it a proper fairy tale, which it is—people in Europe seemed to understand that better than they understood it here (in both the book and the movie). I thought Tony took great risks with that movie and I thought the film was sweet, charming. It had a better beginning and ending than a middle. It was originally going to be in two parts but Tony couldn't solve the two-part screenplay—isn't it hysterical how movie people talk about "solving" scripts?—and he couldn't get anyone to finance a movie in two parts either. Then he truncated what he had into one film, and that hurt; that kind of cartooned the characters, made it too speeded-up, at least for people who didn't know the book. But he made every frame of it with love and zest; there's nothing cynical about Tony.

INTERVIEWER: As far as I know, the stories in *The World According to Garp* are the last you've done. Do you intend to work with short fiction again?

IRVING: No. I can't write a good story. The closest thing to a good story I ever wrote was "The Pension Grillparzer," and the reason I worked as hard as I did on that story was that I was writing it for T. S. Garp—I had to establish that my character was the real thing, that he could really write. I would never have worked on a story of my own that hard. I just don't care for the short story form. The summations, the closed doors, the focus; not for me. I won't ever write another story— except perhaps a story entirely meant to be read or spoken aloud. Something exactly forty-five minutes to an hour in length, and never to be published, just to be *said*. Once I publish something I usually don't enjoy reading aloud from it anymore, but I read "The Pension Grillparzer" aloud, to public audiences, seventy-three times. Once a young woman spoke to me after a reading. "I've heard you read a dozen times," she said. She'd traveled from New York to California, to Vermont, to Missouri, to Iowa, to South Carolina. And all she ever got to hear was "The Pension Grillparzer." She looked a trifle disturbed. "I keep thinking you'll read something different," she said peevishly. I never read the story again. But now I feel like trying it again; the story is simply a length that is perfect, and it's self-contained. I don't have anything else like it. I like public readings, but the chapters of all my novels, lately, are one and a half or two hours of reading; and cutting them down doesn't improve them; and all the necessary things one has to say to introduce chapters, or parts of chapters, from a novel-in-progress . . . it's frustrating.

INTERVIEWER: How about the books of your contemporaries? Are you a good reader?

IRVING: My contemporaries: of course, I read them. Or I begin them. Among my favorites: Kurt Vonnegut, of course— he's the most original American writer since Mark Twain and the most humanitarian writer in English since Charles Dickens. And Günter Grass, of course. I loved John Cheever; I knew his territory and I liked his sense of mischief and fair play—always at war with each other. And I really value my friendships with any number of writers I admire: Joseph Heller, Gail Godwin, John Hawkes, Stanley Elkin, Peter Matthiessen, Robertson Davies . . . well, there isn't a "complete" list. I generally like other writers; I try to meet every writer I can—and read any book that anyone tells me about.

INTERVIEWER: How do you think this period in American literature measures up against earlier ones?

IRVING: As for my view of the contemporary novel . . . well, as I've said so many times: I'm old-fashioned. I believe in plot, of all things; in narrative, all the time; in storytelling; in character. Very traditional forms interest me. This nonsense about the novel being about "the word" . . . what can that mean? Are we novelists going to become like so many modern poets, writing only for and to each other, not comprehensible to anyone who isn't another writer? I have only a prep-school education in the poems of John Milton. Yet I can read Milton; I really understand him. All that time has passed, and yet he's still clear. But when I read the poems of someone my own age and can't understand a single thing, is that supposed to be a failure of my education, or of the poetry?

INTERVIEWER: *Setting Free the Bears*, *The Water-Method Man*, and *The 158-Pound Marriage* were innovative, or at least postmodernist, in their designs, in their mixing of points of view or first- and third-person narrative, in their great concern for language. Your novels after them have been less concerned with experiments in storytelling and more concerned with the story itself. How do you account for that?

IRVING: The novel is a popular art form, an accessible form. I don't enjoy novels that are boring exercises in show-off writing with no narrative, no characters, no *information*—novels that are just an intellectually discursive text with lots of style. Is their object to make me feel stupid? These are not novels. These are the works of people who want to call themselves writers but haven't a recognizable form to work in. Their subject *is* their technique. And their vision? They have no vision, no private version of the world; there is only a private version of style, of technique. I just completed an introduction to *Great Expectations* in which I pointed out that Dickens was never so vain as to imagine that his love or his use of language was particularly special. He could write very prettily when he wanted to, but he never had so little to say that he thought the object of writing was pretty language. The broadest novelists never cared for that kind of original language. Dickens, Hardy, Tolstoy, Hawthorne, Melville: to such novelists, originality with language is mere fashion; it will pass. The larger, plainer things they are preoccupied with, their obsessions—these will last: the story, the characters, the laughter and the tears.

INTERVIEWER: How helpful were your years spent at the Iowa Writers' Workshop?

IRVING: I was not necessarily "taught" anything there as a student, although I was certainly encouraged and helped—and the advice of Vance Bourjaily, Kurt Vonnegut, and José Donoso clearly saved me some valuable time; that is, they told me things about my writing and about writing in general that I would probably have figured out for myself, but time is precious for a young writer. I always say that this is what I can "teach" a young writer: something he'll know for himself in a little while longer; but why wait to know these things? I am talking about technical things, the only things you can presume to teach, anyway.

INTERVIEWER: What are some of the more important "technical" things?

IRVING: "Voice" is a technical thing; the choice to be close to this character, distant from that character—to be in this or that point of view. You can learn these things; you can learn to recognize your own good and bad habits, what you do well in the first-person narrative voice, and what you do to excess, for example; and what the dangers and advantages are of a third-person narrative that presumes historical distance (the voice of a biographer, for example). There are so many stances involved, so many postures you can assume while telling a story; they can be much more deliberate, much more in a writer's control, than an amateur knows. The reader, of course, shouldn't be aware of much of this. It's brilliant, for example, how Grass calls Oskar Matzerath "he" or "Oskar" at one moment, and then—sometimes in the same sentence—he refers to little Oskar as "I"; he's a first-person narrator *and* a third-person narrator in the same sentence. But it's done so seamlessly, it doesn't call attention to itself; I *hate* those forms and styles that call great attention to themselves.

INTERVIEWER: You've also said you made some valuable friendships as a teacher at Iowa.

IRVING: Yes. Especially with Gail Godwin, Stanley Elkin, and John Cheever.

INTERVIEWER: And you met J. P. Donleavy at Iowa.

IRVING: I like meeting other writers, and Iowa City is a good place to meet them, but I didn't enjoy Donleavy. John Cheever and I, who were in a particularly ritualized habit of watching Monday Night Football together, while eating homemade pasta, were happy to hear that Donleavy was coming. We'd both admired *The Ginger Man* and we wanted to meet the author. I went to the airport to meet him; I'd written three novels—but not yet *The World According to Garp;* I wasn't famous. I didn't expect Donleavy to have read anything of mine, but I was surprised when he announced that he read no one living; then he asked if we were in Kansas. I told him a little about the Workshop, but he was one of those writers with no knowledge about writing programs and many prejudices about them: to be a student of writing was a waste of time; better to go out and suffer. He was wearing a very expensive three-piece suit, very handsome shoes, and handling a very posh walking stick at the time, and I began to get irritated. In a meeting with Workshop students, he told them that any writer who was lowering himself by teaching writing wasn't capable of teaching them anything. And so I was quite cross by the time I had

to pick up the great man and drive him to his reading. I said
we would be taking Mr. Cheever with us to the reading, and
that both Mr. Cheever and I were great admirers, and that
although I knew Mr. Donleavy did not read anyone living, he
should know that Mr. Cheever was a wonderful writer. His
short stories were models of the form, I said. But when I
introduced Cheever to Donleavy, Donleavy wouldn't even look
at him; he went on talking to his wife, about aspirin, as if
Cheever wasn't there. I tried to say a few things about why so
many American writers turned to teaching—as a way of supporting themselves without having to place the burden of making money upon their writing; and as a way of giving
themselves enough time to practice their writing, too. But
Donleavy wasn't interested and he said so. The whole trip he
was taking was tiresome; the people he met, the people everywhere, were tiresome, too. And so Cheever and I sat up front
in the car, excluded from the conversation about the evils of
aspirin, and driving the Donleavys about as if they were unhappy royalty in a hick town. I will say that Mrs. Donleavy
appeared to suffer her husband's rudeness, or perhaps she was
just suffering her headache. Cheever tried a few times to en-
gage Donleavy in some conversation, and as Cheever was as
gifted in conversation as any man I have ever met, I grew more
and more furious at Donleavy's coldness and unresponsiveness
and *total* discourtesy. I was thinking, frankly, that I should
throw the lout in a puddle, if there was one handy, when
Cheever spoke up. "Do you know, Mr. Donleavy," Cheever
said, "that no *major* writer of fiction was ever a shit to another
writer of fiction, except Hemingway—and he was crazy?" That
was all. Donleavy had no answer. Perhaps he thought Hemingway was still a living writer and therefore hadn't read him,
either. Cheever and I deposited the Donleavys at the reading,
which we spontaneously decided to skip. It was many years
later that I met and became friends with George Roy Hill, who
told me that he'd been a roommate of "Mike" Donleavy at

Trinity College, Dublin, and that "Mike" was just a touch eccentric and surely not a bad sort. But I remembered my evening with Cheever and told George that, in my opinion, Donleavy was a *minor* writer, a shit, or crazy—or all three. I should add that drinking wasn't the issue of this unpleasant evening; Cheever was not drinking; Donleavy wasn't drunk— he was simply righteous and acting the prima donna. I feel a little like I'm tattling on a fellow schoolboy to tell this story, but I felt so awful—not for myself but for Cheever. It was such an outrage: that Donleavy—this large, silly man with his walking stick—was *snubbing* John Cheever. I suppose it's silly that I should *still* be angry, but George Plimpton told me that Donleavy has a subscription to *The Paris Review**; this presents an apparent contradiction to Donleavy's claim that he doesn't read anyone living, but it gives me hope that he might read this. If the story embarrasses him, or makes him angry, I would say we're even; the evening embarrassed Cheever and me, and made us angry, too.

INTERVIEWER: John Cheever's fiction was frequently informed by a Christian sensibility. How about your own? Are you a religious man?

IRVING: I am *now*. I had the usual, fainthearted church experiences of an average New England Protestant. I was a Congregationalist; then I became an Episcopalian because more of my friends went to that Sunday school than to the Sunday school in the Congo, as we used to call it. And if I have a preference now it's Congregational again, although I'm still cross with them for consolidating—you know, they kind of unionized, like all the other churches, and I liked them better the old way, when they were independent from all the other churches, even all the other so-called Congregational churches; that was more Yankee, that was very New England. I'm actually writing a religious novel now. What I mean by that is that

*A *complimentary* subscription—*Ed.*

I'm writing a novel that begs the reader to believe in a miracle. It's a small enough miracle to be fairly universally believed, I hope; and it's a questionable enough "religious experience" to be exactly that, to a religious reader, and acceptable on other terms to my readers who are not believers. I'm a believer, by the way. Haven't always been. And there's a day every now and then when I'm frankly worried, or just your average doubter. Well, for the sake of the new novel, I am bolstering up what belief I have. I'm a very conventionally religious person—you know, I find it easier to "believe" when I'm physically *in* a church, and I kind of lose touch with the feeling of how to pray when I slip away from the church for very long.

INTERVIEWER: Are you willing to say anything more about the novel you're working on?

IRVING: It will be called *A Prayer for Owen Meany*. It's about this little guy—both a hero and a victim—who believes that he's been appointed by God, that he's been specially chosen; and that the rather terrible "fate" he encounters is all part of his divine assignment. And it's the writer's job, isn't it, to make the readers wonder if maybe this isn't entirely true? Even the doubters. I have to convince them of little Owen Meany's special appointment in the universe, too. In that sense, maybe, writing a novel is always a religious act, in that we have to believe that our characters *are* appointed—even if only by us—and that their acts are not accidents, their responses not random. I don't believe in accidents. That's another aspect of how old-fashioned I am, I guess.

INTERVIEWER: You're a public figure now. Does that interfere with your goals as a writer?

IRVING: No.

INTERVIEWER: You don't have a drinking problem. In fact, your capacity for serious exercise is well-known; you're in good shape. But so many writers drink to excess. I've heard you lay the blame on what's *wrong* with this or that book on the author's drinking problem. You've said, for example, that the reason both Hemingway and Fitzgerald wrote their best books in their twenties (they were twenty-seven when they wrote *The Sun Also Rises* and *The Great Gatsby*) is that they "pickled their brains." Do you really believe that?

IRVING: Yes, I really believe that. They should have gotten better as they got older; *I've* gotten better. We're not professional athletes; it's reasonable to assume that we'll get better as we mature—at least, until we start getting senile. Of course, some writers who write their best books early simply lose interest in writing; or they lose their concentration—probably because they want to do other things. But Hemingway and Fitzgerald really lived to write; their bodies and their brains betrayed them. I'm such an incapable drinker, I'm lucky. If I drink half a bottle of red wine with my dinner, I forget who I had dinner with—not to mention everything that I or anybody else said. If I drink more than half a bottle, I fall instantly asleep. But just think of what novelists do: fiction writing requires a kind of memory, a vigorous, invented memory. If I can forget who I had dinner with, what might I forget about my novel-in-progress? The irony is that drinking is especially dangerous to novelists; memory is vital to us. I'm not so down on drinking for writers from a moral point of view; but booze is clearly not good for writing *or* for driving cars. You know what Lawrence said: "The novel is the highest example of subtle interrelatedness that man has discovered." I agree! And just consider for one second what drinking does to "subtle interrelatedness." Forget the "subtle"; "interrelatedness" is what makes novels work—without it, you have no narrative momentum; you have incoherent rambling. Drunks ramble; so do books by drunks.

INTERVIEWER: How big is your ego?

IRVING: It grows a little smaller all the time. Being an ex-athlete is good for losing ego. And writing, in my opinion, is the opposite of having ego. Confidence as a writer should not be confused with personal, egotistical confidence. A writer is a vehicle. I feel the story I am writing existed before I existed; I'm just the slob who finds it, and rather clumsily tries to do it, and the characters, justice. I think of writing fiction as doing justice to the people in the story, and doing justice to *their* story—it's not *my* story. It's entirely ghostly work; I'm just the medium. As a writer, I do more listening than talking. W. H. Auden called the first act of writing "noticing." He meant the vision—not so much what we make up but what we *witness*. Oh, sure: writers "make up" the language, the voice, the transitions, all the clunking bridges that span the story's parts—that stuff, it's true, is invented. I am still old-fashioned enough to maintain that what *happens* in a novel is what distinguishes it, and what happens is what we *see*. In that sense, we're all just reporters. Didn't Faulkner say something like it was necessary only to write about "the human heart in conflict with itself" in order to write well? Well, I think that's all we do: we find more than we create, we simply see and expose more than we fabulate and invent. At least I do. Of course, it's necessary to make the atmosphere of a novel more real than real, as we say. Whatever its *place* is, it's got to feel, concretely, like a place with richer detail than any place we can actually remember. I think what a reader likes best is memories, the more vivid the better. That's the role of atmosphere in fiction: it provides details that feel as good, or as terrifying, as memories. Vienna, in my books, is more Vienna than Vienna; St. Cloud's is more Maine than Maine.

INTERVIEWER: One of the predominant characteristics of your protagonists is that they gain success in their occupations without any formal training—T. S. Garp skips college altogether, Lilly Berry publishes a novel while still a teenager, Homer Wells practices obstetrics without a medical degree— and yet you earned a graduate degree and you've worked as a professor at a number of colleges. How do you account for this disparity between your own experience and that of your characters? Are you implying that higher education is unnecessary?

IRVING: I needed prep school; I needed the experience of going to school, or having to struggle in school, and I needed that much education. And I got quite a lot of education at Exeter, by the way; at least I learned how to learn, how to find things out. There's another key to education: you learn how to pay *enough* attention, even though you're bored. A very important trick for a writer to pick up. But college was a waste of time for me. I stopped paying attention after I left Exeter—I stopped paying attention in school, I mean. By then I already wanted to write; I was already a reader. I wanted more time—to read more and more novels, and to practice my own writing. That's all I wanted to do, and all that really benefited me: reading lots of other novels, and practicing my own writing. Of course, you do get to read some novels in college, but you also have to waste all that time talking about them and writing about them, when you could be reading more novels.

INTERVIEWER: How about writing classes?

IRVING: Writing classes bought me time, and they gave me a little audience. And Thomas Williams and John Yount at the University of New Hampshire were very important to me; they encouraged me and they criticized me, and that saved me time, too. I would have learned what they taught me somewhere, sometime, eventually, but it was wonderful for me to learn it then, and from them. And Kurt Vonnegut was important to me at Iowa, as you already know. But I'm talking about three other *writers* who patted me on the head and passed a pencil over my sentences—I didn't need the *college* part of the education. I suppose I *did* need those silly degrees, because I wouldn't have gotten a teaching job without those degrees, and teaching was an honorable and not-too-time-consuming way to support myself (which I needed to do) in those years I was writing the first four books. So that's always been true of an education, isn't it? You get one, you get a better job—right? But if I was a good teacher—and I was—it was because I had read a lot of novels and I had written and written and written;

that provided me with the substance, with what I actually taught. I didn't need college to be a writer; I needed what a lot of people need from so-called higher education: the credentials! And let's tell the truth: I wouldn't have been given those college teaching positions simply because I had a B.A. and an M.F.A. I got those jobs because I published. School didn't help me get published.

INTERVIEWER: How did you first get published?

IRVING: I was lucky from the start. Tom Williams sent a couple of my undergraduate short stories to his agent, Mavis McIntosh. She sold one, "A Winter Branch," to *Redbook* for $1,000, and so I had an agent. She retired less than a year later and passed me along to Peter Matson, who's been my agent ever since. That's my longest literary-business relationship, and he's also one of my dearest friends. Now that's lucky, that Peter and I were right for each other; that's good luck. And Peter found me Joe Fox at Random House, and Fox was very good for me, too—a good editor, a good man with a pencil, which I needed. And when Random House wasn't exactly promising to change their ways and pull out all the stops for *The World According to Garp*, it was Fox who gave me the right advice: to leave him. That's class. And Henry Robbins published *Garp* at Dutton, and that was a success. The first unlucky thing that happened to me in publishing was that Henry died. He was a lovely man and it crushed me. But the Dutton people did their best—a very young editor named Jane Rosenman did a good job with me and *The Hotel New Hampshire*. And then I met Harvey Ginsberg, who was actually an old friend of Henry's—a classmate at Harvard—and just when I'm writing *The Cider House Rules*, where does it turn out that Harvey is from? Bangor, Maine. You think that's not lucky? And so now Harvey and I are together at William Morrow, and I'm so happy I don't have plans to change publishing houses. How many writers do you know who'll say that? Hear many happy publishing stories? I've been *very* lucky, and I know it, and I'm grateful. So much bitterness exists between writers and their publishers and representatives, but I've been spared it, and that means I can think about my writing instead of worrying about how I'm published—which provides many writers I know with an absolutely crippling distraction. You have to eliminate the distractions. You've got to keep focused.

—RON HANSEN
Autumn 1986

Notes on the Contributors

SVEN BIRKERTS *(Interview with Joseph Brodsky)* is the author of *An Artificial Wilderness: Essays on 20th-Century Literature.* He presently teaches writing at Harvard University.

FRANK CROWTHER *(Interview with E. B. White)* was an administrator of the National Endowment for the Arts and an editor of *The Paris Review.* He died in 1976.

JONATHAN DEE *(Interview with John Hersey)* is a senior editor of *The Paris Review.* His work has appeared in the *Village Voice,* and he is a recipient of the Henfield Foundation award for fiction.

EDWIN FRANK *(Interview with Robert Fitzgerald)* is a poet who lives in San Francisco. His work has appeared in the *New York Review of Books* and *Sequoia.*

JOHN S. FRIEDMAN *(Interview with Elie Wiesel)* a former journalist and professor at the City University of New York, is a producer of Marcel Ophuls' latest film, *Hotel Terminus: The Life and Times of Klaus Barbie.*

SHUSHA GUPPY *(Interview with Anita Brookner)* is the London Editor of *The Paris Review,* and a contributor to *Harpers & Queen* and *The Independent.* Her memoir, *The Blindfold Horse,* was published this year by William Heinemann in Britain.

RON HANSEN *(Interview with John Irving)* was a student of John Irving's at the University of Iowa from 1972 to 1974. He is the author of *Desperadoes, The Assasination of Jesse James by the Coward Robert Ford,* and a children's book, *The Shadowmaker,* and he is editor of *You Don't Know What Love Is,* an anthology of contemporary American stories.

EDWARD HIRSCH *(Interview with Derek Walcott)* is the author of two books of poetry, *For the Sleepwalkers* (Knopf, 1981), and *Wild Gratitude,* which Knopf published in spring 1986.

ANDREW MCCORD *(Interview with Robert Fitzgerald)* is a reporter for the weekly newspaper *India Abroad.* He lives in New York.

JEANNE MCCULLOCH *(Interview with Leon Edel)* is the managing editor of *The Paris Review.* Her fiction and nonfiction have appeared in *The North American Review, The Paris Review, The New York Times Book Review,* and *Vogue.* She is currently completing her first novel.

GEORGE PLIMPTON *(Interviews with E. B. White and E. L. Doctorow)* is the editor of *The Paris Review.* His most recent book is a novel, *The Curious Case of Sidd Finch* (Macmillan).

TOM TEICHOLZ *(Interview with Cynthia Ozick)* is a writer and attorney in New York. His work has appeared in *New York Woman, Channels, The Forward,* and *Interview.* He is currently at work on a book about the John Demjanjuk Trial for St. Martin's Press.

WILLIAM CRAWFORD WOODS *(Interview with Robert Stone)* is a novelist and a journalist who teaches at Longwood College in Virginia.

RICHARD ZIEGFELD *(Interview with James Laughlin)* has published nine books on topics such as author–publisher relationships, literary history and criticism, and biography.

DATE			